DIAMOND COAST

A MILO DECOGAN THRILLER

BOOK ONE OF THE RELIEF SOLUTIONS SERIES

ROBERT COLE

Ebook ISBN: 978-1-964981-07-9
Paperback ISBN: 978-1-964981-08-6

KINDLE EDITION, LICENSE NOTES

ALSO BY ROBERT COLE

To those who go and help others where the world won't—and to those who protect them.

PROLOGUE

1 MARCH 0617 hrs

Gangura, South Sudan

In the ten months since Caitlin Bishop had arrived in South Sudan, she had come to love this hour more than any other. The world between dawn and daybreak was the one time the refugee camp felt truly at peace: before the noise, before the chaos, before the endless demands of need and suffering pressed against her like heat.

Lying on her narrow wooden bunk, she listened to the first stirrings of life outside her tukul: soft footsteps on dirt, the faint bleating of goats, a distant cough followed by laughter. The sounds drifted through the wooden shutters like a song she'd learned by heart. Warm morning light seeped through the cracks, catching the pale veil of mosquito netting above her, scattering it with soft gold.

For a fleeting moment, she felt content, as if the world had remembered how to be kind.

She turned on her side and closed her eyes, smiling. The air was already thick and warm, the kind of humid heaviness that clung to her skin no matter how early it was. But she had grown used to it. She could almost taste the camp's routine before it unfolded.

In her mind's eye, she pictured the two Sudanese cooks, lean men with weathered hands, crouched over the fire pit beside the kitchen hut. One stirred a battered iron cauldron suspended by a metal frame, waiting for the water to boil. The other rolled out dough with a bottle, shaping small rounds of mandazi bread that would soon puff golden brown in the oil. The smell would drift across the camp—yeast, smoke, honey. Caitlin's mouth watered at the thought.

It was this quiet rhythm she'd come to depend on, the fragile structure of normalcy that made everything else about the Sudan bearable. For all its hardships, Gangura had become home.

The World Refugee Committee compound sat in a shallow clearing surrounded by jungle, its perimeter fenced with twelve-foot bamboo poles lashed together with rope and wire. Inside were twenty tukuls, round, mud-walled huts with thatched roofs that gleamed like old straw under the sun. Her own hut was near the eastern edge of the compound, a few meters apart from the others. She'd chosen it for the solitude, for the peace it offered after long days spent mediating disputes, distributing food, and treating dehydration under a tin-roofed clinic that baked like an oven.

The camp itself was roughly the length of a football field, with winding dirt paths connecting the huts, the communal kitchen, and the central meeting shelter where a sagging tarpaulin bore the faded blue letters WRC. Beyond the fence, dense teak and mahogany trees pressed close, their shadows thick and secret.

Among the eleven full-time staff, Caitlin was one of only three Westerners. The others, Melissa Jenkins, a bright-eyed twenty-year-old intern from Michigan, and Dr. Sebastian Forrester, the British country director, had become her family in this isolated outpost. Eight Sudanese nationals completed the team: translators, field officers, and logistical staff, men and women who had once been refugees themselves.

They were the heart of the camp. Without them, nothing worked.

And at the center of it all was Festus, by position the WRC operations manager, but in truth the camp's backbone and soul. Broad-shouldered, with skin the deep sheen of mahogany and a scruffy beard that framed his constant smile, Festus possessed both strength and grace. Educated in Uganda after fleeing the civil war as a child, he had returned to South Sudan not out of obligation, but love—a fierce devotion to his people and to rebuilding what had been broken. His laugh, rich and disarming, brightened the compound, and his ability to turn tension into laughter was legendary. When tempers flared, it was Festus who calmed them; when supplies fell short, it was Festus who somehow found more.

To Caitlin, he was more than a colleague; he was her mentor, protector, and teacher, guiding her through the unspoken codes of Sudanese life with patience and humor.

And then there were the daily laborers: the guards, cooks, drivers, and the shy teenage helper, Taibi, who came each morning carrying two steaming buckets of water for her wash. He'd rap gently on her doorframe and murmur, *"Miss Caitlin, time to wake."*

But today, there was no knock.

The sound that woke her was wrong: fast, heavy footsteps outside the fence. Too many of them.

She frowned, sitting up, her heart already quickening. The footsteps came from the northern side, beyond the road. Then came the voices, urgent, breathless, speaking in low bursts of Sudanese Arabic. She strained to listen, but the words blurred together. Something about "moving now," and "the gate."

Then the crash.

A single, thunderous impact shattered the morning calm, the unmistakable sound of wood giving way under the brute force of a charging vehicle.

The front gate.

Caitlin froze, every muscle taut. Another crash followed, louder, splintering, then angry shouting, commanding, overlapping in chaos.

Gunfire ripped through the air. Three sharp cracks, then a long burst.

She threw off her blanket, her breath shallow and ragged. Her hands shook as she yanked a sweatshirt over her tank top and pulled on the first pair of pants she could find. Her boots lay by the bed, half-buried in dust. She jammed her feet into them, not bothering with socks.

Outside, screams.

Male voices, guards, maybe Festus, yelling orders she couldn't make out. Then the distinct, mechanical clatter of assault rifles, close now, echoing against the bamboo fence.

She moved to the door, pulling aside the woven blanket that hung there as a curtain. The morning light was gone, replaced by smoke and dust kicked up from the dry earth.

The camp was under attack.

Men in mismatched fatigues and headscarves poured through the broken gate, their AK-47s raised. She counted at least a dozen, maybe more. Some wore bright red cloths tied around their forearms—a tribal marker, she realized. Lord's Resistance Army.

They fired as they advanced, shouting over each other, dragging terrified workers from huts. A woman screamed as she was pulled to the ground near the kitchen. Caitlin's breath caught. Near her, the cooks dropped to their knees, hands raised. One of them was shot anyway, a single round to the chest. Caitlin stifled a scream as she watched him fall face-first into the dirt.

Caitlin's pulse hammered. Her brain screamed at her to move, but her body refused.

A shout—"*Out! Everyone out!*"—and another series of shots cracked across the compound. She ducked instinctively, heart pounding so hard she could feel it in her ears.

Through the open flap of her hut, she saw Festus, broad-shoul-dered, kind-eyed Festus, being shoved forward with the barrel of a rifle pressed to his back. Blood streamed down his face. Behind him, Sebastian stumbled from his office hut, his khaki shirt unbuttoned, one hand raised, the other clutching his ever-present medical bag.

"Please," Sebastian called. "There are civilians—"

A gunman struck him hard across the jaw with a pistol, the crack of bone echoing. Sebastian fell to his knees.

Festus lunged forward, shouting something Caitlin couldn't hear over the noise, and then came another burst of gunfire. The bullets caught him squarely in the chest, lifting him off his feet. He hit the ground in a spray of red.

"Festus!" Caitlin whispered, the word breaking out of her like a sob.

She wanted to run to him, to help, to do anything, but her mind was screaming *you'll be next, you'll be next*.

She dropped back into the shadows of her tukul, her whole body trembling. The gunfire seemed to vibrate through the walls.

Training. Remember your training.

The voice came from memory, the security officer from Rhode Island, a former military contractor, green-eyed, blunt, and relentless. He'd drilled them for hours on what to do in an incursion: *Stay low. Stay quiet. Don't panic. Observe. Plan. Move.*

She forced herself to breathe. Slowly.

Her go-bag sat beneath the bed, a small canvas pack with water, flashlight, knife, her passport and other papers she'd never thought she'd need. She snatched it up, slung it across her shoulder, and crawled toward the window on the far wall. The rear of her hut faced the jungle, opposite the main gate.

A glance outside showed chaos: two huts burning, smoke rising black against the sky, gunmen tearing through possessions, hauling people out by their hair. One rebel dragged a woman across the dirt, her arms flailing. Another fired into the air, laughing.

This wasn't a raid.

It was a purge.

Caitlin's breath hitched as she spotted movement beyond the next hut, a flash of pale hair.

Melissa.

The girl was peering from behind a curtain, frozen. She looked impossibly young, her face streaked with tears.

Hesitating a fraction of a second, Caitlin reached up, tore the screen from her back window, and squeezed through the narrow opening, scraping her arms on the frame. She tumbled out, falling awkwardly to the ground.

She crouched low, darting across the gap between huts, her boots silent in the red dust. The smell of smoke and cordite filled her nose.

"Melissa," she hissed, pressing herself against the mud wall of the next tukul. "Melissa, it's me."

The girl's frightened face appeared at the window. "Caitlin! They...they shot Festus! Oh my God, they shot him!"

"Listen to me," Caitlin said, forcing her voice steady. "We don't have time. Do you have your bag?"

Melissa shook her head, trembling. "Sebastian said I wouldn't need one. I...Caitlin, I can't—"

"Shoes, sweatshirt, now." Caitlin's tone left no room for argument. "We're leaving. There's an escape route near the latrine, but we need to go. Now."

Melissa hesitated, eyes wide. "They're everywhere—"

"I know. Trust me."

Inside, Melissa scrambled. Caitlin could hear her rummaging through her things, sobbing to herself. The gunfire hadn't stopped; it just moved farther away for a moment before surging back, closer, louder.

A scream tore through the air. Then another.

Caitlin flinched. "Now, Melissa!"

Melissa climbed through the window, nearly falling before Caitlin caught her, pulling her down into a crouch. The girl's breath came in ragged bursts.

"What if they see us?"

"They won't," Caitlin said. She hoped she was right.

The escape hatch was thirty meters away, a small, hidden panel built into the bamboo fence, disguised with mud and vines. It had been the security consultant's idea, approved reluctantly by Sebastian after a previous ambush on an NGO compound up north. Caitlin had opened it once during a drill, but she'd never imagined she'd have to use it.

They moved in short bursts, ducking from shadow to shadow. The compound was chaos now. Smoke drifted low, acrid and thick, stinging her eyes. She could hear the rebels shouting orders: *find them, find the white women.*

Her stomach twisted.

As they reached the southeast corner, Caitlin spotted the latrine huts, their thin tin walls shimmering in the rising heat. Beyond them, half hidden by foliage, was the small patch of mud concealing the hatch.

"Here," she whispered. She dropped to her knees, scraping away the mud with her fingers until she found the wooden latch. Her hands were slick with sweat. Behind her, the rhythmic thud of boots approached again.

Melissa grabbed her arm. "They're coming!"

Caitlin turned the latch. It jammed. Panic surged. She hit it again, harder.

A burst of gunfire tore through the latrines, sending shards of tin spinning into the air. Melissa screamed, clutching her head.

"Down!" Caitlin hissed, dragging her to the ground. The next volley tore through the bamboo fence, wood splintering inches above them.

The latch gave. The panel shifted open.

"Go," Caitlin ordered, shoving Melissa toward it.

Melissa crawled through, disappearing into the dark foliage beyond. Caitlin followed, wriggling through the narrow opening, her bag catching on the wood. She yanked it free, her chest scraping the frame.

Then they were outside the compound, on their knees in the dense undergrowth, the world suddenly smaller, suffocatingly close.

Caitlin turned back just in time to see the compound's gate engulfed in flame. The rebels had set the kitchen hut ablaze; the fire was spreading fast. She could hear someone—Sebastian, maybe— shouting defiance before being silenced by another gunshot.

Tears blurred her vision, but she didn't stop.

She grabbed Melissa's hand. "Move."

They plunged into the jungle.

The foliage closed around them, thick with vines and wet leaves. The air smelled of sap and gunpowder. The sun, rising through the canopy, painted everything in shifting gold and green. Every sound, every bird call, every rustle, made Caitlin flinch.

Behind them, the camp burned.

Melissa stumbled, almost falling. "I can't—"

"Yes, you can." Caitlin hauled her upright. "We follow the sound of water. There's a river southeast. Stay close."

The jungle swallowed the path behind them. Gunfire echoed once more, then faded into the distance.

Caitlin didn't look back.

1

1 MARCH 1447 HRS

PRUDENCE ISLAND, **Rhode Island**

Forget Gatorade. Ice-cold lemonade is the ultimate thirst quencher, especially on a hot August day in New England. I had just completed a six-mile run around Prudence Island, and the heat radiating from my body demanded refreshment. I relished the sharp, sweet bite of fresh lemonade, savoring each cold, tangy sip as it slid down my throat, soothing muscles fatigued from miles of pounding pavement. The run had been invigorating, my breathing rhythmic, feet steady on familiar paths winding around the island's quiet roads, each mile releasing stress built up from weeks of intense travel and relentless work.

It felt as if I'd scarcely spent any time at home this entire summer. My cottage on Prudence Island had become more of a fleeting sanctuary rather than the restful retreat I intended it to be. Today, however, would be different. Today was meant for relaxation and indulgence.

I envisioned a perfect afternoon ahead: reclining into my beloved, overstuffed leather chair, eyes fixed on the massive seventy-five-inch flat-screen television, an extravagant Christmas gift I had bestowed upon myself. The Red Sox were struggling to defend their lead in the standings from a determined Yankees team, and today's showdown at Fenway promised to be a gripping battle. With no plans, obligations, or urgent demands looming, I could already picture myself drifting off into a well-earned nap.

I switched on the television, punching the buttons for NESN from memory. The game was already underway, scoreless at the top of the second inning. The familiar crackle of the announcer's voice and the gentle murmur of the crowd provided an immediate sense of comfort. I stepped into the kitchen and built a tuna sandwich overflowing with chunks of white albacore, crisp lettuce, and thick slices of ripe tomato. I poured myself another generous glass of lemonade from the sweating pitcher on the granite counter, beads of condensation forming a cool puddle beneath it.

Walking into the adjoining great room, still dressed in running shorts and an old, faded Georgetown t-shirt, I relished the refreshing breeze drawn in by the attic fan, carrying the salty tang of the ocean. Settling into my chair, I let my gaze wander toward the expansive bay window framing a breathtaking view of Narragansett Bay and the iconic Newport Bridge arcing gracefully in the distance. Though I had owned this cottage for years, its picturesque vista never failed to captivate me.

The bay was a living canvas of vibrant activity. Sailboats with billowing sails skimmed across the water, each vessel adorned in bright, lively colors. Across the bay to the east, golfers strolled along the final hole of the renowned Carnegie Abbey golf course. I could almost hear their relaxed laughter drifting over the water as they headed toward the inviting glow of the outdoor bar.

Bright sunlight reflected off clusters of colorful lobster pots bobbing in the green-tinted waters, creating a dazzling mosaic. The beauty of the scene coaxed the accumulated tension of the past week from my muscles, replacing it with a profound, peaceful calm.

I had returned late the previous evening from Guyana, still nursing the lingering exhaustion of an unexpectedly challenging assignment. A valued client—a British election-monitoring non-profit working to strengthen democratic institutions—had received disturbing threats of kidnapping and extortion. My assignment was straightforward: coordinate with local authorities and enhance security measures. But a simple week had transformed into a harrowing experience when the police vehicle I occupied came under a hail of gunfire from a local drug lord determined to thwart the democratic process.

Bullets had riddled our sedan, shattering windows and piercing doors, forcing us to abandon the vehicle and escape on foot through dense, unforgiving jungle terrain. For hours, we navigated the unfamiliar landscape, adrenaline surging, nerves frayed, yet we emerged unharmed, albeit covered in mud, sweat, and mosquito bites. Following a whirlwind of debriefings, paperwork, and a lengthy flight back to Boston, I had earned the right to several uninterrupted days of rest.

Tam, my efficient and protective executive assistant, knew to safeguard this time, interrupting me only if the situation was life or death. Visions of lazy afternoons golfing, boating excursions around the bay, sun-soaked naps, and informal meals of crispy fried clams accompanied by ice-cold drafts at the Carnegie Abbey bar filled my mind.

As the Red Sox game unfolded, Chris Sale's masterful pitching drew my attention back to the television. I enjoyed my tuna sandwich, sipping lemonade until my eyelids grew heavy. The last conscious memory was J.D. Martinez lofting a routine fly ball toward right field.

The next sensation I registered was a cool, gentle breeze brushing my skin, rousing me from a deep, restful slumber. Despite the oppressive heat of earlier, August nights along Narragansett Bay were refreshing and cool. Rather than closing the windows and sealing out the ocean's lullaby of lapping waves, I reached for the soft woolen blanket draped over the back of the chair.

Glancing at the clock, I blinked in surprise. It read 8:34 pm. I'd slept for over five hours, evidence of just how much rest my body needed. My stomach growled, reminding me of its emptiness. I needed dinner.

Living on Prudence Island simplifies decisions about dining out; there are no options. The general store, charming and convenient, was the island's only source of sustenance and closed promptly at six pm. Fortunately, my mainland condo at the Carnegie Abbey Club across the bay included a car, making trips into town simple and enjoyable, but first required a short boat ride across the narrow part of Narragansett Bay to reach the club.

Refreshed by a quick shower, I dressed in comfortable khaki shorts and a well-loved, faded Oxford rugby pullover. Exiting through the screened porch, I walked down the gentle slope toward the wooden dock extending forty feet into the bay. Cradled on its lift sat my pride and joy, a sleek, elegant 36-foot Hinckley picnic boat, its polished teak gleaming under the moonlight. While I wouldn't call myself a passionate boat enthusiast, there was undeniable pleasure in commuting by water, a luxury I treasured.

The summer evening was spectacular, stars brightening the night sky as they mirrored their celestial glow on the bay's calm waters. With a practiced ease, I stepped onto the deck of the Hinckley, feeling the familiar gentle sway beneath my feet. As I prepared to set out across the moonlit Narragansett Bay toward dinner, a quiet, contented smile settled across my lips.

Life, at this precise moment, felt close to perfect.

2 MARCH 0714 HRS

PRUDENCE ISLAND, **Rhode Island**

I was already awake when the phone rang. Dawn had slipped quietly into my bedroom, bathing the walls in gentle shades of gold and pink, stirring me from sleep. Rather than rising, I allowed myself the rare indulgence of lingering, eyes half-closed, savoring the tranquility of the early morning hours. My thoughts drifted, meandering between daydreams—a peaceful sail to Sakonnet Point perhaps, or idle speculation about whether the Patriots' offseason moves would finally yield results in the coming season.

The unexpected ring shattered the peace of my contemplative morning. With mild irritation, I reached over to pick up my iPhone, the screen glowing with Tam's name. My executive assistant, Tam, was efficient and professional to a fault. She rarely disturbed my mornings unless something urgent demanded immediate attention.

"Who died?" I answered sarcastically.

"Sorry to interrupt your morning, Milo," Tam replied, bypassing any pleasantries. Her voice carried its usual brisk efficiency, betraying no hint of the hour's inconvenience. "We've just received an urgent call from the Secretary of State. George Bishop insists on speaking with you as soon as possible."

"The Secretary of State? Can't Nate handle this?" I asked. Nate, my operations director, was far more suited to handling diplomatic interactions and the tedious bureaucracy often associated with government calls. His patient demeanor made him the perfect choice for delicate diplomatic dialogue.

"Not just State Department," Tam clarified, her voice firm and precise. "George Bishop himself. He specifically said it's urgent and personal."

Now fully alert, I sat upright, my mind racing to comprehend the significance. Direct calls from cabinet-level officials weren't common, despite the solid reputation Relief Solutions had established within international humanitarian circles. In fact, this would be a first.

"Did he offer any more context?" I probed.

"None at all," Tam answered. "I've sent you his direct number. I'll be in the office should you need anything further."

"Thanks, Tam," I acknowledged, disconnecting the call and turning to my laptop. My curiosity and unease demanded that I refresh my memory regarding Secretary George Bishop.

Like most Secretaries of State, Bishop was not a career diplomat. Instead, he was a product of one of America's oldest and wealthiest families, deeply embedded in the maritime industry and politics. Born into privilege, Bishop had transitioned from managing his family's extensive maritime enterprises to a highly successful political career. He served six productive and popular years as a Massachusetts senator before a family tragedy altered his path.

His only son, serving as a Marine lieutenant in Iraq, had been killed by a roadside bomb. The devastating loss had prompted Bishop to abruptly withdraw from political life, shunning public attention in favor of quiet introspection. After several years of relative obscurity, President Franklin nominated him as Secretary of State. Despite widespread speculation about political maneuvering, Bishop's reputation for decisive leadership quickly earned him respect in his new role.

With a deep breath, I picked up my phone and dialed the

number Tam provided, expecting an aide or secretary to answer. Instead, after a single ring, a deep, authoritative voice unmistakably tinged with a Boston accent responded.

"Mr. deCogan, thank you for returning my call."

"My pleasure, Mr. Secretary," I responded. "To what do I owe the honor?"

"I'll get straight to it," Bishop began, tension evident in his voice. "You come with the highest recommendations of Joshua Gale and General Jack Donovan. Both assure me you're uniquely qualified. Right now, I urgently need your help. My daughter Caitlin has been kidnapped in South Sudan. I need you to find her and bring her home safely."

I took a moment to process the gravity of his request. General Jack Donovan was not only my former commanding officer during my Special Forces days but also my supervisor during my subsequent tenure in the CIA. Over years of serving under him, he'd become more than just a mentor; he'd become a surrogate father figure whose opinion I deeply valued. If Donovan had recommended me, it was serious indeed.

"Can you provide more details, Mr. Secretary? Are you certain it was a kidnapping?" I questioned.

"Yes—," Bishop's voice faltered, heavy with emotion. "Yesterday, Caitlin's humanitarian compound came under violent attack. Initially, we thought it might be local unrest. Diplomatic Security Service dispatched a response team from our Kampala embassy to investigate."

"The WRC compound, correct?" I interjected, recalling my previous consultancy work with the World Refugee Committee. A distinct image of Caitlin surfaced—young, spirited, confident, and committed to her humanitarian role. At the time, I had no idea she was Secretary Bishop's daughter.

"Exactly," Bishop confirmed, no doubt aware of my familiarity. "My daughter oversees their gender-violence initiatives. DSS arrived to find a massacre, nineteen staff executed with chilling precision.

Caitlin and another American volunteer, Melissa Jenkins, were missing. One surviving local cook described how attackers demanded Caitlin's location, executing everyone else when they couldn't find her."

The brutality Bishop described shook me. "Did DSS manage to track Caitlin's escape?" I pressed, hoping for a lead.

"They found evidence suggesting Caitlin and Melissa used an emergency exit," Bishop explained. "Local villagers saw two women fleeing, pursued by armed men in vehicles. Unfortunately, our DSS team subsequently lost contact."

"Lost contact?" I echoed.

"Yesterday afternoon, a South Sudanese patrol found our DSS team dead," Bishop revealed, his voice tight with anger and frustration. "Ambushed and executed on the roadside."

This startling revelation caused my pulse to quicken. Such blatant aggression towards American security personnel was unusual in the region.

"Attackers left behind a note addressed directly to me," Bishop continued. "It stated they had Caitlin, warning against further rescue attempts. There have been no ransom demands yet. While the note is real, we aren't sure if they have Caitlin or if she escaped."

I exhaled, weighing the complex circumstances unfolding. "How specifically can I assist you, Mr. Secretary?"

"I want to hire you directly," Bishop stated. "You will have full logistical support from the State Department and my personal resources, but officially, you'll have no government affiliation. This matter requires absolute discretion."

"Understood," I replied, already shifting into operational planning mode.

"Excellent," Bishop said with evident relief. "I've dispatched a private jet to Newport along with my aide, Jessica Reid. She'll provide every scrap of intelligence we possess. Embassies in South Sudan, Uganda, and the DRC are awaiting your requests. Do you have immediate questions?"

His tone implied none were expected, but I clarified one critical detail. "How should I update you?"

"Jessica will provide a satellite phone pre-programmed with my direct number," Bishop answered. "Call immediately with any developments."

His voice softened, raw emotion bleeding through. "Milo, please find my daughter. Bring her back safely. I'm counting on you."

"I promise, sir," I responded. "I'll do everything possible."

The call ended abruptly, leaving only silence.

Sitting quietly for a moment, I allowed the gravity of the Secretary's request to sink in. The face of Caitlin Bishop lingered in my memory, her vibrant determination etched clearly in my mind. My thoughts drifted back to General Donovan, contemplating the weight of his recommendation and the implicit trust he placed in me.

I stood, feeling the full urgency of the situation compelling swift and decisive action. This was no ordinary operation. Lives hung in the balance, and failure was not an option. Caitlin's life depended on my skill, experience, and resolve.

Moving swiftly, I began assembling essential gear and reviewing the initial steps required for rapid deployment. This operation had suddenly become personal. Western NGOs, especially those with American or European staff were rarely the targets of such brutality. A heavy sense of responsibility pressed on me. I had been the one who trained the staff here on how to prevent and survive precisely this kind of attack, and now they were the ones paying the price for failure. As I prepared, my determination hardened with each passing moment.

I knew what needed to be done, and I had every intention of succeeding.

3

2 MARCH 0723 HRS

PRUDENCE ISLAND, **Rhode Island**

While finding the kidnapped daughter of the Secretary of State was not an everyday occurrence for Relief Solutions, rapidly organizing overseas response missions was a core part of our operational DNA. As any seasoned commander knows, the critical first step is mobilizing your team.

As usual, Tam answered my call on the first ring.

"Good morning, Milo. Did you speak to Secretary Bishop?"

"I did. His daughter's been kidnapped."

In any other office, this would have elicited dramatic exclamations or at least a shocked gasp. But Tam was unflappable, her steady silence confirming her instant absorption and processing of the situation.

"I assume you want the full staff assembled immediately?" she asked.

"Yes. Exactly," I replied, smiling to myself, impressed yet again by her prescient action.

"Nate's already en route, and Stacy's here preparing the situation room," Tam informed me. "Anything else you need?"

"Tell Nate to pick up some Dunks on his way in," I added,

knowing food might be scarce in the urgency of the upcoming mission. "I'll be there in thirty."

"Understood, Milo. See you shortly."

I disconnected the call, turning toward the shower, but stopped mid-step. Realizing the urgency, I knew the best use of my time was to reach out to Josh Gale at WRC headquarters in Detroit.

The World Refugee Committee operated in some of the most volatile corners of the globe—South Sudan, Yemen, Sierra Leone, Somalia, Afghanistan—places where governments had failed and survival depended on improvisation. WRC wasn't a political organization, but a humanitarian lifeline, focused on medical, health, and sanitation support for the millions displaced by war. Its field teams built clinics out of shipping containers, trained midwives under trees, and purified water from rivers choked with ash. I'd worked with a dozen NGOs in my career, but WRC was among the few that actually delivered on its promises, however imperfectly.

Josh Gale, the organization's president, had spent thirty years toggling between academia and the field, a scholar's mind trapped in a humanitarian's body. He'd first heard of me through mutual contacts at State and the UN, then brought Relief Solutions on last year to improve WRC's security footprint. Josh was a good man, one of the few who still believed decency could survive in the world's darkest places. But like many in his line of work, he struggled with the ambiguity of command, always weighing ethics against survival. That tension made him thoughtful, but slow when speed mattered most.

Josh answered after the first ring, his voice edged with tension. "Milo! Thanks for calling. I assume you've spoken with the Secretary?"

"Just finished with him," I confirmed. "Josh, what the hell happened? Why wasn't I looped in sooner?"

"I wanted to call you," Josh began, frustration clear in his tone. "Secretary Bishop insisted we wait until DSS had reported back. He wanted to avoid triggering false alarms. But now, it's a complete disaster." His voice rose, anxiety evident. "Jesus, Milo. What do we do now?"

"Take a breath, Josh," I advised, steady and reassuring. Josh Gale was a talented physician who had dedicated his life to humanitarian service, but the brutal realities of violent conflict had shaken him. Massacres were well outside his emotional or professional comfort zone. "You hired Relief Solutions for situations like this. You're in good hands. Later this morning, Stacy Greene will contact you directly. She's our top crisis manager, and she'll coordinate closely with your team. We'll also send a liaison to your office by the end of the day."

"Okay," Josh said, regaining some composure. "But what about Caitlin? And my local staff? Their families will need answers. How do I handle that?"

"I'll personally oversee Caitlin's recovery," I assured him. "Trust my team's expertise in handling sensitive situations like these. Focus on keeping the Detroit office calm and organized, and we'll handle the rest. Stacy will call shortly to start managing information flow and media inquiries."

Josh exhaled audibly, relieved to share the burden. "Thank you, Milo. I mean it."

"This is what we do, Josh. Anything else I should know?" I asked. "Any details that could make a difference right now?"

Josh hesitated. "No, not that I can think of. The attack blindsided us. DSS hasn't provided anything beyond what the Secretary already told you."

"Understood," I reassured him. "Stay strong, Josh. Stacy will be in touch soon."

I hung up, closing my eyes as I mentally transported myself back to the World Refugee Committee compound in Gangura. I'd spent several days there months earlier during an extensive security assessment covering South Sudan, eastern DRC, Rwanda, and Somalia. Memories flooded back, underscoring the gravity of our mission.

The compound had been modest yet efficient, a cluster of tukuls encircled by tall bamboo fencing. Its heart was the communal tukul, an expansive, open-air gathering space where staff congregated for meals and downtime. At its operational helm was Sebastian Forrester, the program director. Sebastian was a wiry British doctor, mid-fifties, with an acerbic wit and an unyielding commitment to his humanitarian calling. His initial reception to my security assessment had bordered on dismissive. Sebastian had spent decades navigating sub-Saharan Africa's volatile environments and saw external security consultants as largely unnecessary.

However, Sebastian's skepticism gradually softened. My straight-forward, practical approach, emphasizing vigilance and preparedness without heavy-handed militarization, seemed to resonate with his own philosophy. Sebastian particularly valued my insistence on robust security awareness training for his local staff, the most vulnerable personnel, living outside compound walls and confronting risks daily.

But perhaps most memorable was Festus, the compound's local Sudanese manager. Jovial and rotund with an infectious laugh, Festus had instantly made me feel welcome, bringing much-needed levity to the heavy atmosphere of refugee work. His genuine warmth transformed evening meals into vibrant events, punctuated by laughter and camaraderie. The night I arrived, Festus had orchestrated an impromptu talent show that left everyone, Sebastian included, doubled over with laughter.

Festus's relentless humor eventually targeted me, especially after my cautious reaction to dinner preparations. Witnessing two scrawny chickens hastily prepared for dinner, I'd feigned vegetarianism to avoid offending my hosts or facing gastrointestinal distress, admitting only to eating the occasional fish while swearing off any two- or four-legged creatures. Festus had been amused, teasing me to no end. My deception held firm, sustained secretly by protein bars tucked away in my backpack, a trusted travel companion for remote assignments.

On my final evening, Festus surprised me by arranging a meal of tilapia caught from the nearby White Nile, and humorously prepared as traditional fish and chips to honor my Irish ancestry. The entire staff gathered, decorating the communal tukul with improvised balloons, hilariously fashioned from the compound's plentiful supply of condoms from their reproductive health program.

That evening, I sat across from Festus and Sebastian, while Caitlin Bishop occupied the seat beside me. Over the previous several days, I had observed Caitlin as she worked, impressed by her intellect, resolve, and passionate commitment to humanitarian causes. Her presence was striking, confident, articulate, but also compassionate toward those she served.

Yet beneath her warmth was a clear, unmistakable disdain for violence or any profession remotely associated with it. Early conversations revealed her skepticism toward those who relied on force, with ex-military individuals like me near the top of her negative list. Her perspective, born of youthful idealism and unblemished hope, was both admirable and naïve.

Throughout our interactions, Caitlin maintained respectful cordiality, appreciating my security expertise while disapproving of my past affiliations. Though she never challenged me, her polite distance signaled unmistakable disapproval of my CIA and military background.

Still, the memory of that evening, filled with laughter, camaraderie, and vibrant optimism, lingered. Festus's hearty laugh, Sebastian's dry humor, Caitlin's earnest passion were the faces and voices I now carried with me into this urgent, perilous mission.

Reflecting on the situation's gravity, my training kicked in. My career had been a mosaic of intense experiences—combat zones, clandestine operations, humanitarian emergencies—each demanding swift, decisive action amid chaos. My reputation had been built for these moments.

My previous assignments had ranged from extracting aid workers trapped in conflict zones to negotiating tense hostage situations. Each scenario sharpened my instincts, deepened my resilience, and reinforced my confidence in Relief Solutions' capabilities. And yet, despite this formidable experience, the personal connection I had forged with the WRC team in Gangura added an emotional connection I seldom felt on an operation.

As I moved to shower and dress, my mind was already formulating strategic plans—routes, contacts, logistics, backup contingencies. Caitlin's kidnapping wasn't just another job. The faces, voices, and laughter shared in that remote compound now carried a haunting urgency, propelling me forward with unwavering determination.

Checking my watch, I realized time was short. The staff awaited my arrival, ready to mobilize. Our mission was clear: Find Caitlin Bishop, reunite her with her father, and ensure justice for those who had suffered in the senseless violence.

Failure was never an option, and in this case, even less so. The stakes had never felt higher. I took a deep breath, shouldered the weight of responsibility, and prepared myself to lead my team into action.

4

2 MARCH 0730 HRS

PRUDENCE ISLAND, **Rhode Island**

My company, Relief Solutions, was born from a sincere desire to make a difference, tempered by the futility and grief that followed personal tragedy. We were small, lean, agile, and uniquely positioned to respond without hesitation to crisis situations around the globe. Our strength lay not just in our operational capabilities but also in the deep networks my colleagues and I had established over our combined years of military, intelligence, and humanitarian service.

My worldview underwent significant shifts during several intense deployments as a military officer, especially in Afghanistan and Iraq, and later as a paramilitary officer with the Central Intelligence Agency. My experiences at the CIA took me across five continents, engaging in clandestine operations designed to apply surgical military force to support the strategic interests and national security goals of the United States. A fancy bureaucratic way of admitting that I had witnessed humanity at its absolute worst, though occasionally, I also saw courage, resilience, and genuine sacrifice.

In graduate school at Georgetown, I enrolled in a course on ethnic conflict, becoming engrossed in the tragic history of Rwanda, specifically the 1994 genocide. Years after the slaughter had ended, I had the sobering opportunity to visit Rwanda in my capacity as a CIA paramilitary officer, allowing me to see firsthand several genocide memorials. One particular site, the Ntarama Church, left an indelible and haunting mark on my soul.

My first impression upon arriving at Ntarama was the understated simplicity of the site: a modest cluster of brick buildings set beneath a tranquil canopy of trees atop a gentle hillock. A faded sign outside stated simply, in both English and French, that approximately five thousand people had been killed there in April 1994, plus or minus. But it wasn't the stark number that caught my attention; it was the unnerving use of the phrase "plus or minus." I remember feeling puzzled, unsettled by the vagueness.

Did they not know exactly how many innocent souls had been murdered here?

And if not, why?

The church itself was relatively small, no more than sixty feet in length and half that in width. Its interior was hauntingly stark, containing little more than two rows of wooden pews and a simple altar. Yet upon entering, my senses were overwhelmed, not by visuals, but by the visceral smell of decay and mold that lingered, ten years after the tragedy.

At the back of the church, piles of shoes and clothing, thousands of items rotting quietly, stood as a grotesque monument to lives violently interrupted. The sheer volume was overwhelming, and I recall how small the room felt, raising immediate skepticism about whether five thousand people could even physically fit inside this space. Perhaps hundreds, crammed tightly, but certainly not thousands.

I began to understand the ambiguity of the "plus or minus."

The imprecise number brought to mind broader questions surrounding the Rwandan genocide. To this day, estimates vary between eight hundred thousand and one million Tutsis slaughtered by Hutus over the bloody months from April to July. The uncertainty gnawed at my sense of justice and accountability.

Lost in contemplation, I barely noticed the woman who entered silently behind me. Tall, painfully thin, wearing a simple gray dress and worn leather sandals, she watched me with eyes that spoke volumes, deep pools of profound sadness and loss. Her presence was calm, patient, and filled with quiet dignity.

As I moved toward the back of the church, she finally spoke, her voice soft yet commanding, the accent heavy but clear enough. "What do you think?" she asked, gesturing at the bare pews and discarded clothing around us.

"It's powerful," I replied, unable to articulate the profound sorrow pressing on my chest. "And sad."

Her gaze lingered on mine, evaluating me carefully before signaling me to follow her outside. Behind the church stood several plywood structures, hastily erected and barely sturdy. She led me into the first shack, her eyes holding mine in an unbroken, silent challenge.

"I was here when it happened," she began, her voice devoid of emotion but carrying immense weight. "I am one of the few who escaped."

I stared at her, unable to find adequate words of response.

Inside the shack, plywood shelves lined every wall, stacked with human skulls, more than anyone could feasibly count. The sight was overwhelming, the silent testimony of unimaginable violence palpable in the fractured bones. Many skulls belonged to children, their tiny forms grotesquely punctured and shattered.

She spoke again, the soft intensity of her voice captivating me. "We kept them all. No burials. So you can count," she challenged, eyes burning with unresolved grief. "You'll find five thousand...plus or minus."

I had stood there frozen, the gravity of her words pressing heavily upon me.

Her voice echoed in my mind, haunting me still to this day.

2,977. Two thousand, nine-hundred and seventy-seven. That number resonates for many Americans. It is exact number of known victims of September 11th, each meticulously honored at the memorial in New York.

Yet here, in Africa, thousands of murdered souls were reduced to a chilling approximation.

"Plus or minus."

The genocide's most haunting aspect, for me at least, was the United Nations' acknowledgment that a mere hundred well-trained soldiers could have mitigated or even prevented the mass killings. By targeting radio stations broadcasting hatred, capturing influential agitators, establishing secure safe havens, and neutralizing key leaders, the genocide could have been curtailed by just a few dozen well-trained, well-intentioned men. Yet, during those horrific months beginning in April 1994, the international community stood by, doing nothing but observing the bloodshed through their television screens each night.

These reflections profoundly shaped my academic pursuits. My graduate thesis at Georgetown and later my doctoral dissertation at Oxford explored privatizing peace, the provocative concept of employing private military organizations ethically and strategically to reduce violence and genocide in conflict regions. My work on these topics eventually sparked the idea for Relief Solutions.

While completing my studies at Georgetown's Edmund A. Walsh School of Foreign Service, my life took another dramatic turn. Unlike most students, I balanced academics with a full-time career as a clandestine services paramilitary officer within the CIA's Special Activities Division, Ground Branch. My team conducted precision strikes against terrorist threats, working in tight-knit groups to tackle global crises. Initially, I found this work satisfying, believing our missions genuinely mattered.

My life then was stable and fulfilling: a townhouse in northern Virginia, strong friendships within the CIA, mentors guiding my career trajectory, and a wonderful wife named Shannon, whom I adored. Together, we discussed building a family, both of us enjoying mapping out our lives and growing old together.

Tragedy, however, blindsided me while on a clandestine assignment in the Philippines. A call from the CIA's Deputy Director shattered my world—Shannon had been killed by a drunk driver, a Qatari diplomat loosely affiliated with their royal family. Shannon's death was sudden, brutal, and irrevocably life-changing.

The following weeks and months blurred, grief numbing me to daily routines. Although supported by friends and colleagues, my enthusiasm for my role waned. The once-fulfilling work felt hollow and insignificant in the shadow of my loss. The nagging thought that Shannon would have wanted me to pursue something more meaningful haunted me.

An unexpected consequence of Shannon's death was newfound financial independence. Eager to avoid litigation and public embarrassment, the Qatari diplomat's family offered an eight-figure settlement. Furthermore, Shannon's wealthy parents had established a considerable trust fund for her, which passed to me after her untimely death.

Financial freedom and profound grief fueled a powerful impulse to create meaningful change. Determined to channel my despair into something constructive and inspired by my academic work on privatizing peace, I founded Relief Solutions. My vision was clear. Build an agile, responsive organization capable of rapid global intervention, leveraging strategic networks from my military and intelligence careers, and filling the operational gaps left by traditional humanitarian organizations.

My approach combined precision, pragmatism, and deep compassion, honed by experiences in military conflict, intelligence operations, and direct observations of human tragedy. Relief Solutions quickly became known for navigating bureaucratic hurdles and deploying tailored resources into crisis zones, resources other organizations couldn't provide, and always guided by clear ethical standards.

At the core of Relief Solutions' mission remained lessons learned from Rwanda and the haunting ambiguity symbolized by that "plus or minus." The indelible memories of genocide, compounded by personal loss, crystallized my resolve to ensure that future crises received prompt and effective response, never again reduced to an approximation.

Relief Solutions became my life's purpose, driven by Shannon's memory, shaped by profound global experiences, and motivated by an unyielding belief that decisive, ethical action could indeed change the world. And in my darkest moments, I found solace in knowing Shannon would have been proud.

5

2 MARCH 0755 HRS

NEWPORT, **Rhode Island**

I arrived at the office just before 8 a.m., having showered, dressed, and completed the fifteen-minute commute from Prudence Island to downtown Newport. Relief Solutions occupied the entire top floor of the U.S. Post Office building at the intersection of Thames and Memorial, situated in the heart of Newport's historic seaside district. The granite building had been erected in 1921, and from appearances, it seemed the dimly lit post office lobby and aged stairwells hadn't received attention or renovation in the hundred years since.

Yet I enjoyed climbing those three flights of stairs each morning, the worn stone treads polished smooth by decades of foot traffic, the risers much shorter than today's standards, and the solid, lacquered banisters that had guided countless hands. An elevator, rumored to be original as well, was tucked away in the corner, but I'd never had the nerve to test its reliability.

Upon reaching the third-floor landing, I paused at our old wooden door, its frosted glass pane etched with the subtle Relief Solutions logo. The nostalgic impression always reminded me of a detective's office from the 1930s, right down to the subdued lighting and musty scent of historic buildings. A closer inspection, however, revealed our high-tech entrance system, an expensive biometric palm scanner installed on the adjacent wall. Placing my palm against the smooth black panel, I waited for the quiet hum and decisive click of the magnetically-controlled lock before pushing the door open.

Stepping into Relief Solutions felt like stepping into another world. Though the original hardwood floors gave the room historical character, everything else in the spacious area was meticulously modernized. Directly ahead, Tam sat behind her large, immaculate receptionist's desk, headset on, directing incoming communications with practiced efficiency. Beyond her, the expansive bullpen stretched thirty feet square, housing a half-dozen state-of-the-art workstations, each equipped with dual 45-inch curved monitors. Dominating the far wall were twelve oversized flat-screen monitors arranged seamlessly, capable of displaying a single panoramic image or subdivided into multiple feeds. This morning, the screens displayed a satellite-rendered global map, while CNN, BBC, and Al Jazeera broadcast on smaller sections along the left.

The scene was intentionally reminiscent of a high-tech tactical operations center, which indeed it was.

I gave Tam a brief nod, which she returned without breaking stride in her conversation. Across the bullpen, Stacy and Nate were seated at the large conference table, positioned in front of the command monitors, tapping away on their laptops. A large box of Dunkin' donuts sat open between them. The remaining workstations, typically occupied by junior analysts who wouldn't arrive for another hour, stood vacant.

Tam Minh was the quiet engine that kept Relief Solutions running. At twenty-seven, she was barely five-two and weighed maybe ninety-five pounds, but her presence filled every inch of the office. With her dark hair pulled back in a sleek knot and those sharp, almond eyes that seemed to read a situation before anyone spoke, she was part assistant, part strategist, and part shadow. Tam was a control freak in the most useful sense—precise, unflappable, and always one step ahead of me, often handing me a document or briefing I hadn't yet realized I needed. Her loyalty bordered on instinct, her efficiency almost unnerving. No one, not even me, knew how many moving parts she effortlessly kept in motion. Beneath that professional calm, though, there was something else I sensed but never acknowledged, a depth of feeling toward me that she guarded with military discipline. If she was aware I'd noticed, she never let it show.

Stacy Greene, my deputy, took point on all operational briefings. A Naval Academy graduate and former Navy Intelligence analyst, Stacy had earned national recognition as an NCAA Division 1 All-American swimmer. That athletic intensity and discipline had accompanied her into her professional career. Tall, broad-shouldered, with caramel skin and hair pulled back in a pony-tail, Stacy had a quiet authority that filled any room. She had made a name for herself coordinating intelligence for SEAL teams in hotspots worldwide. Fluent in French, Arabic, and Swahili, she'd been my first hire at Relief Solutions. Since coming on board, her analytical rigor and calm leadership had proven invaluable time and again.

Then there was Nate Delman, our Operations and Intelligence specialist. A former Army Special Forces officer, Nate possessed a lean build and perpetually sun-bronzed face from too many years in the world's equatorial conflict zones. He was restless, his hands or feet constantly moving, a man whose boundless energy was both a blessing and an annoyance to those who worked closely with him. Nate's military reputation was stellar; he'd led countless special operations missions throughout the Middle East and Africa. When I established Relief Solutions, his was one of the first phone calls I made. Loyal, dependable, and fiercely dedicated, Nate was the perfect man to handle the high-stakes fieldwork and logistical complexities that defined our missions.

Sitting down next to Nate, I tossed my small backpack onto the polished table, reaching into the donut box to retrieve my current obsession, a maple-glazed delight. As I leaned back, savoring the first sugary bite, I felt Tam slip into the seat beside me. A familiar sound, a cold can of Diet Coke, clunked onto the table in front of me, condensation already forming along its surface.

"Thanks, Tam," I said, cracking open the chilled soda. Tam knew all our individual quirks, right down to my peculiar preference for ice-cold Diet Coke over morning coffee.

"Okay, folks," I said after a satisfying swallow. "Any updates?"

Predictably, Stacy took control. "Actually, we have quite a bit," she said, standing up while tapping a few keys on her keyboard. The large wall display immediately transitioned to an enhanced satellite image of South Sudan, zooming in on Gangura.

"Thirty-three hours ago," Stacy began, "the World Refugee Committee compound in Gangura was attacked by unidentified assailants, believed to be members of the Lord's Resistance Army. Witnesses reported at least a dozen heavily armed men in multiple vehicles. Nineteen staff members were confirmed killed, and two— both young American women—are missing, presumed kidnapped. Caitlin Bishop, daughter of Secretary of State George Bishop, has been working with WRC for fifteen months on gender-based violence initiatives. Melissa Jenkins, a 20-year-old University of Michigan student, was volunteering for her spring semester."

Nate, predictably impatient, interrupted. "How'd the embassy first learn about this?"

Unfazed, Stacy continued. "World Vision's local director, who has a compound north of Gangura, informed a contact at the British Embassy in Juba. Recognizing a U.S. NGO involvement, the Brits promptly contacted Diplomatic Security at our embassy. DSS tried unsuccessfully to contact WRC's Gangura compound and then deployed their quick-reaction team when no response was received. They arrived yesterday afternoon local time, confirming nineteen killed and found evidence that Caitlin was the intended target. An eyewitness described that the attackers were specifically looking for the white woman, executing staff members when unable to locate her."

"Any confirmation that Caitlin or Melissa were definitely kidnapped?" I asked. "Is there a chance they escaped?"

"No proof yet either way," Stacy replied. "DSS located an open escape door in the rear of the compound, and local villagers reported seeing two white women heading south along a remote trail. DSS pursued, but their comms ceased abruptly. Subsequently, their entire six-man team was found dead four kilometers from the compound. Ambushed by the same attackers seems most likely. No further updates from the embassy yet."

"Good rundown, Stacy," I said. "Nate, anything to add?"

Nate leaned forward, elbows resting on the table, tapping a pen rhythmically against his notebook. "Not much yet. I've reached out to our contacts in Juba and Kampala for the usual logistics and security support, so we'll hit the ground running. Tam booked our flights, so everything is in motion. I'm finalizing our logistics checklist for Tam and Stacy now."

"Good. Stacy, reach out personally to Joshua Gale at WRC. He's rattled and needs our steady hand. Is Lynn Davies available?"

Lynn was our go-to crisis-management consultant. A former communications director for major international NGOs, Lynn had an unmatched ability to keep client messaging controlled and calm under extreme pressure. A striking redhead with intense green eyes, Lynn projected the perfect balance of empathy and authority, making her indispensable in managing sensitive situations.

"I'll call her after we wrap up here," Stacy replied.

"If she's available, get her to Detroit ASAP. Nothing leaves WRC without our vetting it first."

Stacy nodded, taking quick notes.

"Tam, when's our flight?"

"You depart Logan tonight at eight, first class, overnight to Heathrow, connecting to Kampala. You're on the first flight into Juba the following morning."

"Nothing sooner?" Nate asked, irritated at the delay. "That's twenty-four hours of downtime. We probably won't get to Gangura for two days!"

Tam's eyes narrowed, her voice sarcastic. "Oh, Nate. I'm sorry. Yes, there were several earlier flights, but I had no idea this was a project that required any urgency."

Nate reddened, lowering his gaze and mumbling an apology.

Tam spoke softly, but she carried a big stick.

Suppressing a smile, I stood up. "Great job, everyone. We know this is all part of operating in this part of the world. If it were easy, they wouldn't need us. So stay flexible. Nate and I will make calls from here before we leave for the airport tonight."

Grabbing another donut, jelly-filled this time, I walked toward my office at the far corner. Stepping inside, I placed my backpack on the oversized antique desk, sighing appreciatively at the familiar surroundings. Several months earlier, during one of my extended absences, Tam had redesigned my formerly sterile workspace into what felt like a sophisticated 19th-century English club. Floor-to-ceiling bookshelves covered three walls, housing hundreds of books collected during my career. A pair of comfortable burgundy leather chairs flanked a small polished coffee table, while a thick Persian rug anchored the warmly lit space. The view from my third-floor window overlooked Newport Harbor, sailboats bobbing, reminding me why I'd chosen Newport for Relief Solutions' home.

Tam had transformed my office into a sanctuary, an inviting retreat that somehow managed to calm even my most stressful days.

Settling into my luxurious leather chair, I mentally shifted gears, preparing for the difficult work ahead. Caitlin Bishop needed us, and despite all our resources and talent, we were already behind the curve.

But we would find her. I was certain of it.

. . .

I knew my three senior staff would handle almost everything related to our rapidly unfolding crisis, but there were two calls I needed to make myself. The first was to Jessica Reid, Secretary Bishop's assistant. From experience, I knew that building a strong, immediate rapport with the principal assistant, or "dog robber," in military parlance, was critical. Assistants often possessed more influence than their official titles implied, controlling direct access to their superiors. Starting on a solid footing with Ms. Reid was therefore essential. My second call would be to Tony "Stitch" Bostich, my senior security manager and former team sergeant, currently home in North Carolina on extended personal leave.

As I pulled my laptop from my bag and settled it onto the polished wooden surface of my desk, Tam's familiar, clipped voice buzzed through the office intercom. "Milo, Jessica Reid from the State Department is holding on Line One."

I smiled, shaking my head in amusement. It appeared Jessica had the same idea regarding our initial contact. "Thanks, Tam. I've got it."

I lifted the phone handset to my ear. "Milo deCogan."

"Hi, Milo. It's Jessica Reid from State." Her voice caught me off-guard, soft, clear, and friendly, with the kind of warmth that hinted at youth. Without meaning to, I imagined her appearance, assuming she was likely attractive and confident. Young and hot, my man-brain summarized bluntly. I was torn between chuckling or scolding myself for jumping to that assumption.

"Hello, Jessica. You beat me to the punch. I was just about to call you."

She laughed, her voice holding a familiar note that gave me sudden pause. "I'm sure you're super busy, Milo. But I wanted to reach out right away to make sure everything's on track, and, honestly, just to say hello again. It's been, what, six years?"

Alarm bells rang in my head!

What the hell was she talking about?

My memory scrambled, desperately seeking any fragment from my past involving a Jessica Reid. It was a common enough name, but six years placed me squarely at Georgetown during graduate studies. Frantically, my mind flipped through recollections of professors, fellow students, and colleagues until the memory jumped to the forefront with painful clarity.

Jessica Reid. Georgetown. *Damn!*

"Yeah," I replied, keeping my voice calm as realization rushed in. "I suppose it has been about that long. How've you been?"

Despite my smooth outward demeanor, internally I was reeling.

Jessica Reid had been an undergraduate student enrolled in one of my advanced graduate seminars—a bright, attractive junior whose intelligence had matched her confidence. Our final group project required long study sessions, and Jessica's youthful energy was magnetic. Despite her obvious allure, at that time my life was devoted to Shannon, my wife, and our fledgling plans for the future. Jessica's playful advances, though flattering, had ultimately resulted in one painfully awkward conversation in the noisy corner of a Georgetown bar, a memory I'd buried deep beneath the weight of subsequent tragedy.

Jessica seemed unaware of my internal turmoil. "I've been great, Milo. I joined the Foreign Service right after graduating, spent a couple of years posted overseas, and for the last two years I've served as personal assistant to Secretary Bishop. And you? Of course, I was very sorry to hear about your wife."

Her words pierced the practiced armor I wore to keep Shannon's memory at a manageable distance. It had been just over three years since Shannon had been killed, and while most days I found comfort in memories of her laughter, intelligence, and contagious optimism, unexpected mentions of her still caught me off guard, scraping open wounds that I mistakenly thought were healing. I steadied my voice, forcing back the flood of memories that Jessica's innocent words had summoned.

"Thanks, Jessica. I appreciate it." I paused, recomposing my thoughts and bringing myself back into the present. "Congratulations on your quick rise at State. Clearly, you've made quite the impression. I'm genuinely happy for your success."

There was a brief pause, as though my praise had caught her by surprise. Her voice softened. "That means a lot, coming from you. I can admit it now, but I idolized you at Georgetown. You probably don't realize it, but you influenced my choice to go into government service. I briefly considered joining the CIA, like you, but I eventually decided the Foreign Service was the better fit." Before I could respond, she deftly shifted gears back to the topic at hand, reminding me that Jessica Reid had matured into a skillful and polished diplomatic professional.

"So? Do you have an update yet for the Secretary?" She continued. "He's understandably anxious. Do you know your arrival timeline in South Sudan?"

"We just booked our flights," I said, glad to have the conversation back in professional mode. "Unfortunately, commercial flights to Juba aren't frequent or convenient. Nate Delman and I will arrive in Kampala tomorrow evening. After that, we'll charter or catch the earliest possible flight north into Juba. I'd obviously have preferred to leave sooner, but this is the fastest commercial option we've got."

Jessica's response was immediate, confident, and decisive. "What if you didn't have to rely on commercial flights? Could you leave sooner? Like, in four hours?"

I glanced at the clock on my laptop's screen, calculating the myriad logistical details we'd need to address to make that timeframe. Despite the logistical complexity, I felt an immediate sense of relief. Getting on the ground as quickly as possible was always preferable in a kidnapping or hostage situation; the first seventy-two hours were crucial.

"If you can manage that, it would save us a tremendous amount of critical time," I responded. "Can you swing something that quickly?"

"Milo, remember this involves the Secretary's daughter," she replied with quiet authority. "I assume the Secretary made clear that you have the full resources of the State Department at your disposal. I will have a Gulfstream G650 on the tarmac at T.F. Green Airport in Providence at one p.m. sharp. Can you make that?"

"Absolutely," I said, feeling a rush of adrenaline. "That would be ideal. It's just myself and Nate, so two passengers total."

"Perfect. The jet will be waiting at the Fixed Base Operator terminal at T.F. Green," she continued, as though arranging private international travel were a routine item on her daily agenda, which it probably was. "It's thirteen hours flight time direct to Juba. You should plan on touching down around eight a.m. local time tomorrow morning."

"That's outstanding. I owe you one for the help. I'll be sure to update you personally when we depart and again when we arrive."

She laughed once again into the phone, a warm, comfortable sound that reminded me of our youthful interactions six years prior. "I'm confident you will, Milo. Stay safe, and we'll speak again soon."

As Jessica disconnected, I sat in silence, trying to recalibrate my expectations. My earlier mental image of Jessica had shifted during the course of our conversation. Jessica Reid had grown into a seasoned professional, calmly confident and efficient under pressure. Secretary Bishop was fortunate to have someone so capable at his side.

At the same time, a subtle unease tugged at my mind regarding our shared Georgetown history. In a mission as sensitive and potentially dangerous as rescuing the Secretary's kidnapped daughter, personal entanglements, even minor ones, had the potential to complicate matters. Jessica's reappearance in my life was unexpected, and while she came across as mature and professional, I resolved to proceed with caution.

I pushed those thoughts aside for the moment, turning instead to the immediate task at hand. Our departure schedule had just accelerated, and there was substantial work yet to do before wheels-up. Relief Solutions thrived because we were nimble, flexible, and responsive. Jessica's offer of the State Department jet provided exactly the agility we needed, significantly improving our chance of resolving Caitlin's kidnapping safely and quickly.

Still, a part of me couldn't help but reflect again on the passage of six years. Back then, Jessica had been eager, idealistic, and perhaps a bit impulsive—a bright undergraduate student flirting with the exciting, dangerous, clandestine world of intelligence and security. Now she was poised, professional, and self-assured, navigating the complexities and pressures of diplomacy at the highest levels of government.

Time, I thought wryly, had changed us both, though perhaps more so her than me. For me, the past six years had brought tremendous personal loss, professional growth, and relentless challenges. I wasn't the man Jessica had once known, certainly not the same optimistic grad student whose life had seemed charmed and exciting. And yet, as always, the job now demanded absolute clarity of purpose and unwavering focus.

I pushed Jessica Reid from my mind, resolving to compartmentalize any lingering uncertainties about our past. At this point, Jessica was simply an asset, a valuable resource to help expedite our mission. I stood from my desk, ready to brief the team on our adjusted timeline, already preparing for my next call to Tony "Stitch" Bostich. Time continued to slip away from us, and Caitlin Bishop's life depended on every second.

As I reached for the intercom to inform Tam and Nate of the revised departure schedule, a quiet voice whispered at the edge of my consciousness, reminding me of Shannon, and of just how rapidly and unpredictably life could change.

I quickly silenced that voice, focusing instead on the mission ahead. Shannon had taught me that in life's most difficult moments, strength was found in decisive action. I intended to honor her lesson once more, by acting swiftly, skillfully, and decisively, just as she would have expected of me.

. . .

After briefing the staff on our adjusted plans, Nate seemed thrilled at the prospect of a private jet, and Tam and Stacy began adjusting timelines for our expedited departure. Given the fully equipped locker room at our Newport office, returning home was unnecessary as all my gear and clothes were on hand. Leaning back in my over-sized chair, I gazed out across the swaying sailboats moored in Newport Harbor, mentally cataloging everything required before wheels-up.

A sharp rap at my door disrupted my thoughts.

"Sorry to interrupt, boss," Nate said from the open doorway. His lean, restless frame was already dressed in tactical cargo pants and a snug-fitting black polo bearing our discreet Relief Solutions logo. "Just to confirm. You want the full K&R kit for this op, right? Now that we've got private transport, weight won't be an issue."

On every Relief Solutions mission, we carried a basic load of essential equipment and supplies tailored to each crisis. "K&R," short-hand for "kidnap and ransom," meant a using our specialized packing list that included surveillance gear, encrypted communications, medical kits, and weapons. Nate's real question was whether we'd be bringing guns, something international commercial flights made impossible.

"Yes, full K&R. And Nate?" I paused, leaning forward to empha-size the point. "Double everything. Use your imagination, especially drones and comms gear. I've got a funny feeling about this one, and I want every possible advantage if things go sideways. I'll call Stitch shortly; might need him on standby if this gets complicated."

"Roger that." Nate gave me a decisive nod before vanishing down the hallway. Seconds later, I heard the faint beep of the biometric scanner as he accessed our secure equipment vault and armory.

I turned my attention to the sleek, high-tech office phone resting on my antique desk, my eyes scanning until I found the button labeled "Stitch." Pressing it, I inserted an AirPod into my ear, allowing the digital magic to route the call.

The phone rang twice before the deep, unmistakable southern

drawl of Tony "Stitch" Bostitch answered smoothly. "Hey brother, a bit early for our usual morning chat, isn't it?"

Stitch's voice carried a familiar warmth that instantly eased my tension. Retired Army Sergeant Major Tony Bostitch had been more than my senior enlisted advisor during my tenure commanding a Special Forces A-Team. He was my confidant, protector, and, above all, my best friend. Stitch had spent over two decades in elite military units, including the prestigious 1st Special Forces Operational Detachment–Delta, better known as Delta Force. With countless deployments, dozens of high-stakes missions, and an unparalleled record of battlefield success, Stitch was the man you wanted beside you when things went sideways.

Yet beneath the hardened exterior of a career soldier, Stitch possessed a quiet depth that few ever saw. Tall, powerfully built, and with his signature Fu Manchu mustache, Stitch radiated a calm authority born from years of commanding men under fire. Those fortunate enough to know him well, myself included, understood that his dry humor and quick wit often masked the heart of a fiercely loyal, deeply compassionate man. He'd stood by my side through the grief of losing Shannon, and now, ironically, it was my turn to support him in an even greater tragedy.

Three months earlier, Stitch had taken a leave of absence to return home to Southern Pines, North Carolina. His thirteen-year-old son, Logan, had been diagnosed with a devastatingly aggressive brain tumor. After a courageous fight, Logan had passed away just shy of a month ago, exactly twenty-six days prior, a count I silently kept in sympathy. For Stitch, a man who had triumphed against impossible odds on countless battlefields, the helplessness he'd faced against Logan's illness was unimaginably painful.

"Not too early, I hope?" I joked. "Did I catch you sleeping in?"

Stitch's deep chuckle resonated through the line, easing the tension. "Nah, brother, you know better. Been up since 0500. Got in ten miles before sunrise."

His predictable reply made me smile. Stitch's relentless discipline was legendary, matched only by his devotion to classic rock trivia. It was an eccentricity of his that had become a hallmark of our conversations. I waited, suspecting what might come next.

"You know what they say. 'When the morning light comes streaming in, I'll get up and do it again.'" He immediately starting humming the tune to Final Jeopardy, expecting me to try and name the song and artist.

I rolled my eyes, secretly enjoying being baited into yet another lyrical guessing game. "Jackson Browne, 'The Pretender.' C'mon, Stitch, challenge me, man. That was too easy. I grew up on Jackson Browne and Fleetwood Mac."

"Damn, you're good, brother," Stitch laughed, delighted. "I guess I've trained you well. So what's up? Everything squared away up in Newport?"

I shifted gears to a more serious tone. "Just got back from Guyana and thought I'd be taking some downtime. But things changed this morning. I received a direct call from the Secretary of State."

Stitch paused. "George Bishop himself?"

"The one and only," I confirmed.

"No kidding? So what did the SecState want with you?"

"His daughter, Caitlin, was kidnapped in South Sudan. She was working for the World Refugee Committee. Attackers hit their compound, slaughtered the entire local staff, and Caitlin, along with another young American woman, are missing and presumed kidnapped."

There was a pause on Stitch's end, followed by a low whistle. "Sounds messy. But why us, Milo? Bishop's got the entire Diplomatic Security Service at his fingertips."

As expected, Stitch understood the complexity of the situation immediately.

"DSS dispatched their quick reaction team, and they got ambushed. All six DSS guys are dead. Bishop now thinks we're his best bet, off the books, discreet, plausible deniability. I'm pretty sure General Donovan put my name forward."

Stitch snorted. "Jack Donovan's behind this, huh? Figures. You know Jack thinks you're the second coming of Colonel Kurtz."

I ignored Stitch's playful jab referencing *Apocalypse Now* and continued. "Anyway, Nate and I are wheels-up to Juba in a few hours. Jessica Reid, the Secretary's assistant, just arranged a State Department Gulfstream for us."

"Fancy," Stitch teased. "You sure you don't need another set of boots on the ground? I've already checked. There's an afternoon nonstop from Raleigh up your way. I can be in Newport before dinner."

"Stay put for now," I instructed firmly but gently. "Honestly, Stitch, you're plugged in with Tam and Stacy from your house, and you can coordinate anything that's needed from there. If things go sideways and we need you in-country, flights are just as quick out of Charlotte as they are out of Boston."

"You sure?" Stitch's voice carried genuine concern. "I know I've been out of pocket lately, but my head's back in the game. Put me in coach; I'm ready to play, today."

I laughed aloud at Stitch's perfectly timed lyric drop from John Fogerty's baseball classic, "Centerfield." This quirky habit had become endearing to everyone at Relief Solutions, even if it often required humoring his relentless musical trivia quizzes.

"Fogerty? Really?" I teased. "You're making this way too easy today."

"Just testing you, brother," Stitch laughed, pleased to lighten the mood. Then his voice turned serious again. "But really, brother—no bullshit. If you need me, say the word. I can head to the airport in an hour."

I felt a rush of gratitude, realizing once again how fortunate I was to have someone like Stitch at my side. His loyalty, strength, and calm presence had seen me through more impossible situations than I could count. But now, it was my turn to return that loyalty.

"I know. But it's important you spend this time with your family.

I promise I'll call the minute we know more. And keep your phone close; you never know how fast this might escalate."

"Okay, man. I'll be ready. I'll give Stacy and Tam a call and help coordinate logistics. Whatever you need, I'm your guy."

I smiled, grateful as always for Stitch's calm strength. "I know you are. I appreciate it, Stitch, more than you realize."

We fell into a brief silence, a quiet acknowledgment passing between us of all the hardships we'd faced and overcome together. Finally, Stitch broke the silence in typical fashion.

"You know, speaking of Fogerty, I think he put it best: 'Someday never comes.' You remember that song?"

I laughed. "Of course. You know you're not going to stump me with Creedence Clearwater Revival, right? My parents were Boomers. I grew up on this shit."

"Damn straight," Stitch laughed. "From CCR's Mardi Gras album, 1972. Always sharp, Milo. Guess some of my brilliance rubbed off."

"Must have been accidental," I chuckled, shaking my head. "All joking aside, give my best to your family. And Stitch...thank you."

"Anytime, brother," Stitch replied, voice serious once more. "You watch your back in Sudan. Keep that head on a swivel, you hear me?"

"Roger that. Will do."

"Good. Talk soon."

The line disconnected, and I sat back, feeling better after our conversation. Stitch had that rare gift—the ability to infuse even the most difficult conversations with quiet strength and humor. It was why he was invaluable to Relief Solutions, but far more importantly, it was why he was invaluable to me.

We had shared everything: combat, grief, triumph, loss. Losing Shannon had been devastating, and Stitch had carried me through those darkest days. In return, I would always have his back, especially now, as he navigated his profound loss. He needed time to heal, even if he wouldn't admit it himself.

Reluctantly, I stood, shaking off those reflections. There would be time later to ponder the weight of friendships, memories, and loss. Now was the moment for action. With less than three hours before takeoff, it was time to get moving.

Yet as I left my office and walked toward the armory, Stitch's words echoed in my mind, almost as if he'd deliberately chosen lyrics that now resonated more deeply:

"Put me in coach—I'm ready to play today."

I smiled. Someday, Stitch, very soon, I'll take you up on that offer. But not today. Today, Nate and I would play centerfield ourselves, because lives were on the line, and we couldn't afford to drop the ball.

6

1 MARCH 0705 HRS

SOMEWHERE SOUTH OF GANGURA, **South Sudan**

She ran until she could no longer hear anything beyond her own jagged breathing and the strained wheezing of Melissa stumbling behind her. Caitlin's legs burned, her lungs protesting against every ragged breath. Still, she pushed on, driven by a raw mix of fear and survival instinct. As she slowed slightly, her senses returned just enough to note the unexpected openness of the terrain, more a lightly wooded forest than the dense, tangled jungle she'd imagined.

Pausing for a brief moment, Caitlin glanced at her watch. Barely thirty minutes had passed since their chaotic escape from the camp, but each of those minutes felt stretched into hours, distorted by adrenaline and fear. Her thoughts flickered dangerously toward the horrific scene she'd left behind. Festus collapsing lifelessly against the communal hut, Sebastian struck down and beaten. She fought to suppress those memories, knowing that allowing herself to dwell on the horror would paralyze her.

Was Festus really dead? Had Sebastian survived? And the others?

A deep pang of guilt clawed at her heart, but she quickly clamped down on the surging emotions. Survival was the only priority now. She had spent her months in South Sudan immersed in stories of resilience, bravery, and endurance among the refugees. It was time she drew strength from their examples.

Attempting to anchor her racing mind, she estimated they'd run roughly a mile from the WRC compound, maybe more. It was difficult to tell in the rolling, jungle terrain. Caitlin had done her best to maintain a steady direction, vaguely south or southeast, but as she scanned the featureless horizon through the trees, a gnawing doubt crept in. She strained to recall the area map pinned to the wall of Sebastian's office. Where was the nearest village? Five miles? Ten? She silently cursed herself for not paying closer attention.

A sudden, sharp sound jarred Caitlin from her thoughts. Turning quickly, she saw Melissa doubled over, heaving violently into the sparse underbrush beside her. Melissa's slender frame shook uncontrollably, her blonde hair tangled and damp with sweat, sticking awkwardly to her pale, tear-streaked face.

"God... I—I can't..." Melissa gasped between convulsive heaves. "Please, Caitlin, we need... to stop. I can't breathe..."

Caitlin moved to her, placing a gentle hand on Melissa's trembling back, feeling the warmth radiating through the thin, damp fabric of her shirt. With tenderness that surprised even herself, Caitlin brushed away a tangled strand of Melissa's hair, gently tucking it behind the young woman's ear.

"It's okay," Caitlin whispered, forcing calm into her voice despite her own trembling hands. "Just breathe slowly. We're going to be alright. We just need to catch our breath, okay?"

Melissa shot her a look filled with a mixture of incredulity and anger. Her eyes, normally bright with youthful idealism, were wide with fear and disbelief. "Are you kidding me?" she managed bitterly, her voice cracking. "Caitlin, we are definitely not okay right now."

Caitlin opened her mouth to respond, but Melissa doubled over again, retching dryly, her stomach already emptied from sheer terror. Caitlin winced, feeling helpless as she watched her younger colleague struggle against panic and exhaustion.

She searched for reassuring words, something to bolster Melissa's dwindling confidence, but her mind was blank. *What can I possibly say? That it's fine? That we're safe?* Caitlin knew these assurances would ring hollow, yet Melissa needed something, anything, to hold onto.

"Look, Melissa," Caitlin began again, speaking more assertively despite her own doubts, "I know it looks really bad right now, but people will come for us. They'll realize we're missing and send help. We just have to find a safe place and lay low for a while. As long as we avoid whoever attacked us, we'll be okay."

No sooner had the words left her mouth than a sudden burst of gunfire shattered the stillness, echoing harshly through the sparse trees. Automatic weapon fire, sharp and rapid, filled the air for several tense seconds. Then came more gunshots—single, deliberate shots punctuating the air, spaced apart just enough to suggest methodical precision. Twenty, maybe thirty individual rounds.

Caitlin's pulse quickened, the gunfire far too close, far closer than she'd expected. Was she mistaken in how far they'd run? Or was it simply the cruel acoustics of the open landscape, the sound carrying further in the still morning air? Whatever the reason, Caitlin knew these weren't the sounds of combat, but something far worse. She imagined her colleagues lined up, defenseless, executed one by one in cold blood by merciless attackers.

Bile rose sharply in her throat, and Caitlin fought desperately to push down the vivid images of carnage and betrayal. She needed clarity, not despair.

Melissa sank to her knees, sobbing, head buried in her trembling hands. Her small body shook with uncontrollable grief and fear, finally overwhelmed by the gravity of their situation. Caitlin's heart twisted at Melissa's obvious despair. Yet she also knew staying here, frozen in fear, was a death sentence.

Caitlin knelt beside Melissa, gripping her shoulders firmly. "I know how terrifying this is," she whispered. "But sitting here won't change anything. We need to keep moving. Do you understand me? The attackers could already be searching for us."

Melissa raised her head, tear-streaked eyes swollen, pleading. "But why us? Why did this happen?"

Caitlin hesitated, the question hitting too close to a truth she'd been avoiding since the first shots rang out that morning. Her father's position as Secretary of State made her a target, a fact she'd conveniently disregarded during her fifteen months in-country. Caitlin rarely mentioned her father to coworkers. She'd always wanted to stand on her own merits, not lean on her father's shadow. But she wasn't naïve enough to believe others hadn't talked. Word travels fast, especially in a close-knit camp.

Was this her fault? Had these people died because of who she was?

"I don't know why. Truly, I don't. But right now, figuring out why doesn't matter. Staying alive is all that counts." Her voice was firm, stronger now with resolve. "We need to move. Slow is fine, but we can't afford to stay here."

Melissa blinked several times, swallowing hard. Caitlin offered her hand, gripping firmly and pulling the younger woman to her feet. Melissa's body shook visibly, but she steadied herself, wiped away fresh tears, and nodded hesitantly.

Caitlin felt a fleeting moment of pride for Melissa's courage, then quickly turned her attention to their immediate surroundings. She tried to recall the overhead map once more. *Was there a village nearby? Had Sebastian mentioned one?* Yes, she remembered something about a settlement perhaps two miles south of camp. If they could reach it, maybe they could find shelter or help.

"Listen," Caitlin said, trying to instill confidence with her tone, "I think there's a village about two miles from here. If we keep moving, we should reach it soon. We'll find help there."

Melissa met her gaze with renewed determination, breathing deeply. "Okay. Let's do it."

They set off cautiously, walking now rather than running, Caitlin taking the lead while Melissa followed closely behind. Every step heightened their sense of vulnerability, every rustling branch or crackling twig sending spikes of anxiety surging through their bodies.

Minutes dragged on agonizingly slow. As they moved, Caitlin's thoughts returned to her colleagues—Festus's jovial laugh, Sebastian's quiet strength. The grim reality of their likely deaths clawed at her conscience. Had they sacrificed themselves unknowingly simply by association with her? Could she ever forgive herself if that was the case?

"Caitlin," Melissa's voice broke through her spiraling thoughts, quiet and cautious. "Do you really think someone will find us? I mean, who even knows we're alive?"

Caitlin swallowed hard, wishing she could provide more certainty. "When we miss check-ins, people will notice. Our Nairobi office tracks us closely. My father—" she hesitated, feeling uncomfortable mentioning him, but continuing regardless. "My father won't rest until we're found. Trust me."

Melissa nodded, clearly drawing comfort from Caitlin's words, though Caitlin herself felt anything but certain. Still, she knew she had to maintain an outward appearance of calm determination, for Melissa's sake as much as her own.

She found herself desperately wishing for Sebastian's guidance. He'd always known what to do, where to go, whom to call. Without him, Caitlin felt painfully inexperienced, vulnerable. Doubt began creeping insidiously into her mind, questioning whether she had the strength or wisdom to lead them both safely through this nightmare.

No, she told herself. *Stop. You can't think like that.*

She'd spent countless hours speaking to refugee women, survivors of unimaginable horrors who had somehow persevered against incredible odds. She'd listened, admired, learned from their stories of courage and resilience. Now, she had to embody that strength herself. There was no other choice.

"We'll get through this. I promise you," Caitlin spoke firmly, pushing aside her fears and doubts.

Melissa gave her a hesitant smile, trying to muster bravery. "I know we will."

As they continued through the sparse forest, Caitlin's mind remained on high alert, scanning their surroundings for danger. Every shifting shadow, every faint sound sent adrenaline surging through her veins. Yet beneath her outward vigilance, a quiet determination grew stronger, a refusal to surrender to fear or despair.

She would find a way to protect Melissa and herself, no matter what it took. Festus, Sebastian, and the others had not died in vain. Their sacrifice would give her strength, sharpen her resolve, and guide her actions.

As the oppressive stillness of the morning wrapped around them once again, Caitlin led Melissa forward step by cautious step, driven by an unspoken promise, a silent vow to honor those she had lost, and a fierce determination to survive whatever challenges awaited them.

7

2 MARCH 1300 HRS

T.F. GREEN AIRPORT, **Warwick, Rhode Island**

I exited the FBO terminal at T.F. Green Airport, the late-morning sun glinted off the streamlined fuselage of the waiting Gulfstream G650, parked about fifty meters away on the apron. Even from a distance, the jet looked extraordinary—long, elegant, and gleaming white with a narrow stripe of deep navy blue accenting the sleek body. It exuded power and speed, a confident symbol of governmental might.

Beside the open hatch at the rear of the plane stood a young man wearing black slacks and a crisp white short-sleeved shirt. He waved politely as Nate and I approached.

"Good morning, Mr. deCogan," the man said, extending a friendly hand. "My name is Jason, and I'm your co-pilot for today's flight. Hand me your bags and take any seat you like. We'll have wheels-up within minutes."

I shook Jason's hand and offered a wry grin. "Nice to meet you, Jason. Do they make you pump the gas too?"

He chuckled. "Hey, I'm from the government; I'm here to help."

I introduced Nate as we placed our bags in the spacious cargo hold near the rear of the jet. It seemed odd to me that a highly skilled pilot was handling baggage duties, but I knew better than most the paradoxes of government service. The U.S. government could spend fifty million dollars on a cutting-edge jet but balked at staffing it properly. Strategic vision and common sense were always in short supply among bureaucrats, and despite knowing many exceptional government servants, I remained cynical about the system itself.

Stepping aboard, my cynicism briefly faded in admiration. The interior of the G650 was breathtaking. Plush, cream-colored leather chairs sat tastefully spaced throughout the cabin, each adorned with polished wood detailing that matched the panels lining the walls. Smooth, pale carpeting cushioned my footsteps as I entered, my eyes taking in the separate lounge area at the rear, where two couches sat opposite a state-of-the-art entertainment system. Every inch of the jet whispered luxury and refined taste. This was no typical government transport. Clearly, diplomatic travel had some hidden perks.

As I placed my backpack onto one of the forward seats, a familiar yet unexpected voice caught me by surprise.

"Well, hello there, Milo. It's been a very long time."

My breath momentarily caught as I looked up to see Jessica Reid walking down the aisle toward me, a half-empty champagne flute casually in hand. Her emerald eyes sparkled with barely-contained delight, a playful smile dancing across her lips. She hadn't changed much. If anything, she had become more captivating, more self-assured, more dangerously beautiful than the ambitious undergraduate I'd known at Georgetown.

Before I could process the unexpected encounter, Jessica had closed the gap and wrapped her arms around my neck, drawing me into an embrace far more intimate than anticipated. Without hesitation, she placed a deliberate, lingering kiss squarely on my cheek—not the polite greeting kind, but the kind certain to leave a lipstick mark.

"I missed you. It's really good to see you again," she murmured.

Heat surged into my face, and I felt my heartbeat quicken. Her proximity was intoxicatingly disorienting. "Ah, hi," I managed awkwardly, mentally chastising myself for losing composure so easily. "We weren't expecting you here."

Jessica took another casual sip from her champagne flute, her gaze never wavering from mine. "Secretary Bishop insisted you have every bit of support possible," she replied. "So, here I am."

Suddenly, memories flooded back, moments I'd successfully buried until this moment. At Georgetown, Jessica had been an enticing yet dangerous distraction. Her attraction to me had been bold, unapologetic, and hard to ignore. I vividly recalled her sharp intellect, quick humor, and striking beauty—qualities that had made resisting her advances a significant personal test. Yet my marriage to Shannon had always been my North Star, guiding me away from temptation, no matter how flattering or relentless Jessica's pursuit had been.

Jessica stepped even closer, reasserting the subtle dominance she always managed in social interactions. My instincts reflexively pulled me back, yet she matched my movement, maintaining her position mere inches from me. I became painfully aware of the delicate scent of her perfume and the gentle touch of her fingertips tracing a slow, deliberate path along my arm.

I noticed Nate's curious gaze fixated on us, a barely suppressed smirk playing across his face. Before the situation grew even more awkward, he stepped forward, extending his hand warmly toward Jessica.

"Jessica, Nate Delman, operations director. Pleasure meeting you."

Jessica finally broke eye contact with me and shook Nate's hand. "Thank you both for your quick response. Settle in. I'll brief you both fully once we're airborne." She shot one last provocative smile my way and headed towards the cockpit, leaving Nate and me to exchange glances.

Nate's mischievous smile broadened as he slid into a chair. "So, boss, when exactly were you planning to mention Jessica? Nice lipstick souvenir, by the way. Guess being a Georgetown alum has perks." He chuckled to himself, retrieving headphones from his bag. Nate had learned in combat to sleep whenever possible, so I knew he'd soon be out cold.

Shaking my head, I chose a seat in the next section behind Nate. As I settled into the comfortable recliner, I marveled again at the G650's interior. Eight luxurious seats grouped around polished wooden tables, a private lounge area behind a divider, and technological amenities discreetly embedded throughout. The plushness stood in stark contrast to the gritty, minimalist environments of my usual operations. For once, I'd travel in unaccustomed luxury, though given our purpose, comfort seemed almost inappropriate.

Moments later, the jet's engines purred to life, quickly rising into a confident roar. Jessica returned, gracefully slipping into the seat facing mine rather than the open chair across the aisle I'd expected her to take. Her intentional proximity unsettled me, a clear message that she intended to pick up where we left off years ago.

As we buckled up, the aircraft began taxiing toward the runway. Gazing outside, I watched the terminal buildings slide past, the vivid Rhode Island sky filled with wisps of high-altitude clouds. The jet paused momentarily, then surged forward with a breathtaking thrust. The G650 leapt from the tarmac, and in seconds, the sweeping panorama of Narragansett Bay stretched out beneath us, dotted with countless sailboats glittering against the sapphire water.

For a moment, I allowed myself the pleasure of that spectacular view: boats bobbing at anchor, the ribbon-like Newport Bridge arched in the distance, and the familiar coastline receding below. Then, reluctantly turning from the scenery, I faced Jessica again, readying myself for the conversation I knew was coming.

"Jessica, thanks again for arranging this jet. You've saved us crucial time."

Her eyes gleamed playfully, though beneath her charm lay unmistakable purpose. "No trouble at all. It's genuinely wonderful seeing you again. You haven't changed a bit."

I nodded. "Likewise. Though I'll admit your being aboard came as a surprise."

She smiled, her eyes briefly distant, as if recalling a memory. "Secretary Bishop insisted on me being available. He's understandably frantic over Caitlin. Anything you need, just ask. I'm at your complete disposal." Her emphasis left little doubt that her offer extended beyond purely professional support.

I met her gaze carefully, remembering the last night we'd spoken at Georgetown, our last day of classes, and the booze-soaked celebration at The Tombs. Jessica had cornered me late in the evening, pressing herself close, whispering provocatively in my ear, quoting the iconic line from Top Gun: "Take me to bed or lose me forever." It had taken considerable willpower to gently decline her bold offer. I'd chosen my marriage vows over momentary temptation, but the look of stunned hurt in Jessica's eyes that night still haunted me. She had stormed away angrily, our friendship severed in an instant.

"I appreciate your support," I began carefully, steering our conversation back to safer ground. "We've already coordinated ground logistics, but your connections at the embassy might be useful."

She leaned forward, her expression earnest. "I'm staying with you in Juba. Secretary Bishop expects hourly updates. I'll be your direct liaison."

Her revelation wasn't entirely unexpected but still unwelcome. This mission required independence and discretion. Having a high-profile State Department aide shadowing me risked alienating essential local contacts.

"Jessica," I said, controlling my tone, "while your offer is generous, we work best with complete autonomy. Some crucial sources won't cooperate if they see a government presence."

Her eyes narrowed, emerald irises sharpening with irritation. "Secretary Bishop specifically requested my involvement. I'm to accompany you personally."

I took a slow breath, carefully framing my response. "I understand. Believe me, I'm grateful. But my sources trust Relief Solutions precisely because we maintain independence from official channels. They'll clam up instantly if they sense government influence. Surely you see that?"

She hesitated, frustration flickering across her features before finally nodding reluctantly. "I suppose you're right. But we must stay in constant contact."

"I promise to keep you continuously updated," I assured her. "Your most critical role is coordinating from the embassy. It helps more than you realize."

She seemed somewhat mollified. Yet lingering disappointment shadowed her eyes as she stood. "Fine. You always were persuasive. Let me grab the Secretary's dossier for you."

As Jessica passed, she placed a gentle, almost possessive squeeze on my shoulder, an unexpected intimacy that sent warmth flooding through me despite my best efforts. Our past tension, it seemed, was not entirely forgotten.

I watched her move gracefully down the cabin, the soft sway of her pencil skirt drawing attention. Memories of Georgetown returned in waves—her brilliance in class debates, her mischievous sense of humor, and that final painful night at The Tombs. Guilt still tugged at me; my rejection had obviously wounded her pride deeply.

As she returned, dossier in hand, our eyes briefly met, reigniting unspoken tension. Jessica Reid was still accustomed to getting her way, and the intensity of her attention worried me. Managing the delicate emotional landscape between us would add unnecessary complexity to an already challenging mission.

Yet despite my apprehensions, another part of me acknowledged the simple truth: Jessica remained an undeniably compelling presence. Her charm, intelligence, and subtle determination resonated powerfully, recalling exactly why I'd found her tempting years ago. I resolved to tread carefully around Jessica, maintaining the fragile boundary between past and present, personal feelings, and professional obligations.

As the sleek jet hurtled eastward, carrying us toward a perilous unknown in South Sudan, I forced my wandering thoughts back to the daunting task at hand. Caitlin Bishop needed our unwavering focus. Emotional entanglements from the past had no place now.

I opened the dossier Jessica handed me, immersing myself in the pages of reports and briefings. Yet despite my efforts at professionalism, the subtle fragrance of Jessica's perfume lingered tantalizingly close, reminding me that old memories, however deeply buried, had a way of resurfacing precisely when they could complicate life most dangerously.

8

2 MARCH 1724 HRS

GANGURA, South Sudan

The oppressive afternoon heat clung mercilessly to Caitlin's body, a heavy, unrelenting weight that pressed down on her with each breath she took. Her skin felt raw, scraped by countless thorny bushes and baked red by the harsh South Sudanese sun. Crouched low beside Melissa in a cluster of sparse bushes, Caitlin stared anxiously at the tiny hamlet before them—a pitiful scattering of three weathered tukuls and a single squat cinderblock building, looking abandoned and forgotten in the vast emptiness.

The dirt road that wound through the hamlet was little more than a thin, faded scar in the earth, stretching endlessly toward an uncertain horizon. Caitlin's gaze flickered nervously back and forth, searching for signs of life, signs of safety, or signs of danger.

Melissa shifted uncomfortably beside her, licking cracked, swollen lips. "We should just go in," she whispered hoarsely, her voice strained and desperate. "Caitlin, please, I...I don't think I can walk another step without water."

Caitlin looked at her friend, taking in Melissa's hollow cheeks, sunken eyes, and the exhausted slump of her shoulders. Guilt twisted Caitlin's stomach. They'd been moving since dawn the previous day, staying hidden deep within the bush, avoiding roads and paths. Every step had been an agonizing battle against hunger, exhaustion, and the crippling fear of discovery. But Melissa's suffering was becoming unbearable. They had no food, and they'd finished the two bottles of water stashed in Caitlin's go-bag yesterday afternoon. Caitlin knew dehydration was deadly, and Melissa was teetering dangerously on the edge.

Still, an instinctual sense of caution surged through Caitlin's veins, screaming silently for her to wait, to hide, to observe before blindly entering the unknown. "I don't like it," she murmured quietly, eyes narrowing as she scanned the hamlet once more. "We don't know who lives there. It's too risky. Let's wait, maybe go in after dark."

Melissa turned to her, eyes dull with exhaustion, barely a spark of life left in them. "They're just kids, Caitlin. Look—two boys and a girl. There aren't any adults around. We'll be okay."

Caitlin followed Melissa's gaze, her heart aching as she saw two young boys laughing softly by a small cooking fire, kicking a faded ball between them. A teenage girl, maybe fifteen or sixteen, moved between the tukuls, carrying a battered plastic bucket. No other movement, no other adults in sight. It seemed safe enough.

Caitlin hesitated, torn between caution and compassion. But Melissa's suffering overrode her instincts. "Fine," she finally relented. "But we stay alert, and at the first sign of trouble, we run. If we get separated, meet right back here after dark."

Melissa nodded weakly but moved quickly, stumbling from their hiding spot before Caitlin could second-guess herself.

They approached with caution, legs trembling, exhaustion heavy on their limbs. The children noticed them as soon as they walked out of the woods. With delighted shouts, the two young boys rushed forward, wide-eyed and smiling broadly, their laughter carefree and welcoming. Caitlin felt a flicker of relief at their youthful innocence.

"Sene oo," Caitlin said hesitantly, recalling one of the few Zande greetings she'd managed to pick up during her months in South Sudan.

The boys grinned, amused at her accented words, and quickly thrust a plastic jug toward Melissa. She seized it eagerly, drinking messily, water streaming down her chin. Caitlin accepted another jug, taking careful sips, savoring the warm, earthy taste. It felt miraculous on her parched throat.

The teenage girl watched from a distance, eyes sharp and wary. She turned abruptly and disappeared into the cinderblock building. Caitlin stiffened, nerves flickering back to life, but moments later, the girl reappeared carrying a battered tin plate filled with boiled maize and beans.

"Eat," she commanded in halting, cautious English, placing the food before them.

Caitlin hesitated only briefly before hunger overcame her caution. She and Melissa sat down, scooping the bland but nourishing food gratefully into their mouths. Despite its simplicity, the meal felt wonderfully restorative, each bite returning a small measure of strength to their weary bodies.

"Thank you," Caitlin murmured, feeling a bit more relaxed. "Tambuahe foro," she added, hoping it was correct. The girl nodded silently, observing them closely.

For the first time in what seemed forever, Caitlin allowed herself to breathe deeply, a small spark of hope flickering in her chest. Perhaps they'd finally found safety, however fleeting.

"I go more," the girl suddenly said, turning and walking back toward the building.

Caitlin watched her disappear, mentally reviewing the few Zande phrases she remembered, feeling regretful she hadn't made more effort to learn the language. Melissa closed her eyes, sighing in relief, unaware of the tension reasserting itself within Caitlin.

In a heartbeat, everything changed.

The girl reemerged from the building doorway, but this time she carried a battered AK-47 rifle cradled in one arm, and a satellite phone clutched in her other hand. Caitlin's breath froze in her chest, her stomach twisting violently. Melissa choked on the last bite of food, eyes widening in pure terror.

"Sit!" the girl barked, raising the rifle in clear threat.

Neither Caitlin nor Melissa hesitated; they obeyed immediately, sinking back down onto the dusty ground. Caitlin's pulse pounded as she struggled to maintain composure. The girl dialed the satellite phone, speaking urgently, not in Zande, but Swahili, a language Caitlin understood far better. Her blood ran cold as she heard the unmistakable words: *"mzungu dem wa mana"*—*important white girl.* The message was chillingly clear. Whoever was on the other end of that call, they were coming...soon.

Minutes passed with torturous slowness, each second feeling like an eternity as Caitlin carefully observed their captor. The girl's stance, initially firm, gradually relaxed; the rifle slowly lowered as confidence replaced caution. Caitlin felt a surge of desperate hope. This was her chance. The teenager was armed but inexperienced, her attention divided, her grip loosening.

Caitlin silently signaled Melissa with her eyes, communicating the urgency of her plan. Melissa nodded subtly, understanding dawning on her exhausted face. Caitlin knew the risk was enormous, but it was their only hope.

Time seemed to slow, each breath measured, calculated. Caitlin watched intently, waiting until the girl's attention drifted toward the empty road, perhaps straining to hear the distant sound of approaching vehicles.

In the tiny instant between one heartbeat and the next, Caitlin lunged forward.

Her muscles screamed in protest as she propelled herself from the dirt, her exhausted body exploding into a desperate burst of energy. The girl reacted too slowly, startled, and stumbled backward. The AK-47 clattered noisily to the ground, the satellite phone tumbling away, spinning across the dirt.

"Melissa, run!" Caitlin shouted, her voice echoing across the empty hamlet, as she scrambled to gain her balance and begin running, propelled by sheer terror.

The boy was faster than she'd ever anticipated.

Caitlin barely reached the shadowy edge of the tree line before he slammed into her from behind, his wiry arms wrapping tightly around her waist, momentum sending them crashing hard into the dusty earth. The impact knocked the wind from her lungs in a ragged gasp. Twigs, leaves, and dirt filled her mouth as they tumbled together, rolling in a chaotic tangle of limbs. She clawed blindly at the earth, panic rising sharply in her throat.

Despite his size, the boy was fierce, all sharp elbows and determined strength. His small fingers scrabbled desperately, attempting to seize her wrists and pin her down. Caitlin kicked wildly, her feet skidding uselessly against loose dirt. Adrenaline surged through her body, heightening every sensation: the rough scrape of rocks against her skin, the boy's breath hot and ragged in her ear, and the acrid tang of fear.

As they rolled again, Caitlin's right hand brushed something hard —a stone, its sharp edge jagged beneath her fingers. Without conscious thought, driven solely by a primitive urge to survive, she seized it, swinging upward with desperate strength.

A sickening, wet crunch echoed sharply through the air.

Immediately, the boy's grip went slack, his body collapsing onto hers like a rag doll. Gasping, shaking uncontrollably, Caitlin shoved him aside, scrambling backward, eyes wide in shock. Blood stained the stone in her trembling hand, dripping onto the parched ground in tiny, dark spots. Nausea twisted sharply in her gut.

She couldn't look directly at him. Couldn't bear to check whether he was still breathing. There was no time for guilt, no room for hesitation. Not now.

Heart pounding, Caitlin stumbled to her feet, dropping the bloody rock, her mind spinning with horror and disbelief. She turned and plunged blindly deeper into the dense bush, branches tearing at her skin, panic lending speed and recklessness to her steps. Behind her, the fading daylight cast long, distorted shadows across the landscape, amplifying her terror and sense of isolation.

It was only moments later when Caitlin realized with sickening clarity that Melissa had not run.

Caitlin's heart twisted painfully when she heard the distant but unmistakable grinding of engines approaching rapidly. Her pace slowed, her mind screaming warnings. Then came the jarring roar of men's voices, sharp and cruel, shouting in excitement and aggression. She stopped, breath catching painfully, and dared a quick glance through the sparse foliage behind her.

Pickup trucks surged into the small hamlet, tires skidding against dirt, dust billowing into the sky like smoke from a burning village. Men leapt eagerly from the vehicles, rifles brandished, their movements arrogant, predatory. Even from this distance, their laughter cut sharply into Caitlin's ears, sending icy tendrils of dread slithering through her veins.

At the center of the chaos stood a figure Caitlin recognized immediately, despite never having laid eyes on him in person.

Major Ébi. Deputy commander of the Lord's Resistance Army.

He stood tall and imposing, his figure commanding instant attention. Dark sunglasses obscured his eyes, but his mouth twisted in a contemptuous smirk of absolute self-assurance. Caitlin's stomach churned in recognition, his face had been prominently displayed on crude posters in every village and hamlet she'd visited in South Sudan. Those crude drawings never adequately captured the cold aura of authority he radiated, nor the casual cruelty evident even in his stance.

She had heard countless whispered stories about Ébi: a feared rebel leader responsible for endless suffering, cruelty, and violence. The very personification of everything Caitlin and her organization had desperately worked to prevent. Now he stood right there, mere yards from Melissa, his presence transforming a dangerous situation into a living nightmare.

Caitlin's stomach twisted as recognition struck like a blow. She was certain now. These were the same men who had stormed the Gangura compound the day before.

Melissa stood frozen at the center of it all, her pale figure trembling visibly as Ébi's men descended upon her. They seized her roughly by the arms, dragging her forward as though she were nothing more than an animal. Their coarse laughter and crude jokes about her helplessness echoed loudly, filling Caitlin with bitter, impotent rage. Her blood boiled painfully at their callousness, her fists clenching in helpless fury.

Yet Melissa did not scream. Caitlin wasn't sure whether the younger woman's silence was shock, fear, or resignation. Whatever it was, the quiet acceptance of her fate cut Caitlin more deeply than any scream ever could.

Caitlin found herself rooted helplessly to the spot, unable to move, unable to tear her eyes from Melissa's suffering. Every fiber of her being shouted at her to run, to flee while she still had a chance. Yet her feet refused to obey. Her mind revolted at the thought of abandoning Melissa.

It wasn't love or friendship that froze her there. It was guilt, a crushing, suffocating guilt born of responsibility. Melissa had looked to her for guidance, for protection, and Caitlin had failed her. Even now, knowing that any attempt to help Melissa would only result in her own capture or death, Caitlin could not yet tear herself away.

She sank to her knees in the dirt, trembling, hating her own helplessness even as she accepted it.

In the clearing, Ébi stepped deliberately closer to Melissa, leaning down to speak softly, too softly for Caitlin to hear. But whatever venom he uttered caused Melissa to visibly flinch, shrinking back instinctively. Caitlin watched helplessly, desperately wanting to charge forward and defend Melissa, knowing it was impossible.

Then Ébi straightened abruptly, turning to bark sharp commands at his men. They scattered immediately, surging eagerly into the surrounding jungle, weapons raised, shouting gleeful threats. Hunting.

Caitlin pressed herself deeper into the brush, panic rising sharply once more. She understood; they were hunting her. Her chest tightened, breath hitching with renewed fear.

She should run, flee deeper into the jungle, and distance herself from the danger. Yet she remained frozen, her body rebelling, her eyes fixated on the scene unfolding before her. Melissa was roughly dragged to one of the tukuls, shoved brutally through the door like a piece of cargo. Caitlin could see Melissa's pale face clearly, framed by her tangled blonde hair, eyes wide yet strangely vacant, staring blankly into nothingness. She offered no resistance, no protest.

Tears burned hotly in Caitlin's eyes, helplessness and fury mingling bitterly. She knew, deep within her heart, there was nothing more she could do now. She had failed Melissa, failed the others she had lost, and failed herself. The bitter taste of defeat filled her mouth, as tangible and suffocating as the heat still lingering heavily in the air.

9

3 MARCH 0858 HRS

JUBA, **South Sudan**

The flight to South Sudan was long but mercifully uneventful. After twelve hours airborne, the sleek Gulfstream descended gradually toward Juba International Airport. From altitude, the landscape stretched below in shades of ochre and muted green, marred occasionally by dusty roads and clusters of low-slung buildings that seemed randomly scattered, a testament to the city's haphazard growth and constant instability.

Through the aircraft window, I studied the airport terminal, which resembled nothing more glamorous than a cluster of oversized Quonset huts arranged side by side. Corrugated steel roofs glinted harshly beneath the sun's relentless gaze, rust-stained in places, and the rudimentary construction gave a stark contrast to the sleek luxury of our aircraft. The apron below was dominated by large cargo planes painted stark white, each emblazoned with bold black letters spelling "UN." They sat quietly on the tarmac, stark reminders of the international community's attempts to inject order into chaos.

I recognized two older, twin-engine commercial jets parked haphazardly alongside the terminal. One wore the yellow-and-blue livery of Sudan Airways, faded and peeling from too many hours beneath the harsh equatorial sun. The other bore the unmistakably bright colors of Uganda Airlines, its bold yellow, red, and black tail standing out vibrantly, hinting at optimism that seemed out of place here.

Juba's passenger terminal was known for its utilitarian bleakness. Having traveled here multiple times, I recalled the bare concrete floors, the sweltering, overcrowded waiting areas, and the confusion of travelers—local families clutching overstuffed suitcases, weary international aid workers, and clusters of Chinese oil and gas employees attempting to navigate the bureaucratic chaos. It was always a scene marked by frustration and quiet desperation.

But today, as the aircraft rolled to a stop just off the edge of the main commercial apron, things appeared calm. As the engines wound down, I spotted the welcome sight of four waiting vehicles on the tarmac below: a sleek gray Mercedes sedan flanked by a white Land Cruiser, both idling quietly, and two imposing black Range Rovers positioned slightly apart, their tinted windows concealing whoever was inside.

I exhaled a silent sigh of relief. Stacy and Tam had come through yet again, orchestrating complex logistics flawlessly from Newport. The sight of those vehicles meant we were off to a better start than many of my previous trips to Africa, where improvisation and adaptability had often been my only logistical assets.

As the Gulfstream's copilot cracked open the door, the thick, oppressive heat surged inward, followed immediately by a distinctive aroma—an unforgettable blend of wood smoke, jet fuel, dust, sweat, sewage, and the faint but unmistakable hint of desperation. Jessica stood quickly, gathering her bag and descending the stairs first, her confidence unwavering.

As Nate and I followed her down onto the hot, cracked tarmac, two men exited the Mercedes sedan and stepped toward us, hands extended. Both were clearly embassy staff, their crisp dress shirts, polished shoes, and cleanly pressed khakis painfully out of place against the grimy backdrop of Juba's airport.

Jessica greeted them with familiarity, exchanging brief pleas-antries before turning toward me. "Milo," she said formally, "allow me to introduce Ambassador Jim Jameson. Ambassador, this is Milo DeCogan from Relief Solutions."

Ambassador Jameson was older, perhaps mid-sixties, with thin-ning white hair combed carefully to disguise advancing baldness. His handshake was firm yet diplomatic, his manner practiced and polished, honed by decades in State Department roles around the globe. His blue eyes, sharp and observant, assessed me carefully.

"Mr. DeCogan, it's a pleasure to finally meet you," he began with practiced politeness, though his voice betrayed a faint tension. "Your reputation precedes you. I've spoken extensively with Secretary Bishop and have given him my personal assurance you'll receive the embassy's complete support."

"Thank you, Ambassador," I replied. "I greatly appreciate your cooperation and the embassy's resources. Your support will be critical."

I introduced Nate, the ambassador nodding politely. Next came his younger consular aide, a thin, nervous man who seemed out of place and slightly unsure of his role, stepping awkwardly forward to shake our hands. He quickly busied himself directing embassy drivers and the Gulfstream's co-pilot, unloading our bags, anxious to appear useful.

Meanwhile, Ambassador Jameson stood close by, clearly uncom-fortable but trying not to show it. He eyed the nearby black Range Rovers suspiciously, curious but hesitant to pry openly. Finally, unable to resist, he gestured toward the imposing vehicles. "May I ask who these gentlemen are?"

His question lingered delicately, the careful diplomacy of someone long practiced in nuance. I smiled politely but revealed nothing more than necessary. "Just some friends arranged by a trusted local contact, Ambassador."

Jameson held my gaze for a long moment, expecting further explanation that I did not offer. An awkward silence hung heavily between us, the ambassador finally relenting, nodding stiffly. "Very well. Please remember that my entire embassy staff remains at your disposal. I've known Caitlin since she was just a child, and I will personally ensure you have every resource necessary to find her."

"I appreciate that," I replied sincerely. "I assure you, we'll keep you updated."

With another stiff handshake and a quick nod to Jessica, Ambassador Jameson retreated gracefully into the Mercedes, clearly unsatisfied with the sparse information provided. The junior consular officer held the sedan door open, glancing nervously back toward us before slipping into the passenger seat himself.

Jessica turned back to me with an amused smirk. "So," she asked, her eyes sparkling with curiosity, "who exactly is in that Range Rover?"

"An old friend," I answered, intentionally vague.

"Does your old friend have a name?" she pressed, clearly accustomed to extracting information.

"Crispus Oryema," I admitted, knowing the name would mean little to her and preferring to avoid unnecessary evasiveness. "He's well-connected locally, someone who can truly help."

She raised an eyebrow. "And yet he didn't come out to greet you personally?"

I shrugged. "Maybe he's cautious. Maybe he's not here personally, but sent his men instead. People in Juba are wary about openly associating with U.S. embassy personnel."

Jessica nodded, absorbing my subtle rebuke. "No need to get defensive," she said, smiling to defuse tension. "You're sure you don't want me to come along?"

"I appreciate your willingness," I said. "But it's best you head to the embassy. Coordinate with Stacy and Tam back home. We'll be in touch as soon as possible."

"Alright," she said, almost reluctantly. "But call me soon, Milo."

"I promise."

She lingered just a moment longer, eyes lingering, before turning abruptly toward the Mercedes. The vehicle quickly departed, turning sharply and vanishing into the crowded Juba traffic beyond the airport gates.

Nate and I picked up our bags and Pelican cases, moving slowly toward the waiting Range Rovers. As we approached, their doors opened in near unison. Several local men, all powerfully built, wearing navy blue tactical fatigues, emerged quietly, spreading out to flank the vehicles. Sidearms were holstered securely at their hips, and several carried AKMS rifles slung comfortably across their chests.

From the lead Range Rover emerged a tall, powerfully built figure, instantly recognizable despite the years since our last encounter. Crispus Oryema looked unchanged, as though he'd somehow remained immune to the ravages of time and stress. Tall and athletic, his strong frame clad in pressed khaki cargo pants and a perfectly tailored navy polo shirt. Graying at the temples, his goatee trimmed neatly, Crispus radiated calm confidence and unwavering authority.

He approached quickly, his deep, rich voice booming cheerfully across the dusty tarmac. "Brother Milo!" he declared warmly, his laughter resonating through the heavy heat. "It is truly wonderful to see you again, my friend!"

We met midway, embracing warmly, the hug fierce and heartfelt. Crispus's arms encircled me, holding longer than any American greeting would typically endure, his affection sincere and deeply African. Finally, he released me, gripping both my shoulders tightly, holding me at arm's length as his eyes searched mine.

"It is good you are here," he said, seriousness overtaking the initial exuberance. "Anything you need, Milo, anything at all, you know you have but to ask."

"I know," I replied, moved by his sincerity. "Thank you, Crispus. Truly."

His smile returned. "Mary and the children send their greetings. Mary insists you come to our home for dinner. I explained it may be difficult given the circumstances."

"I'd love to," I assured him. "But first things first. Let me introduce you to my colleague, Nate Delman."

Crispus turned graciously, greeting Nate warmly with another enthusiastic handshake and a clap on the shoulder, welcoming him with the warmth reserved for family. He gestured to his waiting men, who began loading our gear into the waiting Range Rovers.

"Come," Crispus urged, his tone urgent again. "We have much to discuss. Events here are moving quickly, and I fear time is not on our side."

I stepped toward the open vehicle door, glancing once more around the hot, dusty airfield. Crispus's urgency unsettled me, his seriousness indicative of just how precarious Caitlin's situation truly was.

As I moved to climb into the Range Rover, Crispus leaned in, lowering his voice. "I believe I know where Ms. Caitlin Bishop has been taken," he whispered, his eyes dark with concern. "But Milo, you must understand. The men who took her are not simple bandits. This is Ébi's doing. LRA. He has grown powerful, dangerous, and utterly ruthless."

My chest tightened painfully at Crispus's words. Ébi's reputation for cruelty and brutality was legendary, and I knew instantly the urgency Crispus felt was warranted. As our vehicles pulled away from Juba International, the harsh reality settled heavily upon us all: we had entered dangerous territory, and the fight to save Caitlin was just beginning.

We headed for the airport exit, the sun now low enough to cast long, distorted shadows across the dusty airfield. As Nate and Crispus engaged in idle conversation about local conditions, my mind drifted inexorably to the vivid memories of my first encounter with Crispus Oryema, a meeting forged in blood and chaos during the brutal, brief South Sudanese civil war four years earlier.

I had been deployed as a team leader with the CIA's Special

Activities Division—a clandestine paramilitary unit designed for the kind of messy, ambiguous situations unfolding in South Sudan. My orders were simple: make direct contact with key South Sudanese commanders, assess the deteriorating situation on the ground, and report back to the seventh floor at Langley. At the heart of my assignment was Colonel Crispus Oryema, then commanding South Sudan's only Special Forces brigade. Years before, Crispus had led an elite militia within the Sudanese People's Liberation Army, pivotal in South Sudan's brutal struggle for independence from the north.

Our first meeting occurred outside the embattled city of Wau, twelve exhausting hours after leaving Juba along roads that were scarcely more than rutted tracks. The conflict was spiraling out of control, civilian casualties mounting daily, and the small UN peace-keeping force stationed near the Wau airfield was helpless to intervene. Crispus openly expressed disgust at their ineffectiveness and resolved instead to lead his battalions on aggressive operations to protect civilians by actively hunting the rebel forces terrorizing the region.

As I approached his temporary field headquarters, little more than a canvas tarp stretched between two battered trucks, Crispus had looked up from a briefing, his penetrating gaze cutting sharply through me. He paused dramatically, then addressed the half-dozen officers around him with sardonic humor.

"Oh look, gentlemen," Crispus had announced loudly. "The war must finally be over; the Americans have arrived to take credit!"

His men laughed, but beneath his sarcasm was a wary assessment of yet another foreign operative whose usefulness remained to be proven. Despite his politeness, Crispus had kept me carefully at arm's length, permitting my presence without encouraging familiarity or trust.

For ten days, I shadowed him, watching his leadership style—a combination of stern discipline and profound empathy toward his men. His reputation as a fearless leader was evident from the deep respect his troops held for him, a loyalty earned through shared hardships and unwavering courage.

On the tenth day, our relationship, and both our lives, changed forever.

We were traveling toward Bentiu, a northern city wracked by ethnic violence, in a three-vehicle convoy. Brendan, a young, inexperienced consular officer assigned from the embassy, sat beside me, trying to hide his nervousness. Crispus sat in front, calm but distant, communicating sparingly. Our lead vehicle was a battered Toyota Hilux, known colloquially as a "technical," armed with a heavy 12.7mm machine gun mounted atop its bed. Behind our vehicle rolled an open-bed truck carrying half a dozen seasoned Special Forces soldiers.

The road to Bentiu was monotonous, oppressive heat and boredom our constant companions. Brendan fidgeted beside me, clearly out of his element, while Crispus stared impassively out the window. Suddenly, through the haze of boredom, my instincts screamed danger.

I caught movement in the dense tree line ahead, figures shifting, metal glinting sharply under sunlight. "STOP!" I shouted urgently at our driver, grabbing his shoulder. "Brake now!"

The driver's reflexive panic reaction was instantaneous. He slammed on the brakes, sending our Land Cruiser skidding violently across the loose gravel. Simultaneously, four rocket-propelled grenades streaked from the trees with a chilling hiss, trailing thick plumes of smoke. My heart froze as one passed mere inches in front of our vehicle, exploding harmlessly in the brush.

But luck was not universal. The technical ahead detonated spectacularly, engulfed instantly in roaring flames. Gunfire erupted from the left side of the road, punching violently through our vehicle. The driver's head snapped sharply, and his lifeless body slumped forward, splattering blood across Crispus and Brendan.

Chaos erupted. "Get out now!" I screamed at Brendan, who sat frozen in shock, his face pale and eyes blank. I seized his arm roughly, yanked open the door, and half-threw him into the roadside ditch. Bullets whizzed overhead, snapping viciously through the air as we sprawled in the shallow trench. Brendan trembled violently, disoriented, while I pulled my Glock from its holster, my pulse hammering in my ears.

"Are you injured?" I demanded, gripping his shoulder tightly. Brendan merely shook his head weakly, too overwhelmed to speak. "Stay down!" I hissed.

Crispus appeared beside us moments later, miraculously unharmed, calmly dialing his satellite phone, requesting reinforcements from Bentiu. Despite the chaos surrounding us, his voice remained composed, authoritative. "We are under heavy attack," he said, unfazed. "Send everything."

His calmness steadied my nerves momentarily until I glanced toward the far tree line, my heart freezing once more. A dozen rebel fighters charged forward, weapons blazing indiscriminately. Amid them, a teenage boy knelt, steadying an RPG launcher, its deadly rocket aimed directly at our position.

"Incoming!" I shouted desperately, burying my face into the dust-filled ditch just before the SUV above us erupted in a thunderous explosion. Concussion slammed into me, a wave of pressure overwhelming my senses, ears ringing violently as the world briefly turned white.

Shaking off disorientation, I quickly checked Brendan. He was curled up tightly, clutching a minor head wound, terrified but stable. Crispus lay nearby, pistol drawn, face set grimly but still remarkably composed despite the violent chaos. We exchanged a brief, silent acknowledgment, both understanding the situation's severity.

A fresh wave of rebels closed in rapidly, AK-47 fire intensifying. Crispus glanced at his watch, calmly saying, "Reinforcements—five minutes."

"We don't have five minutes," I replied, knowing our survival hung by mere seconds.

Crispus's eyes met mine, resolute, unafraid. "I'll get you five minutes," he said.

Before I could object, he began crawling away, positioning himself strategically farther down the ditch, directly opposite the advancing rebels.

I searched desperately for weapons, ammunition, cover—anything to improve our odds. But flames consumed our vehicle, weapons inside useless. The roaring fire's heat, however, formed a protective barrier, preventing the rebels from charging our position.

Suddenly, Crispus fired three precise pistol shots in quick succession, three rebels dropped immediately, each hit cleanly through the head. Two more rapid shots, two more rebels fell. But return fire was overwhelming; bullets slammed into Crispus's body, staining his clothes red. Yet he did not falter, raising himself defiantly, firing again and again.

Two rebels sprinted across the road toward us. I snapped up my pistol, dropping one instantly, but the second disappeared into our ditch, dangerously close to Crispus. With no choice, I squeezed two shots, striking the rebel in the back before he could fire. I dashed forward, tackling his dying body and grabbing his AK-47 rifle.

Ignoring standard procedures to check the weapon before firing, I immediately aimed across the road, unleashing automatic fire. Rebels scattered, several falling under my fire, but the magazine emptied too quickly. I drew my Glock again, acutely aware I had limited ammunition remaining.

More rebels emerged from the far woodline, swarming toward us. My blood froze. I knew we were about to be overwhelmed. Just as despair took hold, a deep, rhythmic staccato echoed sharply:

Bam! Bam! Bam!

The unmistakable sound of a heavy M2 Browning .50 caliber machine gun ripped through the advancing rebels, tearing bodies apart and shattering their momentum instantly. American-supplied Humvees raced into view, their armored gunners methodically cutting down the remaining attackers, driving the survivors fleeing into the bush.

Dust settled slowly. Shaking with adrenaline, I turned immediately to Crispus, who lay motionless, wounds bleeding badly, but his eyes still bright with defiance. Brendan hurried over, still shaken but now active, assisting me as we urgently applied pressure bandages.

I leaned close. "Stay with us, Crispus," I urged.

He managed a faint smile, his voice weak but determined. "I'm fine, Milo. You won't be rid of me this easily."

True to his word, Crispus survived those wounds, astonishing doctors in Juba with his swift recovery. From that day, our relationship transformed irrevocably—from distant colleagues to lifelong friends, bonded irrevocably through combat and mutual sacrifice.

Back in the present, I blinked away vivid memories, feeling Crispus's firm hand now gripping my shoulder, sensing exactly where my mind had drifted.

"You're remembering Bentiu," he said quietly, understanding fully.

I nodded. "You saved our lives that day."

He smiled, shaking his head. "I can say the same for you."

I met his eyes. A moment of silence passed between us, filled with shared memories, gratitude, and the deep bond forged through fire and bloodshed.

Crispus finally broke the quiet, his voice solemn. "Milo, this situation with Caitlin Bishop. I fear it will be every bit as dangerous as that day in Bentiu. Perhaps even worse."

I met his gaze unflinchingly. "Then it's good we have you on our side again, brother."

Crispus smiled warmly, clasping my shoulder firmly. "Together, my friend. Always."

10

3 MARCH 0922 HRS

JUBA, **South Sudan**

A sudden, jolting swerve by the driver snapped me out of my vivid memories and back into the gritty, harsh reality of Juba, the bustling capital city of the world's newest nation. South Sudan had only recently emerged onto maps as a recognized sovereign state, but driving along these crowded, chaotic streets, one could hardly guess we were navigating the center of national governance.

Outside the SUV's window, a vivid tapestry of life surged by in a riot of color, sound, and ceaseless movement. Ebony-skinned women draped in flowing dresses of vibrant reds, yellows, blues, and greens moved gracefully despite the dust, balancing impossibly heavy loads atop their heads with practiced ease. Some carried armloads of fire-wood, while others balanced large baskets filled with vegetables, fruits, or textiles, their faces stoic yet resolute. Small children darted among them, chasing each other playfully, oblivious to traffic dangers, while merchants shouted, hawking everything from roasted peanuts to cheap plastic toys.

A thick, choking haze of red dust hung perpetually in the air, churned up by each passing vehicle. The hard-packed dirt road had long since surrendered any semblance of pavement, giving way to deep ruts, potholes, and random mounds of compacted earth. Each vehicle kicked up a fresh cloud of fine red powder, coating pedestrians, storefronts, and everything in between with a gritty film that clung to the skin and burned the nostrils.

Buildings lining the street were mostly crude, single-story structures fashioned from cinderblock and corrugated metal, patched together without any discernible pattern or zoning regulations. Rusted tin roofs were weighted down with worn tires or piles of stones to prevent sheets from blowing away in storms, and many walls were crudely plastered with faded hand-painted advertisements for Coca-Cola, mobile phone services, or political campaign slogans. Makeshift wooden stalls crowded street corners, selling everything from mobile phone SIM cards to fried dough balls, creating a constant buzz of economic activity amid the poverty and chaos.

Though I'd visited Juba numerous times, the scene always struck me with fresh poignancy. This street, this slice of vibrant, struggling humanity, could easily have existed in countless other small cities across the Sahel, the harsh and unforgiving transitional belt spanning from the Atlantic Ocean in the west to the Red Sea in the east, a region marked by poverty, conflict, and immense resilience.

It wasn't lost on me how many of the world's brutal conflicts had their origins or played out tragically within this fragile, turbulent zone of human civilization. South Sudan was just the latest in a grim line of unstable nations struggling for identity, stability, and survival.

The quality of the roads deteriorated as we moved farther from the airport, our vehicle bouncing roughly with every meter traveled. After fifteen minutes of navigating Juba's congested, winding avenues, our driver swung the vehicle sharply left onto a narrower road, the tires grinding harshly through gravel and red clay. I braced myself against the seat in front of me as we skidded to a halt outside a formidable-looking steel gate, at least ten feet high, reinforced and imposing.

Four heavily armed sentries stood alertly in front of the gate, each wearing crisp navy tactical fatigues, web belts loaded with ammunition pouches, and AK rifles held confidently at a low ready position. Their eyes were hidden behind dark sunglasses, and their posture radiated disciplined readiness. Each man's expression relaxed noticeably the moment they recognized Crispus seated in the front passenger seat.

Through my window, I glimpsed the walls flanking the gate—tall, solid concrete painted a subtle shade of tan, meticulously maintained and topped with several coils of gleaming razor wire. It stretched unbroken into the distance, clearly enclosing an extensive compound. As soon as the sentries confirmed Crispus's identity, they quickly swung open the heavy steel gate, snapping sharp salutes as we rolled slowly forward.

Entering through the gate felt as if we'd crossed a secret border into a completely different country. Instantly, the clamorous, dusty streets of Juba receded behind us, replaced by a peaceful, shaded driveway that curved gracefully beneath the spreading branches of mature mahogany trees. The sudden quiet was startling, the cacophony of the city replaced by birdsong and the soft rustling of leaves overhead. To the side, vivid green acacia and tamarind trees stood guard along the banks of the Nile, their lush foliage providing a stark, tranquil contrast to the gritty chaos we'd just left behind.

Crispus turned around from the front seat, watching my reaction with an amused smile. "Welcome to the headquarters of Panther Security Group," he announced with unmistakable pride in his voice. "My home—and yours, for as long as you wish to stay."

"It's impressive," I replied, gazing appreciatively out at the tranquil scene passing by outside my window. "You've built yourself quite an oasis here."

He smiled again, eyes twinkling. "When the world outside is chaos, Milo, it helps to have someplace orderly to retreat to. You and Nate will find our guesthouse very comfortable, and we have several secure conference rooms where you can set up your operations."

"Thank you," I replied. "I appreciate your hospitality more than I can say."

Crispus waved dismissively. "Nonsense, my friend. You are forever welcome in my home. You have earned that right a thousand times over."

Two hours later, I found myself once again in a large SUV, this time settled in the passenger seat, as Crispus expertly navigated the chaotic streets of Juba. I'd asked Nate to remain behind at our newly established operations center. There, he was coordinating with Stacy in Newport and ensuring our equipment was ready for what we anticipated would be a complex, rapidly developing operation. Having been awake for nearly twenty-four hours straight, I could feel exhaustion creeping into every muscle, despite my attempts to push it aside. Noticing my weariness, Crispus had suggested we grab a quick meal at a local place he assured me was safe, comfortable, and close enough that we wouldn't lose valuable time.

The previous two hours had been a whirlwind of preparation and strategic planning. The Panther Security Group compound, universally known simply as "PSG" or "the Panthers," was impressively expansive, a world unto itself, tucked neatly along twelve hundred feet of prime Nile riverfront. Spread over fifteen meticulously maintained acres, the compound provided a secure haven, isolated from Juba's incessant chaos.

Earlier, Crispus had shown us around the well-secured campus, detailing each structure with evident pride: administrative offices housed in a solid two-story concrete building, an expansive warehouse stacked with supplies, and neatly ordered barracks capable of comfortably accommodating over one hundred security personnel at any given time. Farther within the compound, beyond manicured lawns and shaded groves, stood half a dozen beautifully constructed cottages nestled among lush stands of papyrus reeds lining the banks of the Nile.

Our assigned guest cottage, built of solid stone and teak, cooled by ceiling fans spinning lazily above polished wooden floors, provided a much-needed respite. After a hurried shower to rinse away travel fatigue, Nate and I had turned Crispus's largest conference room into our temporary operations nerve center. Nate unpacked and configured the specialized electronics and satellite comms gear we'd brought, while I established secure, encrypted links back to Stacy at our Newport headquarters.

Despite it being just past three a.m. Newport time, Stacy appeared onscreen looking as sharp and energized as if she'd just stepped into the office for a routine morning briefing. Her face was illuminated by the glow of multiple screens around her, and as she spoke, it was clear she and her team had worked tirelessly through the night to provide us with critical intelligence.

"We're fairly certain Caitlin initially escaped the compound," Stacy explained. "But after that, it gets less clear. It's still unknown whether she's actively evading capture or if she was later intercepted by the attacking forces."

"The attackers?" I prompted, hoping for clarity.

Stacy hesitated only slightly before answering. "The best intel right now strongly indicates involvement from an element of the Lord's Resistance Army, although we have no specifics regarding the exact unit or their motives behind targeting the WRC."

Following Stacy's succinct briefing, Crispus stepped forward, projecting a satellite image onto the screen. His authoritative presence immediately commanded everyone's attention.

"Our local contacts across South Sudan, northern Uganda, and into the DRC have been working nonstop," he began, his voice steady but urgent. "We have a lead, credible but not yet fully confirmed. It comes from a trusted source near the border region, a small hamlet just inside the DRC, south of Gangura. Two white women matching Caitlin and Melissa's description were sighted, heading south on foot."

The implications of Crispus's briefing were stark. Time was slipping away.

"Let's move on this," I said. "How quickly can we get there?"

Crispus nodded. "We can reach Yambio by air within two hours. But the major complication—the 'long pole in the tent,' as you Americans say—is arranging reliable ground transport once we land. Without vehicles pre-staged, we risk sitting idle on an exposed airstrip."

I grimaced, knowing all too well the vulnerabilities posed by inadequate logistics.

Crispus quickly added, "I've already dispatched two fully equipped SUVs with reliable men from Panther Group. They left less than an hour ago on the six-hour drive to Yambio. Assuming no delays, they'll arrive by five p.m. If we take off from Juba no later than three, we'll land just as they're arriving."

I didn't like the enforced wait, but I trusted Crispus implicitly. I'd learned long ago that in Africa, patience and adaptability were often the only advantages one had.

Noticing my exhaustion and tension, Crispus had suggested we grab an early lunch, and despite my desire to press on, hunger eventually won out.

As we drove through the chaotic streets of Juba, our vehicle jostled among throngs of vendors, shoppers, and street hawkers. The thick, acrid scent of diesel fumes mingled with smoky charcoal fires and freshly grilled meat, drifting through our open windows. Crispus maneuvered confidently, one hand casually draped over the steering wheel, the other resting lightly on the window frame, eyes vigilant, constantly scanning mirrors.

After several minutes of navigating the dense city traffic, Crispus abruptly swung the vehicle onto a gravel parking lot shaded by sprawling acacia trees. The lot was uneven and pitted, scattered with a haphazard collection of dusty Land Cruisers, Hilux trucks, and motorcycles that had clearly seen more jungle tracks than urban roads.

Ahead stood a modest single-story building with an old, weathered wooden sign bearing the faded words, "Notos Lounge Bar & Grill." The entrance was covered by sagging tin roofing, rusted from years of rainy seasons. Despite its outward shabbiness, the place seemed oddly welcoming, a quiet refuge from the chaos just outside its perimeter.

Stepping inside was like entering another world. Immediately, the oppressive heat receded several degrees, replaced by cool shadows and a pleasant blend of teakwood, tobacco smoke, and distant aromas of grilling meat. The interior was dimly lit, fieldstone walls lending it a cave-like coziness. At the room's center, a large teak bar dominated the space, ringed by high-backed wooden stools, many occupied by locals and expatriates quietly conversing over cold beers and worn cell phones.

Crispus moved easily through the establishment, clearly a regular patron. The aging proprietor greeted him warmly, clasping Crispus's shoulder with genuine affection.

"You've brought guests, I see," he teased. "Do they pay double today?"

"Only if you water down the karkade again," Crispus shot back, laughing. The proprietor waved us toward a set of French doors leading to a courtyard patio.

We stepped out onto a shaded patio, protected from the harsh sunlight by a rusted tin awning overhead. The enclosed courtyard was ringed by pale yellow concrete walls, faded and chipped by years of tropical sun and monsoon rains. Wooden tables and benches were neatly arranged throughout, many occupied by tired-looking NGO workers, contractors, and security types, their weary faces hinting at the difficult places from which they'd recently emerged.

We chose a table near the back wall, shaded beneath the spreading branches of a large tamarind tree. The cool, tranquil atmosphere was an immediate relief, and as we sat, a waiter hurried over with a worn pad in hand.

"Cold lemonade," I ordered, wiping sweat from my brow. "Tall glass. Plenty of ice, real ice, not a solo cube floating in warm water."

The waiter smiled politely, though I was sure my humor was lost in translation. Crispus interjected, "Bring him some karkade as well. Let him experience how we survive the heat here."

"Karkade?" I asked, raising an eyebrow.

"It's hibiscus tea. Tart, sweet, quite refreshing," Crispus explained. "You'll either love it or regret ever hearing its name."

I leaned back, stretching tired muscles, relaxing into the pleasant ambience. "Fair enough. While we wait, tell me more about this hamlet near Yambio. Your men have eyes on the village?"

Crispus leaned forward, his expression suddenly serious again. "Not direct eyes-on yet, Milo, but we've established solid communications with local contacts in the area. We're piecing together their movements. What we know so far indicates Caitlin and Melissa fled the Gangura compound to the south, directly into rebel-controlled territory across the border. The hamlet itself is barely more than a few huts and a crossroads, but the LRA's presence is strong. Locals have confirmed seeing two young white women moving south along remote footpaths."

"How reliable is the intel?" I pressed cautiously.

"Third-hand," Crispus admitted. "But I trust the sources. It's the best lead we have. And knowing the LRA's patterns, the sooner we get to them, the better."

I took a slow breath, considering the implications. The LRA's reputation for brutality was infamous, their tactics savage. Caitlin and Melissa's survival was anything but guaranteed.

"Once we hit the ground in Yambio," I asked. "What's our contingency plan if things go south quickly?"

Crispus met my gaze squarely, voice calm but resolute. "If there's trouble at the landing site or along the route, we're prepared. We'll have a quick-reaction force on standby. Panther's best fighters are already gearing up. We go in strong, prepared for anything."

"Air support?" I inquired.

Crispus shook his head. "Limited to none. UN's rules of engage-
ment are restrictive, and we can't count on the South Sudanese military to move quickly enough. It'll be us, on the ground, moving fast
and quiet. I won't lie to you, Milo, once we cross into the DRC, we're
entirely on our own."

I considered the odds, knowing they were steep but unwilling to
back away. Caitlin Bishop's life depended on our success. "Then we
move decisively," I said. "Quickly in, quickly out. No wasted time."

"Exactly," Crispus agreed. "And remember, my men will follow
your lead without question. You have complete authority. They know
your reputation and trust you implicitly."

I felt the heavy weight of responsibility settle onto my shoulders
once again, but alongside it was deep gratitude. "I appreciate your
confidence, Crispus."

He smiled. "You've earned it a hundred times over, my friend."

Our drinks arrived—a sweating glass of lemonade with blessedly
real ice, alongside a smaller glass filled with deep red karkade. I took a
careful sip, pleasantly surprised by the tart, refreshing tang of
hibiscus.

Crispus raised his glass. "To swift success...and the safe recovery
of Ms. Caitlin Bishop."

"To success," I echoed, clinking my glass against his.

We drank quietly, two old comrades preparing themselves for the
dangerous, uncertain journey ahead.

Before I could press Crispus for more details, the entire courtyard
atmosphere seemed to shift. It was subtle at first, a faint drop in
conversation volume, a slight turning of heads, but unmistakable in its
intensity. It was the kind of charged stillness I'd felt in dark alleys and
border crossings right before everything spiraled into gunfire or
worse. Or right before meeting someone powerful and ruthless
enough to trigger violence with a casual word.

Two Asian men entered the courtyard first, instantly marking themselves as security. They wore black fatigues tucked neatly into polished tactical boots, both men moving with the relaxed yet precise gait of professionals accustomed to violence. Their eyes were masked by mirrored sunglasses, their expressions impassive yet alert, continuously scanning the patio for threats.

Following closely behind them was a third man whose presence was immediately imposing. Dressed impeccably in pressed black trousers and a tailored white button-down shirt, open slightly at the collar, revealing a thick, muscular neck. The newcomer radiated power and menace simultaneously. He looked to be in his mid-forties, barrel-chested, and powerful in a way that suggested both disciplined training and an innate brutality. His broad shoulders strained slightly against the fabric of his shirt, hinting at significant upper-body strength, while his large, thick-knuckled hands swung casually at his sides, exuding casual confidence and latent danger.

His face was sharply defined: high cheekbones above a granite-like jawline so pronounced it seemed carved from dark volcanic rock. A jagged, ugly scar traced a violent path from just above his left eyebrow, slicing downward across the empty, staring socket of his left eye, clearly glass, and continuing down his cheek to end at his angular chin. That lifeless eye, opaque and unsettling, reflected our courtyard surroundings coldly, predatorily. Beneath his composed, almost businesslike demeanor lurked the unmistakable air of someone whose profession involved violence, someone accustomed to ruthlessly removing obstacles from his path.

He was the kind of man you instinctively didn't turn your back on, not unless you harbored a death wish.

Beside me, Crispus visibly tensed, subtle but clear enough for me to notice. Not fear, exactly; more a heightened alertness, like a wolf who'd just sensed another predator lurking at the edge of its territory.

"Friend of yours?" I asked, keeping my tone neutral but alert.

Crispus's expression tightened. "Jimmy Liu. Operations manager for Jinhai Holdings. You know the type—logistics, security, enforcement. The shadowy side of Chinese investment in Africa. He's their fixer here. Whenever Jinhai needs to smooth the path for a mining contract, oil concession, or infrastructure deal, Liu and his men make sure it happens. One way or another."

I nodded. "I thought Jinhai was officially state-backed."

Crispus gave a bitter smile, his eyes never leaving Liu. "Officially. But in practice, companies like Jinhai employ men like Liu to ensure profitability, by any means necessary. He's widely hated by locals but equally feared. He's ruthless, efficient, and completely without remorse."

By now, Liu was already striding toward us, each step measured, confident, and heavy with implied threat. His two bodyguards peeled off, casually taking seats at nearby tables, positioning themselves with clear sightlines to our conversation. Their practiced ease was deceptive. Both remained tense and vigilant, ready to spring into violence at the slightest provocation.

"Mr. deCogan," Liu greeted me warmly as he stopped near our table, his voice impeccably smooth, an upper-crust British accent wrapping effortlessly around every word. His English was flawless, almost overly polished, reminiscent of a private boarding-school education. "Welcome to Juba. It's a pleasure to finally meet you."

He paused deliberately, clearly waiting for me to stand. I rose slowly from my chair but pointedly did not extend my hand. "You have me at a disadvantage, Mr. Liu. How do you know of me?"

His smile widened, charming yet predatory. "You're taller than I expected." He turned toward Crispus, nodding with calculated respect. "Crispus."

"Liu," Crispus responded curtly, neutral but guarded.

Liu indicated an empty chair at our table, though his gesture was merely a formality. He had every intention of joining us regardless. "May I?"

I hesitated, weighing my options, knowing full well my consent or refusal wouldn't alter his intentions. "Please," I said finally, nodding toward the chair.

Liu settled into the seat, carefully adjusting his cuffs and casually leaning back, projecting ease and authority. His dark hair, neatly trimmed and streaked subtly with silver, matched the thin, precise mustache above his lip. Up close, I noticed the fine details of his appearance: polished gold cufflinks, an expensive wristwatch, and manicured nails. Everything about Jimmy Liu spoke of deliberate, meticulous care, masking the underlying brutality of his true nature.

"Word travels fast in this part of the world," Liu began conversationally, eyeing me with his good eye, the glass eye reflecting us coldly. "You're here because of the tragic events in Gangura. Unfortunate situation indeed."

I kept my expression deliberately neutral. Crispus shifted slightly again, clearly uncomfortable at the mention of Gangura, the edges of his patience fraying.

Liu continued, unfazed by our silence. "You're looking for Secretary Bishop's daughter, yes?" He leaned back further, fingers interlaced. "Relax, gentlemen. We have ears in many places. When an incident involving an American with high-profile connections occurs, even subtle ripples reach our shores."

I finally spoke, cautious yet direct. "What exactly is it you want, Mr. Liu?"

He gave a slight, knowing smile. "It's not about what I want, Mr. deCogan. It's about how I can help you."

"Out of the kindness of your heart?" I asked skeptically.

He chuckled, as if amused by the idea. "Out of simple efficiency and mutual interest. You're traveling to Yambio, aren't you? A time-sensitive operation. Every moment counts."

I remained silent, waiting.

Liu leaned forward, his voice lowering. "My employer is a generous and compassionate man. He instructed me to provide you whatever assistance you require. As it happens, we have an aircraft fueled and ready right now—no bureaucratic delays, no red tape. Several of our armored SUVs are already staged in Yambio, fully fueled, equipped, and waiting. My logistics team stands ready to assist your mission."

He paused, letting his words sink in before continuing, "In situations like these, Mr. deCogan, knowing when to accept an advantage is crucial."

I studied him, weighing his offer, trying to discern hidden motives beneath his carefully crafted charm. Beside me, Crispus remained still, silent yet alert. Tension crackled palpably between the three of us, the stakes quietly escalating with every passing second.

Finally, I gave a slow nod. "We genuinely appreciate your offer, Mr. Liu. But forgive my skepticism. Men rarely offer such generous assistance without expecting something significant in return."

Liu's smile widened slowly—predatory, knowing, untroubled. "Ah, but therein lies the beauty of diplomacy in our line of work. My employer recognizes your capabilities, Mr. deCogan. He believes building goodwill with a man of your reputation and skill is valuable. Today, we help you. Perhaps tomorrow, circumstances reverse."

I raised an eyebrow. "And what if there is no tomorrow?"

He shrugged, indifferent, confident. "Then consider it our small gesture of goodwill. Nothing more."

Crispus finally broke his silence, voice low but firm. "Jimmy, your sudden generosity feels suspiciously timed."

Liu turned his head, focusing his unsettling glass eye on Crispus, the effect disquieting. "Suspicion is a healthy trait, Crispus. But I assure you, my motivations are purely pragmatic. The LRA creates instability, chaos. Their unpredictability damages business interests in the region, mine and yours alike. Eliminating or containing them aligns with our mutual interests."

He leaned closer, lowering his voice further. "And surely, Crispus, even you understand the advantages of pragmatism. Your men are good, but my resources are deeper. Take advantage of this."

A tense silence filled the courtyard, broken only by distant chatter and the gentle hum of Notos's generator. Crispus and I exchanged a brief, charged glance, both recognizing the perilous position Liu's offer placed us in, yet equally aware of our urgent need for immediate resources.

I spoke first. "Alright, Mr. Liu. Your assistance is accepted, with gratitude. Please inform your logistics team that we'll be ready for immediate departure."

Liu stood, carefully adjusting his pristine white shirt cuffs again. "Excellent. My people are at your disposal. Mutual cooperation benefits everyone, especially in uncertain times like these."

He turned, his bodyguards rising fluidly, instantly alert. "Gentlemen, safe travels. And Mr. DeCogan, I look forward to speaking with you again very soon."

He departed swiftly, leaving behind lingering tension thick enough to touch. As Liu exited, Crispus released a quiet, frustrated sigh, clearly unhappy with our newfound alliance.

"You trust him?" I asked.

Crispus shook his head. "Not even a little. Liu's dangerous—calculating, ruthless, and always playing multiple angles simultaneously. But he's right about one thing: we need speed. And Liu's help may just save Caitlin's life."

"I don't like it either. But if the LRA really has Caitlin, we have no choice but to move fast."

Crispus met my gaze. "Agreed. Just stay vigilant. Accepting Liu's help comes at a price—perhaps not today, but someday soon he'll come collecting."

I nodded, knowing full well Crispus was right. Jimmy Liu's generosity wasn't altruism; it was calculated, strategic leverage. Still, Caitlin Bishop's life hung precariously in the balance. Moral compromises, even dangerous ones, were the currency we had no choice but to spend.

I drained my glass, feeling the weight of our choices settle heavily upon us. "Then we'll pay Liu's price when it comes," I said. "But right now, let's bring Caitlin home."

Crispus nodded. "Agreed. One crisis at a time."

With that, we rose from the table, steeling ourselves for the dangerous journey ahead, a journey now complicated by the unsettling alliance forged moments ago with Jimmy Liu, one of East Africa's most dangerous and ruthless operators.

11

3 MARCH 1300 HRS

SOUTH OF GANGURA, South Sudan

Caitlin lay flat on her stomach, her chin pressed into the dry, unforgiving dirt as she peered through the sparse underbrush at the quiet hamlet below. Her muscles protested every slight movement, a relentless ache running through her arms, legs, and spine. The cluster of three tukuls and the single, nondescript cinderblock building appeared unchanged from when she'd fled in terror the previous night, but an unsettling chill seemed to cling to the morning air—a silent, oppressive tension that felt dangerous, suffocating.

She exhaled slowly, tasting grit and the acrid tang of dust. Fatigue gripped her body like a vice, making each breath feel labored and heavy. The relentless jungle had drained her overnight; the cold darkness had seeped through her bones, and the jungle floor had been lumpy, uncomfortable, and crawling with insects. Her clothing was torn and dirt-stained, her skin scratched raw by branches and thorns. Every muscle fiber was stretched taut from hours of forced, fearful movement. Her throat was parched, her tongue swollen and cracked, her lips feeling brittle enough to crumble. The emptiness in her stomach twisted painfully, yet hunger was nothing compared to her searing thirst.

Worse than the physical pain was the gnawing fear and guilt she felt about Melissa's capture. Throughout the previous night, Caitlin had been haunted by vivid, terrifying images of her friend being dragged away. Melissa's wide, pleading eyes had burned themselves into Caitlin's consciousness—the panicked, desperate look of betrayal as she'd watched Caitlin flee, powerless to help her friend. Caitlin shuddered now at the fresh memory, remembering how Ébi's men had greedily grabbed Melissa, rough hands roaming freely over her trembling body, voices mocking her frightened sobs.

That guilt was the real torment, stronger even than thirst and exhaustion. It was the reason Caitlin was still here, crouched in the bushes near the hamlet instead of fleeing deeper into the jungle. She refused to abandon Melissa. *Not yet, not like this.*

As the morning sun climbed higher, painting the jungle in harsh golden light, Caitlin maneuvered to her vantage point on the north side of the hamlet, her muscles screaming with each subtle, painstaking movement. The hamlet remained oddly still; yet just as her breathing steadied, the distant hum of approaching engines snapped her attention sharply into focus.

Her pulse quickened, adrenaline surging through her veins as a small convoy of three black SUVs appeared in the distance, grinding slowly along the dirt road, kicking up plumes of fine red dust. Caitlin's heart sank and rose simultaneously; these weren't the ramshackle vehicles Ébi's rebels favored. They were well-maintained, modern, authoritative. A glimmer of desperate hope sparked inside her chest. Perhaps these were government forces? Maybe mercenaries hired by the embassy to rescue her and Melissa? Or was it something far more sinister?

Holding her breath, Caitlin crawled closer through the underbrush, ignoring the stabbing pain of twigs and rocks beneath her body. Each movement was agonizingly slow, her weakened limbs trembling, her heart pounding in her ears. The SUVs stopped abruptly at the hamlet's center. Men poured out, their disciplined movements unmistakably professional. They were dressed in black tactical fatigues, each step calculated and precise as they secured their immediate surroundings.

Caitlin pressed herself even flatter against the earth, narrowing her eyes, trying to identify insignias, patches, or any clue that might reveal who these men were. Their professionalism suggested military training, but whose army? Her mind raced, analyzing possibilities, clinging to the hope that rescue had arrived.

Two men raised binoculars, scanning through the trees surrounding the hamlet. Others swiftly entered the cinderblock building, weapons held low but ready, moving with practiced ease. Caitlin's mind buzzed: were they here to free Melissa? Or had the situation worsened somehow?

A sharp crack, a branch snapping somewhere close behind her, froze her heart in mid-beat. Ice flooded her veins, her muscles tensed. Before she could react, a second sound—closer now, too close—sent her pulse racing again. Slowly, fearfully, she turned her head, her eyes widening in pure dread at the sight behind her:

Two men, both Asian, clad in identical black fatigues as the men in the hamlet, their assault rifles aimed directly at her.

In an instant, pure panic exploded within her. She pushed herself up, not thinking, just moving, survival instinct screaming in her head. Caitlin bolted, arms pumping wildly, eyes fixed desperately on the thick jungle ahead.

She barely made it three desperate strides before agonizing pain tore through her body, electric shock seizing every muscle, her limbs collapsing uncontrollably beneath her. Caitlin's body jerked, collapsing forward, face slamming into the dirt, every nerve ending ignited in an unbearable blaze of agony. Her vision blurred, the world spinning nauseatingly around her, yet she couldn't scream, couldn't breathe, her body betrayed by her own muscles spasming uncontrollably.

In that awful moment, she understood—she'd been hit with a taser.

Slowly, agonizingly, the brutal spasms subsided, leaving Caitlin limp, breathless, and temporarily paralyzed. Her mind screamed in desperation, urging her limbs to move, to run, but nothing obeyed. Tears of frustration and terror blurred her vision as heavy boots approached rapidly through the brush.

Hands roughly flipped her onto her back, forcing zip-ties tightly around her wrists, pinching painfully into her skin. She strained to focus, her blurry vision slowly clearing. The two Asian men spoke in low voices—Mandarin perhaps, or Cantonese. She couldn't be sure, her ears still ringing from the electric shock.

One of them grabbed a radio clipped to his belt, speaking sharply into it. Caitlin fought panic, forcing herself to take steady breaths, fighting through the disorientation and weakness.

"Who...who are you?" Caitlin croaked, her throat raw, voice barely audible.

The man binding her wrists ignored her question completely, pulling her roughly upright by one arm. Her legs shook violently, threatening to collapse again beneath her. The second man kept his weapon steadily trained on her, his expression cold and utterly indifferent.

The first man nudged her forward. They began marching her roughly toward the hamlet, toward the waiting vehicles and the other armed men. Caitlin's stomach churned; her heart pounded. *Who were these people? What did they want with her?*

12

3 MARCH 1405 HRS

YAMBIO, South Sudan

The Britten-Norman Defender shook violently as we descended through rough, turbulent air, metal panels rattling with an unsettling intensity. My fingers tightened reflexively on the seat, knuckles whitening. Below, the narrow airstrip of Yambio stretched before us, a raw, dirt-baked scar slicing through a dense sea of emerald jungle. From altitude, it seemed impossibly small, swallowed by the sprawling landscape of wilderness. The sun blazed down, creating shimmering waves of heat that danced deceptively above the parched earth.

My shoulders felt weighed down by the gravity of our mission. This was the closest I'd come yet to locating Caitlin Bishop, and the relentless anxiety had begun to gnaw at me. I forced myself to remain alert, pushing aside fatigue from two sleepless days. Nate sat beside me, inspecting his compact surveillance drone for perhaps the sixth time since we'd departed. He double-checked each component with obsessive precision—wires, battery compartments, and sensor arrays —muttering under his breath. Nate had never fully trusted electronics, not even his own, especially on missions like this. His constant checks were part routine, part superstition, and I'd long ago learned not to interrupt.

Across from us, Crispus leaned in toward his men from Panther Security Group, speaking quietly yet intently, his voice commanding and authoritative. The men listened closely, nodding gravely at his instructions. These men were former military, disciplined professionals who carried themselves with calm confidence, prepared to face whatever lay ahead. It wasn't their first operation in hostile territory, and it certainly wouldn't be their last.

The pilot guided us lower, banking sharply. My stomach lurched as we descended toward the uneven runway, the aircraft wobbling on the currents of hot air rising from the jungle. Finally, wheels touched ground with a jarring bounce, the Defender skidding on loose gravel before coming to a halt in a choking swirl of dust.

Stepping down from the aircraft, I shielded my eyes from the blazing sunlight, scanning the makeshift airfield. Sitting there waiting for us, engines idling patiently in the oppressive heat, were two black SUVs, sleek and out of place amidst the rough surroundings. Jimmy Liu's logistics had indeed come through, as he'd promised, though I felt uneasy knowing we now depended on his questionable generosity.

Turning toward Nate, I murmured under my breath, "I still don't like working with Liu."

Nate snorted, shaking his head as he carefully stowed the drone case inside his pack. "You don't like working with anyone. But be honest. With his logistics, we're already a day ahead of schedule. Otherwise, we'd still be stuck at the airport in Juba, arguing about fuel and permits."

I grunted noncommittally, knowing he was right, even if admitting it grated on my nerves. Liu represented a dangerous wildcard. Crispus finished speaking to one of the men by the lead SUV, then motioned for us to join him.

"Vehicles are clean," he reported. "Fuel tanks topped, engines checked. Air conditioning's weak, but we can't exactly afford to complain."

The three of us and Crispus's men quickly piled into the vehicles, slamming doors shut against the stifling midday heat. Soon we were roaring down the dusty track toward Gangura, a dense cloud of red dust billowing in our wake.

As we drove, I stared out the tinted windows at the jungle pressing in on both sides of the road. Branches reached overhead, creating dark tunnels of shadowy vegetation, thick and oppressive. The air in the SUV quickly became stifling, despite the AC turned to a weak full blast. We rode in tense silence, each man absorbed by private thoughts about the coming task.

Twenty minutes later, the SUVs slowed, coming to a gentle stop at the edge of what had been the World Refugee Committee compound. I stepped out, bile rising in my throat at the devastation before me. The vibrant place I remembered was now a ghost town, shattered, burned, stripped. A feeling of bleak emptiness hung heavily over everything.

I moved cautiously through the wreckage, scanning the debris: shell casings littered the ground like metallic seeds; smashed generators lay twisted beside fragments of electronics; the acrid smell of burnt wood mingled unpleasantly with the iron-rich scent of dried blood. Flies swarmed over disturbed earth, drawn to spots marked by dark stains left behind after bodies had been removed. The rebels had stripped everything of value, leaving only destruction in their wake. Authorities had come earlier, taking away the victims' bodies to Yambio, yet the lingering violence was palpable.

I stepped forward, reconstructing in my mind the assault's chaotic timeline, the initial moments of terror, the panicked flight of Caitlin and Melissa. Memories surged clearly now. I had been here just last summer to conduct security assessments and train local staff, never imagining it would come to this.

"Check the tukuls on that side," I instructed Crispus, pointing toward the far end of the compound. "Caitlin's room should be down there."

His men moved swiftly, systematically searching until one raised his hand. "Here!" he called out. "We found women's clothing!"

I hurried over, stepping carefully into the circular mud-walled hut, my eyes adjusting to the dim interior. Caitlin's personal items were still arranged neatly—folded clothes, a few personal photographs, a University of Michigan sweatshirt draped over a wooden peg. I scanned the room, feeling a quickening pulse as I noted the absence of one specific item.

Caitlin's go-bag was missing. I felt immediate relief, knowing it contained enough critical survival supplies of water, food, and first-aid materials to keep her alive and functioning for at least another day or two.

I exited quickly, walking slowly around the back of the tukul. My heart leapt as I spotted the small door built into the back fence, exactly as I'd insisted during my earlier risk assessment. It was ajar, clearly forced open from within. I knelt down, inspecting footprints leading straight into the jungle.

"She definitely escaped," I murmured aloud, tracing the tracks carefully. "She got out during the chaos."

Crispus approached, assessing the situation. "Matches what our informants suggested," he agreed. "We should head south."

Minutes later, we were roaring along dirt roads toward Duru, red dust billowing behind us. Crispus's satphone never left his ear as he coordinated updates with his local network. Intelligence indicated Caitlin and Melissa might still be somewhere nearby, but details remained sketchy.

I pulled out my encrypted satphone, dialing Stacy back in Newport. Her voice came through clearly, fatigue evident despite her best attempts to mask it.

"Any new intel, Stacy?" I asked.

She exhaled. "Nothing concrete. But locals are buzzing that

Major Ébi himself has been sighted moving through the area. You're headed straight into his territory. Watch your six."

Ébi's reputation with the LRA was brutally clear in the intelligence dossier Stacy had provided—infamous for violence, known specifically for savage cruelty toward women. The thought of Caitlin in his hands twisted sharply in my gut. If she'd been captured by him, I knew her survival odds were plummeting by the hour.

"Copy that," I replied. "We'll proceed carefully. Keep lines open."

"Be careful," Stacy's voice softened, genuine worry breaking through her professionalism. "We don't have many allies down there."

"Understood." I disconnected, heart heavy with the gravity of our situation.

Across the seat, Crispus ended his own brief satphone call almost simultaneously. He turned toward me, his expression composed but his eyes alive with something new: hope edged with urgency. A faint smile tugged at his mouth as he slid the phone into his vest pocket.

"I think we've found her," he said, voice low but steady. "But it appears Ébi has as well. My informant just got word. Ébi's men located the girls at a hamlet a few kilometers south of here."

For a long second, the sound of the SUV's engine filled the silence between us. Then I met Crispus's gaze and gave a single nod. Whatever happened next, we were out of time.

I signaled for our small convoy to halt, bringing the vehicles to a slow, dusty stop along the overgrown jungle road. The heavy heat pressed down on us like an iron fist, sweat dripping down my back, soaking through my shirt as I stepped from the vehicle. We were almost fifteen kilometers south of the WRC compound and nearing a hamlet that seemed in the direct path of Caitlin's route south. This was the closest we dared approach before risking detection.

Nate moved quickly, pulling out the EVO Max drone, carefully assembling and preparing the tiny surveillance device with his characteristic, obsessive precision. Within moments, it rose from his palm, a soft humming barely audible above the dense buzz of insects. We clustered around the handheld screen, watching intently as the drone's camera feed provided us with high-resolution imagery from above.

The hamlet appeared small and insignificant from altitude, a trio of weathered tukuls surrounding a squat, sun-bleached cinderblock structure. Armed men lounged idly in the courtyard's shade, weapons propped carelessly against trees or walls. Several children played innocently nearby, seemingly oblivious, or perhaps immune, to the violence and cruelty surrounding their lives.

"They're relaxed," Crispus murmured, voice low and steady as he studied the screen. "Clearly not expecting trouble."

"That's their mistake," I replied, a tightness in my voice betraying the tension inside me. "We'll use it."

For several minutes, we sketched out an assault plan while Nate flew the drone back along our approach path, ensuring the route was clear. Crispus assured me his men were well versed in this type of mission, and given the few rebel personnel on site, we all felt confident that our advantage of surprise would more than make up for our lack of numbers.

We moved the vehicles a kilometer back, parking them discreetly in a hidden clearing. Nate and one of Crispus's men remained behind as backup, setting up comms and secondary drone surveillance. Crispus and the rest of his Panthers moved swiftly, forming an armed perimeter, weapons at the ready, alertness radiating from each of them. These were seasoned warriors, and their confident precision was unmistakable.

Together, Crispus and I advanced silently through the dense foliage, the jungle's oppressive heat wrapping tightly around us. Humidity clung to our skin, insects humming in our ears. My pulse quickened, adrenaline sharpening every sense, as we crept forward toward the hamlet.

At a concealed vantage point, I gave a hand signal to Crispus. He nodded, understanding my intent. This was our moment.

Then, with ruthless precision, Crispus's team opened fire, bursts of automatic gunfire shattering the oppressive stillness. Chaos erupted instantly within the hamlet, guards scrambling desperately for weapons, caught completely off-guard. Several dropped immediately, bullets punching into their chests, limbs flailing, weapons scattering uselessly into the dirt.

One rebel fell near the courtyard well, never managing to lift his rifle. Another attempted to sprint toward the cinderblock building but was cut down mid-stride, bullets tearing through his torso. The air filled with the harsh crack of rifles, shouts of confusion and fear. We pressed forward, using the chaos as our cover.

Reaching the cinderblock structure, my breath caught in my chest. The building had no secondary exit, just one single door, standing solidly shut. A fatal funnel that I had no choice but to breach. Weapon raised, adrenaline surging, I slammed my boot against the door. The wood splintered, makeshift hinges shattering as the door burst inward with explosive force.

Inside, amidst shadows and stifling heat, stood the man I instantly recognized: Major Ébi. His brutal reputation surged through my mind, filling me with cold, deliberate purpose. Ébi's weapon rose swiftly, but I reacted quicker, training and reflex taking control. My rifle snapped forward, muzzle flashes erupting bright in the dim room. Two rounds slammed into Ébi's chest, staggering him backward. Before he could fall, my aim adjusted, placing a third bullet through his forehead. Ébi's body collapsed, lifeless eyes staring blankly upward as blood pooled beneath him.

One of Ébi's men lunged violently from my peripheral vision, a knife blade raised threateningly. Crispus's operator behind me fired once with ruthless efficiency. The rebel collapsed mid-stride, skull ruptured, body crumpling in grotesque silence.

Heart pounding, I turned quickly, scanning the room. And then I saw her.

Melissa lay on a filthy, stained mattress in the corner, clothes torn and dirtied, wrists tightly bound. Her face was swollen and bloodied, eyes swollen shut, bruises marring her pale skin. A surge of rage and protective fury filled me, overwhelming all else. I rushed to her side, pulling out my knife and cutting through the cruel plastic bindings digging into her wrists.

Her eyes fluttered open, glazed and unfocused. She flinched at my touch, instinctively recoiling.

"Melissa," I whispered, gently gripping her shoulder. "My name is Milo. We're here to get you out. You're safe now."

Her cracked lips moved slightly, a faint, incoherent murmur escaping. She was dazed, barely conscious, traumatized by unimaginable suffering.

With infinite care, I lifted her into my arms, her body alarmingly fragile, trembling weakly. Outside, the violent chaos had subsided. Crispus and his men had regained full control, securing the perimeter, checking bodies, and confiscating weapons. Crispus was already speaking rapidly into his radio, likely calling our vehicles forward to extract us.

Carrying Melissa carefully, I stepped out into the bright courtyard sunlight. Crispus approached, rifle hanging at his side, a grim but satisfied look etched deeply into his features.

But before I could speak, a sudden movement drew my attention to the right. My stomach plunged.

From the shadows of the nearest tukul emerged a teenage girl, young—no older than fourteen—her small hands gripping an oversized AK-47. Her wide eyes were wild, frightened yet determined, her posture rigid with desperation.

"No!" I shouted desperately, heart frozen in shock.

She fired immediately, the weapon jerking in her inexperienced hands. Bullets ripped toward us, chaos erupting anew. Crispus staggered backward, a sickening, wet hole opening abruptly in the back of his skull. His body crumpled lifelessly to the dusty ground at my feet, blood pooling around his shattered head.

My mind barely registered the volley of gunfire erupting around me as Crispus's men reacted instinctively, riddling the young girl's small body with dozens of bullets. She danced grotesquely for a horrible second, limbs flailing as bullets tore through her fragile form, before collapsing backward into the dark tukul doorway.

Heart hammering, I knelt beside Crispus's fallen body, briefly frozen by shock and grief. He'd survived so many horrors, only to fall now, here, at the end of a minor firefight.

Nate arrived from the perimeter, urgency etched into his face. He knelt beside me, shaking his head grimly. There was nothing to do; no amount of bandages or first aid could bring life back to the eyes of my friend.

"No sign of Caitlin anywhere," he reported. "We've searched every building and into the jungle a hundred yards in every direction. I've put the drone in thermal mode and have no heat signatures from anywhere around the hamlet."

I took a deep, ragged breath, turning my attention back to Melissa, who lay weakly on the ground nearby. Kneeling beside her again, I gently supported her head, whispering urgently. "Melissa, listen to me. Please. Where's Caitlin? Is she here?"

Her eyes opened slowly, pain and fear filling them. Her voice came out faintly, barely audible:

"They took her..." she mumbled. "A man...he spoke English... British accent...Asian."

A coldness settled sharply in my chest. My mind flashed immediately to the man we'd encountered in Juba, Jimmy Liu. It was the only possible explanation. His offer of assistance was nothing more than an attempt to keep tabs on us while we searched for Caitlin. But why? Why would the henchman of of a large Chinese mining magnate kidnap the daughter of the Secretary of State? It made no sense.

My pulse quickened dangerously, fury mixing with dread. Liu had betrayed us, manipulated us, and now he had Caitlin.

I rose, determination solidifying within me. Melissa was alive, safe now. But Caitlin remained in grave danger, captive somewhere under Jimmy Liu's ruthless control.

Nate saw my expression, reading the sudden shift. He knew exactly what I was thinking.

"Milo, what's our next move?" he asked, though I could see the anger in his eyes matched my own.

I met his gaze, voice cold and steady. "Our next move? We get Melissa to safety, then we find Jimmy Liu. Whatever it takes, we get Caitlin back. No matter the cost."

He nodded, eyes narrowing with grim determination. "Understood. We'll do it your way."

I glanced once more at Crispus's body, now covered respectfully by his grieving men, a pang of guilt and sorrow gripping my chest. His sacrifice had saved Melissa, but we couldn't pause long to mourn, not yet.

"Let's move," I said, my voice hardened by loss and resolve.

As we carried Melissa toward the waiting SUVs, I felt a dangerous calmness settling into me, a quiet rage tempered by clear, unshakable purpose. Jimmy Liu had made a terrible mistake. He'd stolen someone I'd sworn to rescue, betraying trust and honor.

And for that mistake, I would make him pay dearly. No matter what it took, no matter the sacrifice, I would bring Caitlin Bishop safely home.

13

3 MARCH 2240 HRS

JUBA, **South Sudan**

"A bottle of White Bull, please," I said, sliding wearily onto the worn leather stool at the rooftop bar. After a day like today, I craved something stronger, but knew better than to surrender to hard liquor in my current state.

The barman, a wiry South Sudanese man with weathered skin and tired eyes, regarded me apologetically, speaking in a gently accented African-British lilt. "Sorry, suh," he murmured. "White Bull brewery shut down back in 2016. Long time now."

I sighed, glancing beyond him at a cluttered shelf stacked high with bottles of varying labels and sizes. Ugandan beers, Bell and Nile Special, stood alongside the familiar elephant-head logo of Tusker, Kenya's iconic lager found everywhere across East Africa.

"A Tusker then," I replied, my voice carrying a weary resignation. "Cold as you've got."

"Yes, suh," he said, pulling a chilled bottle from beneath the counter along with a clean pint glass. He placed them gently in front of me, then retreated, clearly reading the subtle cues that I wanted solitude. Ignoring the glass, I grabbed the cold, sweating bottle, pressing it momentarily to my forehead before taking a long, grateful swig. The beer was crisp and refreshing, but it did little to ease the weight pressing on my chest or the thoughts racing through my mind.

It had been a hell of a day.

The images replayed in my mind on an endless loop: Crispus's lifeless body sprawled in the red dust, the teenage girl's vacant expression as she fired, Melissa's battered, traumatized face. After securing Melissa and the bodies of Crispus and his guard, we hurried back to the small dirt airstrip near Yambio. While Liu's plane was still waiting for us at the airstrip, I had no intention of getting on it and had instead coordinated with Stacy to send another plane from Juba to pick us up.

During the tense flight to Juba, I'd sat hunched in solemn silence beside Nate, listening absently to the droning engines, staring blankly out the small window at the green, seemingly endless expanse of jungle below. The weight of guilt and grief hung heavily upon my shoulders. Crispus had died saving us, saving Melissa, perhaps even me. I knew the familiar, awful sensation: a good man gone because of a mission I'd accepted. Another comrade sacrificed. Another debt owed to a grieving family.

We touched down in Juba to find two ambulances already waiting. Jessica, standing crisply efficient in the oppressive heat, directed the loading of Melissa's battered body into one ambulance, Crispus's and his guard's remains into the other. I had to admit, reluctantly, that Jessica's efficiency was impressive. She sliced effortlessly through layers of local bureaucracy, ensuring everything moved smoothly and discreetly. Without her presence, we might still have been stuck at the airstrip, fighting useless red tape.

At the hospital, a U.S. embassy doctor immediately took charge of Melissa's care, swiftly guiding her into a secure, private room. I stood numbly in the waiting area, eyes drawn to a familiar figure, a woman standing alone, rigid, her eyes fixed blankly ahead. Mary, Crispus's wife. Her proud bearing now seemed fragile, barely masking the depth of her pain. Her lips trembled, her head shook gently from side to side as she murmured, "No, no, no..."

I approached quietly, my heart heavy. "Mary, I'm so sorry," I whispered, opening my arms gently. She turned slowly, eyes filled with tears, then suddenly buried herself against my chest, her shoulders shaking uncontrollably with silent, dignified grief. There were simply no words adequate for this moment. We stood in silence, connected by the shared weight of loss.

After consoling Mary as best I could, the rest of the evening blurred into a chaotic mix of questioning Melissa, briefing Jessica and the ambassador, and urgent strategy sessions with Nate and Stacy. I made the painful decision to move Nate and myself out of Crispus's compound; the thought of further burdening Mary or the Panther Security Group seemed unbearable. Instead, we relocated hastily into the Pyramid Continental, Juba's large, imposing modern hotel favored by diplomats and expats.

Nate had excused himself, collapsing exhausted into his room. But sleep felt impossible for me. Restless and deeply troubled, I found myself drawn to the rooftop bar, seeking a measure of quiet solitude among the city lights and oppressive heat. I knew this ritual too well, a silent farewell to yet another comrade lost, the lonely toast of grief and memory shared only with shadows and ghosts.

I raised the Tusker bottle slowly, murmuring to myself, "I knew you, Crispus. I'll remember you. You won't be forgotten."

I took another deep pull, swallowing the bitter grief along with the cold beer. This was a ritual that never became easier, one I knew would continue repeating as long as my line of work remained what it was.

As I drank, my mind drifted from the raw memory of Crispus's lifeless form back to the hospital room, where I'd questioned Melissa with gentle urgency. She had lain there broken and battered, a shell of the vibrant young woman she had been. Her eyes were swollen nearly shut, dark bruises marring her pale, trembling limbs. The thin hospital gown barely covered the evidence of the terrible abuse she'd endured. Every word she spoke came through cracked, swollen lips, pain etched across her young face.

Through whispered conversations, careful questioning, and patient listening, I'd pieced together the harrowing timeline. Melissa had confirmed Major Ébi and his brutal LRA gang had attacked the WRC compound, forcing her and Caitlin into a desperate flight through the jungle. Caitlin had guided them to a hidden door I'd insisted be installed months earlier, a small relief that my advice had at least bought them an initial escape.

Melissa remembered fragments of the nightmare—the quiet hamlet, the children, the teenage girl who had betrayed them—but after that, her memory dissolved into disjointed fragments and black holes. Her trauma was raw, overwhelming; I knew better than to push her memories too far, too quickly.

Still, certain details had emerged with chilling clarity. Melissa insisted, fiercely and repeatedly, that Caitlin had initially evaded capture by Ébi's rebels at the hamlet. Yet she also swore she had heard Caitlin's voice again, just shortly before we rescued her. Her recollection of this was feverish and vague, but her insistence was unwavering.

Melissa described Caitlin speaking outside the hut, arguing with a man whose voice she described as "British-accented, precise, authoritative." She said Caitlin mentioned "the Ambassador" several times, though she couldn't recall the context. But Melissa's most chilling memory was of the man who entered the small hut that had become her prison shortly afterward to speak sharply with Ébi himself.

Melissa had barely been able to see through swollen eyes, but she was certain the man was Asian. Her words echoed clearly in my mind even now, as I sat nursing the Tusker in thoughtful silence: "An Asian guy...strong...muscular. A scar down his face."

My gut churned uneasily. Jimmy Liu again sprang to mind. Liu, who had appeared conveniently, offering resources with suspicious ease. Liu, whose background as the enforcer and fixer for the shadowy Jinhai Holdings fit precisely Melissa's fragmented description. Liu, whose impeccable British accent had stood out to me in Juba.

Cold realization settled over me like frost. Liu had orchestrated everything. Manipulating us, positioning himself carefully, masking his ruthless agenda behind false generosity. He had Caitlin now, I felt certain. We'd been played, tricked into trusting a dangerous and clever enemy.

My fingers clenched involuntarily around the cold beer bottle, anger rising sharply inside me. Liu had made a serious mistake by crossing me, and it would cost him. Yet the fury in my chest was tempered by deeper anxiety. Caitlin was still alive, in grave danger, held by men whose violence and cruelty knew few bounds.

I took another slow drink, trying to gather my thoughts. Jessica was already en route, having promised to meet me here at the Pyramid Continental. My mind swirled, doubt and determination warring within me. Trust was now a luxury I couldn't afford, and the stakes had risen dramatically. Every second counted now.

I raised the beer bottle again, taking another bitter swallow, hoping the alcohol might dull the ache of loss and anger. It didn't. Crispus's face remained vivid in my mind, alongside the image of Caitlin trapped and afraid, awaiting rescue.

I whispered into the warm night air, a quiet vow forged from grief, rage, and unwavering determination: "Crispus, you won't have died in vain. I promise. Whatever it takes, I'll find Caitlin, and I'll make Liu pay."

The dark rooftops of Juba stretched silently beneath the hotel's rooftop terrace, shadows mixing uneasily with dimly lit streets. I felt isolated, haunted by ghosts and guilt, the weight of my choices heavier than ever.

But beneath it all, a clear resolve formed: Caitlin Bishop would be brought home, and Jimmy Liu would face justice, no matter the personal cost.

I drained the bottle, steeling myself for what lay ahead. The battle was far from over, and I had every intention of seeing it through to the end.

My mind inevitably drifted back toward Jimmy Liu. There was something about his presence that unsettled me; his willingness to step forward and provide assistance was almost too convenient. Melissa's vague mention of an "Asian guy, muscular, British accent" echoed in my mind like a warning bell, suggesting a connection that couldn't simply be ignored.

Before I could chase the thought further, a pair of slender arms slid softly around my shoulders from behind. The unexpected warmth caught me off guard, briefly dissolving my tightly wound tension. I stiffened instinctively, my muscles tensing, then relaxed just enough to look over my shoulder.

Jessica's striking aquamarine eyes met mine from mere inches away, her face gentle yet intense. Her embrace was firm, almost possessive, and there was a tender sympathy in her voice as she murmured into my ear. "I'm so sorry about your friend, Milo. But I can't even tell you how relieved I am that you're safe."

Her arms tightened around me, and for an instant, her lips hovered perilously close to my cheek. I felt a stirring of attraction, a natural response given her undeniable beauty, but I quickly suppressed it, acutely conscious of the day's tragedy.

Jessica released me slowly, sliding gracefully into the stool beside mine before I could utter a reply. "Mind if I join you for a nightcap?" she asked with a knowing half-smile, already gesturing to the bartender for two more beers. The casual assumption in her manner irritated me slightly, but I lacked the energy or desire to argue.

The bartender set two fresh Tusker bottles before us, condensation glistening on the brown glass. Jessica lifted her bottle toward me in a subtle, silent toast, eyes bright and hopeful. I simply nodded, taking a slow pull, savoring the cold beer as it washed down my throat, soothing but not quite easing the ache that lingered in my chest.

Jessica seemed unperturbed by my reserved silence. "I spoke at length with Secretary Bishop," she began, her voice carefully neutral. "He asked me specifically to pass on his deepest condolences for Crispus's loss. But he also wanted me to convey his sincere gratitude to you for ridding Africa of one of its worst terrorists."

She paused, letting her words settle. I continued staring into my beer, expression unreadable.

"Major Ébi was on the International Criminal Court's Most Wanted List," Jessica continued, her tone turning slightly more formal. "The U.S. government had offered a million-dollar reward for his capture or death. Secretary Bishop instructed me to assure you that, in addition to your normal fees, the reward money is yours. He wants you to know how much he values your service."

I finally looked at Jessica directly, struck again by her exceptional beauty, yet troubled by the blunt insensitivity of her remarks. I had just comforted a grieving widow, informed her that her husband would never return to their children, and here was Jessica, casually handing out commendations and monetary rewards. Obtuse was the word that sprang to mind, though Jessica was not slow; rather, she was dangerously intelligent, perhaps lacking only a degree of empathy.

"Tell Secretary Bishop thank you," I said, measuring my voice carefully. "But please make sure that the entire reward goes directly to Mary Oryema, Crispus's widow."

Jessica's perfectly arched brows lifted slightly, her eyes assessing me. "Are you absolutely certain, Milo? That's a tremendous amount of money."

"I'm positive," I replied. "She needs it far more than I ever would."

"Fine," Jessica said, clearly uncomfortable yet unwilling to argue the point further. She shifted tactically to another topic. "Secretary Bishop also emphasized that he still has full confidence in you and

Relief Solutions. He wanted me to ensure you knew that he wants you to continue searching for Caitlin."

Her phrasing caught me by surprise, and I halted mid-swallow, setting my bottle down on the polished bar. "Was there ever a question?" I asked, unable to mask my irritation. "I've barely been on the ground for twenty-four hours. Did he think I'd just pack up and leave?"

Jessica met my challenging stare, frustrated that her carefully prepared message had landed so poorly. "No," she responded with exaggerated patience. "The Secretary simply wanted you reassured of his continued support."

I shook my head in mild exasperation, not quite sure why her statement annoyed me so much. Jessica was trying to be helpful, I knew, but every word from her mouth seemed to rub against the raw edges of my nerves tonight.

The bar had grown quieter, the late hour thinning out patrons, leaving only a trio of expats at a distant table murmuring in low voices. Jessica's presence beside me felt charged with unspoken expectation. Her proximity, the soft fragrance of her perfume, and the smooth skin visible along her elegant neck were undeniably distracting.

I glanced toward the barman, who was drying a glass and watching us with subtle amusement. I'm sure we presented an intriguing pair—Jessica's poised beauty and my weary, tense demeanor. He gave me a knowing nod before discreetly turning away.

"So," Jessica pressed, breaking the silence, "what's your next step? Any leads yet?"

I sighed, rubbing my temples. "Stacy and the team back in Newport are digging through every lead they have," I admitted. "We've got to get a location for Caitlin quickly. I have a call scheduled with Stacy at four a.m. our time, so I should probably grab a few hours' sleep. Once we get solid intel, Nate and I will move immediately."

Jessica leaned forward, eyes sparkling with determined intensity. "I'm coming with you," she said.

I studied her for a moment, weighing my reply. Arguing would be futile. Jessica was stubborn, influential, and had the explicit backing of Secretary Bishop himself. Besides, having her diplomatic clout could prove invaluable, even if her presence complicated things personally.

"I'm glad you'll be with us," I said, removing all traces of irony from my voice. "Be ready to leave by six. It's probably going to be a very long day."

Jessica smiled, clearly satisfied. "The embassy's Gulfstream is scheduled to return to Europe tomorrow. If we need it, I'll see if I can hold it another day or two. Just say the word."

"That'd be good," I agreed. "Meet for coffee downstairs at six sharp. Have your bags packed."

She hesitated for a moment, then reached over, lightly placing her hand on my thigh. Her fingers rested there softly, yet the gesture carried unmistakable intent. "I took a room here tonight, rather than stay at the embassy guesthouse," she said softly, voice lowering slightly. "If you want some company tonight, just ask."

I felt my pulse quicken involuntarily at the warmth of her touch and the quiet suggestion in her voice. Her attractiveness was undeniable—vivid green eyes, long graceful neck, delicate yet confident posture. My body, emotionally drained from the day's brutal events, reacted instinctively to her proximity.

But my mind flashed to Crispus, my friend, dead barely six hours. The image of his lifeless body haunted me. The raw pain in Mary's eyes was fresh in my mind, and the turmoil within me surged to the surface.

Gently, I covered Jessica's hand with mine, lifting it away. "I appreciate that more than you know," I said. "But tonight...after everything that's happened...I wouldn't be good company. Can we please take a rain check? I've got to coordinate with Stacy and try to grab at least an hour or two of sleep before tomorrow."

Jessica studied me, searching my eyes, weighing my sincerity. Slowly, she nodded, a slight disappointment flickering behind her carefully controlled expression. "I understand. Please forgive my timing. But...I do hope we get another chance soon to talk privately. There's still so much I want to learn about you."

"Likewise," I replied neutrally, careful not to close any doors.

Jessica leaned in suddenly, her lips brushing intimately close to my ear, sending an involuntary shiver down my spine. "And there's so much more of myself that I'd like to show you," she whispered, voice dripping sensual promise.

God, she never quits, does she?

I offered a slight, friendly smile. "We'll have plenty of time. I promise," I reassured her. Finishing my beer, I set the empty bottle down decisively on the polished wood bar top. "But now, I really should get back to the suite. Tomorrow will be a very long day."

She smiled coyly. "I'll be ready for you," she said, leaving the double meaning hanging provocatively between us.

As I stood, an uneasy thought rose urgently in my mind, one I'd been debating internally all evening. Turning slightly back toward Jessica, I decided to trust my instincts and press forward.

"Jessica, just one more quick thing," I began carefully. "Jimmy Liu. What exactly can you tell me about him?"

Her bright green eyes hardened instantly, the playfulness vanishing. "Why do you ask?"

"I just want to better understand all the players involved here. Liu seemed remarkably eager to help, and he clearly knew a lot about Caitlin's situation. Thought maybe you'd have some insights."

Jessica's expression grew guarded, distant. "Jimmy Liu's a well-connected local businessman. That's all I can really share, Milo. Sorry."

She was holding something back, unwilling or unable to divulge more. The question was why.

"No problem," I replied, forcing casualness into my tone. "Just thought I'd ask. See you in the morning."

Without waiting for further response, I turned and strode purposefully from the rooftop bar. Back in my suite, Nate was sleeping deeply, oblivious. Before collapsing onto my bed, I took out my secure satphone and dialed Stacy.

"Milo?" Stacy answered immediately. "Everything alright? Thought you'd be asleep by now."

"Almost. I need a quick favor. Get me everything you can on Jimmy Liu, a Chinese businessman here in Juba. See if you can put eyes on him without him knowing."

"Consider it done."

"You may already be doing this, but pull everything you can on his employer, Lin Jinhai, as well. These guys are behind this mess, and it's critical we understand why."

"I've already started. Jinhai's conglomerate of companies has its fingers everywhere in sub-Saharan Africa—anywhere where there's money to be made below ground, you can find a trail to Lin Jinhai's money. I'll keep working and get you a more polished package in the morning."

"One other thing," I said. "Something that's been nagging me all day but I just couldn't quite put my finger on it 'til now. Why did Jimmy Liu have several armored SUVs sitting in Yambio? There were two for our use, but Jimmy must have had his own transportation waiting for him as well. Gangura and Yambio are in the middle of nowhere. There's no mining there. So why have such a heavy logistics package on site?"

I could almost hear the gears turning on the other end of the line, the quiet stillness that came when Stacy's mind locked onto a problem. For a long moment, she said nothing, the silence stretching taut between us. Then she spoke. "I think you may have come up with the exact right question to figure this whole thing out. I don't have the answer, but I will. Soon."

I thanked her, disconnected, and fell back onto the bed. Tomorrow would be another long, dangerous day, and Jimmy Liu's role in this was becoming clearer.

14

4 MARCH 0420 HRS

JUBA, **South Sudan**

I woke well before my alarm could sound, staring upward into the dim ceiling of our suite. Sleep had come in fragmented bursts, interrupted by memories of the raid near Gangura—the rapid gunfire, the hollow look in Crispus's lifeless eyes, the haunting image of Melissa's battered body. It had been a restless night, my mind tortured by a cycle of guilt, grief, and frustration.

My brain churned, running scenarios—alternate decisions, different angles of attack, faster reactions—all ways I might have changed the tragic outcome. Yet the past was immovable, etched in stone, unforgiving and permanent. Crispus was gone, and no amount of self-torture could alter that fact. Still, I couldn't silence the insistent voice questioning if his death might somehow have been prevented.

I pushed myself up, muscles stiff and body heavy. The spacious suite at the Pyramid Continental Hotel provided luxury without comfort. The plush sofa, fine wooden furniture, and tasteful décor seemed incongruous given my dark mood. Nate sat quietly at the small dining table, sipping strong black coffee, the dim glow of the laptop illuminating his rugged face as he clicked through secure video channels.

"Call's coming up," Nate said, glancing at me with his usual cool practicality. Despite everything, Nate's calm presence provided grounding, a stable counterweight to my internal chaos. He sipped from his mug, eyes focused, prepared as always. Nate was methodical and reliable, never one to let emotions cloud his judgment.

I pulled an armchair next to Nate, positioning myself so I could see the laptop screen. He opened the secure video link, connecting to our Newport headquarters. The familiar image of Stacy filled the screen, her composed face framed against a detailed map of central Africa hanging behind her. Even late in the evening Rhode Island time, she appeared focused, alert, professional. That was Stacy—efficient, razor-sharp, reliable.

Sitting beside Stacy was Stitch. My eyebrows rose in mild surprise. I'd specifically instructed him to remain at home with his family in North Carolina. But Stitch hated being left behind, particularly during critical operations. He leaned toward the screen, one hand habitually stroking the Fu Manchu mustache that had become his trademark over the years. Stitch's quiet presence reassured me, even from thousands of miles away.

"Hey guys," I began, raising a tired hand in greeting. "I'm counting on you having something good for us."

Stacy nodded, organized, ready to deliver her usual exhaustive intel briefing. "We've made significant headway. But first—"

Stitch interrupted, a somber look crossing his weathered face. "Hey, Milo. Before anything else—I'm sorry about Crispus. He was one hell of a good man."

Stitch's sincerity struck me deeply. His bond with Crispus had grown from their shared military history and a previous Relief Solutions operation where he'd worked closely with Crispus. The loss was clearly weighing on him. I nodded in acknowledgment, not trusting myself to speak further on that topic.

"Thanks, Stitch," I said, pushing past my grief. "He was. Now let's hear what you've got, Stacy."

Stacy took a steady breath, eyes sharp, ready to present. "Okay, bottom line first: we've gathered strong intel that Caitlin was in Goma roughly six hours ago. More importantly, we've confirmed that Jimmy Liu arrived there simultaneously, and it seems unlikely this is a coincidence."

Nate leaned forward, intrigued. "Goma? How could they move her that far so quickly?"

Stacy nodded. "Great question. At first, we believed the captors might move her by road deeper into northeastern DRC. But that's challenging terrain, hours of driving through territory held by various rebel groups, all at odds with each other. The only viable alternative was aerial extraction. So that's where we focused our search, looking at everything that flew into or out of that area. And bingo. A Bell 412 helicopter registered to Green Kivu Mining departed Goma Airport yesterday afternoon, landing briefly in Bunia. Concurrently, a Britten-Norman Defender—the same aircraft model you flew into Yambio, of which Liu controls several—departed Juba, landing simultaneously with the helicopter."

My pulse quickened as I listened. "You think Caitlin was transferred between these aircraft?"

"I do," Stacy affirmed. "The helicopter refueled in Bunia and took on passengers from the Defender; passengers who had arrived from your area of operation. The helicopter returned to Goma late last night, fitting perfectly with the timeline of Caitlin's disappearance. Given the timeline of the flights, Liu likely took the Britten-Norman plane to Bunia, and hopped a flight to a makeshift landing zone south of the hamlet where you found Melissa. He and his men grabbed Caitlin from Ébi and were gone shortly before your arrival. Liu then took her back to Goma in the helicopter. We believe they're still there."

Nate frowned. "Visual confirmation?"

Stacy shook her head. "Not yet, but I'm confident we'll confirm visually soon. We have extensive contacts at Bunia and Goma airports. As airport personnel start their shifts today, we'll have direct confirmation."

"Samuel Kaziye," Stitch interjected, eyes brightening with recognition. "Remember him, Milo? Old Sammy still owes us."

I nodded, recalling Sammy clearly. He managed Goma's chaotic airport, and Stitch and I had once assisted his family with critical immigration issues. Sammy would definitely have intel, and he did indeed owe us.

"Good catch, Stitch," I said. "Let's prioritize Sammy for immediate contact as soon as operations start today."

Stacy shifted, poised to move on. "Now, let's talk about Jimmy Liu." On the video monitor, she looked to Stitch to pick up the briefing.

Stitch leaned forward, his weathered features tightening into a serious, almost grim expression. "Alright, Milo, we spent the past several hours digging deep into Jimmy Liu's background. To be blunt —this guy is a certified badass, a ruthless operator."

He shuffled several printed pages laid on the conference room table in front of him. Stacy sat silently beside him, her expression neutral but watchful. Stitch adjusted his reading glasses, cleared his throat, and then spoke deliberately.

"I reached out to some contacts at Langley and Anacostia," Stitch began, referencing the CIA and DIA headquarters, respectively. "Their dossiers on Liu were extensive and deeply troubling. Jimmy Liu was not just some mercenary who lucked his way into power. He was a seasoned, battle-hardened special operator who earned a reputation for ruthlessness during his tenure with the PLA's elite Snow Leopard Commando Unit."

Nate leaned in closer, intrigued, his analytical mind working overtime. "Snow Leopard Commandos...that's serious. Those guys are top-tier PLA special forces."

Stitch nodded, adjusting his glasses again. "Exactly. Liu's military dossier describes him as one of their most decorated operators. Grad-

uated at the top of his training class, adept in explosives, close-quar-
ters combat, counterterrorism tactics. Highly intelligent, highly
disciplined, but also known for brutal efficiency in combat. The
Chinese brass respected him deeply but also feared him."

He flipped a page, finding a highlighted section. "But the incident that sealed his reputation happened in June 2020. Galwan
Valley, high up on the mountainous border between China and
India. A flashpoint that ignited into a brutal, no-holds-barred battle
between Chinese and Indian troops."

I listened closely, feeling a chill down my spine despite the
oppressive Juba heat outside. Stitch's voice lowered slightly as he
continued, pulling me deeper into the intensity of his description.

"The Galwan clash was unique because both sides had agreed to
avoid firearms, fearing escalation to war, so they engaged in a primitive, vicious hand-to-hand battle. Imagine it: 14,000 feet above sea
level, limited oxygen, freezing darkness, no firearms allowed, just
fists, rocks, and improvised weapons. For six long hours, men from
both sides fought brutally, relentlessly, driven by pure survival
instinct."

Stitch paused, no doubt picturing the horrific scene as vividly as
if he'd been present himself. Nate remained silent beside me, eyes
locked onto Stitch's face, absorbed.

Stitch continued, eyes narrowing. "Jimmy Liu was leading one of
the Chinese advance squads. According to the dossier, during the
initial skirmish, Liu was struck violently in the face with a heavy iron
bar swung by an Indian soldier. The blow was brutal, immediately
rupturing his left eye socket. The eyeball itself was partially torn
from its socket. He suffered what they described as 'traumatic
enucleation.'"

Nate winced, drawing a deep breath, but said nothing. Stitch's
voice took on a steely intensity, clearly affected by the graphic details
he recounted. "Despite unimaginable pain, blood pouring down his
face, Liu refused to withdraw. Instead, he charged straight into the
Indian soldiers, fighting furiously with bare fists and improvised

weapons. One eyewitness account from a Chinese soldier claims Liu personally killed at least five enemy combatants that night."

I exhaled slowly, processing this image in my mind—a man fighting ferociously, brutally, despite an injury that would incapacitate most people. The sheer savagery and determination it would take seemed almost superhuman.

Stitch leaned back, setting down the dossier pages for a moment. "According to CIA analysts, Liu's actions directly turned the tide of that fight in the Chinese forces' favor. But the fighting continued for hours, vicious and desperate on both sides. By dawn, twenty Indian soldiers lay dead, along with numerous Chinese casualties. Jimmy Liu, half-blind and severely wounded, had survived. His actions earned him the PLA's highest commendation, personally awarded by Xi Jinping."

There was a heavy silence around the table. Nate rubbed his jaw before speaking. "So Liu's not just dangerous, he's battle-tested, capable of astonishing violence, and respected by his country's highest leadership."

"Exactly," Stitch confirmed. "The glass eye and facial scar were permanent reminders, but they also became symbols of his ferocity. The dossiers suggest he embraced them as part of his persona, as if the injuries granted him more power, more intimidation."

Stacy leaned forward now, her eyes sharply analytical. "Langley and DIA assessments both suggest Liu's deployment to Africa was strategic, a deliberate placement. He didn't fall from grace; he rose through it. Jinhai Holdings, the corporation Liu represents, operates under Beijing's tacit support, funneling resources back to China. Liu serves as their chief enforcer and fixer across the continent, Africa's equivalent of the boogeyman. He's ruthless, smart, disciplined, and now running lucrative operations involving gold, minerals, oil, and infrastructure throughout central Africa."

I leaned back, considering their words carefully. Liu had presented himself so casually in Juba, yet the reality was unsettling.

"So why is Jimmy Liu personally invested in Caitlin Bishop's kidnapping? What does he gain by taking the Secretary of State's daughter?"

Stitch exchanged a meaningful glance with Stacy before responding. "That's the million-dollar question, Milo. Liu is not known for making tactical errors. If he took Caitlin, it was calculated, strategic, serving a specific purpose."

"Which would suggest," Stacy added, "either money or power. Jinhai Holdings—and Liu—are financially motivated. George Bishop, prior to becoming Secretary of State, was a major global businessman. There's a high probability that their paths crossed professionally in the past, possibly a business deal, a debt, something unresolved."

I nodded. "And politically?"

Stacy shook her head, eyes narrowed in analysis. "That seems unlikely. Kidnapping Caitlin brings enormous diplomatic risk and no tangible political gain for Jinhai or Beijing. Their strategy would likely focus on less overtly dangerous methods."

"So," Nate interjected, summarizing, "money, power, or leverage over Secretary Bishop personally. Something unresolved, something Liu's willing to gamble heavily on."

"Yes," Stitch affirmed. "But Liu doesn't gamble, not without an almost certain payout. Whatever his endgame, we should assume he's calculated carefully. Caitlin isn't simply a hostage; she's likely key leverage in a much larger negotiation."

I absorbed their insights, knowing we'd gained critical intelligence but also realizing the stakes had risen sharply. Liu's willingness to directly involve himself meant Caitlin's kidnapping was no ordinary event. My pulse quickened as I realized the implications.

I sighed, addressing everyone. "Alright. We keep digging into Liu, his connections, and Bishop's past. But our immediate priority remains finding Caitlin. What intel do we have on her location right now?"

Stacy nodded. "As of six hours ago, all available intel places Caitlin in Goma. We've tracked an aircraft belonging to Liu's mining operation flying her into Goma late last night. We've confirmed Liu himself arrived simultaneously. Goma's our clear next step."

I checked my watch: almost five a.m. "Jessica's still holding the State Department jet. We'll be airborne within the hour. Nate, grab your gear. Let's move."

Nate stood, ready to go. Stitch leaned in toward the camera. "Milo—be careful in Goma. Liu's powerful there. He's surrounded by his own private security, likely former PLA special forces or mercenaries. Confronting him directly might be very dangerous."

I met Stitch's gaze, voice steady with resolve. "Duly noted. But Liu's made this personal. Caitlin's coming home, and Liu will answer for Crispus."

Stitch nodded. "Then we're here, Milo. Whatever you need."

I gave a final nod, signaling Nate to finish packing. As we prepared to leave, I couldn't shake the cold dread and fiery anger building inside me. Jimmy Liu was not just another opponent. He was an adversary uniquely ruthless, battle-hardened, and strategically formidable—a man who had killed trained soldiers in pitch-black, bare-handed combat. But Caitlin Bishop was my responsibility now, and nothing, not even a man like Jimmy Liu, was going to stand in my way.

We quickly gathered our gear, heading downstairs to rendezvous with Jessica. Despite my mixed feelings, her diplomatic clout and logistical access made her indispensable now.

In the lobby, Jessica stood poised beside two stacked suitcases, her posture crisp and controlled. She wore a tailored ivory blouse tucked into charcoal slacks, a thin leather belt cinched at her narrow waist, every line of her outfit pressed to perfection. Her carry-on sat upright beside her, straps coiled neatly, passport balanced on top. As we approached, she drew a measured breath, the faintest smile breaking through the tension in her face, a smile edged more with impatience than warmth.

"Milo," Jessica began, stepping intimately into my personal space. "I'm glad you finally came down. Sleep okay?"

"Not really," I admitted. "But it'll suffice."

Jessica placed her hand on my arm, her voice dropping. "You don't always have to be the hero, Milo. Sometimes, accepting comfort is perfectly alright."

I hesitated, her closeness and sincerity briefly tempting me. But my thoughts quickly flashed to Crispus's widow, Mary, and my lingering doubts about Jessica's motives. I carefully removed her hand with a polite smile.

"I appreciate that, Jessica. Maybe later. Right now, Caitlin is my only focus."

She nodded, understanding but not quite hiding her disappointment. "Fair enough. The plane's waiting. We should move."

I agreed, pushing aside distractions. We loaded quickly into the embassy SUV, moving swiftly toward Juba airport. The embassy Gulfstream was already fueled, engines idling patiently as we boarded. Jessica took a seat opposite me, legs crossed elegantly, her eyes subtly studying me throughout the short flight.

I deliberately focused outward, staring through the small window at the sprawling jungle below, mentally preparing myself for Goma. Jessica eventually broke the silence gently.

"You seem troubled," she said. "Is everything alright?"

"Jimmy Liu," I replied, observing her. "I still feel like we're missing something. Can you find out more about him from your contacts in the State Department? I feel like someone must know more."

"Yes, of course," she answered, but not before I caught the slight hesitation. "I'll see what I can find out."

She was withholding something; I could sense it. Ever careful with her words, her reply to me last night kept churning through my mind—"that's all I can really share." She didn't say she didn't know; she said she couldn't share. I knew I wasn't going to get anything from her sitting on the plane, so for now, I let it slide, determined to focus solely on Caitlin's rescue.

The jet descended toward Goma airport, tension rising within me. Soon, we'd be on the ground, facing Liu directly.

And no matter the cost, Caitlin Bishop would be coming home.

15

4 MARCH 0805 HRS

GOMA, Democratic Republic of Congo

Stepping off the Gulfstream onto the cracked and faded tarmac of Goma International Airport felt like entering a different world. Though situated picturesquely along the northern shore of Lake Kivu, Goma embodied every stark contrast imaginable. A city twice the population of Juba, and more than twice its suffering, Goma was home to countless refugees, crushing poverty, and escalating violence. Standing here, it was hard to imagine a city built upon such hardship and chaos also sat atop some of the richest deposits of minerals on Earth.

The city derived its name from the Bantu word for drum, a nod to the distant rumbling of Mount Nyiragongo, a volcano that towered ominously on the northern horizon. Its frequent eruptions had painted much of Goma's history in smoke and fire, reshaping lives and livelihoods for over a century. The city itself was an intricate patchwork of bustling markets, sprawling shantytowns, and remnants of French colonialism reflected in buildings and roads worn down by decades of neglect.

Goma was the capital of North Kivu province, a region cursed with unimaginable wealth. Coltan, gold, diamonds—vast riches lay beneath its fertile soil, valued at an estimated $24 trillion. Above ground, however, the city existed in permanent crisis, its poverty and desperation in stark contrast to the wealth lying beneath. Millions displaced by ongoing conflict crowded into Goma's fringes, forming sprawling camps where suffering and struggle had become a way of life.

Nate and Jessica descended the jet's stairs behind me, Nate efficiently managing equipment and logistics while Jessica stepped up beside me, adjusting her sunglasses and gazing skeptically at our surroundings. She had announced earlier that the State Department jet was required back in Europe, news I welcomed. Luxury jets were a liability in a place like Goma, drawing unnecessary attention. I preferred slipping quietly under the radar, especially on operations as delicate as this.

I had filled Jessica in on everything Stitch and Stacy uncovered, particularly the emerging involvement of Jimmy Liu and Green Kivu Mining. At first, she had shown interest, excusing herself to the back cabin to call Secretary Bishop despite the late hour in Washington. But afterward, she seemed strangely withdrawn, skeptical even, suggesting that a major Chinese mining firm was an unlikely kidnapper. I'd pretended to sleep after that, avoiding further conflict.

Two embassy-marked Range Rovers now approached across the tarmac, tires crunching gravel as they drew close. Jessica pointed them out with satisfaction. "Our welcoming committee," she said. "I figured we'd avoid immigration hassles this way." She glanced meaningfully toward Nate unloading Pelican cases packed with sensitive gear. "I don't know exactly what you guys have stowed in those, but I assumed customs would pose a problem otherwise."

"Just standard contingency gear," I replied, hoping to deflect her curiosity. "Nothing too alarming."

Jessica arched a delicate eyebrow, clearly unconvinced. "Why do I find that hard to believe?"

I shrugged, offering no further clarification. Instead, my attention shifted toward a battered white pickup truck now pulling slowly toward us from the direction of the terminal. A familiar yellow airport light atop its roof flashed intermittently, lending the vehicle an air of modest authority.

"Looks like our man," I said, feeling a flicker of relief. Sammy Kaziye had always been reliable. More than a friend, he had become a trusted ally during my many trips through Goma.

Jessica, handing off our passports to an embassy driver, then returned quickly to my side, watching curiously as the ancient truck rumbled to a stop just before us. The driver's side door creaked open, and a slight, slender black man in his late fifties stepped onto the tarmac.

Sammy Kaziye, the civilian manager of Goma International, was instantly recognizable by his prematurely receding hairline, gleaming ebony forehead, and irrepressible smile. His teeth flashed brilliantly against his dark skin as he strode toward me, arms already open wide in an enthusiastic embrace.

"Brother Milo!" Sammy's deep voice boomed warmly as he wrapped me in a hearty hug. "Far, far too long since you last visited! You mustn't keep Sammy waiting so many months, my friend!"

I smiled genuinely, warmly embracing Sammy in return. Sammy's friendship was rooted in mutual respect and shared history. Stitch and I had once helped his younger sister navigate difficult immigration issues in the U.S., ensuring her safety and stable reloca-tion. Ever since, Sammy's loyalty had been fierce, his assistance invaluable. He'd always claimed we'd given his family a second chance at life. I knew he'd never forget it.

Sammy turned his exuberance toward Jessica. "Ms. Reid, welcome to Goma. Your embassy called ahead. Your arrival is eagerly awaited. Anything you need, please just ask." Jessica smiled, charmed by Sammy's graciousness, shaking his hand warmly and thanking him.

As Sammy turned away briefly to discuss details with Jessica, he pressed something discreetly into my palm—a small, folded piece of paper. I kept my expression neutral, closing my fingers

tightly around the slip of paper, feeling an instinctive thrill of anticipation.

After introductions and quick exchanges with Sammy, we
followed him inside the airport to a cramped conference room tucked
near the terminal's administrative offices. The scent of mold and dust
filled the air, mingled with the whine of an ancient air conditioner
struggling noisily against oppressive heat.

As we took seats around a scarred wooden table, Sammy closed
the door behind us, providing privacy.

"I received your message earlier, Milo," Sammy began, his usual
smile fading into seriousness. "Since early this morning, I've inter-
viewed every member of my staff on duty last night. The Green Kivu
Mining helicopter you mentioned landed precisely at 11:17 p.m.
There were four passengers, one a white female."

Nate leaned forward, his expression intense. "It has to be Caitlin.
Did she appear injured? Did anyone try to intervene?"

Sammy shook his head regretfully. "My fuel truck driver
approached closely enough to notice her, but reported no obvious
distress. The passengers quickly entered two SUVs marked with the
Green Kivu logo and departed at 11:24 p.m. Beyond that, we have no
further knowledge of their destination."

I sat back, digesting Sammy's confirmation. "This strongly
confirms Caitlin's presence here," I said.

Jessica, however, seemed agitated, frowning. "Wait. This doesn't
make sense. Green Kivu is a massive, reputable mining corporation.
Why on earth would they abduct the Secretary of State's daughter?
It's absurd—this isn't the nineteenth century. It's business, not Joseph
Conrad's Heart of Darkness."

"Jessica," I responded evenly, not wanting to provoke her further.
"I'm following facts, leads, evidence. This intel is credible. If Caitlin
were here, we would need to track her now."

Jessica shook her head. "I just find it highly improbable. Are we
sure this is not some kind of mistake?"

Frustration boiled silently beneath my surface. "Jessica," I spoke, measured and calm, "the Secretary hired Relief Solutions specifically for our proven track record. I've never sent us chasing false leads. What I do is follow intel, verify facts, and act swiftly. Caitlin was almost certainly here—your disbelief won't change facts."

Jessica remained silent, sensing she'd pushed me far enough.

I glanced at my watch. "Look, it's already morning. Sammy, thank you for all your help. Do you mind if I freshen up before we proceed?"

Sammy nodded. "Of course, Milo. Restroom's down the corridor on the right."

I shook his hand firmly once more, thanking him for everything. Sammy squeezed my hand, holding my eyes meaningfully for an extra second. "Anything, anytime," he murmured, reaffirming his unwavering support.

Walking toward the restroom, I felt anticipation building. Inside, I locked the door carefully, unfolding the slip of paper Sammy had discreetly passed me earlier.

The handwriting was Sammy's unmistakable, careful print. I read it quickly. The hunt was on.

16

4 MARCH 0835 HRS

GOMA, Democratic Republic of the Congo

Wrestling the ancient steering wheel of Sammy's battered Renault sedan, I turned into the wide, rusty iron gates of the Amahoro Guesthouse. The car, devoid of power steering, groaned in protest, resisting the abrupt movement until I forced it onto the gravel driveway leading into the compound. A cloud of volcanic dust billowed behind me, settling on the cracked leather seats and worn dashboard. I exhaled slowly, steadying myself after the drive through Goma's chaotic streets.

The guesthouse stood solid and unchanged, a rare island of permanence amid the turbulent seas of Goma's endless upheaval. Nestled in five carefully maintained acres of manicured gardens and tall shade trees, the Amahoro Guesthouse seemed untouched by the rapid and sometimes violent transformation that had swept the city over the last three decades. Its name, meaning "Peace" in Kinyarwanda, contrasted starkly with the chaos just beyond its towering iron fences.

The ornate wrought-iron fence encircling the property was perhaps its most impressive feature—ten feet high and topped by pointed spikes, serving as both a practical barrier and a statement of resilience against Goma's outside troubles. The main house, a stately yet weathered colonial structure, stood tall and proud at the heart of the compound, its white plaster walls now stained by time and volcanic ash. A broad, shaded veranda wrapped around the entire building, lined with wooden chairs and tables, creating the air of a private sanctuary.

Adjacent to the main house stood two modest single-story outbuildings, each housing additional guest rooms. These buildings bore chipped paint and peeling shutters, a testament to neglect, yet retained a quiet dignity. I had visited the Amahoro Guesthouse twice before, and I knew that despite appearances, the place held secrets, whispers, and dangerous connections lurking beneath its tranquil exterior.

Twenty minutes earlier, seated in Sammy's ancient Renault in a secluded parking lot near Goma airport, I'd reread the small slip of paper Sammy had pressed into my palm earlier. Sammy, always cautious, had known that Liu's influence extended everywhere, even within the airport itself.

The handwritten note had read, in Sammy's careful, unmistakable hand:

THIS AIRPORT HAS EARS. YOU'RE ON THE RIGHT TRACK. UMWAMIKAZI IS WAITING FOR YOU AT AMAHORO GUESTHOUSE. TAKE THE RED RENAULT PARKED IN MY SPOT.

Those few cryptic lines had electrified my senses, clarifying the gravity of the situation. If Sammy felt compelled to warn me so explicitly, Jimmy Liu's reach was deeper and more dangerous than I'd imagined.

After reading Sammy's note, I'd fired off a detailed text to Nate, instructing him on how best to manage Jessica during my absence, diverting her attention by having her accompany him to the local headquarters of Green Kivu Mining in Goma, asking questions that would inevitably be met with evasive or deceptive answers. I knew that Nate's steady pragmatism and careful diplomacy would handle Jessica's sharp intellect and insatiable curiosity well.

With Nate briefed, I'd started the rattling Renault and driven through Goma's crowded streets toward the Amahoro Guesthouse. My mind churned with the realization that the mysterious figure known as "Umwamikazi"—the Queen—was awaiting me.

The name was a title rather than a given name. "Umwamikazi" translated literally from Kinyarwanda as "Queen," an honorific that was both respectful and deeply symbolic. The woman who bore that title, Rosalie Muhire, was someone whose story was as tragic and ruthless as the city itself. Born into privilege in neighboring Rwanda, Rosalie had been the eldest daughter of the Honorable Mutara Muhire, Chief Justice of Rwanda's Supreme Court, a respected Tutsi family that held considerable influence before the country collapsed into genocidal chaos in April 1994.

When Hutu extremists began the coordinated massacre of Tutsis, Chief Justice Muhire had taken refuge with his family at Kigali's Église Saint-Famille, seeking sanctuary from the killing squads that swept Rwanda's capital with merciless efficiency. They believed the church and its influential priest, Father Wenceslas Munyemana, whose mixed ethnic parentage and prominent role in the community seemed a guarantee of safety, would protect them. That faith was catastrophically misplaced.

On a terrifying April night, as Father Wenceslas quietly fled on a plane bound for Paris, abandoning his parishioners to their fate, the Hutu Interahamwe militia surrounded Église Saint-Famille. Rosalie, then thirteen, sat huddled with her family, crowded among thousands who sought sanctuary. As the militia set up tripod-mounted machine guns on a road embankment overlooking the compound, the priest's betrayal became tragically apparent.

The massacre commenced without warning, machine guns raining indiscriminate fire down upon the trapped civilians below. Rosalie's father died instantly, two bullets tearing violently through his forehead, showering his family with his blood and brains. Her mother fell next, shielding Rosalie and her siblings with her own body, screaming prayers that no one could hear above the slaughter. Rosalie was struck by a bullet that tore through her left wrist, severing her hand, knocking her unconscious as her family collapsed around her.

She awoke hours later, beneath the heavy, lifeless bodies of her parents and siblings, trapped in a surreal nightmare. Her memory of escaping the carnage was fragmented and nightmarish, a blur of blood and screams. Yet somehow, Rosalie survived. Her survival became legend, a chilling tale whispered reverently across Rwanda's mountains and beyond.

Rosalie Muhire had chosen not to follow her father into the judicial profession. Instead, her path had led into darker, more clandestine territory. Settling in Goma amidst the post-genocide chaos, Rosalie quickly rose as a formidable businesswoman. Her influence and wealth expanded dramatically, founded upon extensive real estate and profitable enterprises catering to the region's endless instability.

Yet Rosalie's public life masked a shadowy, ruthless persona. Known simply as the Umwamikazi, she controlled Goma's illicit underworld, trafficking in gold, diamonds, weapons, drugs, and human lives. To most, she was an enigmatic business magnate; to a select few, Rosalie Muhire was a key intelligence operative directing Rwanda's National Intelligence and Security Service interests within eastern Congo. Her hatred for Hutus and the Congolese government, both of whom she blamed for genocide-related atrocities, was widely known. She operated intelligently, mercilessly, and without remorse.

It intrigued me that Rosalie now sought involvement in Caitlin Bishop's kidnapping case. Her assistance was potentially invaluable, but I knew better than to underestimate her ruthlessness or fail to recognize the risks in seeking her aid.

Now, driving Sammy's battered Renault into the peaceful compound, my pulse quickened with anticipation and apprehension. I parked the car beneath a large flame tree whose vibrant blossoms contrasted sharply with the faded paint on the main house. Armed guards stood quietly alert around the perimeter, each carefully noting my arrival, fingers resting lightly near their rifle triggers.

As I approached the veranda, an older, slender Congolese man in a threadbare blue suit emerged gracefully from the main doorway, stepping forward with professional courtesy.

"Greetings, Mr. deCogan," he said, his voice calm and welcoming. "I am André, and it is my great honor to welcome you once again to the Amahoro Guesthouse. The Umwamikazi awaits you on the veranda at the rear of the house. Please follow me."

Though I'd visited the Amahoro Guesthouse twice before, I could not recall ever meeting the thin, middle-aged man who greeted me at the entrance. His suit, threadbare and carefully ironed, marked him as the hotel manager, or perhaps an aide to the mysterious woman I'd come here to see. Clearly, he'd been expecting me, though we'd never personally met. Visitors here were not your average tourists; those who arrived at the Amahoro Guesthouse usually did so discreetly and purposefully, their stays shrouded in secrecy and whispers.

With quiet dignity, and without further pleasantries, the man guided me through the lobby. The place felt caught in time, its interior rich with worn antique furniture, African artifacts adorning faded walls that whispered stories of colonial grandeur long since faded. The warm, dusty scent of polished mahogany and leather mingled with faint hints of spices from the guesthouse's kitchen, adding an exotic yet inviting ambiance to the somber space.

We moved through open French doors onto the expansive rear veranda. It was early enough that the air still carried a coolness tinged with the promise of the coming midday heat. Patrons, a dozen or so, sat scattered at wooden tables across the length of the veranda, quietly engaged in breakfast. Mostly older African businessmen dressed formally despite the rising humidity, accompanied by wives or mistresses whose presence seemed ornamental rather than intimate.

My attention was drawn to a table near the railing, occupied by a woman whose presence dominated the entire veranda. Rosalie Muhire sat with regal composure, her posture impeccable, shoulders gracefully poised beneath the traditional umushanana—a flowing lavender skirt paired exquisitely with a tailored short-sleeved pink blouse, and a multi-colored sash artfully draped over one shoulder. She exuded the natural elegance that had long characterized her presence, her striking emerald-green eyes gazing calmly toward me as I approached.

Rosalie's beauty was undeniable, her flawless mocha complexion and high, graceful jawline complementing her strikingly green eyes. Her refined features could rival those of any international runway model, yet she carried herself with a confidence and poise born not just from beauty, but from power, experience, and tragedy.

As she extended her right hand, the other remained prominently displayed on the table, ending abruptly at the wrist in a stark stump, a constant visual reminder of the brutality she'd endured. It was intentional. Rosalie never hid her injury; instead, she wore it openly as a badge of survival and strength. My eyes were drawn briefly to her left wrist, where a heavy, worn man's wristwatch hung securely, clasped tightly above the scar tissue.

I had heard rumors about that watch. Some whispered it belonged to the Hutu leader responsible for the massacre at Église Saint-Famille, the slaughter that had cost Rosalie her family and, nearly, her life. Rumors suggested Rosalie wore the watch as a grim reminder never to forgive, never to forget. Others claimed a more macabre trophy existed, a second watch, supposedly still strapped to the severed hand of that same man's wife, kept in a jar in Rosalie's private office. True or not, these whispers had solidified her reputation as someone who could neither forgive nor forget betrayal.

"Good morning, Rosalie," I greeted respectfully, stopping beside her table. "Thank you for agreeing to meet me on such short notice."

Rosalie's eyes met mine, a delicate, knowing smile playing across her flawless features. Her English was impeccable, crisp and elegant as British royalty. "My dear Milo, it is I who should thank you," she replied, gesturing toward the empty seat opposite her. "Your visits are always a pleasure, and given all you've done for me and my people, I would never refuse you."

I nodded in gratitude, taking the offered seat. "Your hospitality is as gracious as ever."

Ours was not a new acquaintance. We'd first crossed paths five years earlier, when Relief Solutions had been contracted to assist on a human trafficking case in the Balkans. Albanian syndicates were smuggling young women out of Africa, mostly from Rwanda and the eastern DRC, moving them through transit hubs in Montenegro and northern Greece before selling them across Europe. It was a brutal, systematic operation, cloaked behind false NGOs and shell charities. Rosalie had become our point of contact, feeding us intelligence that local law enforcement either couldn't or wouldn't pursue. Her information had been precise, her motives deeply personal.

One of the missing girls had been her niece, a bright, wide-eyed teenager who vanished after taking what she thought was a domestic job offer in Kigali. Rosalie's grief had hardened into purpose, and together we'd dismantled a trafficking ring that had enslaved dozens. Since then, there'd been a quiet respect between us, an unspoken understanding born of shared victories and scars. Rosalie was no mere informant; she was a force—driven, poised, and dangerous when cornered.

"Would you care for something to drink?" she asked, raising her right hand to signal a nearby server.

"That juice you have looks perfect," I replied, noticing the chilled passion fruit beverage in her delicate grasp.

Rosalie nodded to the waiter, who promptly delivered a glass of the refreshing drink. I sipped it slowly, enjoying its sweet, tangy freshness—a stark contrast to the heavy emotional weight I'd been carrying since landing in Goma.

For a moment, silence lingered between us, an unspoken game of patience. Rosalie expected me to ask the questions first, but I'd learned the importance of patience, waiting carefully for her to speak. It became an awkward yet intentional silence, a game of subtle wills and tactics that both of us understood intimately.

Finally, Rosalie's smile widened, and she broke the silence, laughing softly as she met my eyes. "You always intrigue me, Milo. Perhaps someday we should spend time together beyond mere business?"

Her voice had a gentle teasing quality, yet the underlying sexual tension in her invitation was unmistakable. For a brief instant, I felt myself drawn toward her natural allure, an unintended glance toward her left wrist breaking the moment's intimacy. Rosalie caught my glance immediately, her emerald eyes hardening with defensiveness, a reaction I realized she likely experienced every day.

She raised her scarred wrist, displaying it openly. "You don't need to pretend. I've grown used to people's discomfort."

I quickly clarified my true interest, feeling an urge to bare my thoughts. "Actually, I was looking at your watch," I confessed, holding her gaze. "Wondering what it was like when you finally confronted its owner."

She held my eyes steadily, surprised, before suddenly breaking into genuine laughter—clear, rich laughter that filled the quiet veranda. Her reaction surprised me, but her amusement seemed sincere.

"My dear Milo, no one has ever dared to ask me that question directly," she replied, enjoying my bluntness. "But your honesty is refreshing. Truly refreshing."

I offered a cautious smile, feeling I had narrowly avoided offending her. Rosalie took another careful sip of her juice, then leaned forward, her eyes now thoughtful.

"Would you like the truth about the watch?"

"If you're willing to share, I'm willing to listen," I replied.

Rosalie unclasped the watch from her wrist and handed it to me, her fingers brushing mine briefly. "This belonged to my father. He gave it to Father Wenceslas, the priest at Église Saint-Famille, to ensure our protection during the genocide. That priest promised to keep us safe, then returned it one day later, having decided otherwise. I wear it as a constant reminder that betrayal always comes from those closest to you."

I studied the watch, feeling a newfound respect for Rosalie's complexity. "Thank you for sharing that with me. You're a woman of many layers, Rosalie. Truly fascinating."

Her smile returned, now softer and more genuine. "Perhaps you might enjoy uncovering those layers sometime?"

Without hesitation, I again replied honestly. "I think I would. Maybe we could spend some time together once this matter is resolved, perhaps a quiet getaway in Paris?"

Rosalie's expression darkened, a shadow crossing her beautiful face. "Anywhere but France," she said coldly, voice suddenly hard. "I'll never set foot there."

I hesitated, curiosity overcoming caution. "May I ask why?"

Rosalie's voice softened again, eyes distant with memory. "Father Wenceslas, that priest who betrayed us during the genocide, fled to France. After orchestrating the deaths of thousands, including my family, the French protected him. He continued preaching for decades, a convicted mass murderer given refuge and a parish. Only after he fathered a child out of wedlock was he excommunicated. Twenty years protected by the Church for being a mass murderer, but excommunicated for breaking his vow of celibacy. That is why France disgusts me."

Her bitterness was palpable, the pain of betrayal still sharp. "I understand," I said, unable to offer any additional comfort or insight, but appreciating her openness with me. "There are plenty of beautiful cities not in France. We can pick one at random."

"I'd like that very much," she said, smiling. "Now, tell me about Caitlin Bishop."

I summarized the key events: Caitlin's disappearance in South

Sudan, her last known sighting near the DRC border, the involvement of Jimmy Liu and Green Kivu Mining. Rosalie listened intently, her analytical mind quickly absorbing every detail.

"The helicopter landed here last night," I concluded. "Liu's involvement is beyond doubt."

Rosalie nodded, checking the watch again. "This morning, a King Air registered to Extractive Industries, Green Kivu's parent company, left Goma for Lubumbashi. But that flight is a decoy. An hour later, a Dassault Falcon 2000 flew in from Johannesburg and departed quickly with Jimmy Liu and an elderly Muslim woman in a wheelchair, likely Caitlin. The Falcon's headed back to Johannesburg as we speak."

I absorbed her words carefully. "You're certain?"

"Absolutely. These are powerful and dangerous people, Milo. Be careful."

I nodded. "Thank you, Rosalie. Truly."

"You're welcome," she said. "But please understand this: I've helped you discreetly because I share your enemy. Green Kivu Mining threatens my interests, and weakening them benefits me. I cannot openly move against them. This must remain our secret."

"You have my word," I assured her. "It stays between us."

"Good." She leaned closer, her voice softening, rekindling subtle flirtation. "Once this ends, perhaps we'll find time to peel back more layers of our own."

I smiled, meeting her eyes. "I would very much enjoy that."

She extended her right hand, gently touching mine in a soft, lingering gesture that carried a deep, unspoken promise.

"I look forward to it, Milo."

I left the table feeling a complex mix of attraction, admiration, and urgency. Rosalie Muhire—the Umwamikazi—was complex, beautiful, and lethal.

17

4 MARCH 0925 HRS

35,000 FEET above Zambia

Caitlin's eyes fluttered open, consciousness slowly returning as the low hum of jet engines filled her senses. Her chin rested heavily against her chest, her neck painfully stiff, protesting even the slightest movement. It took several moments for her surroundings to come into focus—a blur of luxurious cream-colored leather seats, polished wood veneer paneling, and drawn window shades shutting out the world. Immediately, she recognized the refined interior as that of a private jet.

Her head throbbed, muddling her thoughts. She had vague, fragmented memories of being wheeled groggily across an airstrip, hands gripping her arms, voices muttering in languages she couldn't identify. But beyond that, everything was hazy, disconnected. Her last clear memory was being thrust violently into an SUV by Asian men in black fatigues somewhere deep in the South Sudanese wilderness.

"Melissa!" The thought jolted her awake, adrenaline piercing through her lingering fog. What had happened to Melissa? Panic surged through her, heart pounding as she tried to piece together those chaotic moments. She remembered the ambush, Melissa's desperate screams, the sudden overwhelming fear, and then nothing.

Caitlin tried to raise her hands but immediately felt sharp pain around her wrists, realizing with a sickening sensation that both arms were tightly zip-tied to the armrests. She struggled against the restraints, feeling panic rise in her chest, her breath quickening. Glancing down, she noticed for the first time that she was clad in a lightweight black robe, one she had no recollection of putting on herself.

A voice from her left startled her into rigid stillness. Slowly, Caitlin turned her head, eyes wide with fear and confusion, toward the source of the sound. Sitting calmly across the aisle in the row just in front of her was a powerfully built Asian man speaking quietly yet firmly into a satellite phone. His British-accented English was precise, refined, and authoritative.

"...you must do exactly as instructed, Mr. Secretary. You entered this agreement willfully and now must uphold your end," the man stated coldly.

Mr. Secretary? Caitlin's mind raced frantically. The only person she had ever heard addressed by that title was her father, George Bishop, the United States Secretary of State. Confusion and dread flooded through her as she realized the Asian man was speaking directly to her father. Her heart thumped painfully against her ribs.

She began tugging more desperately at the restraints, feeling panic begin to surge again. The man glanced toward her, noticing she was awake, and a slow smile spread across his face, unsettling in its casual cruelty. He was intimidatingly muscular, his black shirt taut against a chest and arms rippling with muscle. A jagged vertical scar ran down one side of his otherwise handsome face, from his eyebrow to his square jawline. His one good eye, cold and penetrating, looked straight through her with dispassionate interest, like she was merely a useful object rather than a human being.

The man turned away from Caitlin, continuing his conversation with eerie calm. "I'm not interested in further negotiation, Secretary Bishop. Call off your pitbull deCogan. Fulfill your end of our agreement exactly as we discussed. Consider this a courtesy call to ensure you fully comprehend the consequences."

Caitlin strained to hear her father's voice, but only indistinct murmurs reached her ears. Her pulse quickened further as the man paused briefly, listening attentively before responding. "Yes, of course. You may speak to her yourself. Allow me."

Without hesitation, he stood and moved toward her seat, holding the satellite phone toward Caitlin's face. Her heart pounded as she heard her father's familiar voice, strong yet unmistakably tense.

"Dad?" she whispered urgently, emotion choking her voice.

"Caitlin!" Her father's voice was clear, intense. "Are you hurt? Have they harmed you?"

A rush of conflicting emotions—relief, confusion, fear—overwhelmed her senses, making it difficult to speak. She had so many questions, so many fears. Where was she being taken? Why was this happening?

"Dad? What's going on? Where am I? What happened to Melissa?"

Her father's voice grew firm, commanding. "Caitlin, listen carefully. Stay calm. Are you injured?"

She took a breath, her voice trembling. "No...no, Dad, I'm not hurt. But please—"

"We don't have much time, sweetheart," he interrupted. "Listen to me. You're going to be okay. Just do exactly as they say, and I promise I'll bring you home safely. Do you understand me?"

"Dad," she pleaded. "Do you know who—."

The Asian man abruptly pulled the phone away, switching off the speaker mode and raising it back to his own ear. Caitlin watched helplessly, unable to finish speaking to her father, her mind reeling with confusion and frustration.

"You now have proof your daughter is alive and unharmed," the man informed Bishop coolly. "If you wish for her to remain that way, you'll do precisely as we have agreed."

He ended the call, calmly replacing the satellite phone into its charger. His gaze returned to Caitlin, eyes devoid of sympathy or emotion.

"Who are you?" Caitlin demanded, attempting to conceal her fear behind anger. "Where are you taking me?"

The man regarded her thoughtfully before responding, his voice chillingly composed. "Your location does not matter. Let's just say I'm a business partner of your father."

The implication sent a chill down her spine. Clearly, the man knew who she was and had carefully orchestrated this kidnapping to serve some dark purpose involving her father. Yet even through her terror, a sense of defiance rose within her.

"You realize," Caitlin said, fighting to steady her trembling voice, "that when they find me, and they will find me, you'll be in so much trouble—"

The man's hand flashed forward with brutal swiftness, striking her hard across the face. Pain exploded through Caitlin's skull, causing her vision to blur, the metallic taste of blood filling her mouth from a bitten tongue. Her ears rang, the slap echoing through her entire body. Tears welled uncontrollably in her eyes, shock mixing with physical agony.

He leaned in closely, his voice calm, ice-cold, devoid of remorse. "Ms. Bishop, allow me to make something very clear. We are far past the point where your threats or beliefs matter. Your father has entered an agreement with us, willingly. You are here as collateral. Do as you're instructed, remain quiet, and your experience will be relatively comfortable. Resist, and I will personally keep you heavily sedated. The choice is yours."

He straightened, waiting for her acknowledgment. Caitlin saw in his expression that this man cared absolutely nothing for her well-being. She was merely a pawn, expendable.

She lowered her eyes, overwhelmed by the terrifying realization that she was utterly powerless. She thought of her father's voice, his reassurances seeming distant, hollow. This captor—calm, calculating, dangerous—made one thing abundantly clear: Caitlin was caught up in something much larger, something ruthless and incomprehensible, and she had become nothing more than a bargaining chip.

Her wrists burned where the zip ties restrained her. Her face throbbed from the violent slap. But the fear in her heart far outweighed the physical pain. Glancing at her captor, she made the only decision available to her at this moment.

She remained silent, her gaze lowered to the plush carpeting, her resolve replaced by an instinctual, primal fear.

She knew then, more clearly than ever before, that she was trapped, and in very, very deep trouble.

18

4 MARCH 0950 HRS

GOMA, Democratic Republic of the Congo

"Where the hell have you been?"

Jessica's sharp voice greeted me the moment I emerged from the dusty Renault sedan, her eyes narrowed, arms crossed tightly across her chest. She stood alongside Nate beneath a rusted metal awning outside the terminal, fuming from my sudden and unexplained absence.

Nate caught my eye, eyebrows raised in a silent warning that Jessica was already wound up. Nate was one of the few people whose patience and calm usually served as a balance to my bluntness, but even he seemed wary of Jessica's rising temper.

I approached slowly, careful to keep my own expression neutral, maintaining composure even as Jessica's impatience seared beneath the surface. "Jessica, listen, I can explain—"

"No, you listen," she cut me off, her tone sharply edged. "How dare you leave me sitting here at the airport while you're off playing cowboy! That is not how this works. You're under contract with the Secretary of State, Milo. You answer to him, and by extension, you answer to me as his representative."

I took a slow breath, holding steady against the intensity of her glare. This was the Jessica I'd been cautious of—assertive, intelligent, yet sometimes dangerously unaware of the nuances involved. It was understandable: her frustration sprang partly from genuine concern and partly from a need to exert control over a situation spiraling far beyond her grasp.

Keeping my voice calm, I replied evenly, "Jessica, if you let me finish—"

But she interrupted again, raising her voice. "No! You disappeared without notice, without explanation. Do you know how worried I was? You don't get to vanish into thin air and then act as if it's no big deal."

Nate bit back a small smile, attempting unsuccessfully to hide amusement at our heated exchange. Clearly, he enjoyed seeing Jessica's carefully maintained composure ruffled, but I didn't have time for games right now.

I paused, allowing her temper to cool slightly, watching as she took several deep, controlled breaths. When she finally seemed more receptive, I continued, my voice quiet and measured. "I understand your frustration. But if you'll give me two minutes to explain, without interruption, I think you'll agree my actions were justified."

Jessica hesitated, fighting her own emotions, before reluctantly nodding. "Fine. Go ahead. But this better be good."

I moved closer, lowering my voice, aware that the airport terminal was unlikely to be safe for frank conversation. "I've received reliable intel about Caitlin's whereabouts. Before our plane landed this morning, another aircraft left Goma headed for Lubumbashi, owned by Extractive Industries Limited, Green Kivu Mining's parent company. Witnesses confirmed a Caucasian woman onboard, likely Caitlin."

Jessica's eyes widened, anger replaced by hopeful urgency. "That's fantastic! Wait—why didn't anyone stop them? Surely airport security—"

"No one but us knew Caitlin had been abducted," I interjected. "And she was escorted onto that plane by well-armed Asian operatives, people no local official would dare confront or question. No one was able to positively ID her, but our intelligence strongly indicates it was Caitlin."

Jessica frowned, struggling to process the information. "Lubumbashi? Where's that exactly?"

"It's in the southern Congo, the second-largest city in the country. It's the epicenter of the world's cobalt mining industry. Almost entirely controlled by the Chinese, which fits perfectly with our suspicions. That's likely their strongest base of operations."

Jessica seemed momentarily stunned, processing my explanation. "But why would a major international company, Green Kivu or their parent corporation, get involved in kidnapping the daughter of the U.S. Secretary of State?"

I paused, watching her, measuring my words. "That's exactly the mystery we need to unravel. You've spoken directly to Secretary Bishop. Does he have any idea why they would target Caitlin?"

Jessica hesitated, eyes darting downward, betraying a flicker of doubt or uncertainty. "Honestly, the Secretary claims he has no clue. Perhaps Caitlin was mixed up in something through her NGO work?"

I sensed she might be telling the truth, at least as much as she knew it. But I wasn't convinced Secretary Bishop was being forthright. Someone knew more than they were revealing.

I'd been trying to decipher Jimmy Liu's role since arriving, convinced his involvement was central. A major Chinese corporation and a high-profile kidnapping made sense only if some secret political or business deal had turned dangerously sour. But the Secretary's reticence troubled me deeply. Bishop's vast resources could have instantly been mobilized; instead, he'd turned to Relief Solutions— small, discreet but expendable. Bishop knew more than he was admitting; I felt sure of it.

Jessica studied me intently. "So what now?"

I hesitated, knowing the next step was critical. "We're going to Lubumbashi right away. I've already arranged transportation; we'll leave in an hour."

Jessica straightened, asserting herself. "I'm coming with you."

I shook my head, anticipating resistance. "Jessica, an official representative of the State Department would attract unwanted attention there. Your presence would alert everyone, including those we're tracking."

Her face darkened, frustrated. "Then what would you have me do? I'm not going back to Washington. I refuse to leave until Caitlin is found."

I considered carefully before responding. "The best way you can help now is from Kinshasa, at the embassy. We may need diplomatic cover or quick intervention. Go to Kinshasa and be ready."

Jessica exhaled, considering my words, then nodded. "Alright. But give me a moment to call the Secretary first. He'll want an update."

"Why not wait until you arrive in Kinshasa?" I asked, wary of interruptions or complications.

"No, it'll take just a minute," Jessica insisted, moving away to make the call privately.

As Jessica stepped away, Nate leaned in. "Think she'll follow your instructions?"

"Honestly, I don't know," I admitted. "Do you trust her?"

Nate hesitated. "Jessica's ambitious but not foolish. She wants Caitlin safe as much as we do. I think we trust her, to a point."

We waited quietly, observing Jessica's animated phone conversation nearby. Suddenly, her demeanor shifted dramatically; a radiant smile broke across her face as she hurried excitedly back toward us, clearly elated.

"They found her!" Jessica exclaimed. "She's safe!"

The news stunned me. "Wait—what? Who found her? Caitlin?"

Jessica nodded excitedly. "Caitlin just called her father. She's safe, aboard a flight to Brussels right now. Secretary Bishop is going there to meet her himself."

Confusion surged through me. "Are you absolutely sure? Did

Secretary Bishop speak to Caitlin face-to-face? Was it just a phone call?"

Jessica's smile faltered under my scrutiny. "He said it was Face-Time. He saw her clearly, unharmed, and spoke with her directly. Caitlin said she left the WRC camp before the attack and apologized for losing touch."

My pulse quickened, skepticism sharpening my senses. "Jessica, that doesn't add up. Are you sure—"

"Look," Jessica interrupted. "Secretary Bishop was very clear. Caitlin's safe, and he specifically said your job is complete. He instructed me to accompany you home immediately."

I stood there, processing, alarm bells ringing in my mind. Something felt profoundly wrong.

Jessica's confident facade wavered, sensing my hesitation. "What's wrong, Milo?"

I took a slow breath. "You're being lied to. Something's not right here. Caitlin wasn't free—she was taken. Liu was involved. We're certain."

Her expression shifted from excitement to uncertainty. "But... Bishop spoke to Caitlin."

"I understand what he told you. But ask yourself—why would Liu massacre an NGO compound, take Caitlin, then simply release her hours later? Something's very wrong. You know Bishop wouldn't send me halfway around the world and then suddenly dismiss me, unless there's more to the story."

Jessica's eyes darkened as realization dawned. "You think Bishop's not telling the truth?"

"I don't know. But something doesn't add up."

Jessica glanced away, struggling internally. She seemed sincerely torn, but a small part of me wondered if this was an act. Then she turned back, her voice firm again. "Tell me what you need. You have my support, fully."

I considered her offer for a moment before responding. With Jessica on our side, we had the ability to make Liu think we were sniffing along the wrong trail. "I need you to go to Lubumbashi with Nate. Stay close, coordinate closely with the embassy. Poke around and see what you guys can find on the ground. Trust only Nate."

"What about you?" she pressed. "Where are you going?"

I hesitated, carefully choosing my words, deciding just how much to reveal. Part of me wanted to tell her the truth, but compartmentalization was the foundation of any good operation. She only needed to know what she needed to know. "I'm heading into the bush to meet with some contacts. We need information, and these sources are our best chance to figure out what's going on. I'll explain once I link up with you in Lubumbashi, but trust me, Caitlin's still in danger, and we're running out of time."

Jessica studied me closely, then nodded. "Alright. I trust you. I'll do whatever's necessary."

"Thank you," I said, meaning it. "I'll brief you fully soon."

Jessica's eyes softened, holding mine for a lingering moment, the tension between us evolving subtly into something warmer. "Be careful, Milo."

"I will," I promised.

We moved quickly now, gathering equipment, preparing for the next critical step. The stakes were higher than ever, each decision critical. Yet amid uncertainty, confusion, and hidden agendas, my resolve hardened. Caitlin Bishop would come home safely, no matter what it took.

GISENYI, **Rwanda**

After ensuring Nate and Jessica had boarded their flight to Lubumbashi, I stood on the tarmac long enough to watch the jet's engines fade into the cloud-hazed distance. I couldn't shake the faint unease in my gut. Jessica waved before stepping into the aircraft, that perfectly rehearsed smile hiding something far more intricate beneath it. Nate, on the other hand, looked exactly as I expected—alert, methodical, already thinking two steps ahead.

Once they were airborne, Sammy pulled up beside me in his aging Renault, the same dusty vehicle I'd borrowed more times than I cared to remember. "You're headed to Gisenyi?" he asked, as if the answer mattered.

"Yeah," I said. "Just need to get across before noon."

He nodded, shifting the transmission into gear. "That old strip still running?"

"Rosalie says she has a plane waiting."

He grinned. "Then it'll be running."

The road east wound through the green highlands of Goma, sharp ridges and valleys carved by time and violence. It wasn't a long drive, but it was the kind that stretched the mind. The closer we got to the border, the heavier the memories pressed in.

Crossing into Rwanda always felt like stepping through a veil. Everything seemed cleaner, more orderly, slightly newer pavement, swept roadsides, soldiers at intersections whose uniforms fit a bit better. But beneath it all lay a quiet unease, like a house rebuilt over old graves.

The ghosts of 1994 never left this place.

As the border guard stamped my passport, I glanced down the road into Rwanda and thought of my first trip here. Back then, the highways were lined with men and women in pink, rows of convicts serving their sentences for genocide, repairing roads or clearing brush under the relentless sun. You couldn't drive a mile without seeing them. The pink was deliberate—a mark of guilt, a public confession stitched into the fabric of everyday life.

Now, two decades later, they were gone.

On this visit, the roads were clean but empty. No more pink uniforms, no more forced labor crews. The *inkiko gacaca*—the community courts that had once defined Rwandan justice—had ended years ago. The state had chosen forgiveness over perpetual punishment, or maybe just exhaustion over vengeance. Either way, the absence of pink made the country look calmer, though I wasn't sure it *was*. Some scars heal under the surface.

By the time we reached the Gisenyi Airport—a narrow strip of asphalt pressed between dense neighborhoods, a maze of rusted tin roofs and narrow dirt lanes—the King Air was already waiting. Rosalie had arranged it through one of her contacts, a sleek twin-engine Beechcraft with polished propeller cones that gleamed in the morning sun.

"Safe flight, boss," Sammy said, shaking my hand before I climbed aboard.

"Keep an eye on things in Goma," I told him. "And if anyone asks, you didn't see me."

He grinned, tapping the side of his nose. "I never see you."

Once the door sealed and the engines wound up, I felt the familiar lift in my chest as the wheels left the ground. The plane banked gently over Lake Kivu, its surface a mirror of cobalt and light.

I waited until the pilot leveled off before pulling my satphone from my pack. Connecting the line to my earbuds, I called Newport.

It was still the middle of the night in Rhode Island, but I knew Stacy. Sleep had never been her strong suit.

She answered on the first ring. "Talk to me," she said.

"Morning to you too," I replied. "Or is it still night?"

"I've been up," she said, her voice crisp, alert. "You sound like you're in the air."

"Over Rwanda. Heading south."

"Rosalie pulled it off then?"

"She always does."

There was a pause—long enough for me to picture her at the office, lit by the glow of too many screens. "You didn't call just to chat," she said.

"No," I admitted. "I've been turning something over in my head since Lubumbashi."

"Liu?"

"Yeah. I can't make sense of him. He's too clean, too well protected for the kind of chaos he's creating. And yet he's involved. That much is obvious."

Stacy exhaled. "You're not the only one stuck on him. The part that keeps bothering me is Yambio. Why the hell did Jimmy Liu have multiple armored SUVs staged there? That's not a casual precaution. Yambio's barely on the map, one road in, one road out, and no reason for that kind of footprint."

"Exactly," I said. "Two of the vehicles were meant for us, but he had his own convoy. There's no mining near Gangura, no Chinese projects, no diplomatic presence. He didn't just happen to have that much infrastructure sitting in the bush. That means whatever he was doing, it was already in motion before Caitlin got grabbed."

The sound of typing came through faintly on her end. "I've been cross-referencing Jinhai's logistics manifests," she said. "Nothing for Yambio or Western Equatoria. The only thing remotely connected is a security detail they funded through Green River Mining. But that's a DRC contract, not South Sudan. Green River's technically a subsidiary under Jinhai's investment wing. But get this—Green River has another shell partner: Extractive Industries Africa. Same leadership, different front. Their revenue last year tripled, but operational costs jumped even higher. They're burning money somewhere."

"That doesn't surprise me," I said. "They're using their usual playbook. Bring in Chinese management and skilled labor while keeping the locals at the bare minimum of subsistence wages, with the promise of higher wages always on the horizon. It's colonialism in a new uniform."

"Exactly. And it's not working. Locals are rioting at mine sites in North Kivu, and Beijing's getting nervous. Jinhai's board is under pressure from the Party. They can't afford another public scandal. Just look what they did to Ye Jianming."

"Who's Le Jianming?" I asked, feeling like it was someone I should know, but he wasn't ringing any bells.

"He was the founder and chairman of CEFC China Energy, like number 200 on the Global Fortune 500 and one of the largest privately held firms in China. The U.S. Justice Department leaked that he had given the president of Chad a $500,000 bribe for oil right. A few days later, poof, old Le is officially disappeared."

"Jesus," I exhaled. "Beijing doesn't mess around."

"Exactly," said Stacy. "I think he's officially been detained pending investigation, but the company is now defunct, and it's doubtful we'll hear from Le Jianming again. Oh, and of course, there's no doubt all the company assets now belong to some other Chinese company, maybe even Jinhai."

"Okay," I said. "So ensuring things stay on track in Africa is a powerful incentive for Jinhai, and he sends Liu to keep things quiet. I still can't calculate how things escalate to kidnapping the daughter of the U.S. Secretary of State."

"Jimmy Liu is the cleaner, the problem-solver. But I still can't figure out what Bishop has to do with it. He's not exactly Beijing's type of ally."

"Maybe not directly," I said. "But money has a way of connecting enemies. If Bishop's investments overlap with Jinhai's, that's leverage. Liu takes Caitlin to use as pressure to force the father's hand."

Stacy went silent again. I could almost hear her mind whirring, sorting, discarding, assembling patterns.

"I keep thinking about those early reports from South Sudan around the same time as Caitlin's kidnapping," she said finally. "There were claims of an entire village wiped out north of the camp —men, women, children—hundreds killed. At first, the reports said rebel activity, with possible involvement of foreign mercenaries. Then someone revised them. Said it was ethnic violence. It's an extremely remote area, pretty far north of Gangura, so I'm not sure how it would be related."

"Who revised them?" I asked.

She hesitated, then read from her screen. "Report verified by the East Africa Stability Initiative. Sub-source: Harmony International."

I recognized the name instantly. "Harmony is a 100% Chinese-funded NGO."

"Yes," Stacy agreed. "And that revision came within twenty-four hours of the initial report."

I felt the familiar chill of recognition—the smell of cover-up, bureaucratic and efficient. "So Liu cleaned up more than people. He cleaned the story itself."

"Looks that way," she said.

The engines droned on, steady, hypnotic. Outside, the world had become a pale haze of cloud and light.

"So what's the endgame?" Stacy asked. "Why take Caitlin? Why risk so much for one person?"

"I don't know exactly, but I do know she's leverage," I said. "Collateral to make Bishop do something he doesn't want to. Maybe to stop him from revealing something he already knows. Could be business. Could be politics. Maybe both."

"Then whatever it is, it's big," she said. "Big enough for Jinhai to move people and money across three countries. Big enough to make Beijing nervous."

"And big enough to kill for," I added.

Another long silence passed.

"Keep digging," I said finally. "Look deeper into Green River and Extractive Industries. Follow the cash. If Liu was moving vehicles, fuel, and men in that region, someone paid for it. Find out where it all originated."

"I will," Stacy said. "And Milo—be careful. Liu's the kind of man who kills to erase questions."

"That's why we're the ones asking them," I said.

The line went quiet except for the faint hum of the aircraft.

"You know," she said softly, "sometimes I think you like this part: the chase, the puzzle."

"Maybe," I admitted, as much to myself as to Stacy. "But this one's not a game."

"None of them ever are," she said. "I'll call you when I have something."

"Copy that."

I ended the call and slipped the satphone back into my pack.

Below, the clouds began to break, revealing long ribbons of savanna stretching toward the south. Somewhere far below, the scars of old wars still marked the earth—the graves, the roads, the ghosts. I'd seen this continent from every altitude and every angle, and it never got easier.

Rosalie's plane hummed forward through the sky, heading toward a thin line on the horizon that divided light from shadow.

I leaned back, closed my eyes, and let the rhythm of the engines settle into my chest. We had more questions than answers. But for the first time, I felt the edges of the truth closing in.

20

4 MARCH 1420 HRS

LIMPOPO PROVINCE, South Africa

Though physically tired from the long journey south, my thoughts felt wired, endlessly replaying the events since my landing earlier that day in Goma. We had meticulously orchestrated a high-risk deception to evade scrutiny from Jimmy Liu and Secretary Bishop by sending Nate and Jessica off to Lubumbashi, where we hoped to divert attention. I had remained behind in Goma, secretly crossing the border into Rwanda to board a flight south arranged by Rosalie Muhire, the formidable woman known throughout eastern Congo simply as "Umwamikazi"—the Queen.

The Rosalie-arranged flight had taken me discreetly into South Africa, landing at Polokwane,a private airstrip used by game preserves in South Africa's northern province of Limpopo. At Polokwane, I'd disembarked with the help of the copilot, slipping from the aircraft at the runway's edge to be met by Thabo, a former South African Recce sergeant major, now working with Dominic and Deangelo Thornton. No need for customs or immigration, and no trace of my entry into South Africa.

My thoughts circled the Thornton brothers, the men upon whom the next phase of the operation depended. Dominic and Deangelo

Thornton were South African-born brothers with distinguished military backgrounds. Born and raised on a remote farm south of Johannesburg, they'd traded farm life for elite military training, attending the Royal Military Academy at Sandhurst in the UK. Their Commonwealth citizenship allowed entry into the British army, where both had excelled in the Light Infantry, later undergoing the arduous selection process for the elite Special Air Service.

My bond with Dominic stretched back years. It began during a brutal firefight on an Afghan mountain where Dominic's SAS troop, overwhelmed by insurgent forces, had called for emergency extraction. I'd led a Special Forces A-team to their rescue, battling fiercely together through a freezing, pitch-black night, securing the survival of both British and American soldiers. That harrowing experience had forged a bond between Dominic and me, an unspoken mutual loyalty that remained ironclad.

After returning to South Africa following their parents' tragic deaths, Dominic had left the Army, joined the South African Police Service, and quickly risen within the SAPS' elite Special Task Force, the nation's foremost tactical police unit. Dominic now served as deputy commander, an influential position that provided invaluable strategic leverage for sensitive operations like this one.

Deangelo, younger and perhaps even more restless, had transferred his own considerable experience from the British SAS into South Africa's renowned Recce Special Forces. After early retirement, he had established Apex Security, a firm rapidly growing in prominence throughout South Africa. Though private, Apex had gained a reputation for skilled, disciplined operators and impeccable reliability—a reflection of Deangelo's own exacting standards. Dominic's position within SAPS and Deangelo's private-sector resources combined into a powerful network that made the Thornton brothers critical allies in complex situations across Africa.

I was acutely aware, however, that leveraging Dominic's official police authority and Deangelo's private security apparatus brought significant political and operational risks. The situation involving

Caitlin Bishop was increasingly precarious, drawing in powerful players like Jimmy Liu, Green Kivu Mining, and Secretary Bishop himself. The entanglement of governments, powerful corporations, and personal vendettas demanded a delicate touch. My earlier conversation with Rosalie echoed in my mind, her subtle warnings about the powerful entities involved and their reach extending beyond conventional limits.

I hadn't been in the Range Rover ten minutes before my satellite phone buzzed in my jacket pocket. I glanced at the caller ID and saw Nate's name flashing. Not a good omen. Nate wasn't scheduled to check in until tomorrow. I quickly clicked the green answer button.

"What's up, Nate?"

Nate's voice was tense, underscored with caution. "The jig is up on our end, boss."

I hesitated, eyeing Thabo in the driver's seat next to me. Though Dominic and Stitch had vouched unequivocally for the former South African Recce sergeant major, old habits died hard, especially caution regarding sensitive information.

"Give me the details," I replied, my voice deliberately neutral.

Nate exhaled audibly. "Jessica told Secretary Bishop you and she flew into Lubumbashi because we'd chartered a flight there. Bishop apparently bought it at first, but then he tracked Jessica's satellite phone. Either that, or Green Kivu tipped him off after we went sniffing around their offices asking about Liu, just as you'd directed."

"I figured that might happen," I muttered, absorbing the implications. "Go on."

"When we missed two flights to Kinshasa and one to Addis Ababa, Bishop called Jessica. Apparently, he wasn't diplomatic, accusing her outright of playing games. Jessica pushed back hard, demanding to speak directly to Caitlin. By then, Caitlin should've landed safely in Brussels if the Secretary's claims were accurate."

Nate paused, allowing me to process.

"What did Bishop say?"

"He lost it. Told Jessica point-blank that if she wasn't on the midnight flight out of Lubumbashi, connecting through Addis to JFK, she'd be terminated immediately. Non-negotiable."

I felt a slow chill build in my chest, deeply troubled by the turn of events. "Where is Bishop now?"

"Jessica says he's en route to Brussels himself. She mentioned he was already planning on being there for scheduled EU meetings. Caitlin's sudden reappearance in Brussels just in time for his arrival seemed way too convenient to Jessica. She's convinced Bishop's lying about Caitlin being safe."

"Do you think Bishop still believes you're me?" I asked. "Has our deception held up?"

"So far, yes. You were right. The flight to Lubumbashi was domestic; no IDs were requested. But once I board a commercial flight to Addis Ababa, I'll need to present identification. We might get burned then."

I considered that carefully. "Understood. That's a chance we have to take. I doubt the Secretary can access airline systems instantaneously, especially in a place like Lubumbashi."

"So you want us to proceed?" Nate asked.

"Affirmative. Get back to Newport as soon as possible. I've already mobilized Stitch for backup, anticipating our cover might be compromised. You and Stitch help Stacy. This situation is far from over."

Nate hesitated. "Are you sure you don't want me heading south to join you? I don't like leaving you without backup, especially given the circumstances."

"I'm fine," I reassured him, glancing sidelong at Thabo, whose face remained impassive as he expertly navigated the Range Rover down the cracked pavement of the N1 toward Johannesburg. "I've got Thabo here, former South African Special Forces. Dominic vouched for him personally."

At this, Thabo's lips curled into a subtle grin, though he kept his eyes locked firmly ahead, carefully scanning the road. I sensed pride behind his otherwise stoic exterior.

Nate sighed, uneasy. "Copy that, boss. Be careful down there. I'll drop a text from Addis Ababa with our ETA back to Newport."

"Good. How's Jessica?"

Nate chuckled. "She's furious at Bishop. But right now, she seems more worried about what's happening with you and Caitlin than her career."

"Keep her focused," I instructed. "Make sure Jessica doesn't set foot anywhere near Johannesburg. If she won't return to DC, keep her traveling north. I can't have her jeopardizing this operation further."

"Roger that," Nate confirmed. "Stay safe, boss."

"You too, Nate." I disconnected, taking a moment to digest the conversation, before glancing over at Thabo.

"Dominic's certain about the house?" I asked. "He positively identified the young woman?"

Thabo's grip tightened on the wheel, his large hands effortlessly guiding the Range Rover along the potholed highway. Thabo was lean yet muscular, with powerful shoulders, a chiseled jawline, and dark eyes set deep into a leathery, weathered face—earned from decades spent outdoors beneath Africa's relentless sun. Though he seemed anywhere between fifty and ninety-five, his posture and physicality still radiated unmistakable strength and competence.

"Yes, sir," Thabo replied. "Dominic's intel is reliable. He's certain the woman is there, and he has the location secured. He's ready to act on your orders."

"Anything else you can tell me? Dominic must have passed along additional intel."

Thabo cracked a wry smile, his white teeth starkly contrasting against his dark skin. "Nothing additional, sir. The major only relayed what I've already told you. He said he'd brief you fully in Johannesburg, face-to-face."

I chuckled. "You're a man of few words, Thabo."

His grin widened, a hint of genuine warmth breaking through his disciplined exterior. "I prefer actions to words, sir. Words get men killed."

"Fair enough," I replied. "How long until we reach Joburg? Three hours?"

"Maybe longer," Thabo cautioned. "This stretch through Limpopo Province is hazardous at night. I'd prefer not to collide with anything larger than a jackal. Elephants crossing here at night are not uncommon, and hitting one would be problematic even in a Range Rover."

I nodded, remembering how dangerous African roads could be, especially at night. Of all the dangers I'd faced throughout my career, driving at night in Africa ranked high among those I actively avoided.

"Take your time, Thabo," I said. "We're in no rush. Wake me if you start getting tired."

"Understood, sir."

Settling back against the worn leather seat, I closed my eyes, attempting to find some measure of rest. But sleep eluded me. Instead, my mind replayed recent events over and over—the brutal attack on the WRC compound, Crispus's sudden death, Caitlin's abduction, and Jessica's growing suspicions about Bishop. Now, the puzzle pieces involving Jimmy Liu seemed increasingly sinister and dangerous.

Thabo broke the silence, sensing my tension. "Deangelo told me about your work on the Continent over the years. Says you've always kept your promises, even at great risk."

I opened my eyes, studying Thabo carefully. "Deangelo exaggerates, but I appreciate the compliment."

"It wasn't meant as flattery, sir," Thabo responded, eyes still scanning the dark road ahead. "We've both known many foreigners promising help, very few actually deliver. Deangelo and Dominic trust you deeply. That speaks volumes."

I nodded, accepting Thabo's cautious endorsement. "They're both good men, as are you. You Recce operators earned my respect long ago."

Thabo smiled. "I appreciate your trust. Dominic says you're determined, stubborn, occasionally reckless, but always driven by a clear sense of purpose."

I chuckled, appreciating Dominic's candid assessment. "That's a fair summary. It's not always pretty, but it gets results."

Thabo gave a brief, approving nod. "Dominic mentioned your friend Crispus, the man you just lost. He said you two were close."

I felt a pang at the mention of Crispus. "Yes, Crispus was a good man. Loyal, brave, dependable. His loss has left a void."

Thabo glanced my way, his tone sincere. "I'm very sorry for your loss, sir. I know what you did for Ellie Thornton in Goma years ago. They won't ever forget your loyalty and courage."

Memories surged sharply—Dominic and Deangelo's younger sister, Ellie, had been trapped behind rebel lines while working in the DRC. As everything turned to chaos, she was kidnapped by militants from a small rebel group. I happened to be in Goma at the time for another client when I'd received the call from Dom. Dropping everything, I'd crossed into hostile territory alone, retrieving her safely after a tense and dangerous confrontation. Dominic had never forgotten it, swearing his eternal loyalty from that day forward.

"That was just doing the right thing," I replied.

"Yes, sir. And that's why Dominic trusts you," Thabo said. "He rarely speaks highly of outsiders, but you're different. That's why I agreed when he asked me to assist you. Anything you need, just say the word."

I nodded gratefully, feeling an immediate bond of trust and respect with Thabo. "Thank you. Let's get Caitlin safely home. That's all that matters right now."

"Understood, sir."

As the vehicle carried us southward, I leaned back once more, attempting to close my eyes. Exhaustion finally overtook me, my consciousness slipping gently into uneasy sleep, troubled dreams haunted by faces: Crispus, Caitlin, Jessica, Bishop, and most dangerously, Jimmy Liu.

21

4 MARCH 1745 HRS

LIMPOPO PROVINCE, South Africa

I stood in the modest kitchen at Apex Security's well-guarded facility in Parkmore, a quiet suburb of Johannesburg. Despite the exhaustion tugging at my shoulders, my mind remained locked in a relentless replay of the day's unfolding chaos. A half-eaten sandwich lay forgotten on a small plate next to a chilled can of Coke Light, both brought earlier by a thoughtful member of Deangelo's staff. The sandwich tasted good—bologna perhaps, or something close. In my experience, some things in Africa were best left unquestioned. And at the top of that list, I'd learned long ago never to ask what type of meat I was eating.

The sound of a vehicle pulling into the gravel parking lot interrupted my contemplation. Glancing through the kitchen window, I watched as a black Range Rover arrived, Dominic stepping out from the driver's side. Tall, lean, and commanding, Dominic radiated authority even in casual clothing. His precise movements and calm demeanor belied the immense stress he shouldered. Simultaneously, Deangelo exited the passenger side. Slightly shorter and more muscular, Deangelo carried himself with a casual confidence, his demeanor more relaxed than Dominic's formal precision.

Seeing them brought an immediate sense of relief. The Thornton brothers, "Tweedle Dee and Tweedle Dom," as some jokingly called them (though never within earshot), were precisely the kind of men needed now. Professional, capable, loyal to a fault. The Thornton brothers' loyalty to me had been sealed forever after I helped resolve a dangerous incident involving their family years earlier near Goma. Their younger sister, kidnapped by militants while doing humanitarian work, had faced almost certain death. Without hesitation, I'd personally extracted her safely, a deed Dominic and Deangelo had never forgotten.

Both brothers shared a profound sense of duty, forged through years of military service, combat, and close calls. Dominic's stoic discipline complemented Deangelo's rugged charisma. Though their paths had diverged, Dominic into elite law enforcement and Deangelo into private security, their bond remained unbreakable, their effectiveness unquestionable.

In recent hours, Dominic had arranged surveillance on Caitlin's suspected location in Sandhurst, confirming her presence at the house used by Jimmy Liu. His Special Task Force operatives had discreetly monitored the premises, reporting activity and ensuring Caitlin was still on-site. Deangelo had assisted with deploying additional security resources, coordinating closely with Dominic to keep surveillance low-profile yet robust. Both men knew the stakes— Caitlin's safe rescue, the complex political implications, the risk inherent in confronting powerful global entities.

But now, standing here awaiting the Thornton brothers, I felt the weight of it all—the loss of Crispus, the dangerous deception involving Jessica, and the uncertain intentions of Secretary Bishop. Each element added another complicated layer to an already volatile situation.

I heard voices in the corridor approaching, Dominic's low timbre resonating clearly, punctuated by Deangelo's unmistakable laughter. Despite the seriousness of the moment, their easy camaraderie brought me a momentary sense of reassurance. The Thornton brothers were not just allies; they were trusted friends, battle-hard-ened and unwavering.

I drained the last of my Coke Light, took a final bite of the sand-wich, and steadied myself for the discussion ahead. Our operation to retrieve Caitlin Bishop would require absolute precision and discre-tion. I trusted Dominic and Deangelo implicitly, but from here forward, every step was critical, every detail mattered.

Dominic and Deangelo's entrance into the living room provided a rare moment of genuine warmth and camaraderie after a series of relentlessly tense couple of days. I hadn't seen either of the Thornton brothers in almost six months, and as they strode confi-dently through the doorway, smiles lighting their rugged faces, I felt a rush of comfort in their presence. Dominic's broad shoulders and disciplined bearing were immediately familiar, a throwback to our earliest days serving together in dangerous corners of the world. Deangelo followed closely, more animated, his demeanor looser than his older brother's, eyes sparkling with good-natured intensity. The affection we all shared was obvious in our robust greetings, firm handshakes quickly dissolving into hearty back-slaps and unreserved man hugs.

It felt good, reassuring, to stand beside men who understood the weight of the situation, who had faced danger before and had come through with their honor and loyalty intact. With pleasantries exchanged, Dominic took command of the situation, stepping seam-lessly into a professional mode befitting his position as the deputy commander of the SAPS Special Task Force. Meanwhile, Deangelo moved effortlessly toward the kitchen refrigerator, pulling open the door and retrieving a pre-made sandwich. He seemed relaxed, unfazed by the gravity of the operation unfolding around him, a calm confidence gained from years in the Recce, South Africa's elite Special Forces.

Dominic's gaze settled on me as he began the briefing. "As soon as Stacy contacted me early this morning with details of the inbound Dassault Falcon, we immediately deployed surveillance at Lanseria.

Tracking their arrival wasn't difficult; however, it became immediately apparent we weren't the only ones watching closely."

I arched an eyebrow. "What do you mean?"

Dominic's expression turned serious, his voice steady. "We observed two Asian men conducting surveillance as well. We've since confirmed both are Chinese nationals. They seemed intent on spotting anyone who appeared interested in that plane."

"Did they notice your men?" I asked, momentarily forgetting Dominic's reputation for absolute discretion and competence.

Dominic's gaze hardened just slightly, a flicker of mild offense shadowing his eyes. It was the look of someone unaccustomed to his professionalism being called into question, even unintentionally. Catching myself quickly, I withdrew my concern with a faint smile. "Forget I asked, Dominic."

He nodded, accepting my apology without comment. "The Falcon 2000 jet landed precisely as expected," he continued, his voice matter-of-fact, all business. "It's registered locally to a company named Global Explorations. Interestingly enough, both Chinese operatives are here in Johannesburg under work visas sponsored directly by that very company. Even more telling is the fact that the residence currently holding Caitlin is also owned by Global Explorations."

"Well, that's significant," I said, processing the implications. "How did they clear Customs?"

Dominic smiled grimly, anticipating my question. "Good question. Lanseria is privately owned but operates standard Customs and Immigration checkpoints. Protocol dictates these officials meet arriving private aircraft directly on the tarmac, boarding the plane to inspect passports."

I narrowed my eyes. "But that didn't happen?"

Dominic shook his head, disturbed by the breach in his country's security. "No. Instead, our two Chinese friends intervened directly. They met the customs officials at the plane's stairs. Passports were simply handed down to the immigration officers. Given local protocols, I have little doubt those passports contained a substantial cash incentive. After stamping them without stepping onboard, the officials drove away, no questions asked."

I took a moment to absorb Dominic's description, weighing the risks implied. "Did they stamp Caitlin's passport too?"

Dominic shook his head. "No. Officially, there were five individuals aboard, two pilots and three passengers, all listed as Chinese nationals. Customs and Immigration made no note whatsoever of a woman being onboard."

My thoughts were racing. "Was Jimmy Liu among the passengers?"

Dominic nodded. "Yes. Positively identified. Liu was traveling under his own passport."

I leaned in closer, tension rising. "And your surveillance team? Did they actually see Caitlin?"

Instead of immediately responding, Dominic retrieved his phone, swiping through images captured by his surveillance operatives. Without a word, he turned the phone toward me, showing me a clear, carefully zoomed photo.

My pulse quickened. Caitlin Bishop's face was unmistakable beneath the fabric of a full-length black chador and headscarf. Her expression was tight, subdued, and clearly frightened—exactly as I'd imagined. There was no mistaking her identity or the seriousness of her situation. She was clearly here, clearly captive, and clearly being moved against her will.

"Bingo," I murmured.

Dominic echoed my sentiment, a faint smile of satisfaction flickering across his serious features. "Exactly. We followed the SUVs directly to a private residence on Coronation Road, in Sandhurst. They seemed confident no one was following. Since arriving, no vehicle has entered or left the premises. Our surveillance remains active, tight, and undetected."

I took a deep breath, assessing the situation. Back during my military and CIA days, we would have immediately assembled an assault team, geared up heavily, and conducted a swift, decisive extraction. Simplicity had been the hallmark of such operations. But my years with Relief Solutions had taught me something different—nuance, subtlety, and finesse mattered, especially in circumstances as delicate and politically fraught as this one.

We faced complications beyond any operation I'd previously encountered. Caitlin's father, George Bishop, was the U.S. Secretary of State, a man with immense political power and substantial private business dealings. His involvement added an opaque layer of political complexity. Additionally, we were dealing with Jimmy Liu, representing powerful Chinese business interests connected to high-level Chinese officials. The convergence of business, politics, and personal stakes was explosive, potentially catastrophic if mishandled.

Moreover, this operation had already cost us dearly. Crispus had lost his life, sacrificed while rescuing Melissa. My actions over the last days had committed immigration offenses across multiple borders, involved a firefight on foreign soil, and now risked entangling Dominic, an influential senior officer in the South African Police Service, in unauthorized surveillance operations that would be exceptionally difficult to justify politically, especially given China's considerable influence in South Africa. And still, Caitlin remained captive, her safety uncertain.

I gathered my thoughts before continuing. "Dom, is there any immediate indication that Caitlin's life is in danger?"

Dominic considered my question, his voice measured. "Not at the moment, no. They seem unaware of our surveillance. She appears safe, at least for now."

Deangelo leaned forward, finally speaking up, his tone practical and confident. "We'll have more precise intel after midnight. Apex Security provides perimeter security for two neighboring properties. When the midnight shift change occurs, I'm placing my best personnel on duty equipped with infrared and thermal imaging gear. We should confirm Caitlin's exact location within the compound or at least narrow it significantly."

I nodded. "That's invaluable intel."

Dominic leaned in, his voice lowered and pragmatic. "Milo, you know our situation is sensitive. But you also know we'll do anything within our capabilities to help. I've prepared a Special Task Force tactical assault team on twenty-four-hour standby. If you make an anonymous tip, we can raid that property in minutes."

"Or, Milo, Apex Security has two fully-equipped ten-man armed response teams downstairs, ready to roll instantly. Three minutes maximum response. That's how fast we operate," Deangelo interjected, his voice carrying the characteristic boldness I'd grown to admire.

Dominic raised a careful eyebrow at his brother. "But Apex doesn't have official authority for that sort of operation."

Deangelo shrugged, unbothered. "Authority is overrated. If those Chinese guards resist or threaten us, my men are licensed to respond with force in self-defense. Believe me, we won't hesitate. We've done it before, and local authorities generally give us wide latitude."

I studied both brothers, weighing their proposals. Deangelo was serious and capable, and his men could indeed handle the situation. Yet, Dominic's SAPS Special Task Force was among the finest tactical police units in the world, highly trained, disciplined, and fully authorized to conduct raids. Keeping this fully legitimate and above board would minimize fallout afterward.

"Dominic, let's stick with your Special Task Force," I said. "I'll provide whatever anonymous tip you require. Once Caitlin's safely extracted to police custody, even the Chinese can't touch her."

Dominic nodded. "Agreed. We'll execute quickly once everything aligns."

We spent the next several hours carefully fine-tuning the plan, evaluating every possible scenario and contingency. With the groundwork laid, we decided to rest briefly before initiating the operation.

The key would be Jimmy Liu leaving the compound. Once that occurred, the moment would be perfect. If at any time surveillance reported immediate risk to Caitlin, Dominic's team would execute the raid instantly.

Our plans were in place. Now we could only wait.

For a brief moment, I felt a flicker of cautious optimism. Caitlin was close. Dominic and Deangelo's unwavering support had brought me to the precipice of successfully retrieving her from harm's way. The next step was crucial, but with the Thornton brothers at my side, I had never felt more confident.

I glanced at Dominic and Deangelo, seeing in their steady, determined gazes the depth of trust and mutual respect forged through years of shared struggle.

It was time to bring Caitlin Bishop home.

JOHANNESBURG, **South Africa**

Caitlin's eyelids flickered open, her chin pressing into her chest as she stirred from the murky haze that had clouded her mind for hours. Her head throbbed, her body weary and disconnected. Since waking aboard the private jet earlier, she'd felt trapped inside a thick mental fog, a fog she was increasingly certain had been chemically induced. Each thought came slowly, reluctantly, as if wading through mud.

She was seated on the edge of a large bed, blinking slowly to clear the lingering confusion. The room around her was spacious, stark, and minimally furnished. Its only amenities were the imposing king-sized bed beneath her and an adjoining ensuite bathroom with simple porcelain fixtures—a bathtub, a modest sink, and toilet. The bed itself featured only a plain sheet and pillow; the lack of any comfort or decoration underscored her captivity.

She guessed she had been in the room anywhere between six to ten hours, judging from the muted daylight filtering through the gaps of boarded windows earlier, now replaced by darkness. Time had become a blurred concept, distorted by the drugs and exhaustion, measured by the periodic visits from her captors.

Twice they had fed her since her arrival. Initially, she had been ravenous, so consumed by hunger and thirst that she devoured the first meal without hesitation. Only afterward, when an overwhelming drowsiness overtook her, did she realize her mistake. They had drugged her food, or drink, or possibly both. She'd fought to stay awake, resorting to painful self-pinching and deliberate pacing to resist slipping into unconsciousness again.

The second meal they provided went straight into the bathroom. She had carefully flushed most of it down the toilet, praying fervently that no hidden cameras observed her private act. The mere thought of constant surveillance sent shivers crawling along her spine. She had arrived in the room wearing a lightweight black robe, hastily thrown over her original clothes, and she was grateful to finally discard her dirt-stained garments in favor of a fresh set from a small pile of new clothing placed neatly on the bed. Joggers, T-shirts, underwear, socks—all meticulously packaged. A thoughtful provision, if one overlooked her confinement.

The shower had been a small mercy, the cool water washing away layers of grime and some of the persistent haze clouding her mind. She emerged refreshed, the fresh clothes offering a fleeting illusion of normalcy, though her heart still raced at the thought of what lay ahead.

As hours passed, she alternated between sitting restlessly on the bed and curling up in the bathtub, desperate to find a modicum of privacy from prying eyes. Her thoughts churned, replaying the cryptic phone call aboard the jet, her father's voice strained with tension, the questions unanswered. What promises had he made? What agreements had he broken to warrant such violent consequences?

In a sudden instant, angry shouting from beyond her locked door snapped her back to the present. Her heart jolted with sudden dread as heavy footsteps echoed through the hall, approaching swiftly. Voices barked orders in English, harsh, commanding, aggressive. Fear surged through her veins, adrenaline instantly clearing the lingering fog.

She leapt from the bed, crouching behind the far side, her breathing ragged with panic. A key twisted in the lock; the door swung inward, revealing the muscular Asian man with the prominent scar who had haunted her since their encounter aboard the plane. His presence filled the doorway, imposing and frightening, his dark eyes cold and detached.

Behind Scarface stood another Asian man, smaller and silent, watching her every move. Scarface spoke furiously into a satellite phone clenched in one powerful hand. In the other, he brandished what appeared to be large pruning shears, cold metal gleaming ominously beneath the harsh fluorescent lighting. Caitlin's stomach knotted in immediate dread; the sight felt unreal, nightmarish.

"I'm tired of your bloody games, Bishop," the man growled into the phone, anger sharpening his precise British accent. "You know very well the consequences of failing to uphold your end of this arrangement. Demanding to see your daughter wasn't part of the deal. But if you'd like proof of what I'm capable of, perhaps I'll send you a piece of her."

Caitlin gasped as the man lunged forward, seizing her roughly by the arm and pulling her forcefully onto the bed. Her heart hammered in her chest as he thrust the phone into his associate's hand, the screen showing a live Facetime connection. For an instant, Caitlin glimpsed her father's horrified face, etched with pain and helplessness.

The man forced her facedown onto the mattress, pressing one heavy knee brutally into her back to immobilize her. Her cheek pressed harshly against the coarse sheets, her breath coming in panicked, shallow bursts.

"Dad!" Caitlin shouted desperately, voice muffled by the mattress, panic surging. "Dad, what's happening?"

"Caitlin!" George Bishop's voice, strained yet authoritative, crackled clearly through the phone's speaker. "Are you hurt? Are you injured?"

She fought back tears, heart aching at hearing her father's voice.

"Dad, please...what's going on? Where am I? Where's Melissa? Tell me what—"

"Caitlin, listen closely," her father interrupted, his voice firm yet trembling with controlled anxiety. "Are you physically injured? Please just tell me if you're okay."

"I'm not injured...physically," Caitlin stammered. "But Dad, please—"

"We don't have much time," Bishop said, voice thick with urgency. "Listen to me. Please. You must do exactly as they say. Everything will be alright. Just cooperate, Caitlin, and I promise I'll get you home."

"Dad, what promises did you make? Why—" Before Caitlin could finish, the phone was abruptly yanked away, the speakerphone disabled. Scarface raised the phone to his ear once more.

"You have visual proof your daughter is alive," the man said, tone chillingly calm. "Now, Bishop, keep your end of this arrangement precisely as agreed. If you don't, you'll receive your daughter in installments."

With startling speed, the man twisted Caitlin's arm painfully behind her back, pulling her left hand sharply upward. Pain radiated through her shoulder, causing her to cry out involuntarily. She felt the sharp steel of the pruning shears pressed firmly against the joint of her smallest finger, the cold metal cutting into her flesh as a trickle of blood flowed warmly down the back of her trembling hand.

"Stop!" Bishop's voice shouted through the phone. "Goddammit, Liu, you've made your point!"

The pressure of the blades vanished immediately as Liu released her hand, though he remained kneeling heavily upon her back.

"You know exactly what is required, Secretary Bishop," Liu said calmly, his voice carrying controlled menace. "We have a precise agreement. Keep your promises, or I will destroy everything you hold dear."

"I just need assurances she won't be harmed," Bishop pleaded through the phone.

Liu's tone turned mocking. "You have no assurances. Let's clarify. If you fail to uphold your end, the next time you see your daughter, it will be in a video entertaining Nigerian oil ministers, or perhaps Mr. Lin's most enthusiastic soldiers. Only then will I send her home in pieces. Are we entirely clear, Mr. Secretary?"

There was a moment of tense silence on the phone, broken finally by a resigned sigh from Bishop. "Understood."

Liu ended the call abruptly, stepping casually away from Caitlin and tossing the phone onto a nearby table. He studied Caitlin silently as she lay shaking and disoriented on the bed.

"Sit up, Ms. Bishop," Liu instructed.

Slowly, Caitlin pulled herself into a sitting position, shaking uncontrollably. Her hand throbbed where the metal blades had cut her skin. Liu stared at her, eyes cold and unfeeling, assessing her without emotion.

"Why are you doing this?" Caitlin asked, voice trembling with confusion and fear. "Who are you? What could my father have possibly agreed to?"

Liu tilted his head, considering her question before replying. "Where you are is unimportant. And who I am matters even less. Simply consider me a business associate of your father's."

Caitlin fought a surge of defiant anger. "You realize when they find me, and they will find me, you'll be in tremendous—"

In an instant, Liu's open palm flashed forward, striking Caitlin brutally across the side of her face. Pain exploded in a white-hot flash, her vision briefly blackening, blood seeping into her mouth as she bit her tongue. Tears blurred her eyes, her ears ringing from the unexpected violence.

"Listen carefully," Liu said, his voice devoid of emotion. "We're past any point where threats or pleas matter. Your father has obligations. Fulfill your part by staying quiet, and things will remain manageable. Resist, and I'll sedate you until this ordeal ends. Your choice." He paused, measuring the effect his words were having. "Oh,

Ms. Bishop? There's no need to flush your meals down the toilet. Behave, and your stay here need not be uncomfortable."

She lowered her eyes, helpless. His casual violence and indifference were chilling. The reality was stark, her life now depended on her father's mysterious dealings, transactions made far beyond her knowledge or control. Caitlin understood, painfully, that her survival hinged on obedience and silence.

As Liu left the room, Caitlin's heart sank further. She sat motionless, her body trembling uncontrollably. She knew her father, his power, and his ambition. And now, she knew the ruthless nature of her captor.

She felt a deep, paralyzing terror realizing the magnitude of her predicament. The luxurious surroundings were meaningless. She was wholly alone—trapped, terrified, and entirely at their mercy.

JOHANNESBURG, **South Africa**

Sleep had remained a cruel illusion, as elusive as the truth that had tangled itself into this complicated web. The hours spent staring at the cracked ceiling of the modest bedroom Dominic had provided me at Apex Security's discreet compound in Parkmore had yielded little rest. Instead, my mind had been caught in a relentless churn, evaluating possibilities and mapping potential outcomes to a game whose pieces remained hidden and whose players concealed their true intentions.

The complexity of the situation weighed heavily on my chest. At its core, this was no ordinary operation. It had become an elaborate, dangerous chess match, involving multiple players on multiple levels, many of whom I couldn't identify. But if this was indeed chess, it wasn't the simple kind played on a board with clear lines and rules. It was three-dimensional, unpredictable, and chaotic—each move I made could trigger unforeseen consequences, and the stakes were unimaginably high.

The linchpin to understanding this complicated puzzle was, unquestionably, Secretary of State George Bishop's motivations. Stacy had worked tirelessly trying to uncover any connection between Bishop and the mysterious Chinese magnate, Lin Jinhai, but so far had turned up nothing concrete. What leverage did Lin have over Bishop that was so powerful it could force the U.S. Secretary of State into sacrificing his own daughter's safety?

I tried to break down the motivations systematically, considering the most common reasons powerful men acted against their own interests: personal safety, family, wealth, reputation, freedom, and honor. The first step was to dismiss the obvious non-factors. Bishop himself would never prioritize personal safety over his daughter. His decorated military background and career had proven he was a man not easily intimidated. Family didn't fit either, since Caitlin was now apparently expendable, at least to him, and his only other child, a son, had been tragically lost in Iraq years before.

Next, wealth and reputation seemed improbable motivators as well. George Bishop, born into New England affluence that traced its origins back to before the American Revolution, had little need for more riches. He had already reached the pinnacle of personal and professional success, serving at the highest levels of government after an enormously successful business career. If he were protecting a financial or reputational interest, Bishop possessed more than enough resources and clout to weather any scandal or monetary setback.

This left freedom and honor as the most plausible motivators. The concept of freedom resonated deeply, men would do nearly anything to avoid a lifetime in prison, sacrificing even family bonds when faced with lifelong incarceration. It seemed plausible at first. Perhaps Bishop had been involved in dealings so unethical, or outright illegal, that exposure would mean inevitable imprisonment. Yet even that felt somewhat inadequate, an incomplete picture.

I rose from the bed and stood by the window, staring out at Johannesburg's awakening skyline, a gentle haze softening the harsh lines of buildings slowly taking form against the early morning sky. Then suddenly, something clicked.

Honor.

It was honor that Bishop would prioritize above all else. He had served his country valiantly in Vietnam, earning a Silver Star as a young infantryman, no small feat for a privileged man who could have easily avoided military service. Later, he'd sacrificed again through the loss of his son in Iraq, yet Bishop never allowed personal tragedy to derail his service to his country. He had accepted the Secretary of State position, not for financial gain, but out of genuine patriotic commitment. Duty. Honor. Country. The old West Point creed fit George Bishop far better than any simple greed or self-preservation.

The realization brought both clarity and complexity to my analysis. If Bishop acted out of honor, placing national security above even the safety of his own daughter, then rescuing Caitlin alone would not necessarily solve the core problem. The leverage Lin Jinhai and Jimmy Liu held was perhaps greater than just the kidnapping of a daughter. They were most likely using Caitlin's captivity to influence broader geopolitical outcomes. The implications were daunting.

Yet even if rescuing Caitlin wouldn't entirely neutralize Lin's leverage, it was still the right move. With her safely away from immediate harm, we could reassess the chessboard. The Chinese players might be angered, might shift their pressure directly onto Bishop himself, but Caitlin would no longer be a pawn. She would be safely off the board.

I exhaled, feeling confident in that analysis, although aware that even these conclusions were still speculation. This game remained dangerously complex and unforgiving.

As I dressed, preparing to head downstairs, I reflected on the meticulous plan we had developed with Dominic and Deangelo Thornton the previous night. The Thornton brothers had devised a straightforward tactical approach that should free Caitlin from Jimmy Liu's grip. Yet even their carefully structured plan remained two-dimensional, a direct assault relying on local security resources and the authority vested in Dominic as a senior officer within the South African Police Special Task Force.

The complications beyond the tactical assault were my responsibility: navigating political sensitivities, immigration violations, South African-China diplomatic ties, and avoiding a massive international incident. Dominic had risked his career and reputation by launching unauthorized surveillance operations to locate Caitlin, while Deangelo had leveraged Apex Security's private resources, risking scrutiny and potential backlash. We were all stepping onto precarious ground.

I dressed quickly, pulling on the crisp polo shirt Deangelo had provided, identical to those worn by Apex supervisors, to help maintain my low profile during the impending operation. I glanced at the clock, realizing I needed breakfast and coffee to sustain me through the long, tense hours ahead.

As I walked toward the open-plan living room, I passed a framed photograph mounted on the wall near the hallway's end. The image depicted Dominic Thornton and several other young men, each wearing the coveted tan beret of Britain's 22 SAS regiment, gathered together on a mist-covered hillside in the rugged Brecon Beacons. The men appeared weary, exhausted from the grueling selection course, yet their expressions radiated quiet pride, camaraderie, and achievement.

I paused, looking closely at Dominic's young face in the photograph. It took me back to our first meeting, a freezing mountainside in Afghanistan's Hindu Kush, where Dominic's SAS troop had been trapped under heavy insurgent attack. My team, acting as the Quick Reaction Force, had been dispatched on a dangerous rescue mission. The successful operation had bonded the two of us forever, solidifying trust and respect through mutual survival.

As I stood reflecting, it hit me, a sudden realization about Secretary Bishop's actions. A sense of duty and honor motivated him deeply, so much so that it meant Bishop might reluctantly sacrifice Caitlin, and perhaps even me, to protect national security and our nation's honor. My pulse quickened as I grasped the gravity of this new insight.

I quickly retrieved my satellite phone and dialed Secretary Bishop's private number. He answered instantly, his voice terse and strained.

"Mr. Secretary, this is Milo deCogan," I began without preamble.

Silence hung heavily on the line.

Finally, Bishop spoke. "You shouldn't be calling. I'm confident Jessica explained everything to you. Caitlin is safe, and your services are no longer required."

"You know Caitlin isn't safe," I pressed. "I can help. This is what I do. Tell me what's really going on, sir. You trusted me enough to hire me; you should trust me now to help you through this."

Bishop's voice sharpened with suppressed anger and perhaps fear. "You know nothing of what's happening. I've given instructions to Jessica. You are to stand down. Immediately. For your sake, deCogan, follow orders."

The line went dead. As I sat there analyzing Bishop's reaction, the phone rang again—Jessica's caller ID. Her voice, strained with anxiety, echoed clearly through the satellite connection.

"Milo, Bishop just called me. Where are you? He's revoking your passport immediately. He insists you remain in Ethiopia and return to the United States under embassy escort."

I absorbed her words, attempting to keep the bile from rising in my throat. Revoking my passport? This could severely limit our options. "He's lying, Jessica. Caitlin is not safe. I'm in South Africa, and we believe Jessica is here as well. We're still trying to track down her exact location, but she's definitely not en route to Brussels."

I wasn't sure if it was my innate sense of compartmentalization or the leftover seed of mistrust toward Jessica, but I was reluctant to let her know that we had found Caitlin. I needed her on my side, but she didn't need to know everything.

Jessica hesitated before responding, her voice steady. "Okay, Milo, I trust you. Bishop is acting very strange, and everything you've told me makes sense. Just tell me how I can help."

"Get to Maputo, Mozambique, with Nate. Rent a large villa,

somewhere secure, remote, and quiet. I'll contact you both with the next steps. This will all be over soon."

I ended the call, immediately dialing Stacy in Newport. "Stacy, things are escalating. Bishop revoked my passport. Keep Stitch ready. Monitor Jessica closely, and ensure Nate is secure. We have to be prepared." We spoke briefly for two minutes—Stacy concerned about my lack of a valid passport, but assuring me that she and Stitch were working on all available options.

As I hung up, Dominic and Deangelo entered the room, their eyes determined, ready to act.

The next steps would be perilous, but the pieces were falling into place.

JOHANNESBURG, **South Africa**

"No plan survives first contact with the enemy," stated some nine-teenth-century Prussian general and paraphrased a bit more recently by Mike Tyson and something about a punch in the face. In my experience, it was a prophetic remark, and I had little doubt it would again hold true today.

Since speaking with my Relief Solutions team earlier that morning, I had spent several painstaking hours going over every aspect of the operational plan with Dominic and Deangelo Thornton. Dominic had left an hour ago to position himself at the Special Task Force command post, ready to receive my call. Deangelo had his two armed-response teams, our backup force in case anything went sideways with the SAPS operation, standing by in the climate-controlled offices downstairs.

I sat in the living room, poring over surveillance imagery of the Sandhurst compound, when Deangelo bounded up the stairs, a squawking radio gripped in one hand and his iPhone in the other. Our surveillance team had pinpointed Caitlin's likely location to one of two ground-floor rooms on the north side of the main house, and I had mentally traced my intended path to her via a concealed rear entrance through the backyard.

Deangelo moved toward me, urgency etched on his face. "We just got the call. A Mercedes SUV just left the compound. Jimmy Liu was in the passenger seat."

I sprang to my feet. "Are they certain?"

"Positive ID," Deangelo affirmed. He thrust the phone toward me, displaying a photograph showing Jimmy Liu sitting comfortably in the passenger seat of a black Mercedes SUV. Liu wore sunglasses, but his distinctive facial scar was visible, confirming beyond doubt that it was him.

Without hesitation, I picked up my cell phone and texted Stacy back in Newport: **We're a Go.**

We had established last night that my phone call would trigger the Special Task Force's assault. Dominic would openly acknowledge our relationship, leveraging my credibility for the operation.

I turned to Deangelo. "Ready?"

"Do it," he replied without hesitation.

I punched the speed dial to the Special Task Force's direct command center line.

"SAPS Special Task Force," a woman answered, her South African accent clear and composed.

"Is this line recorded?" I asked.

"Yes," she answered, her tone cautious now. "Please state the nature of your call."

"My name is Milo deCogan with Relief Solutions. I'm a security specialist calling to report the confirmed location of a kidnapped victim here in Johannesburg. Caitlin Bishop, an American citizen, was forcefully abducted on March 1st from the World Refugee Committee camp in Gangura, South Sudan. Her kidnapping was widely documented in the media. She was transported via private jet to South Africa and is currently being held at 11 Coronation Road in Sandhurst."

"Very well, sir," she replied. I heard hurried movements and muffled voices in the background. "Could you please confirm the name of the kidnapped individual and the precise address again?"

"Caitlin Bishop is the victim's name. She's being held captive at number 11 Coronation Road, Sandhurst. Is Captain Dominic Thornton there? He knows me and can verify my credentials."

There was a brief pause, followed by several audible clicks as another individual came onto the line, Dominic, I presumed.

"This is Major Thabiso Dlamini, commanding officer of the STF. With whom am I speaking?" His voice was deep, authoritative—the voice of a man accustomed to power and cautious decision-making.

"Major, my name is Milo deCogan. I'm a private security consultant with Relief Solutions, contracted to locate and retrieve Caitlin Bishop, who was kidnapped from a humanitarian compound in South Sudan. I have positively confirmed her current location here in Sandhurst, and I'm requesting your immediate assistance. Captain Dominic Thornton can vouch for me personally and professionally."

"Mr. deCogan, I would request you come to our headquarters to verify this information," Major Dlamini stated, his voice cautious and measured.

"I understand, sir," I said, urgency edging my tone. "However, we must act now. Caitlin Bishop is in immediate danger at 11 Coronation Road. Half of her kidnappers have just left, and only three guards remain. I know Captain Thornton personally. He'll confirm my credentials and reliability."

"It is not a matter of belief," Major Dlamini replied. "But we cannot deploy an armed police assault team into Sandhurst based on an anonymous call. Come to the station, and I promise we will investigate thoroughly."

"Sir, with respect, this is not an anonymous call. I'm telling you who I am, and I'm telling you that this woman is in grave danger."

"So you've said. We will be happy to discuss this at the station. If things are as you say, we will respond immediately."

Frustration surged within me. Where the hell was Dominic?

Before I could respond, Deangelo stepped forward, urgently displaying his phone so I could read a text from Dominic himself:

TELL MILO TO SAY HE'LL COME IN. SWITCH TO PLAN B. I'LL MEET YOU THERE IN 10.

My heart skipped a beat. Plan B was not what I'd hoped for, far riskier than our carefully laid-out original operation. My stomach tightened, but I spoke quickly into the phone.

"Understood, Major. I'll head to your location now."

"Very good," Major Dlamini responded. "We are at 2 Summit Road, Morningside. Report promptly, please."

"I'll be there shortly. Thank you, sir."

I disconnected, turning toward Deangelo. "Plan B?"

He nodded confidently. "It'll work. You ride with Thabo in the SUV. Follow closely behind the assault teams. Dominic will rendezvous with us on-site."

Deangelo was dressed similarly to me in khaki cargo pants and a white Apex Security polo. His only additional gear included a utility belt equipped with a radio, first aid kit, and pistol holster.

I gestured to his pistol. "Any chance I can get one of those?"

"Absolutely," Deangelo replied. "I have one prepared for you downstairs. You'll need the radio, but hopefully not the sidearm."

Downstairs, Apex Security's response teams moved quickly and efficiently, loading into two heavy-duty assault trucks. Each vehicle carried eight heavily armed rapid-response guards, back-to-back seating in their open beds. I secured a utility belt from Thabo, buckling it carefully around my waist. Pulling the sidearm from its holster, I recognized it instantly, a Vektor Z88 9mm semi-automatic, essentially a Beretta 92F clone. While not my preferred Glock 19, the Z88 was familiar, solid, and reliable. I knew if I had to draw this weapon, our situation would already be critically dire, and there would be a strong likelihood that I'd end up in a South African prison.

"Ready to move, sir?" Thabo's voice was calm, professional. He had driven me from the airstrip yesterday and would serve again as my driver.

"Ready," I said. "The satchel?"

"Already secured in the backseat," he confirmed.

We hurried into the parking area, where Deangelo ensured everyone was loaded securely into their vehicles. With a decisive wave, he jumped into the lead vehicle, and our convoy surged out the compound gates. My radio earpiece crackled, linking me into Apex's secure operational communications as we moved.

Our staging compound was less than five minutes from Coronation Road. Moving swiftly west down 4th Street, we took a quick maneuver onto Sandton Drive, followed by a sweeping left turn onto Winnie Mandela Drive. Moments later, the lead vehicle braked sharply, cutting east onto Cromartie Road. We were rapidly closing in on our target, and my pulse quickened as we approached Coronation Road.

Suddenly, ahead, blue SAPS police lights flashed reassuringly.

Our convoy screeched to a halt outside the target compound. Apex's armed teams leapt from their vehicles, deploying quickly and confidently. Thabo parked the SUV beside the gated entrance, and I calmly exited onto the neatly kept grass verge.

Plan B hinged on creating deliberate confusion.

Apex Security provided armed response services for 17 Coronation Road, the property adjacent to Caitlin's location. Conveniently, the residents of number 17 were currently overseas. Earlier, an Apex guard had intentionally triggered their security alarm, necessitating an armed response check.

However, Deangelo purposefully mixed up addresses. Instead of entering number 17, Apex trucks pulled into number 11's driveway, the Chinese-owned compound. The security alert that triggered the Apex response also simultaneously summoned local police, and Dominic, waiting nearby for this very call, responded in seconds with his SAPS patrol cruiser. He followed the Apex vehicles *mistakenly* into the wrong compound, further escalating confusion. The charade wouldn't hold up under scrutiny after the fact, but the rescue of

Caitlin should absolve everyone of any misconduct; the ends justify the means. At least that was our hope.

As planned, the chaotic scene drew two armed Chinese guards outside in response to the dozen armed Apex security guards piling into the front yard. Dominic and his fellow SAPS officer immediately disarmed and detained the Chinese guards, neutralizing them with flex cuffs. Amidst the orchestrated distraction, we were confident no one would notice my presence.

Dressed as an Apex Security supervisor, carrying a heavy canvas satchel, I exited the SUV and jogged around the side of the house, maintaining the appearance of conducting a security check of the backyard. Quickly rounding the rear of the house, I assessed the expansive property: immaculate gardens, a stone patio, and a pristine lap pool. A tall concrete wall topped by concertina wire enclosed the luxurious estate.

I ran to the rear door closest to the room we'd identified as containing Caitlin. Finding the door locked, I extracted a Halligan tool from my canvas bag. The Halligan, a stout, forged-steel breaching bar with an adze, pick, and fork all in one, was standard issue for firefighters and tactical breachers, made to punch locks, pry frames, and split jambs with controlled force. With practiced ease, I inserted the tool and violently leveraged my body weight backwards; the doorframe splintered, and the door swung inward.

Entering a basement living area, I moved quickly down a short corridor to my left. Rounding the corner, I came face-to-face with the remaining Chinese guard stationed in front of Caitlin's door, an MP5K slung across his chest.

"Hey!" I said, smiling. "They told me to show you this."

Before he could react, I tossed him the Halligan tool, lobbing it upwards for him to catch. As his hands reached instinctively to catch the 3-lb modified sledgehammer before it hit him in the chest, I surged forward, swiftly delivering a precise strike to his throat. The guard gasped, clutching his damaged windpipe, all thoughts of defending himself instantly erased as he tried to breathe. Before he could recover, I gripped the back of his head and drove my knee upwards into his face, feeling his nose cartilage collapse under the impact. Sweeping his legs from beneath him, I subdued and restrained him with flex cuffs. I almost felt sorry for the young man as he struggled to breathe through his swelling windpipe and crushed nose. Almost.

Moving to Caitlin's door, I was glad to see the door didn't require a key. It was latched with a reversed deadbolt.

"Caitlin!" I called as I entered her room. "It's Milo deCogan. I'm here to get you out!"

JOHANNESBURG, **South Africa**

Caitlin heard muffled voices approaching from the hallway and assumed they were bringing lunch. She had received breakfast several hours earlier, and now seemed the logical time for the midday meal. The indistinct voices rose abruptly into a sudden commotion, and she heard a heavy, ominous thump against her door. Her senses jolted awake, sharpening with anxiety.

She heard the door lock disengaged, followed by the door swinging inward.

"Caitlin?" shouted a male voice from the doorway. "It's Milo deCogan. I'm here to get you out."

Milo deCogan? The security consultant who had visited the WRC compound back in Gangura? Her mind reeled in disbelief. Was it really him? How could he possibly be here?

She rose from where she had been sitting on the stark, king-sized bed, eyes wide, pulse quickening. She spoke cautiously, disbelief and hope tangled in her voice.

"Milo?" she shrieked, scarcely daring to trust her ears.

The door pushed fully open, and the man she remembered from

those security training sessions appeared before her, even taller than she remembered. He had been the one who stressed the importance of keeping a go-bag, who had shown her the secret escape door in the Gangura compound, advice that had saved her life.

Her relief was overwhelming. She rushed toward him without thought, throwing herself into his arms as he entered the room. His strong embrace enveloped her, firm and reassuring, and she buried her face against his chest, surrendering to uncontrollable tears streaming down her cheeks.

"It's alright, Caitlin," Milo murmured, stroking the back of her head. "You're safe now. I've got you."

He held her for several long seconds, allowing her breathing to steady. Then, carefully, he placed his hands on her shoulders and gently pushed her back so he could look into her eyes.

"Caitlin, listen carefully," he began with gentle urgency. "I'm here to get you out of this place, but we still have work to do. Do you have any personal belongings we need to take?"

She shook her head, her mind racing, still trying to grasp this miraculous turn of events. "No. Nothing. They didn't let me keep anything."

His eyes glanced down to her bare feet. "Shoes? Do you have shoes somewhere?"

"No," she admitted, embarrassed, looking down at her feet. "They took my shoes away, and I haven't had them since I've been here."

"Okay, no problem," he said, his voice calm yet authoritative. "We need to move fast. Stay close and follow me."

Milo turned swiftly, stepping out of the room into the corridor, and Caitlin followed closely behind, her heart pounding with a mixture of relief and renewed tension. She recoiled upon seeing the third Chinese guard, lying face down in the hallway, restrained with flexcuffs and gasping for air like a fish out of water. Recognizing him as the armed man who had accompanied Scarface into her room the previous night, she stepped carefully over him, hurrying to catch up with Milo.

They hurried through an expansive living area furnished lavishly with couches and a polished mahogany bar, out a rear door into a well-maintained backyard. Caitlin struggled to keep pace as Milo picked up a heavy canvas satchel, which had been positioned outside. Loud voices echoed from the front of the house, sounding angry and authoritative. Yet the backyard remained eerily empty, untouched by the turmoil beyond.

She followed Milo at a run, adrenaline surging through her veins as they raced across the patio toward a tall, imposing wall marking the property boundary. The wall was topped with razor wire; she saw its glint ten feet above them. Milo stopped at a spot where the wire had sagged and tangled, hanging loose like coils of barbed metal ribbon.

He reached into the canvas bag, extracting a heavy contraption consisting of metal poles held together by stacked black plastic segments. She stared in confusion as Milo yanked the top crossbar upward, causing the telescoping segments below to fall into place. Within seconds, the device transformed into a solid, fully-extended ladder which he positioned at an angle against the wall.

Milo grabbed her arm and propelled her onto the bottom rung. "Let's go," he commanded. "Climb quickly. I'll be right behind you."

Caitlin hesitated briefly when she noticed a large black man peering down at her from atop the wall. Fear froze her in place.

"Move, Caitlin!" Milo insisted from below. "He's with us! He'll help you over."

Without waiting, Milo put his hand on her rear and pushed her upward, urging her higher. She climbed rapidly, her bare feet scrambling against metal rungs. Fear and adrenaline combined to drive her higher.

Within seconds, she reached the top, and the large man above extended powerful hands, grasping her firmly beneath her arms. With a sudden, effortless pull, he hoisted her over the top, expertly navigating her body through the gap in the razor wire. Her breath caught as he pulled her close, descending the ladder with her securely tucked against him.

Reaching the ground on the other side of the wall, she glanced upward. Milo swung himself over the top and descended to where she waited below on this side of the wall. Before she could catch her breath, both men grasped her arms, lifting her off the ground and propelling her at a sprint along the side of a neighboring house toward a waiting white SUV marked with Apex Security's distinct logo.

As they approached the vehicle, she heard the shouting behind them growing louder, more frantic, but felt no bullets or threats of pursuit. The entire extraction unfolded with stunning precision. Milo quickly bundled her into the rear seat, the large man taking the passenger side, and a driver already gripping the wheel.

The engine roared as the SUV surged forward, tires squealing against pavement. Milo pushed Caitlin's head downward between the seats, positioning himself protectively on top of her. She felt his steady breathing, his weight reassuring even as her heart raced, fearing bullets would shatter the windows and tear into the vehicle.

But nothing happened. The SUV made several rapid, sharp turns before Milo finally lifted himself off, gently pulling her upright onto the seat beside him.

She exhaled deeply, trying to catch her breath. Milo's eyes met hers, a reassuring half-smile crossing his face as he spoke.

"It's a real pleasure to see you again, Caitlin," he said, with understated humor in his tone. "I apologize for the messed-up circumstances."

Despite herself, Caitlin felt the tension suddenly release, allowing herself a brief smile. The reality of her rescue finally sank in —she was safe.

"Thank you," she whispered, struggling for words as tears welled again. "I can't thank you enough, Milo. I can't believe you came for me."

He squeezed her shoulder, a silent reassurance as they sped onward. "We take care of our own. It's going to be alright now."

She wanted desperately to believe him. And as Johannesburg blurred rapidly past the SUV windows, she allowed herself a sliver of cautious optimism.

26

5 MARCH 1226 HRS

JOHANNESBURG, South Africa

"Albatross, Albatross, Albatross."

I repeated our prearranged code word into the radio handset the instant we cleared the gates and accelerated away from the compound. My eyes were locked intently on the rear window, scanning the street behind us as our driver turned onto Winnie Mandela Drive. After several tense seconds, I allowed myself to breathe, satisfied we weren't being pursued.

Plan B had worked, at least for the moment.

Up front sat two men I'd never met before today. Beside the driver sat a large, muscular black man, whose powerful presence and calm demeanor suggested considerable experience. He caught my gaze in the mirror and nodded reassuringly, offering a broad, genuine smile of relief.

"Thank you," I said, leaning forward, extending my hand towards him in gratitude.

"My pleasure," he replied, gripping my hand. His voice resonated with a deep, confident timbre. "Been a while since I've enjoyed myself that much. Felt like the old days back in the Recces."

Caitlin, sitting beside me in the rear seat, leaned forward

earnestly. Her voice trembled, the cumulative emotion of recent days bubbling toward the surface. "Thank you both so much," she said, eyes glistening as she turned to me. "Milo, how did you even find me? What's going on? Please...tell me something."

I felt her emotions surging, saw the fatigue, fear, and confusion etched into her expression. She had endured more than anyone should have to: her friends murdered, Melissa brutalized, herself kidnapped, held captive without explanation. The past week had taken a terrible toll.

Her eyes filled with tears, and they began streaming unchecked down her cheeks. Seeing her distress, my instinctive response was to take her hand in mine, holding it firmly.

"Caitlin, I'll explain everything soon, I promise," I said, reassuring her. "First, we need to get someplace safe. Once we're secure, we'll talk through everything. You have my word."

She squeezed my hand harder, desperation and relief mixing in her tear-filled gaze. "What about my father?" she asked, her voice breaking. "Is he okay? Is he here in Johannesburg?"

"Your father isn't here," I answered, choosing my words carefully. "But we'll contact him once we reach safety. Right now, we just need to get clear and get you somewhere secure. Can you trust me on that?"

She nodded, holding onto my hand, unwilling to let go. Her trust moved me profoundly, and I knew I'd protect her at all costs.

Our SUV surged onward, navigating through the well-tended streets of Sandton, heading toward the safe location Deangelo had arranged. Turning onto Republic Road, we passed the busy intersections of Sandton Drive, buildings gradually thinning out into more suburban surroundings. Deangelo had carefully selected this site, one of Apex Security's discreet warehouses in the Ferndale neighborhood, to serve as our immediate safe haven.

I had never visited this particular location, but Deangelo assured me it was secure, off-record, and entirely separate from official Apex operations. Dominic and Deangelo would rendezvous with us there once they cleared the aftermath at Coronation Road and confirmed there were no lingering tails or threats.

This phase of Plan B carried significant risk. Under our initial plan, Dominic's Special Task Force would have conducted an official, sanctioned rescue. Caitlin would have been in police custody, safe and secure, simplifying her return to the U.S. But Plan B had unfolded differently. Major Dlamini had demanded my physical presence at STF headquarters. With my passport now revoked and my immigration status questionable at best, stepping foot inside a South African police station posed a high risk of immediate detention or worse.

Moreover, the authorities had not officially recognized Caitlin as a kidnapping victim. Dominic's unofficial surveillance and unauthorized operation placed us all precariously outside the lines of formal approval, especially given China's powerful and influential presence in South Africa. Our situation was complex and volatile, fraught with risks that extended far beyond mere rescue logistics.

I took solace, though, knowing Jessica and Nate were safely en route to Maputo, a strategic location just a short flight or a manageable drive from Johannesburg. Stitch remained in Frankfurt, primed and waiting should we require further assistance. My immediate priority was getting Caitlin safely out of the line of fire. Once she was secure, she could communicate directly with her father, Secretary Bishop, whose troubling and contradictory actions continued to mystify me. His reasoning for calling off our search and misleading us about Caitlin's safety remained unknown and unsettling.

At length, our SUV slowed in front of a nondescript compound, surrounded by a tall security wall topped with razor wire. An electronic gate slid open on rickety wheels as our driver approached, the SUV rolling through the opening and into a large gravel parking area. Before us stood a modest but sturdy warehouse, fronted by several oversized garage doors designed to accommodate large commercial trucks. One of the doors was already raised, waiting for our arrival.

Without hesitation, the driver maneuvered our vehicle into the open bay, the overhead door lowering immediately behind us. A sense of calm isolation settled over the vehicle, providing momentary comfort.

"We'll wait here for the others," the large man in front announced, glancing back at Caitlin and me. "There's an office and lounge area over there. Comfortable seating, tables, and everything you might need. Go relax a bit; we'll stand watch outside."

We stepped out onto the clean, stained concrete warehouse floor. Caitlin moved gingerly, conscious of her lack of shoes. I made a mental note that we'd need to get her shoes. The large man and the driver positioned themselves near the garage entrance, watchful and alert.

Placing a guiding hand on Caitlin's shoulder, I led her toward the lounge. Her eyes were wide, taking everything in, processing the rapid change from captivity to freedom. I hoped the lounge might offer a small measure of comfort and normalcy.

Inside, the lounge area was plain yet welcoming—comfortable sofas, sturdy tables, and basic office amenities. A refrigerator hummed in the corner, and I hoped it contained something cold and refreshing. Caitlin's ordeal demanded immediate physical and emotional care, and I was determined to provide it.

"Caitlin," I said, watching her closely, "are you holding up okay? How do you feel?"

She turned to face me, her eyes reflecting exhaustion, fear, and profound relief. "I...I don't even know how to begin answering that. This all feels so unreal. I was certain I might never get out of there alive. I have so many questions, but I'm not sure I'm ready for the answers just yet."

I gently squeezed her shoulder. "You're safe now. We'll get you home, Caitlin. But I need you to hold tight just a little longer, okay?"

She nodded, gathering herself, her strength impressing me despite everything she'd endured.

I guided her toward one of the couches, and she sank into it gratefully. Her breathing was steadying, and her tense posture began to relax.

"I'm so grateful you came," Caitlin whispered, her voice breaking. "I still can't believe it's you who got me out."

"That's what we do," I replied, attempting to put on the most reassuring face possible. "You're safe, and nothing else matters right now. We'll figure everything else out together."

She nodded, looking down at her hands. "My father...he must know what's going on. I just can't believe he'd abandon me like this. Something's terribly wrong, Milo. I mean...something is *seriously* wrong!"

I hesitated, choosing my words carefully. "We'll get answers. Your father may have complicated motives, but I assure you, our first priority is your safety. That's what matters now. We'll sort out the other answers later."

Caitlin leaned back, eyes briefly closing, struggling with overwhelming emotions. I sat beside her, quietly supportive, knowing that for the moment, silence and presence offered more comfort than words.

We sat in the dim lounge, the warehouse's thick walls muffling external sounds, providing a sense of temporary security. For a few precious moments, Caitlin seemed to find a semblance of peace, her breathing calming steadily.

Still, my mind raced, calculating the next moves, carefully weighing our options. Dominic and Deangelo would soon arrive, and we would need to quickly decide our next steps. Secretary Bishop's puzzling actions weighed heavily on my thoughts, his cryptic motivations adding layers of complexity to an already volatile situation.

I glanced at Caitlin, seeing her momentarily relaxed, regaining some composure, and resolved once more to see her safely home, regardless of the obstacles ahead. For now, we waited, knowing our brief respite in this quiet, safe house was merely the calm before the inevitable storm.

. . .

"Hello, Milo," the tall blonde woman greeted me as she entered the lounge, two large paper shopping bags clutched in her hands.

"Victoria!" I replied, caught off guard but standing and opening my arms to receive her warm hug and a kiss on each cheek. "What a pleasant surprise."

Victoria Thornton was Deangelo's wife. Though I had met her a handful of times, we weren't particularly close. Dominic and I had formed a special bond forged in combat years earlier, and we had remained extremely tight. That closeness extended somewhat to Deangelo, but our interactions had mostly been limited to guys-only gatherings, and I had seen Victoria only briefly during my visits to Johannesburg.

"Dee filled me in on your situation," Victoria said knowingly. She turned toward Caitlin, realizing the oversight. "Forgive my rudeness, I'm Victoria Thornton. You must be Caitlin."

"Nice to meet you," Caitlin replied softly, reaching forward to shake Victoria's extended right hand.

"I'm terribly sorry for your ordeal," Victoria continued. "I've brought you a selection of clothes, shoes, and other essentials I thought you might need. I had to guess your sizes based on the description Dee got from Milo, but I'm hopeful they'll fit." Victoria guided Caitlin to a large conference table, upon which began unloading the items from her shopping bags..

As Victoria began laying out the new clothing options for Caitlin, I heard the outside door open. Curious, I moved into the adjacent garage bay, assuming Dominic or Deangelo had arrived.

"We did it!" Deangelo's voice boomed as he entered, laughter punctuating his words. "You should've seen the look on that guy's face when he arrived. I swear he was so angry, his face turned so red, I thought his scar might split open."

I paused, perplexed. "Wait a second...Jimmy Liu showed up? I thought he'd already left."

"Yeah, bru," Deangelo confirmed. "He must have turned around.

He arrived just minutes after we got there. We'd already zip-tied his men, and his local security guards were too terrified to intervene. Liu and Dominic got into a huge shouting match. We knew you were still inside, and Dominic wouldn't let Liu enter the premises until he could prove he lived there. There was a tense moment when I seriously thought things might go kinetic. The only reason Liu and his driver didn't draw weapons was the sixteen rifles we had aimed right at them."

"So, tell me what happened," I said, processing the unexpected twist. "When I went around the back, you'd just restrained the Chinese guards. What happened after that? Liu just showed up out of nowhere?"

Deangelo nodded, recounting the events. "The first part went precisely as planned. The Chinese guards seemed to understand English, although I wasn't entirely sure how fluent they were. They complied with Dominic's instructions, no doubt having been instructed to be fearful of SAPS, and we easily disarmed them. But a couple minutes later, just after you went around back, the whole thing went sideways when Jimmy Liu himself showed up. He drove right up onto the grass beside the gate, jumped out, and marched straight toward the house. Dominic confronted him, playing the official SAPS policeman role perfectly. Dominic claimed he was investigating a reported burglary alarm. At first, Liu kept his composure, thanked Dominic for responding, and assured us it was just a false alarm. He insisted we could all leave immediately. But Dominic knew you needed more time, so he pressed Liu aggressively, demanding identification and proof of property ownership. The situation escalated quickly from there."

"Did anyone get hurt?" I asked, suddenly anxious.

"No," Deangelo reassured me. "Nothing turned physical. Dominic and Liu just yelled at each other for a couple of minutes, Dominic acting like a stubborn, by-the-book cop. When I heard your Albatross code word over the radio, I signaled Dominic we were good to go. At that point, we all just pretended to realize the misunderstanding and apologized profusely. No harm, no foul, and we just loaded up the trucks and left."

I laughed, more from relief than actual amusement. Considering how close we'd come to absolute disaster, it seemed incredible. Had Liu arrived even a minute earlier, or charged directly into the house instead of engaging with the SAPS, I would never have managed Caitlin's rescue without a violent confrontation.

At that moment, I heard a car pull up outside, and Dominic walked into the garage bay, a triumphant smile across his face.

"Everything okay, Milo?" Dominic asked as the three of us exchanged fist bumps. "How's the young lady holding up?"

"She's tough," I replied. "Handling this like a true warrior. Caitlin's inside with Victoria right now, changing into new clothes. I haven't fully debriefed her yet, but physically she seems unharmed."

"Excellent news," Dominic responded

"I heard you had quite the encounter with our friend Jimmy Liu?" I prompted.

I expected Dominic to laugh, but instead, his expression sobered instantly. "That man's a stone-cold killer," Dominic said. "I honestly believed he was going to pull a weapon on me."

"We would've dropped him immediately," Deangelo interjected.

Dominic shook his head. "I don't think Liu was concerned about that. He looked at us like we were insignificant, ants he could crush anytime he pleased. But I believe he didn't want to cause a public scene. He couldn't afford letting a SAPS officer enter that house, especially knowing he had kidnapped the daughter of a prominent American official. And he didn't want a bloody shootout occurring on his boss's front lawn."

"But you think he suspected we were there for Caitlin?" I asked, processing the implications.

"Yes," Dominic replied. "I'm quite sure he did. But it hardly matters, because there's no doubt he knows now."

"Do you think we're clear of repercussions?" I asked, looking between the two brothers. "Any potential backlash for you or Deangelo?"

"I believe we're fine," Dominic answered. "What's Liu going to do, file a police report complaining he lost a woman he'd kidnapped? He has nothing legitimate against us."

"No worries on my end, bru," Deangelo added, smiling. "Just a simple address mix-up by Apex Security. Liu may suspect we were involved, but seriously, what can he do about it? It's not like he can call the police."

"Okay," I nodded in cautious agreement. "But both of you be extremely careful. These people are dangerous. Let's head inside. I want you to meet Caitlin."

Together, the three of us walked into the office space. Caitlin stood inside, fully changed into fresh clothing—a crisp pair of jeans and a green Springboks rugby shirt. Her feet now sported white Adidas Ultraboost sneakers. Her hair was pulled back into a tidy ponytail, and she appeared remarkably composed. She was snacking from a bag of cookies placed conveniently on the counter. Anyone seeing her at this moment would never imagine the trauma and captivity she had recently endured.

"Caitlin," I began, gesturing toward Dominic and Deangelo, "I'd like you to meet the two men who assisted me in your rescue this morning: Dominic and Deangelo Thornton. Deangelo is Victoria's husband."

Caitlin stepped forward to greet them, extending her hand politely. Instead of accepting her handshake, Deangelo pulled her into an affectionate embrace, clearly moved by the moment. Caitlin then turned and hugged Dominic tightly. Tears began to glisten in her eyes, and I could sense the pent-up emotions of her recent experiences finally bubbling near the surface.

After a quiet moment, Caitlin stepped back, clearly moved. "Thank you both. I don't even have words to describe how grateful I am."

"So what happens next?" Caitlin asked after we had all settled comfortably around the large conference table. Her voice was steady, but curiosity and uncertainty lingered. "I'd really like to speak with my father. Can I?"

"Yes, of course," I assured her. "We'll arrange a call to your father right away. Our current plan involves staying at a secure Airbnb my company rented just a few blocks from here. It's safe and discreet. Once things settle down, you can decide when you'd like to return home. If your father wants to arrange a plane to pick you up, we can accommodate that at any time. For now, though, it's safest if we wait here a day or two until things stabilize. Dominic has arranged for a medical doctor to visit us there to check you over, and we'll order whatever take-out you're craving. I'm sure you're starving. Our goal is getting you back into a normal routine as quickly as possible."

Caitlin nodded, taking it all in. "I have so many questions," she said. "But first, please, I just need to speak with my father."

I exchanged a brief glance with Dominic and Deangelo, who both nodded.

"Absolutely," I promised her. "Let's call him now."

27

5 MARCH 1250 HRS

JOHANNESBURG, South Africa

"Hi, Daddy," Caitlin began, her voice hesitant as she searched for the right way to address her father, given the ordeal of the past week.

"Caitlin?" George Bishop's voice sounded startled. Instantly, he called out harshly to those around him: "Clear the room! Right goddamn now!"

She could hear muffled sounds of hurried footsteps, then his voice returned with strained urgency. "Sweetheart, are you okay? Where are you? I just received a very disturbing call."

She hesitated, her words catching in her throat. Standing up to her father had always been difficult, especially after her brother Danny died in combat in Iraq. As a child, she'd cherished her role as Daddy's little girl, but as an adult, she often resented his controlling nature over both her personal decisions and professional pursuits.

"I suppose it depends on what your definition of 'okay' is," she replied, attempting to keep bitterness from her voice. "I'm physically unharmed if that's what you're asking. Milo deCogan rescued me from those Chinese thugs. Who were those men, Dad? They weren't the same people who attacked us at Gangura. And what on earth is going on with you? Why was Scarface threatening you on the phone?"

As the words spilled out, a rush of emotions overwhelmed her. Tears welled in her eyes and streamed down her cheeks as the full weight of the past week's trauma finally surfaced. She glanced across the room to Milo, who sat quietly on the couch opposite her, offering emotional support simply by his reassuring presence. The three Thorntons—Dominic, Deangelo, and Victoria—had discreetly stepped outside, leaving them alone. Yet Caitlin had explicitly asked Milo to remain nearby.

Just in case. Of what, exactly, she wasn't entirely sure. She only knew she felt safer with him close.

"Where are you now, Caitlin?" her father asked, ignoring her torrent of questions and reverting to his typical assertive self.

"I'm in Johannesburg," Caitlin answered, struggling to regain composure. "Dad, they killed Sebastian and Festus. They shot them down in cold blood. Melissa and I barely escaped through the hidden back door you had Milo install. We fled into the jungle, walked for days, then thought we found safety in a village. But those rebels captured Melissa, and I was taken by another group, Chinese men who drugged me and threatened to torture me—"

"Did they hurt you?" Bishop cut her off. "Sweetheart, were you harmed?"

She understood what he was asking. Her voice trembled but remained firm. "No, Dad, they didn't rape me if that's what you mean. But they nearly cut my finger off...while you watched! You watched through the phone, Dad! You saw everything!"

Her father's silence echoed painfully across the line. Caitlin felt raw anger and hurt surge to the surface.

Milo leaned forward, offering her a plastic bottle of water. He gestured for her to drink, urging her to regain her composure. She took a slow sip, using the brief pause to steady herself.

"Where are you right now, Dad?" she asked, her voice calmer now. "Are you still in Washington?"

She knew from Milo's earlier comments that her father was in Brussels, but she needed confirmation.

"I'm in Brussels," he replied. "I have critical meetings scheduled with NATO and the European Union."

She snapped, anger returning. "More critical than rescuing your own daughter kidnapped halfway around the world?"

His response was immediate and firm, his voice carrying a stern note. "You don't understand, Caitlin. It's incredibly complicated. You need to trust me."

"Trust you?" she spat, incredulous. "You fired the only person searching for me! You lied to everyone, claiming I was safe while I was locked up, terrified, a thousand miles from where I was supposed to be!"

"Calm down, Caitlin," he replied, trying to reassert control. "You have no idea how complicated this situation has become."

"Oh, you think I'm upset?" Caitlin snapped. "Do you realize what Scarface said to me? He said if you didn't hold up your end of the deal, then he'd send me home to you in pieces. In pieces, Dad! What deal? What could you possibly be doing that someone would cut me up into pieces?"

"I was doing everything possible to resolve the situation," Bishop pleaded, his voice suddenly more vulnerable, anguished, on the verge of breaking. "Please believe me, Caitlin. I made decisions based on what I thought was best for everyone. I never thought you'd become involved. I'm so sorry...so sorry."

Despite her anger, Caitlin recognized sincerity in her father's voice, emotion she'd rarely heard since Danny's death in Iraq. She realized, despite everything, that her father still loved her deeply and had acted out of some profound sense of duty. Perhaps she truly did not understand the broader complexities he was facing.

"So what do I do now, Dad? Where do I go from here?"

"There's a U.S. Consulate right there in Sandton," Bishop said. "Tell Milo to take you there immediately. Can he do that?"

She pulled the phone away briefly and looked at Milo. "My

father wants us to go straight to the consulate. Can you take me there now?"

Milo nodded. "Yes. We can be there in fifteen minutes."

She spoke back into the phone. "Yes, Dad, we'll head over immediately. Milo says we can arrive in about fifteen minutes."

"Good," Bishop replied, his relief evident. "I'll make some urgent calls to ensure they're expecting you. I'll call Jessica and make sure everything is set. Once you're safely inside the consulate, call me back immediately. I'll explain more clearly then. Caitlin, I love you."

"I love you too, Dad," she answered.

The call disconnected. Milo moved toward her, seeing the conflict and pain etched deeply into her features.

"I understand this is incredibly difficult," Milo said. "But this outcome is a best-case scenario. Going straight to the consulate is even safer than staying hidden for a few days. You'll be on American soil, completely secure."

She met Milo's eyes. "But what about you?" she asked, still unaware that her father had revoked Milo's passport. "Will you be safe?"

He smiled. "I'll be right beside you."

Just then, the door opened, and Dominic Thornton stepped in from the garage. His normally confident demeanor was now troubled, his expression unusually grave, reflecting the seriousness of their situation.

Dominic approached Milo, his voice tense, yet steady. "Milo, we need to talk. Right now."

"What happened?" Milo asked.

JOHANNESBURG, South Africa

The past twenty minutes had changed everything. I had been well aware that I was playing a complicated game of three-dimensional chess. Now, however, I understood something crucial: I wasn't nearly as skilled at it as I thought.

The grim news Dominic had brought into the room had dismantled our carefully laid Plan B. We were now scrambling through Plan D, or E, or maybe even Plan F—I was struggling to keep track. Honestly, it probably didn't matter at this stage.

For the moment, the only clear objective was reaching the U.S. Consulate.

When Dominic had walked into the room at the conclusion of Caitlin's call with her father, I immediately sensed trouble. It was etched across his face, betraying the severity of whatever news he carried.

"What happened?" I asked.

Dominic exhaled, shaking his head. "We've been outmaneuvered. I'll be honest, Milo. I didn't see this coming."

"What happened?" I pressed again.

Dominic's voice was steady but grim. "A call came in on the

SAPS 10111 emergency line from 11 Coronation Road in Sand-hurst, reporting an armed home invasion. Responding SAPS officers were met by Jimmy Liu, who identified himself as the property owner's representative. According to Liu, an armed male and female assailant forcibly entered the property after scaling a neighboring wall. Liu presented CCTV footage showing the male intruder strug-gling violently with one of the guards in the home, and later scaling the wall. He claimed one of his guards, a male Chinese national, was shot and killed during the incident. While the woman was unidenti-fied, the man was positively identified as one Milo deCogan, an American citizen."

My blood turned to ice. Checkmate. How had I been so careless, so completely blindsided?

When I failed to respond, Dominic continued, his voice heavy. "Just minutes ago, SAPS issued a general broadcast, a Wanted Person Alert, for Milo deCogan: white male, 1.9 meters tall, approximately 85 kilograms, short light-brown hair, green eyes, last observed wearing a white polo shirt. SAPS officially considers the suspect armed and extremely dangerous."

"Fuck me," I muttered.

"Exactly," Dominic agreed. "You're most definitely fucked."

I looked toward Caitlin, who had overheard the conversation, her expression a mix of fear and confusion. "Caitlin just spoke with her father," I said, regaining composure. "Secretary Bishop requested that she and I proceed immediately to the U.S. Consulate here in Sand-ton. Dominic, what's your assessment?"

Dominic nodded. "Right now, Milo, that seems your safest move. If SAPS apprehends you first, you're facing a significant stay behind bars. I'll help all I can, of course, but the CCTV footage provided by Liu could be sufficient to keep you jailed indefinitely without bond."

I cursed again, furious with myself for not anticipating this scenario. Liu's deft manipulation had accelerated the conflict into an entirely new arena. "Jimmy Liu is forcing our hand. I thought he would want to keep things discreet. I never imagined he would escalate this into a public spectacle."

Dominic's face tightened, acknowledging the severity of the situation. "Yes, it's a bold, unexpected move. But give me some time. I'm certain we can neutralize this threat. Right now, getting to the consulate is critical."

"Agreed," I said, absorbing the situation. "But can you transport us safely?"

Dominic hesitated, weighing the implications. "Not me personally, I can't risk that exposure right now. Thabo can take you discreetly in an unmarked SUV. I can escort you with my SAPS vehicle to ensure you make it safely to the consulate gate. Once you're there, the Marines can take over. The consulate is U.S. soil—SAPS has no jurisdiction."

We spent several intense minutes gathering our gear, briefing Caitlin, and reviewing our planned route. Our only contingency was returning here or to the Apex Security office in Sandton if something went wrong.

Two potential complications stood out in my mind.

First, a SAPS patrol officer could recognize and intercept us. Dominic assured me it was unlikely, and he would intervene directly if it occurred. The consulate lay just eight kilometers away, a drive of only fifteen minutes.

Second, the Marines at the consulate might refuse me entry. Caitlin's admission was assured; mine, with my revoked passport, was uncertain. If refused, I planned to retreat swiftly to our current safehouse, lying low until Stacy or Jessica could sort out the bureaucratic issues. I had little doubt that Jessica would be able to smooth things over, given a little bit of time.

We exchanged sincere farewells with Deangelo and Victoria, and I promised them that I'd return soon under far better circumstances. Thabo awaited us in the parking lot, an unmarked red SUV ready and running. Caitlin and I climbed into the back seat, while Dominic took point in the SAPS police cruiser, escorting us from the premises toward the consulate.

The drive was short but tense, the silence in our vehicle palpable. Thabo concentrated on shadowing Dominic's cruiser, while I scanned our surroundings, watching anxiously for any SAPS vehicles tailing us. Arrest was not on my agenda; while adventurous, I had no desire to experience incarceration within South Africa's justice system.

We retraced the route we had taken just an hour before after rescuing Caitlin. Westward along Republic Road, turning onto Winnie Mandela Drive, we then left onto Sandton Drive, soon entering Sandton proper. Just ahead lay the U.S. Consulate, a bastion of American soil situated prominently on the southwest corner at the intersection of Sandton Drive and Rivonia Road.

Approaching from the west along Sandton Drive, we maneu-vered through traffic, cautiously observing the surrounding area. Our plan involved passing the consulate, executing a careful U-turn, then pulling up directly outside the consulate's walk-up service windows located along the sidewalk.

Everything around us appeared normal. On our left sprawled the expansive Sandton City Mall, bustling with ordinary daily activity. I scanned for U.S. Marines positioned outside, watching protectively for Caitlin's arrival. But there were no visible Marines, just the stan-dard dozen or so people lined up patiently along the sidewalk, awaiting routine consular services.

Our convoy completed the careful U-turn at Rivonia Road, coming to a halt right outside the consulate gate. I studied our surroundings again, noting the reassuring absence of attention toward us.

"Stay seated a moment, Caitlin," I instructed. "I'll come around to open your door."

She nodded, remaining in place, recognizing the gravity of the situation.

Thabo and I simultaneously exited the SUV, stepping onto the roadside, senses on full alert. The breakdown lane provided ample clearance from passing traffic, allowing us to move safely. I exchanged a brief look of appreciation with Thabo, then began moving purposefully around the vehicle's rear to Caitlin's side. That small movement undoubtedly saved my life.

A large-caliber bullet punched through Thabo's right cheek and exited the back of his neck, taking his life in an instant. The driver's side window exploded in a violent burst, showering blood and gore across everything. In that same instant, I felt a sharp tug on my upper arm, followed immediately by searing pain. My door still open, I instinctively ducked down behind it for cover.

"Are you hit?" I shouted at Caitlin, who sat momentarily frozen, unable to process what was unfolding. "Caitlin, get down now!"

I raised my head cautiously to assess the threat and watched in horror as bullets riddled Dominic's SAPS cruiser directly ahead of us. Across the street, a masked assailant astride the back of a motorcycle methodically fired a suppressed MP5K submachine gun into Dominic's body. I saw Dominic's form jerking violently with each impact, several rounds striking him squarely in the head. There was no doubt my friend was dead.

Fuck! This was rapidly spiraling out of control.

I'd faced similar situations before; surviving them required calm decisiveness. One mistake now would mean death. The fact that I wasn't already dead meant I was either extremely fortunate or had done something correct. I needed to capitalize on that slim margin immediately.

Where the hell were the Marines when you really needed them?

With no Marines or friendly cavalry coming to our rescue, the masked attacker began to reload his weapon across the street. Seconds from spraying another lethal volley toward Caitlin and me, he represented an immediate and deadly threat.

Looking downward, I saw Thabo sprawled lifeless at my feet, a spreading pool of blood beneath his head. The grip of his Z88 pistol protruded from a concealed holster inside his waistband. Without hesitation, I reached down and pulled the pistol free.

In a single fluid motion, I rose, took a shooter's stance, leveled the pistol center mass toward the masked gunman, and squeezed the trigger.

Click!

Shit! Thabo hadn't chambered a round!

Without missing a beat, I quickly racked the slide, chambering a round and putting the pistol into battery.

Bang!

The first shot struck the motorcycle's oil pan, harmlessly deflecting off metal.

Taking a deep breath to steady myself, I adjusted my aim as the attacker completed reloading and raised his weapon toward me again.

Bang! Bang! Bang!

Firing three rapid, precise shots, I saw at least two of my rounds strike the masked assailant squarely, knocking him from his motorcycle.

I exhaled, turning back to Caitlin. "Are you okay?" I yelled, desperate for her confirmation.

"Yes!" she responded still ducking down. "Are you?"

Bang!

The SUV's rear window exploded inward, showering Caitlin with shards of glass. Someone else was still out there, a sniper firing at long range.

Without hesitation, I jumped into the driver's seat, slammed the gearshift into drive, and jammed my foot hard onto the accelerator. The SUV lurched forward violently, barely allowing me time to swerve and avoid colliding with Dominic's riddled police car. As we passed, Dominic's vacant, lifeless eyes met mine. Whatever grace awaited him was no longer ours to give.

Tires screeching, we raced west along Sandton Drive. I waited for another sniper round, bracing myself, but none came. My heart pounding, I tried to regain focus.

"Are you hurt?" I asked Caitlin, who shifted anxiously behind me.

"No, I'm not hit," she replied. "But you are!"

Glancing downward, I saw my left shoulder and upper arm soaked in blood. With adrenaline surging, I'd felt nothing but the initial sting; that would soon change.

Fuck! We had no contingency plan for this.

Suddenly, spotting Sandton City Mall, an idea struck. Without warning, I braked sharply and turned the wheel hard right, jumping the SUV over the curb and onto the grassy median. Accelerating again, I aimed for the parking ramp just ahead, which led directly into the mall's enormous underground garage. Driving a bullet-riddled SUV away from a crime scene, I knew we wouldn't last long on Johannesburg's streets.

I slowed slightly as we entered the parking structure, following directional arrows and quickly choosing to descend to the ground level. Finding a secluded space near the rear of the garage, I brought the SUV to a halt, engine still idling.

"What do we do now?" Caitlin's voice trembled, fear and uncertainty clear.

"Honestly, I don't know," I admitted. Even from inside the parking structure, the approaching sirens were audible, echoing with urgency. "But we need to hurry."

I grabbed my backpack from the floorboard, unzipping it and retrieving my first-aid kit. Caitlin immediately took the kit from my hands, clearly wanting to help.

"Let me do it," she insisted. "Can you get your shirt off so I can see the wound?"

"We don't have time for that," I said. "Just apply the pressure bandage as tightly as possible. Don't worry about cleaning or removing the shirt. Just stop the bleeding."

Caitlin prepared the bandage carefully as I briefly examined my wound. It looked like a bullet had sliced cleanly through my deltoid muscle, painful but manageable. No arterial bleeding appeared evident.

I winced as Caitlin firmly pressed the bandage onto my injury, wrapping it tightly around my upper arm. "Make it tighter," I urged, knowing firm pressure was essential. "As tight as possible."

She pulled harder, securing the bandage perfectly.

Reaching back into my backpack, I pulled out a navy-blue windbreaker I always carried. Though designed for rain, today it would conceal my blood-soaked shirt and the pistol now tucked discreetly into my waistband.

I stashed the first-aid kit, zipped up the pack, then drew the Z88 pistol, quickly checking the magazine. Ten rounds remained, plus the one chambered, enough to get us clear, if it came to that.

"Let's move," I instructed Caitlin, shouldering open the rear passenger door and stepping onto the garage floor. I tossed my backpack over my good shoulder.

"Here, let me take the bag," Caitlin said, grabbing it from me. "You need your hands free if there's trouble. What now?"

I appreciated her steadiness. "We need to get distance between us and this vehicle. Follow me."

The shooting had occurred mere minutes ago, and Joburg's police would descend rapidly. I had no clue as to the sniper's identity, though instinct said it was connected directly to Jimmy Liu. The MP5K the motorcycle shooter used matched the weapons held by Liu's Chinese guards earlier. I didn't believe in coincidence.

We moved quickly across the parking garage floor toward the mall entrance. I knew we would blend more easily among Sandton City Mall's bustling crowds.

Caitlin stayed close, moving quickly but carefully across the concrete. It was imperative that we kept moving, staying ahead of the authorities and whatever new threat Liu might deploy.

29

5 MARCH 1348 HRS

JOHANNESBURG, **South Africa**

Transiting through Sandton City Mall proved uneventful. The chaos unfolding outside the U.S. Consulate had not yet penetrated the shopping complex, allowing us to move swiftly and without incident.

We walked briskly past Trump's Grill, one of Joburg's most popular steakhouses, and exited the mall through large glass doors into Nelson Mandela Square. Ignoring tourists posing cheerfully in front of the enormous Mandela statue, we continued north into the Michelangelo Hotel's courtyard. Entering Maude Street, I turned left, cutting across traffic and ascending the steps toward Riff's Bar and Grill in the Garden Court Hotel. I knew this route well; the restaurant led directly into a discreet courtyard that would guide us north toward the intersection of Alice Lane and West Street.

My primary goal was to place as many buildings and obstacles as possible between us and anyone who might be pursuing.

Although Johannesburg boasted a population of nearly five million people, Sandton City, with its upscale business and entertainment district, offered limited cover for pedestrians trying to blend in anonymously. The multi-lane, tree-lined streets were exceptionally broad, sidewalks even wider, and modern buildings often set well back behind gates and walls. Pedestrians were numerous yet dispersed, moving purposefully from place to place.

Unlike bustling cities such as New York, Boston, London, or Paris, here there was no weaving quickly down crowded side streets or slipping unnoticed into buildings. Rapid escape required a taxi. Fortunately, as we stepped onto West Street, one approached immediately. I quickly flagged it down, and we climbed inside.

Without considering a specific destination, I gave the driver the first place that sprang to mind: Northgate Shopping Centre. Located roughly twenty minutes west of Sandton, it would afford me enough time and distance to figure out our next move and evade those who were surely hunting us.

Caitlin, to her immense credit, remained mostly silent throughout the escape. She stayed alert, kept pace, and offered quiet cooperation whenever needed. She was exactly the partner I needed in this scenario. At this point, I still wasn't sure if the sniper had targeted me, her, or both of us.

My first call was to Stacy.

Careful not to divulge sensitive information in front of the driver, I included our prearranged emergency code word "Pineapple" early in the conversation. Immediately afterward, I sent Stacy a brief text summarizing our situation, detailing our current location, and emphasizing the urgent need for extraction or a secure hideout.

My second call was to Deangelo.

The phone rang four tense times before it was answered. I was startled to hear a woman's voice: "Hello?"

"Victoria?" I asked, surprised.

"Milo? Is that you?"

"Yes," I replied. "Why do you have Deangelo's phone?"

"What's going on, Milo? Everything has gone absolutely crazy here. The police stormed in, and Dee handed me his phone and told me to go wait in the car. What the hell is happening?"

"SAPS are there right now?" I asked, my pulse quickening. "Are you both safe?"

"Safe?" Her voice rose, bordering on hysteria. "Dee is inside with the police! More SAPS vehicles have pulled up, and officers are spread all across the parking lot."

Things had spiraled out of control even faster than I'd anticipated. How had they linked Deangelo and Apex Security to this mess so quickly? I knew I should tell Victoria something, but I couldn't bear delivering the news about Dominic, not right now. I doubted she could handle it amidst everything else.

"Victoria, listen carefully," I said, steadying my voice. "Is there any way at all you can get Deangelo on this phone without the police knowing?"

"Are you kidding?" she said. "Deangelo is inside surrounded by at least four SAPS officers, with another half dozen out here in the lot."

"Okay," I conceded, realizing there was nothing more productive I could gain from continuing the call. I didn't want to involve her further. "Just wait—"

She cut me off abruptly. "Hold on. Another police SUV just pulled in, followed by a black Mercedes SUV. That SAPS major, Dominic's superior, the black officer Dominic dislikes, is stepping out of the police vehicle. What's his name again?"

"Dlamini," I said. "Major Thabiso Dlamini, Special Task Force."

"Yes, that's him."

"What about the Mercedes? Could it be someone from the Embassy?"

"Wait, the passenger is stepping out," Victoria said. A tense silence followed before she continued cautiously. "Well, he might be American. He's a muscular Asian man with a long scar on his face."

Jimmy Liu.

How could Liu be arriving at Apex Security, escorted by Dominic's commanding officer? This guy was consistently two steps ahead of us.

I took a deep breath, feeling suddenly defeated. "Victoria," I said.

"Listen to me carefully. If possible, lose this phone immediately. Tell Deangelo I'm sorry...I'm so terribly sorry."

"What exactly are you sorry for, Milo?" Victoria's voice was tense, fearful.

"Just tell Deangelo I'll be in touch as soon as possible. Don't worry about us. Please just take care of yourselves. Promise me."

I disconnected quickly, staring down at the phone, the implications weighing heavily upon me.

Caitlin studied me intently, concern evident in her eyes. "Was that someone from the Embassy?"

"No," I replied. "Jimmy Liu—escorted personally by the police."

Her eyes widened in disbelief. "Are you serious?"

"Serious as a heart attack."

In that moment, my appreciation for Caitlin Bishop deepened profoundly. Over these past frantic days, I'd been solely focused on rescuing her. But Caitlin had endured unimaginable horrors: fleeing ruthless rebels, being drugged, disguised in a burkha, and abducted to South Africa against her will. She'd survived a gun battle, administered first aid to my gunshot wound, and calmly navigated the chaos of the Sandton City Mall escape. Her courage and composure amazed me.

Undoubtedly, countless questions were swirling through her mind, but she hadn't asked a single one. Not one question, not one doubt expressed. Caitlin remained composed, gave me space to think, and showed remarkable resilience. She was quietly trying to process events, just as I was.

My phone buzzed. I glanced down and read the simple message displayed on my screen:

CALL ME, BROTHER

It was from Stitch, who I hoped was staged safely in Germany, awaiting further instructions. He was precisely the person I needed to speak with right now.

I dialed immediately.

"Hey, brother," Stitch said, skipping any greeting. "You safe?"

"For the moment," I replied. "We're in a taxi."

"Understood," he responded. "Stacy briefed me already. This situation is completely FUBAR. Dominic was truly one of the best. I can't believe he's gone."

Stitch's bond with Dominic was almost as close as mine, and I could hear genuine pain in his voice.

"Listen carefully," Stitch continued, refocusing. "I'm texting you an address. It belongs to an old friend, someone not connected from Relief Solutions and entirely untraceable. She'll sell you a reliable vehicle for cash. It's a five-year-old Mitsubishi Pajero in good condition. Ten thousand U.S. dollars cash. She'll hold onto the title; you just drive away. When this is over, I'll let her know where it is. Otherwise, she'll report it stolen."

"Sounds perfect," I replied, keenly aware the taxi driver might be overhearing everything. I was cautious about giving away details that could be shared later with the authorities, or with Jimmy Liu's men, who might well be the same thing now.

"Give her your iPhone, but keep the satellite phone," Stitch instructed. "I have a plan to distract and mislead anyone tracking your phones."

"Got it," I replied, appreciating Stitch's tactical clarity, even though I still wasn't fully aware of his and Stacy's broader strategy.

"Then take Caitlin south. Use the N12 highway through Kimberley. Stay clear of the N1. It'll be longer but with far fewer cameras. Put as much distance as possible between you and Joburg. Once you're at least a hundred miles clear, call Stacy from your satphone. We'll have a solid extraction plan ready."

"Will do," I replied. I didn't need further explanation; my trust in Stitch and Stacy was absolute.

There was a brief silence before Stitch interjected, sensing my exhaustion and tension. "And Milo—stay frosty, brother. Remember, 'the road is long, with many a winding turn.'"

I smiled, recognizing Stitch's characteristic attempt at levity through a cryptic song lyric. "Come on, Stitch. You're quoting lyrics to me now? You seriously think I'm in the mood for riddles?"

"Come on, brother," Stitch said. "You've got this. Just trying to lighten the mood a bit. Call me if you need anything at all." He disconnected the call.

I looked at Caitlin and gave her a thumbs-up, trying to project confidence. She returned a gentle smile, perhaps her first genuine one in a long while.

When Stitch ended the call, I sat there a moment longer, staring at the silent phone in my hand. He'd done it again, dropped one of his damned lyrics, and hung up before I could ask what the hell he meant by it. *The road is long, with many a winding turn.* At the time, it sounded like nonsense, one of his half-poetic ways of telling me to stay sharp. I remember shaking my head, irritated that he could be so flippant when everything was on the line.

In days ahead, I'd learn the line came from an old song: *He Ain't Heavy, He's My Brother*. The irony wouldn't hit me until much later, when the road we were on twisted in ways neither of us could have predicted. If I'd known the song then, I might have understood what Stitch was really saying—that no matter how long or winding the path ahead, he'd be there beside me. Because he wasn't just my team-mate, my second, or my friend. He was my brother. And the road ahead was about to test that bond in every way imaginable.

My phone buzzed again, and I read the address Stitch had texted me. It was in Fourways, a suburban neighborhood northwest of Johannesburg. Whether intentional or fortuitous, it aligned with our current route. I'd have our taxi continue to Northgate Shopping Centre, then pick up another cab from there toward Fourways. The more transportation changes we made, the harder it would be for anyone to track us down.

Twenty minutes later, Caitlin and I approached Montecasino, a large luxury hotel and casino situated close to the address Stitch had provided. A quarter mile south of the casino, I pointed to a sheltered bus stop and instructed our taxi driver to pull over.

Caitlin, uncertain of my intentions, disembarked the taxi without question as I paid the driver in Rand, the local currency. We stepped out onto the sidewalk of Leslie Avenue. Using the Google Maps app on my phone, I navigated toward the address Stitch had sent us, located in a housing development across the street to the south.

We walked down Penguin Drive and turned right onto Darter Avenue. The suburban homes in Joburg resembled those found in Europe or the United States, but each property was distinctive, encircled by a high wall at least eight feet tall, complete with secured gates across every front entrance and driveway. The stark presence of these walls served as a constant reminder of the pervasive threat of crime and home invasions in Johannesburg.

As pedestrians, we saw no welcoming homes, just imposing walls lining both sides of the street. I felt painfully exposed. If a SAPS vehicle rounded the corner, we would have nowhere to run. The narrow street felt more like a constricted alleyway than a suburban avenue.

Through occasional gaps in the gates, I caught glimpses of the homes within, modest brick or stucco houses with neatly maintained yards. Fortunately, nearly every home displayed its address prominently on the gate, making our search straightforward.

In a matter of minutes, we arrived at the pedestrian gate for the address Stitch had provided. I located a button next to the gate and pressed it. Rather than receiving a reply through the intercom mounted above the button, I instead heard the quiet buzz indicating the gate had been remotely unlocked. With complete faith in Stitch's arrangements, I opened the gate, guiding Caitlin inside, and closed it firmly behind us.

We hadn't made it halfway toward the front door when a woman emerged from the carport beside the house. I saw a silver Mitsubishi Pajero SUV parked in the driveway, confirming we were in the right place.

The woman was slight, in her mid-sixties, of Indian descent, with long dark hair pulled back into a bun. She wore no makeup, her appearance natural and elegant, dressed in comfortable clothing suitable for gardening or casual chores. Her expression was warm, welcoming, but observant, and she approached us with confidence.

"Welcome," she said. "You arrived sooner than I expected."

"We're here about the car," I responded neutrally, cautious not to reveal too much too soon. Stitch hadn't given me a contact name, and I remained wary of inadvertently disclosing too much detail.

"Yes, of course," the woman said, smiling. "Tony mentioned you'd be coming."

Tony? Who the hell was Tony? It took me a moment before realizing Stitch's full name was Tony Bostich, something I hadn't heard anyone use in a long time. Stitch had always just been Stitch to me, and it felt strange to hear someone use his real name.

"Yes, Tony sent us," I replied, still off balance.

She paused, openly studying us both. Her gaze lingered appraisingly, and she made no attempt to hide her curiosity. Though petite, her stature conveyed quiet strength. Her expression suggested a mixture of caution and trustworthiness.

"You must be Milo," she said finally, extending a small, delicate hand toward me.

So much for operational security.

"Yes," I admitted, shaking her hand, surprised at the firmness of her grip. "And this is my friend, Caitlin."

"Hello, Caitlin," the woman said, shaking Caitlin's hand as well. "My name is Sunitha, but please call me Sunny. Milo, I've heard so much about you. It's truly a pleasure to finally meet you."

The degree of her familiarity was disconcerting, and my curiosity got the better of me. "If you don't mind me asking, how exactly do you know Tony?"

She smiled, as though recalling pleasant memories. "I've known Tony since he was just a young private in the Army. My husband, Walter, was Tony's very first platoon sergeant, and he took a young, wayward PFC Bostich under his wing. Tony used to spend Thanksgiving and Christmas dinners at our house. We became family, really, and we've stayed close ever since."

The image of Stitch as a young, wayward private nearly made me laugh aloud. To me, Stitch had always been the consummate warfighter, a grizzled senior non-commissioned officer who had spent nearly all of his twenty-five-year military career in Special Forces, including over five years in the elite Delta Force. To imagine Stitch as a wayward young private seemed utterly incongruous.

"I'm sure you have some incredible stories I'd genuinely love to hear," I said sincerely. "But unfortunately, as Tony probably mentioned, we're pressed for time."

"Of course," Sunny replied, understanding immediately. "Please, follow me."

She led us toward the silver Mitsubishi Pajero parked beneath the carport on the side of the house. Another vehicle, a newer BMW sedan, was parked nearby.

I hesitated a moment. "Is your husband here?"

Sunny's gentle smile vanished, replaced instantly by sorrow. "No," she said quietly, her voice subdued. "Walter passed away from cancer over ten years ago. We were living near Clarksville, Tennessee, at the time. We didn't have children of our own, so after Walter died, I moved back here, to South Africa, where I was born, to be closer to my extended family."

"I'm terribly sorry," Caitlin offered, and I added my condolences as well.

Sunny composed herself quickly and spent the next several minutes efficiently showing us the Pajero. I handed her the ten thousand dollars in cash. I always carried significant amounts of cash during operations, and despite what I'd already spent in South Sudan and Goma, I still had over forty thousand dollars in my backpack. Fortunately for us, Sunny harbored little confidence in the South African banking system, and she was happy to exchange the thirty thousand Rand she had on hand for an additional two thousand U.S. dollars.

She had thoughtfully gone the extra mile, providing us with a case of bottled water and some biltong, South Africa's far tastier equivalent of beef jerky. Biltong was a beloved snack in this part of the world, as popular as peanut butter and jelly sandwiches were back home. Caitlin and I both used the restroom, preparing ourselves to depart as rapidly as possible. We had been at Sunny's less than ten minutes.

"Tony asked me to give you my phone," I explained, handing the device over to Sunny. "Did he give you any additional instructions?"

"Yes," she replied, taking the phone. "He asked me to drive two hours east, out to Witbank Nature Reserve in the direction of the Mozambique border, and throw it into the lake."

I couldn't help but smile. Stitch always had a clear plan, even if I didn't fully grasp the exact reasons. I had deleted everything sensitive from the phone already, confident the device's extra encryption would make hacking impossible. I trusted Stitch implicitly and would follow his instructions without question.

Sunny escorted us back toward the car, and we exchanged warm goodbyes. Caitlin and I both promised earnestly that we would someday return to Johannesburg and properly repay Sunny for her kindness and hospitality.

"You both take care," Sunny said, her eyes filled with genuine warmth. "And please tell Tony I said hello. He needs to visit more often."

"We will," Caitlin replied. "Thank you again...for everything."

We climbed into the Pajero, started the engine, and waved to Sunny one final time before pulling smoothly out onto the suburban street. Our next move was uncertain, but at least we now had reliable transport, provisions, and a chance to put some distance between us and those who pursued us.

30

5 MARCH 1532 HRS

KRUGERSDORP, **South Africa**

Thirty minutes later, we were heading west on the N14, just past Muldersdrift, en route to Krugersdorp in our newly acquired Mitsubishi Pajero. I was pleased to find it in excellent condition, complete with reliable four-wheel drive. With confidence, I felt it would carry us safely all the way to Mossel Bay on South Africa's southern coast.

Finally alone and relatively secure for the moment, I took time to brief Caitlin on my previous conversations, aware she had only heard my half of each call and was missing critical details. She also wasn't yet familiar with the Relief Solutions team, so I answered each of her questions, clarifying roles and relationships wherever necessary.

Caitlin was adamant about calling her father, convinced he would solve our problems. It took significant effort, but I successfully persuaded her otherwise. We had no idea how deeply her father might have been involved, directly or inadvertently, in the attack at the consulate, and we couldn't risk the chance that his communications might be compromised.

Caitlin shared my deep concern upon hearing of Jimmy Liu's unsettling presence at Apex Security headquarters. We agreed without hesitation that the Chinese were likely behind the killings of Dominic and Thabo. What remained unclear was whether the sniper's intended target had been me, Caitlin herself, or both. Neither possibility was reassuring.

Our immediate objective now was simply to stay hidden—off everyone's radar, unseen, and untraceable.

One benefit of driving a right-hand-drive vehicle was that it allowed Caitlin to administer first aid to my wounded left arm as I continued steering. With her assistance, we managed to remove my jacket and cut away the sleeve of my shirt. Caitlin might not have been combat lifesaver trained, but the extensive first-aid training she'd received working with the World Refugee Committee made her surprisingly adept. With confidence and efficiency, she applied rapid-seal wound gel and a liquid skin adhesive to close the three-inch gash on my arm. Several horse-pill-sized 800-milligram Motrin tablets soon reduced the sharp pain to something more tolerable.

I found an old-school, foldable paper map of South Africa in the glove compartment, and Caitlin quickly proved herself a capable navigator. We determined we'd reach Ventersdorp in roughly ninety minutes, where we would then turn south onto the N12. That route would take us straight to Mossel Bay on Africa's southern tip. Given the late afternoon hour, I estimated we'd arrive by sunrise tomorrow morning. The goal was simple: maintain our anonymity and put significant distance between us and the chaos behind us in Joburg.

Caitlin broke a brief silence as we drove steadily west. "So what happens when we finally get to Mossel Bay?"

"That's exactly what Stacy and Stitch are working on," I replied. "Our job is to reach Mossel Bay without anyone noticing. Their job is figuring out how to get us safely out from there. Hopefully, your father will be in a position to assist."

As we approached a large green sign on the roadside, yellow letters indicated Ventersdorp to our right, while Krugersdorp and the R28 continued straight ahead.

"Turn here," Caitlin said suddenly, pointing to a road branching sharply to the left.

"But we're heading right," I replied, slightly confused.

"Turn left, Milo. Now!"

Trusting Caitlin, I turned left, unsure of the reason but confident in her instincts. The two-lane road wrapped around a large truck stop or parking area filled with a variety of semi-trucks and trailers.

"Keep going," she urged. "Just ahead."

"What are we—" My question trailed off as a sign on a large building came clearly into view on our left: Cradlestone Mall.

"We need supplies for the drive and for when we reach Mossel Bay," Caitlin explained. "We don't have our cell phones anymore, so we can't just look things up on the way like we normally would. Here's a mall, and there's no way my picture or name has been circulated to the police yet. It's still too soon. You stay here...I'll be back in fifteen minutes."

My arm hurt too much to argue, and Caitlin was clearly right. Quickly, I listed a few essentials I thought might help, though she already seemed aware of what we'd need. As she entered the mall, I used the opportunity to make an important call.

I dialed Stacy.

"It's me," I said as soon as she picked up. "We have the car and are heading west. Stopped briefly outside Krugersdorp for supplies. What's the news?"

"I've got something," Stacy replied, her voice steady yet laced with concern. "The shooting at the consulate is headline news on CNN. By now, every news channel in South Africa is broadcasting it. Thankfully, CNN blurred your face in the CCTV footage. Eyewitnesses have stepped forward, and it's obvious from the footage you and Caitlin were victims, not aggressors."

"Well, that's at least some good news," I said. "Have they identified us publicly yet?"

"Not publicly, no," Stacy answered, "but my contacts in the State

Department and SAPS indicate they're fully aware it was you and Caitlin Bishop."

"What about Secretary Bishop...has he issued a statement?"

"No, nothing at all," Stacy replied. "He's completely silent on the matter."

I sighed. "So, where does that leave us?"

"Unclear," Stacy said. "There's still a Wanted Person Alert for one Milo deCogan, complete with your detailed description. Every police officer in South Africa has that information now."

"Wonderful," I muttered.

"The bad news is the shooting at the consulate has made your apprehension SAPS's top priority. The good news is, word is getting out about Caitlin's abduction in South Sudan. The media are linking the consulate incident to the attack on the WRC compound. Sources say upcoming news stories will speculate you were sent to rescue Caitlin, but something went wrong. Bottom line, Milo—you two need to lay low until we sort this out."

"Understood," I said, mentally processing the situation. "Caitlin should be back shortly, and we'll head south immediately. Hey, can you explain the situation with Sunny throwing my phone in a lake? What's Stitch's plan there?"

"That's Stitch's idea," Stacy replied. "We know your satphone is secure, but your regular phone could technically be tracked through South African cell towers if someone had access. And the Chinese probably have that access."

"So you want them chasing my phone? Won't they realize it's a trick when they find it underwater?"

"We don't think so," Stacy explained. "I'll give Stitch full credit here. The one person whose movements are completely transparent and continuously tracked is Jessica Reid, thanks to her State Department-issued phone. We're positive the Chinese have her monitored."

"Okay, so what exactly is your move?"

"Stitch instructed Nate and Jessica to head west from Maputo toward the South African border. They're on a course that would theoretically link up with your phone, currently being moved by Sunny. Nate and Jessica will stay put in Ressano Garcia, right at the Mozambique-South Africa border. Someone clever enough, like the Chinese, will assume you're fleeing eastward to reconnect with Jessica and Nate. They'll watch them, believing you'll show up eventually. Hopefully, this diverts their attention away from your real route."

I absorbed this, admiring Stitch's tactical thinking. "That's brilliant. Speaking of Stitch...where's he now? And what's our final plan from Mossel Bay?"

Stacy hesitated. "Actually, we've adjusted the plan. We no longer want you heading to Mossel Bay. Continue west on the N14 and go all the way to Port Nolloth."

I frowned, unfamiliar with the name. "Where the hell is Port Nolloth? I thought I knew South African geography pretty well, but that name doesn't ring a bell."

"It's on the Diamond Coast, a quiet fishing town near the Namibian border on South Africa's northwest coast," Stacy explained. "It's isolated and small. I've booked an Airbnb there for a month and coordinated with the caretaker to stock extensive supplies. Your cover: you're a reclusive Canadian author finishing a manuscript. You want absolutely no disturbances."

"Nice," I said. "Can anyone track the booking?"

"I'll ignore that," Stacy replied with mock annoyance, "because I know you didn't just question my tradecraft. The booking was made through a literary agent in Toronto, fully prepaid for thirty days, with a thousand-dollar food and beverage allowance."

"I never doubted you," I said truthfully.

"I'll text you the exact address and the lockbox code. Port Nolloth is quiet; tourists and weekenders are common enough not to raise suspicion."

"Sounds perfect," I said. "Could you also send driving directions? We have a roadmap for the main routes, but we'll need detailed instructions once we get near Port Nolloth."

"Will do. You'll mostly take N14, with a few key turns your map covers. The R382 is your only access road into town, and I'll text specifics from there. Given your current location, expect about fourteen hours driving time."

"Understood," I said.

"It's remote almost the entire way," Stacy added. "Make sure you refuel in Upington, about 650 kilometers from you now. There are two twenty-four-hour stations there. After dark, you won't find much open elsewhere."

"Thanks, Stacy," I replied. "Call immediately if anything new surfaces. I'll check back in a few hours."

After hanging up, I expected Caitlin's imminent return, yet it was another twenty minutes before she finally emerged from the mall. At first glance, I barely recognized her. She wore a wide-brimmed straw hat and large designer sunglasses. Her frizzy light-brown hair was neatly tucked beneath the hat, making her appear nearly ten years older. She looked completely different from the Caitlin Bishop who had entered the mall earlier.

She carried several large shopping bags and moved quickly toward the Pajero. I began opening my door to help her, but a sharp pain from my arm reminded me to remain discreet, avoiding possible CCTV cameras.

"Got everything you need?" I asked as she climbed into the vehicle.

"Oh, definitely," Caitlin replied. "We're all set. Let's go. I'll fill you in once we're back on the highway."

31

6 MARCH 0040 HRS

UPINGTON, **Northern Cape Province, South Africa**

Just past midnight, we'd been driving steadily for over eight hours. The dashboard readout indicated forty kilometers of fuel remained. For the last hour, I had mentally calculated and recalculated our fuel consumption repeatedly, becoming increasingly confident in my estimations. According to Stacy's intel and the mile markers along the N14 highway, a 24-hour gas station was just ahead. The distant cluster of lights emerging through the darkness lent further confidence to my calculations.

For the most part, the drive had proven mercifully uneventful, just as we'd hoped. My arm throbbed, a constant, distracting ache, but at least it kept me awake and alert. Caitlin had wisely stocked up on energy drinks and candy bars during our earlier stop, and those also contributed significantly to my alertness.

Beside me, Caitlin slept soundly in the front passenger seat. Semi-reclined, curled up beneath my windbreaker serving as a makeshift blanket, she seemed finally at ease. Earlier, Caitlin had offered to drive, but maintaining control was second nature to me, and I wasn't nearly tired enough to surrender the wheel. It wouldn't be my first sleepless night, and should anything go wrong with SAPS,

I preferred being in direct control. Still, she had been sleeping peacefully for just over an hour, and although reluctant, I knew I would soon need to wake her before we stopped for fuel.

The first hour had been spent cautiously navigating Johannesburg's suburban traffic. The N14 was technically a highway, though it hardly resembled highways elsewhere in the world. In practice, it was essentially a straight road, one lane in each direction. While the posted speed limit was 120 kilometers per hour, roughly seventy-five miles per hour, our actual speed had fluctuated frequently. For the initial hundred kilometers, numerous small villages along the route required us to slow significantly, sometimes down to just sixty kilometers per hour.

Once darkness fell, the traffic thinned out considerably. Yet, because our primary goal was to remain unnoticed, I avoided passing slower vehicles aggressively. The last thing I needed was a speeding ticket or drawing unnecessary attention. Consequently, our pace had remained careful, steady, and slow.

The real highlight of our drive thus far had been Caitlin's call with her father a few hours earlier. To ensure it couldn't be traced, we had routed the call through Stacy, whose tech wizardry securely patched us into Secretary Bishop's line.

"Hello, Dad," Caitlin said as soon as her father answered.

"Caitlin! Are you okay? Where are you?" George Bishop's voice was thick with genuine concern—a reassuring sign, even though we still weren't sure whose side he was really on.

"I'm safe, Dad. I wasn't harmed."

"Thank God. Caitlin, please tell me where you are," Bishop urged. "I can send help. Are you in Johannesburg? Can you reach the embassy in Pretoria?"

"Dad, for now I'm safe," she responded.

"Can you speak freely?" Bishop pressed. "Are you alone?"

"Whirlibird, Dad," Caitlin said. "Is that better?"

Bishop audibly sighed with relief. I was proud she had set up a prearranged code word, a fundamental technique I taught in every

Working in Dangerous Environments course, including the one Caitlin attended at the World Refugee Committee. Her father, clearly reassured by her use of the code, softened his tone.

"Okay, good. Thank God," Bishop said. "Caitlin, please tell me exactly where you are. I can arrange DSS protection. I'll help you... just let me know."

She glanced toward me, then took a steadying breath. "Dad, I'm with Milo. Right now, I don't know who else I can trust. But I trust him completely."

Bishop's voice cracked with emotion. "You don't think you can trust me?"

"I do trust you, Dad," she said. "But I don't know if this phone is secure, or what exactly I can safely say. Right now, Milo is the only one I'm certain can protect me."

A heavy silence stretched across the line. I anticipated Bishop insisting again that Caitlin reveal her location. Before the call, Caitlin and I had discussed the importance of not sharing our whereabouts, despite her inclination to tell her father everything. At one point, we'd even considered feeding him false information. Ultimately, we had agreed that silence would be safest.

"Alright," Bishop finally conceded. His voice softened, almost resigned. "People I trust told me Milo was the best. I always taught you to trust your instincts. If your instincts tell you Milo is your safest bet, then trust those instincts."

"Thank you, Dad."

He cleared his throat. "Tell me, Caitlin, what *exactly* happened at the consulate?"

She hesitated before answering. "Dad, they were waiting for us. How is that even possible? We didn't tell anyone where we were going, yet armed gunmen were already positioned there when we arrived."

"The footage I've seen shows Milo was shot," Bishop continued, sidestepping Caitlin's pointed question. "Is he okay?"

Caitlin looked toward me. We had agreed not to reveal my injury. "Yes, he's fine," she said, honoring our agreement.

"Dad," she pressed. "Why are the Chinese after me? What's really happening? Why me?"

Bishop exhaled heavily. "It's complicated, Caitlin. Too complicated. You've gotten caught up in something you never should have. I never would have taken the actions I did if I'd known it would put you in danger."

"That still doesn't explain how they knew we were going to the consulate," Caitlin insisted.

"I honestly don't know," Bishop admitted, sounding genuinely bewildered. "I had my rooms and phones swept repeatedly. I never trusted my staff with any details. Jessica was the only one I allowed to call the consulate, strictly to avoid compromise."

He paused, his tone turning urgent again. "Caitlin, please—if you can reach the embassy or consulate, I can protect you."

"Isn't that what you said earlier?" she countered. "It didn't work out too well last time. Two innocent men died trying to protect me. Do you even realize how that feels, Dad?"

Caitlin's voice broke with emotion, tears streaming down her cheeks. I knew the conversation wasn't going to get any better. Gesturing with my hand in the universal signal, I silently advised Caitlin to wrap it up.

"I have to go now, Dad," she said. "I'll call you tomorrow."

"Wait, Caitlin! Just—" He paused, clearly emotional. "I love you. Please call me back as soon as you can."

"I love you too, Dad," Caitlin said, ending the call.

We drove in silence briefly, neither of us learning much new from the conversation. Still, I couldn't shake the impression that George Bishop was caught in circumstances beyond his control. It seemed he would do almost anything to protect his daughter, yet something else severely limited his options. Something perhaps even more important than his daughter's life.

. . .

Just after midnight, the lights of Upington appeared in the distance. It was time to wake Caitlin. I reached over, touching her arm gently, and she startled awake.

"Where are we?" she asked, quickly pulling herself upright and realizing her seat was still reclined. She took a moment to adjust it.

"We're approaching Upington," I answered, scanning the road. No headlights appeared behind us or in the opposite direction, as had been the case for a long stretch. "Are you ready?"

She glanced around, still gathering herself. "You're just going to do it right here?"

"Why not?" I replied. "It's as good a spot as any."

Without further discussion, I pressed down on the brake pedal and brought the Pajero to a stop on the roadside gravel. Earlier we'd debated finding a smaller road to turn off on, but without the benefit of digital maps, we'd always spotted them too late.

The vehicle halted; Caitlin swung open her door and stepped onto the roadside. I put the SUV in park, hopped out, and scanned both directions again. Empty darkness surrounded us, no cars in sight. Above, the stars were so dense they blurred into a silvery haze, a luminous wash across the sky that made the heavens feel closer, like the universe had folded in on itself to watch. We circled quickly around the rear of the vehicle, passing each other near the trunk. A brief urge to high-five her as if we were a relay team flashed through my mind, but I suppressed it, unsure if she would find the gesture humorous.

Caitlin slipped into the driver's seat, and I settled into the passenger side. She adjusted the seat while I helped fasten her seat-belt. In the far distance, faint headlights appeared behind us, urging us onward.

"We should move," I said.

"Got it," she replied, her voice steady.

She shifted the Pajero into gear and pressed the accelerator a bit too firmly. The rear tires fishtailed briefly, then gained traction, propelling us westward on the N14. Caitlin rapidly brought the vehicle up to cruising speed as the lights of Upington gradually transformed into distinct buildings and houses.

In the darkness, the size of the town was hard to gauge, but Stacy had provided mile markers for two 24-hour gas stations, and one was coming up shortly. Caitlin eased our speed down to about seventy kilometers per hour. In the distance behind us, a commercial truck slowly gained ground.

We had developed this plan together earlier. What Caitlin hadn't realized was that South African gas stations were full-service, meaning anonymous fueling would be impossible. When I explained this earlier, Caitlin suggested wisely that she drive. We would appear as an ordinary couple traveling, and I could recline my seat, place my baseball cap over my face, and pretend to sleep. At least that was our hope.

Paying in Rand rather than credit cards allowed Caitlin to remain inside, reducing exposure to CCTV cameras likely placed around the station.

Ahead, blue neon lights came into view, gradually resolving into a canopy above gas pumps. A large white ENGEN sign shone brightly, and the station was set slightly back from the road. Caitlin slowed, turned onto the service road, and entered the station. Brightly lit with four gas pump islands out front, a convenience store labeled BI-LO Shop in bold red lettering stood to the right. At this late hour, it appeared empty.

Caitlin pulled carefully up to a pump and switched off the ignition. No one was visible outside or inside the store, despite its brightly lit interior.

"Shit," I muttered, peering from beneath my cap, positioned in a reclined pose that allowed me some visibility.

Caitlin's voice grew tense. "What should I do?"

I glanced at the fuel gauge. Thirty kilometers of gas remained, enough to reach the next station if necessary, but I preferred not risking it.

"Just wait a moment," I advised. "Maybe the attendant's stepped away."

I counted silently to thirty, noticing Caitlin's anxiety building.

"Should I go inside?" she asked, shifting nervously. "Maybe they need me to pay first?"

"Just tap the horn briefly," I instructed.

"You're joking, right?"

"No," I insisted. "This is South Africa. Say what you will, but we're a white couple in a nice car in the dead of night. Tap the horn. He'll come out."

Caitlin honked the horn.

Peeking carefully beneath the cap's edge, I spotted a young black attendant looking out curiously from the store window. His expression shifted quickly from suspicion to friendliness as Caitlin waved at him from inside. Dressed in jeans, a red t-shirt, and a blue vest, the attendant hurried toward our vehicle.

Caitlin already had her window down. "Good evening," she said, unexpectedly slipping into an awkward Irish accent. I fought hard not to chuckle beneath my cap. The accent hadn't been planned, and I quietly admired her improvisation—though I hoped the young South African hadn't encountered many actual Irish travelers.

"Good morning, ma'am," the attendant replied cheerfully, his voice youthful enough that I wondered if he was even twenty.

"Could you fill it up with premium, please?" Caitlin requested, maintaining the friendly accent.

"Yebo," the attendant replied, moving to the SUV's gas tank at the rear.

Knock, knock, knock!

The attendant tapped briskly on the driver's rear window, startling us both. I stayed perfectly still.

"Ma'am, is there a button? The gas cover won't open."

We hadn't considered this earlier. Caitlin looked down and quickly located the button near her right ankle, pressing it. The gas cover released audibly with a faint pop.

"Thank you, ma'am. Just a moment, please."

Relaxing slightly, we listened to the sound of the gas pump engaging and petrol filling the tank. We weren't sure of the exact cost, but Caitlin had two thousand five hundred Rand already counted out, ready to hand to the attendant.

Suddenly, headlights flashed through the rear window, and a vehicle pulled into the station. Perhaps this was good. Another car could distract the attendant from paying too much attention to us. I carefully peeked again to see a white four-door sedan pull to a stop outside the shop. It took only a split second to register the blue and neon-yellow stripe on the car's side and the large word "Police" printed boldly along the bottom.

Caitlin stiffened beside me.

"Shit," I muttered. Just our luck.

I slid my hand over hers, squeezing slightly to reassure her. Stay calm, my touch hopefully communicated. Stay cool.

I still carried the Z88 pistol, but I had already mentally committed to not drawing it on SAPS officers. They were simply doing their jobs, and harming innocent people was out of the question.

I watched closely as the officer stepped out of his vehicle, an over-weight Indian man who hitched up his gun belt with a practiced motion.

"Sir!" The attendant shouted across the lot, drawing the police-man's attention.

The officer turned toward us, eyebrows raised in question.

"Sir!" the attendant yelled. "The coffee's fresh inside. Help your-self. I'll be right in!"

The cop waved in acknowledgment, heading into the store. After another minute, the tank was full. Relief coursed through my body.

"That'll be eighteen hundred and forty Rand, please," the atten-dant announced.

Caitlin quickly handed over nineteen hundred Rand. "Danke schön, keep the change," she said, still strangely blending her accents.

"Thank you, ma'am!" the attendant replied, heading back toward the store and the waiting policeman.

"Let's move," I urged.

Caitlin started the Pajero, shifted into gear, and eased onto the road, accelerating smoothly south on the N14. As we pulled away, she suddenly began laughing, relief and adrenaline bubbling over. In moments, we were both laughing.

"'Danke schön'?" I asked, raising an eyebrow. "And what about that accent? Was that supposed to be Irish?"

"It wasn't that bad!" she laughed. "I figured if he remembered me, he'd recall the accent first. Plus, don't they have lots of Germans around here?"

"Yes, but not many Germans with Irish accents," I laughed, shaking my head as we sped into the darkness.

32

6 MARCH 0110 HRS
N14 HIGHWAY, NORTHERN CAPE PROVINCE, SOUTH AFRICA

THE ROAD WEST of Upington stretched empty beneath the stars, miles of hard tar and silence. The Pajero's headlights carved a pale tunnel through the desert darkness, the twin beams fading into the horizon where sky and sand fused into one endless line. The hum of the tires was steady and hypnotic, broken only by the low growl of the diesel engine and the occasional clatter of pebbles kicked from the shoulder.

Caitlin sat forward slightly now, her fingers tight around the steering wheel. The relief she'd felt leaving the gas station had faded to a restless edge. Every few minutes, she glanced at the rearview mirror, then at me, then back to the mirror again, as if expecting something to materialize from the night.

"We're clear," I said, trying to sound casual. "Just road and stars."

She nodded but didn't relax. I understood. The adrenaline from the gas station encounter hadn't yet worn off, and exhaustion had sharpened her nerves to a fine point. The night out here was too still, too absolute.

Outside the windows, the desert lay barren and ghostly, a pale world washed in moonlight. A herd of springbok grazed off the roadside, their eyes glowing green when caught by our beams before vanishing back into the scrub. The air felt strangely alive, humming with unseen life and distant heat.

I glanced at the digital display. Six kilometers since we left Upington. Tank full, road empty. We'd be clear of populated areas soon.

"Feels like the world's asleep except us," Caitlin offered.

"Let's keep it that way," I said.

She smiled, then looked into the mirror again. Her brow furrowed. "Milo," she said. "There's something behind us."

I turned my head slightly. At first, I saw nothing but the black ribbon of highway trailing into the void. Then, far back along the curve of the road, a blue-white flash cut the dark, once, then again, pulsing in rhythm.

"Blue lights," she whispered.

My stomach tightened. The flicker came again, closer this time. I leaned forward, narrowing my eyes.

Definitely blue—rotating, steady, and moving fast.

"Shit," I muttered under my breath.

Caitlin gripped the wheel harder. "Police?"

"Maybe," I said. "But we didn't pass a checkpoint. There's no traffic out here." I scanned the mirror again. "And they're moving too fast."

"What do we do?" Her voice was rising. "We can't outrun them."

I weighed options. Evasive driving in open terrain was suicide— flat desert, straight road, nowhere to hide. And we couldn't risk a confrontation if it was real SAPS. I'd already made the decision back in Johannesburg that I wouldn't pull a gun on a South African officer unless he was going to hurt us.

I turned to her. "Keep calm. Don't speed up. Don't brake. Just maintain a steady pace. If they're real, they'll signal us to pull over."

Caitlin nodded, her breathing shallow. "You think they followed us from the station?"

"Doubt it," I said. "But I don't like coincidences."

The lights grew brighter, filling the mirrors with flickering blue. I could see now the faint outline of the vehicle—a small sedan, low to the ground, gaining quickly.

"They're closing fast," Caitlin said, panic edging into her voice. "Really fast."

I looked over. Her knuckles were white on the wheel. "It's okay," I said. "Stay calm. Pull over, and keep the engine running."

"What if—"

"Just do it." I didn't mean to sound harsh, but now wasn't the time for explanations.

I slid my hand down to my thigh, my fingers finding the grip of the Z88 pistol. Habit made me press-check the slide, confirming a round was chambered. The metallic click was soft but loud in the small cabin.

"Okay," Caitlin whispered, inhaling deeply in an attempt to remain calm.

She eased the Pajero to the shoulder, gravel crunching beneath the tires. Behind us, the sedan slowed too, coasting to a stop about fifteen meters back. The blue light bar washed over us in rhythmic pulses, strobing through the interior—blue, black, blue again.

I glanced at the mirror. "Two occupants," I said. "Driver getting out."

Caitlin turned her head. "That's not the same guy from the gas station," she said, voice tight.

"Just stay relaxed. Hands on the steering wheel," I murmured.

Through the glare, I saw the first figure approach—tall, solid build, wearing a dark police shirt but no hat. His flashlight beam cut through the window and swept across the interior, briefly blinding us. The other man circled wide to my side, staying back near the rear bumper, his outline barely visible.

Something about his posture sent an alarm through me. The stance was wrong. Too tense, too deliberate. Then I saw it: a glint of metal slung low at his side, the distinctive folding stock of an AKMS rifle.

"Caitlin," I said. "We've got a problem."

"What?"

"Don't look. Second man—he's armed. Not SAPS-issue."

She stiffened, whispering, "What do we do?"

"Wait," I said.

The driver's-side officer stopped at Caitlin's window, leaning down. The flashlight beam hit her face, then mine. His expression flickered with surprise, genuine surprise, at seeing a woman behind the wheel. For an instant, he even smiled.

"Evening, ma'am," he said, his accent thick and rural. "May I see your license, please?"

"Of course," Caitlin said quickly, her voice wavering.

She fumbled toward the glove box, buying time. I watched his face closely, reading the details. The man was Black, with bushy hair that barely fit under his SAPS cap, mutton-chop sideburns, and a wispy goatee—giving him an unprofessional, almost slovenly appearance. The man's sleeves were too short, his uniform faded and not fully buttoned. No reflective vest, no radio on his belt. And, most telling of all, no name tag.

"Where you comin' from?" he asked in heavily accented English.

"Johannesburg," she said evenly.

"Heading where?"

"Cape Town."

He nodded slowly, his flashlight sweeping again into the car. "Step out, please."

Caitlin froze. "Is there a problem, officer?"

"Step out," he repeated, firmer.

She turned her eyes to me. I gave a slight nod. *Comply, for now.*

As she opened her door, I did the same, the cool desert air rushing in. I kept my movements calm, unhurried. The officer on my side was still just a silhouette against the harsh light from the sedan's beams.

I stepped out, squinting into the glare. The moment I saw it— jeans, sneakers, no duty belt—everything clicked.

These definitely weren't cops.

The rifle wasn't an anomaly; it was the truth.

Blue Light Bandits.

I didn't hesitate, letting my years of training take over.

I pivoted, raising the Z88 in one fluid motion, sight picture locking center mass on the man with the AK. Two quick squeezes of the trigger. The pistol kicked twice in my hand. The man staggered backward, collapsing against the hood of the sedan before sliding to the ground.

I swung over the Pajero's roof, catching the second man's shocked expression—the moment of disbelief frozen in his wide eyes. Before he could reach for the weapon at his hip, I put a single round dead center in his forehead.

He dropped instantly, the flashlight tumbling from his hand and spinning across the asphalt before clattering to stillness.

Caitlin screamed. "Oh my God! You shot them—you shot the police!"

I turned to her, my voice firm, measured. "They're not police. Stay back."

The blue lights still flashed, painting everything in surreal color—the bodies, the road, Caitlin's pale face. I moved quickly, sweeping around to the back of the Pajero. The second man lay sprawled, blood pooling beneath his shirt. His rifle, a well-worn AKMS with a folded stock, was still clutched in one hand. I kicked it free and crouched to check his pulse. Nothing.

I looked over the sedan. The paint was dull, oxidized, and peppered with rust spots. The license plate was half-covered in mud, and the blue light bar on the roof was portable—mounted with suction cups, wires dangling through the window. The interior was stripped, no police radio, no computer terminal.

Blue Light Bandits.

They were a plague on South African highways—criminals dressed as police, targeting travelers on lonely roads, robbing, raping, killing. SAPS was stretched thin, and too often, these impostors operated unchecked.

Caitlin was trembling by the open door, hands over her mouth. I walked to her, my gun still in my right hand.

"They're not cops," I said again, gently but firmly. "Look at their car. Look at their clothes."

She hesitated, then turned her head toward the sedan. Her breath caught when she saw it—the jeans, the mismatched boots, the flashing lights taped to the roof.

Her voice broke. "Oh my God... they—"

"Criminals," I said. "Pretending to be police. They would've killed us, Caitlin. You understand?"

Tears welled in her eyes, but she nodded. "I...I thought you..."

"I know." I holstered the weapon and reached for her shoulders. "It's over. You're safe."

She collapsed against me, her body shaking. I held her there, the desert silence pressing in, the fake police lights strobing like ghosts around us.

After a moment, she pulled back, wiping at her eyes. "What now?"

I crouched again, grabbed the AKMS, and slung it over my shoulder. "Now we go."

I left them where they fell, two bodies in blue and denim, lying under a sky thick with stars. The wind carried the faint hum of insects and the steady pulse of the stolen light bar still flashing on the road.

Sliding back into the driver's seat, I adjusted the seat from where Caitlin had moved it forward. Caitlin climbed in beside me, silent. I put the SUV in gear and eased back onto the highway.

In the mirror, the fake police lights faded behind us until they were swallowed by the desert.

Caitlin turned her face toward me, her voice barely above a whisper. "How did you know?"

I kept my eyes on the road. "I didn't," I said. "Not until I saw the jeans."

She exhaled shakily, still trying to process. "And if they'd been real police?"

I glanced at her. "Then I'd be dead," I said simply. "If not tonight, then as soon as Liu's men got their hands on me in a South African jail."

We drove in silence after that, the road unspooling ahead, an endless black ribbon under the weight of a sky so crowded with stars it looked almost milky, like spilled light. The air smelled faintly of cordite and dust. Somewhere behind us, two men lay cooling on the asphalt, their false badges shining blue in the dark.

For the first time that night, Caitlin reached over and took my hand. I didn't pull away.

We didn't speak again until we saw the faint shimmer of dawn breaking over the western horizon and the outskirts of Port Nolloth ahead.

PORT NOLLOTH, **Northern Cape, South Africa**

I rolled over, instinctively reaching for my phone on the table before remembering I no longer had it. Instead, I checked my watch: 10:37 a.m. It felt odd to be without a cellphone, but at least my watch allowed me to stay oriented with the time.

As my eyes adjusted to the room, my attention shifted toward Caitlin. She was curled into an oversized fabric armchair next to the sofa where I had slept. Her eyes were closed, and she breathed steadily, hands tucked neatly beneath her head and knees drawn up beneath an afghan she had found somewhere in the house.

The drive from Upington to Port Nolloth had been nearly five hours of monotonous darkness punctuated occasionally by terrifying near-misses as animals darted across our path, threatening an abrupt and unfortunate end to our escape from Johannesburg. Most of the route, the N14 resembled little more than a single ribbon of asphalt, often unmarked and barely wide enough for two vehicles to safely pass each other from opposite directions. Few vehicles accompanied us, just an occasional commercial truck lumbering through the darkness.

I drove the entire way, while Caitlin slept fitfully beside me, catching brief moments of rest after the harrowing ordeals she had endured. The candy bars and energy drinks sustained me, although their consumption necessitated two impromptu roadside bathroom breaks. After sharing the intense experience of being shot at and fleeing a nationwide manhunt, something as simple as relieving ourselves on the side of the road felt oddly natural.

The long drive provided plenty of opportunity for conversation. Caitlin gradually opened up, sharing details about her family and upbringing. She spoke of her mother, who had passed away from cancer when Caitlin was young, and the profound impact the loss of her brother had on her as a teenager. She described herself as "daddy's little girl," revealing a deep closeness with her father. Yet, beneath the surface, it was clear that she knew little of his business empire or political dealings.

Caitlin also offered insight into her complex relationship with Jessica Reid, whose presence seemed to evoke mixed emotions. Jessica had become something of a surrogate big sister to Caitlin, who admired Jessica's self-assuredness and ability to carve a space for herself within the traditionally male-dominated diplomatic circles. Jessica regularly stayed with Caitlin and her father in their homes in Martha's Vineyard, Boston, and Washington, D.C., and had even vacationed with them several times.

Still, Caitlin admitted to feeling occasional jealousy toward Jessica's closeness with her father. Although Caitlin trusted Jessica, convinced there was nothing inappropriate in the relationship, she sometimes wondered if Jessica had deliberately ingratiated herself into their family to advance professionally. Caitlin didn't hold it against her; Jessica had proven her loyalty to Caitlin and her father repeatedly, but the transactional nature of their relationship occasionally left Caitlin uneasy.

I swung my legs onto the floor, engaging my core muscles to sit upright on the sofa. My back felt stiff from the nearly fourteen-hour drive. I stretched, flexing sore muscles and taking a deep breath.

We had arrived in Port Nolloth about half an hour before sunrise, slowly navigating down the town's central avenue, fittingly called Main Road. Stacy had provided detailed directions to our rental house, though judging from the town's size, it seemed almost impossible to get lost.

With a fluctuating population between two thousand and five thousand, depending on the season, Port Nolloth presented itself as a typical coastal community, albeit one two hundred miles from anywhere. Cape Town was almost three hundred and fifty miles south, and nothing substantial existed along South Africa's Atlantic coastline once north of Saldanha Bay, two hundred and fifty miles south. Northward lay Namibia, even more barren than this desolate part of South Africa's Northern Cape province.

Everything valuable in this vast, arid land lay beneath the surface —hence the nickname, Diamond Coast.

As we drove into the sleeping town, commercial one- and two-story buildings appeared, clustered primarily around Main Road. Street lamps lit up a modest downtown area, which seemed confined entirely along this central artery. Several small grocery stores gave way to low-rise shops offering clothing, cell phone repairs, freshly cooked seafood, and liquor.

Approaching the ocean, Main Road bent sharply right, just past a modest police station. Heading north, we passed a small church, a gas station, and a sizable whitewashed school building.

According to Stacy's instructions, we followed Main Road north for a quarter mile toward the lighthouse and turned left onto an unpaved sand road that ran parallel to the shoreline. Our rental was situated two blocks north of the lighthouse.

I had anticipated a tall, historic brick lighthouse, painted white with a lantern room perched elegantly atop its structure. I was sorely disappointed. Port Nolloth's "lighthouse" was merely a thirty-foot metal scaffold structure topped with a rotating white beacon—functional, perhaps, but severely lacking in charm or history.

Our rental house was a modest L-shaped cottage. Its primary space comprised an open room that combined a living room, dining area, and kitchen, facing the ocean across the narrow sand road, which dead-ended two houses further north. The furnishings inside were basic, mismatched, yet completely functional. To the right, facing away from the ocean, was the small master bedroom that formed the base of the "L." Two additional tiny bedrooms and the single bathroom extended off the kitchen area, forming the vertical segment of the "L." Behind the cottage, a six-foot-high concrete block wall enclosed a courtyard and parking area.

Upon arrival, we parked the Pajero inside the courtyard, locked the gate securely behind us, and spent about an hour inspecting the premises and checking the extensive supplies Stacy had thoughtfully pre-ordered. We had enough food and essentials to sustain ourselves comfortably for several weeks, provided we didn't grow tired of pasta, rice, and canned soup. Fortunately, our local caretaker had also stocked several pounds of fresh beef, chicken, and flavorful boerewors sausage—more than enough to keep us comfortable as we figured out our next move.

The sofa creaked gently as I stretched, prompting Caitlin's eyes to flutter open slowly.

"Good morning, sunshine," I greeted her, hoping for a cheerful start to the day.

"Morning," Caitlin responded, pushing herself upright in the chair and taking a moment to regain her bearings. It struck me suddenly that she probably hadn't slept in the same place twice over the last week.

"You got about three solid hours of Zzzs. How do you feel?"

She stretched her arms, tilted her head from side to side, then twisted lightly in the chair. "Not bad at all," she replied with a quiet smile. "Considering everything."

"Well, as I always say, any day alive is a good day."

She laughed, and I realized just how important it was to keep her smiling.

"If you say so," she teased.

"I most certainly do," I insisted, standing and glancing out the wide front windows. Sunlight streamed brightly across the sand road and down onto the dunes, illuminating the vast Atlantic beyond. The turquoise sea, topped with white-capped waves, rolled gently against the shore. Despite its beauty, I knew from my previous stays in Cape Town that the water was far colder than it appeared.

Caitlin joined me, standing close beside me as we quietly admired the picturesque scene.

"So, what's next?" she asked. "Hungry?"

"Definitely," I agreed enthusiastically. "Let's raid the kitchen."

We moved toward the kitchen and began reassessing our food supplies. Caitlin pulled out eggs and a block of sharp cheddar cheese, while I reached for a coil of boerewors sausage. I felt slightly guilty cooking it indoors, knowing the traditional method was grilling it over an open braai, but we didn't have that option.

Working alongside each other, we moved effortlessly around the kitchen, playfully nudging each other and laughing at our own antics. The situation seemed almost domestic, and for a moment, we were simply two people enjoying each other's company without the cloud of our circumstances overhead.

Within minutes, the makings of an omelet were coming together nicely. Sausage sizzled enticingly in the pan, while bowls of scrambled eggs and freshly shredded cheddar cheese awaited their turn. Caitlin opened the refrigerator and pulled out a chilled bottle of white wine, Rickety Bridge Chenin Blanc. Given the stress she had endured, a glass of wine seemed entirely fitting for breakfast.

Expertly uncorking the bottle, she poured two generous glasses and handed one to me, lifting hers in a toast.

"I haven't properly thanked you, Milo," she said, suddenly earnest. "I genuinely don't know what would've happened to me without your help."

I hesitated, raising my glass and unsure how best to reply. I wanted to downplay it, to assure her that no thanks were necessary, but I sensed the importance of this moment for her. My mind flashed to Crispus and Dominic, and I saw the emotion brimming in Caitlin's eyes as she remembered her colleagues who'd lost their lives in South Sudan.

"Bitte," I replied, exhausting roughly twenty-five percent of the German vocabulary I knew, hoping she'd catch my playful reference to her earlier German 'thank you' at the gas station.

She smiled knowingly, eyes brightening.

Still got it, Milo.

I opened my arms in invitation, and Caitlin stepped willingly into a warm embrace. I squeezed her tightly as she rested her head gently against my chest. I couldn't begin to fathom the sense of isolation she must feel. While we'd quickly bonded through our intense shared experience, she was still essentially alone, a young woman abducted and seemingly left to fate by her own father, now hiding in a remote house along the Diamond Coast of Africa with a man she'd only recently met.

"Tell me it's going to be okay," she whispered, her voice muffled against my chest.

"I don't know how to say that in German," I joked, drawing out her laughter.

Before she could respond, I added, "It's going to be okay, Caitlin." I stroked her hair, feeling her tension gradually ease. We remained there, quietly holding each other, until the sizzling sound of burning sausage snapped us back to reality.

"Time to add the eggs!" I exclaimed, breaking our embrace with gentle reluctance. We clicked glasses, and I took a satisfying sip.

"Sláinte," I said with a wink.

I finished preparing the omelets while Caitlin took charge of the toast. After downing the wine, I switched to water, while Caitlin opted to stick with another glass of the Chenin Blanc.

It was nearly noon by the time we finished breakfast. Our meal tasted wonderful, and we kept our conversation purposely away from the chaos and danger of our recent ordeal. It was comforting to watch

Caitlin relax, if only momentarily. After we cleared the table, I mentioned needing to make a few phone calls, hoping she might use the opportunity for a much-needed nap.

"I have some calls to make," I announced.

"Nope," she countered, a mischievous smile forming on her lips. "We have something much more important first. The biggest danger right now is you being recognized, so we need to deal with that first and foremost."

Without waiting for my reply, Caitlin jumped from her chair and dashed into the master bedroom, where we'd placed our bags earlier. She returned moments later holding a white bottle and a small bag from Clicks.

"What's that?" I asked, genuinely confused.

"This, my dear Milo," she said with exaggerated seriousness, "is L'Oreal hair coloring. Ever wonder what you'd look like as a blond?"

"Uh, no," I responded. "Does it require sucking out half my brain?"

I couldn't resist making her laugh, and it worked perfectly.

"No," she chuckled, trying to regain composure. "But it does require removing about half your hair."

"My hair's already short," I protested.

"Not short enough," she declared, pulling a pair of hair clippers from the bag. "Come on, take your shirt off and grab a dining room chair. I'll cut your hair, and then we can dye it."

Forty minutes later, I sat in the middle of the main room, shirtless, with a towel draped carefully around my shoulders. Caitlin had ordered me to sit still for another ten minutes, so I watched patiently as she swept up what appeared to be nearly all my hair. It wasn't quite the high-and-tight of my Ranger days at Fort Benning, but judging by the sheer amount of hair on the floor, it must've been close.

She hadn't yet let me see a mirror, and I grew more uneasy each time she murmured "Oops!" under her breath and giggled.

"Ten more minutes," she said, glancing at me. "Then we'll rinse you off, and voilà—you'll be a new man."

"Sure," I said, masking uncertainty. Truthfully, I didn't mind the haircut or even the hair dye. The experience had been surprisingly pleasant, especially when Caitlin abandoned the applicator brush and used her gloved fingers to massage the dye into my freshly shorn scalp. I even tolerated having my eyebrows dyed.

What I hadn't anticipated or particularly enjoyed was the thick layer of Vaseline she spread along my hairline, ears, and neck. The greasy sensation was unsettling, and having never been fond of lotions or creams, Vaseline was certainly not on my list of preferred experiences.

Once the time elapsed, Caitlin guided me to the kitchen sink and thoroughly rinsed my head. As I ran my fingers through my newly short hair, vivid memories flashed through my mind—Sunday afternoon haircuts at Fort Benning, carefree days of being a young Ranger, the world stretching wide open before me.

She led me into the bathroom, and I finally saw myself in the mirror.

"Jesus Christ," I said. "I look like fucking Billy Idol!"

She burst into laughter. "Is he a German porn star? Because you look exactly like one," she teased through her giggles.

"You're kidding me, right?" I asked, barely suppressing a grin. "And how exactly would you know what a German porn star looks like?"

Caitlin continued laughing, stepping close to use the towel to shape my newly blond spikes.

"I'm just kidding," she assured me. "Honestly, it looks great. No one would mistake you for Milo deCogan now."

I peered into the mirror again, turning my head from side to side to get the full effect. I reluctantly agreed with her; it was a good disguise.

"Seriously, Caitlin," I said, raising an eyebrow, "do you really not know who Billy Idol is?"

PORT NOLLOTH, **Northern Cape Province, South Africa**

I placed the antenna extension kit on the window in the living room, allowing me to sit comfortably on the sofa while I used the satellite phone. My first call was to Stacy.

"How's it going?" she asked without preamble. I'd spoken with Stacy briefly when we'd arrived in Port Nolloth, but this would be our first substantial conversation since settling into the safe house.

"So far, so good," I replied. "The house is perfect, and we've got everything we need."

"I don't think you'll have to be there too long," Stacy said. "We're working to get you out ASAP."

"Excellent. Tell me what's happening in Joburg first. Did they arrest Deangelo? Am I still wanted for murder? We have no internet or news access here, so we're in the dark."

"Good news and bad news on that front," Stacy began. "The bad news: our plan to mislead them into thinking you and Caitlin were headed toward Maputo hasn't gained traction. Nate's been monitoring things in the town just inside the Mozambique border, and there's no indication anyone's looking for you in that direction. We've hacked into SAPS databases, and there's no targeted search toward Mozambique. I just sent Nate back to Maputo."

"But there's still a nationwide APB out for me in South Africa?" I asked.

"Yes, technically it's called a Wanted Person Alert, and it's still active."

"Great."

"Here's the good news, though," Stacy continued. "Major Dlamini of the Special Task Force seems to have it out for you, but we've managed to get into his emails and confirm he's bought and paid for by Jinhai and Jimmy Liu."

"That explains why he denied Dominic's request to assault the compound in Joburg. And also how Liu knew to return to the compound on Coronation Road so quickly."

"Yes, it does."

"But that doesn't exactly sound like good news, Stacy. Am I missing something?"

"You are," she said. "The Major's compromised, but his superior officer is Colonel Waldemar DeVries. He's apparently a huge fan of yours. He's now assumed command of both investigations—the shootout at the consulate and the murder at 11 Coronation Road. He's also submitted an order to terminate the Wanted Person Alert. With SAPS being less than efficient, it might take a few hours to process, but at least things are moving."

"DeVries? I don't think I've ever met anyone named DeVries at SAPS."

"You haven't," she said. "Colonel Waldemar DeVries was Dominic's godfather and mentor within SAPS, his guardian angel."

"Interesting," I said, mulling over the new information.

"Even more interesting: he's Victoria Thornton's father."

"No shit?"

"No shit," Stacy confirmed. "She called Daddy immediately when things started unraveling. He got Deangelo out of custody right away. After hearing the whole story, Colonel DeVries has gone all-in trying to undo the damage that Jimmy Liu and the Chinese have caused."

"That certainly counts as good news. Do you think I'll be cleared to travel soon? We need to get Caitlin back home."

"We still have some obstacles," Stacy cautioned. "Our sources in South Africa indicate the Chinese are maintaining a full-court press to locate you two. They're calling in favors across the country, tapping legitimate business contacts and even underground criminal networks. They definitely want Caitlin alive, and you dead."

"Great," I sighed. Just another day in paradise, I thought grimly.

"I confirmed with Jessica that your passport remains suspended. You'll be detained if you try to use it. She's working with the Secretary of State to lift the suspension, but she's had trouble reaching him. Apparently, it's easier to revoke a passport than to reinstate one."

"Okay. And Stitch? Is that part of the plan still on track?"

"Yes, that part is solid," Stacy replied. "You know Stitch. He'll move heaven and earth to stick to the plan."

"Where is he now?"

Stacy paused briefly, likely referencing her computer. "Stitch is about four hours out of Windhoek, driving south fast as he can."

"And the plan is still to—"

"Yes," Stacy interjected. "I'm working on precise routing to ensure the smoothest linkup for you both. It's not as straightforward as you might imagine. This is the most barren place I've ever seen, worse than Libya or western Iraq."

"I know," I agreed. "There's nothing out here but sand and diamond strip mines."

"Exactly. I'm concerned about the sparse road network. You have a handheld Garmin GPS, but the key is getting you and Caitlin across the border discreetly. The best spot we've found is about a three-klick walk for both of you, and you'll have to wade or swim across the Orange River."

"That's manageable."

"Just remember, Milo, you'll be crossing at night. You might be a former Army Ranger and Green Beret badass, but Caitlin isn't. Have you discussed this with her yet?"

"Not yet," I admitted. "But I think she'll be up for it. Stitch will still meet us on the Namibian side, correct?"

"Yes, that's the plan," Stacy confirmed. "Again, my worry is the limited routes. The C13 Highway is essentially the only road heading north from the border, and there's nowhere else to go."

"I agree. Keep looking at options, but I think this is our best bet. Run it by Stitch; his gut feeling is usually spot on. Ideally, I'd love to charter a plane out of Oranjemund, but that would be too easy for our adversaries to track."

"I'll do that," Stacy said. "Milo, there's something else, more bad news. I heard from a contact back in Goma. Melissa Jenkins died earlier this morning."

"What?" I asked, incredulous. "How could that happen?"

"They're not sure yet. My contact said the doctors suspect Melissa went into sepsis overnight. Her body just started shutting down, and nothing they did worked. The embassy is collecting her body, and I'm told they'll do an autopsy when she's returned to the states."

"Jesus," I muttered. "That poor kid. Fuck! I hate these assholes, you know that?"

"I know," Stacy said, giving me a moment to process the news. I took a few deep breaths, regaining my composure. I could do nothing more for Melissa now. I vowed to keep this news from Caitlin until we were safely home.

"Any updates on the Chinese and Secretary Bishop?" I asked, shifting gears. We still didn't fully grasp the situation between the two parties, and understanding their conflict was critical to keeping Caitlin safe. Why did the Chinese want her so badly? And what was Bishop hiding?

"So far, we've gathered a ton of information, but as with most intel operations, the trick isn't just collecting puzzle pieces; it's assembling them into a coherent picture," Stacy explained. "The short answer: we haven't found the smoking gun. However, we do have some intriguing facts. First, George Bishop's business empire is heavily invested in the mining industry throughout Africa."

"Is that a secret?" I asked. "Or illegal?"

"Neither. However, it's not something readily available to the public."

"Is Bishop in business with Lin Jinhai or any other Chinese nationals?" I followed up.

"Not that we can identify, at least not directly. Bishop primarily invests as part of international consortiums partnering with local groups. These groups develop mineral resources while ensuring some profits remain locally. It's not exactly altruism, but it's a far better arrangement for the host countries than what the Chinese offer."

"So Bishop is a competitor to the Chinese?"

"Well," Stacy hesitated, "Not exactly. It's an incestuous business environment, somewhat akin to the Texas oilfields. All the players know each other. There's plenty of profit to go around, so sometimes they compete, and sometimes they collaborate."

"Okay," I said, still uncertain about what this meant for us. "Anything else?"

"Bishop's also been openly critical of Chinese expansion in the South China Sea, and he's become the administration's leading advocate for a harder stance against China. He's also encouraged the President to build closer ties with Taiwan."

"That can't be good for China, but does it impact Jinhai enough to kidnap Bishop's daughter?"

"Milo, nothing we've found rises to a level that would justify kidnapping the Secretary of State's daughter. It's an irrational move, by individuals known for being highly rational players. We're clearly missing something."

"Agreed," I said. "What about those early reports of a massacre north of Gangura? Were you able to get any more details? I know it's a long shot, but it is an anomaly."

"Nothing so far," she replied. "I talked to Crispus' number two guy at Panther Security. He offered to send a team up to put eyes on the ground and find out what's happening, but it's a long drive. They're still enroute."

"Okay, I understand. Keep digging, Stacy. You and your team are doing outstanding work. Something will surface soon; it always does. Caitlin plans to call her father later today; maybe we'll learn more then."

"Okay," Stacy said. "Anything else we can do? You two should be safe in the house. Just lay low."

"That's our plan."

I disconnected the call and spent the next half hour contemplating the many pieces on this ever-changing three-dimensional chessboard. Every time something seemed to make sense and I understood why a specific move had been made, another piece on the board forced me to reconsider my entire strategy.

No matter how long I racked my brain, I couldn't put together a plausible scenario in which the Chinese kidnapping of Caitlin Bishop made sense. She seemed to be merely a pawn with limited strategic value, yet with the potential to bring all of the opponent's attention down upon them. Her work with the World Refugee Committee had no significant global political impact, and her ransom value to the Secretary of State remained unclear. After all, he was ultimately just an advisor to the President, without unilateral power to change U.S. foreign policy toward China. And Lin Jinhai, despite his close ties to the Chinese political leadership, was still fundamentally a businessman. Businessmen made rational decisions based on risk assessments concerning profit and loss. I couldn't see how the kidnapping of Caitlin passed that risk-reward analysis. The potential reward seemed minimal, and the risks appeared overwhelming.

Caitlin had grabbed a paperback from the bookshelf in the corner of the living room and retired to the master bedroom. I noticed it was a novel by Deon Meyer, one of my favorite authors, who just happened to be from Cape Town. The book, Fever, was set in the dry, arid Northern Cape region where we now found ourselves. I sincerely hoped that was the extent of the similarities; from what I remembered, Fever was a post-apocalyptic survival novel, and I had no intention of enduring an apocalypse in Port Nolloth.

If Caitlin was as exhausted as I was, she was likely already asleep. I'd just decided to slough off to one of the back bedrooms to catch a few Z's when the satellite phone buzzed. I quickly grabbed it—Stitch.

"What's up?" I answered.

"Hey, brother," Stitch replied, "how's it hanging?"

"Tired," I said. "I'm hoping to rest soon. It's gonna be another long night. Any change to our link-up time? I talked with Stacy earlier, and she mentioned you two were still pinpointing the exact location."

"Yeah, that's why I'm calling."

I waited for him to continue, knowing from experience that it was never good when Stitch hesitated.

"Go ahead," I prompted. "I'm listening."

"Your buddy Jimmy Liu and his boss seem to always be one step ahead of us. I think—"

"Did something happen? Is that why you're calling?" I cut in, sensing urgency in his voice.

"Yes," he admitted. "Stacy called me. She thought you might be asleep and didn't want to disturb you unnecessarily, but she wanted my opinion. South Africa's Border Management Authority just doubled the manning of its Namibian crossing points in the Northern Cape."

"Okay," I said, struggling to believe the South Africans knew we were already in the Northern Cape.

"I just got off the phone with Deangelo after speaking to Stacy," Stitch continued. "His father-in-law, Colonel DeVries, is on our side. Dee said DeVries passed along that someone high in the South African government wants to stop you and Caitlin from leaving. DeVries oversees all criminal investigations in Gauteng province, the province surrounding Joburg, and he said you've already been ruled out as a suspect in both the consulate shooting and the Chinese compound incident. Video evidence and eyewitness accounts clearly show your innocence, and the CCTV footage the Chinese provided has been exposed as doctored and discarded as fake. Yet, despite all this, someone is pressuring the SAPS general above DeVries to continue pursuing you. The latest alert at the Namibian border specifically includes you and Caitlin."

"Did they mention her by name?" I asked. "Wouldn't that draw the U.S. State Department's attention pretty quickly?"

"That's just it. They didn't mention her by name or include her photograph. They've only provided a description and stated she's traveling with you. But they do have your name and photo."

"Shit," I muttered, realizing how complicated things had become. "So, what do you think? Is our cover blown?"

"That's why I'm calling. You're safe there for now, as long as you don't leave the house—at least for a little while. Our original plan was for you to drive up to the border tonight, cross on foot, and for me to pick you up on the C13 highway east of Oranjemund."

"Right," I said. "We weren't planning to use the official crossing at Alexander Bay, so does it really matter how many guards they post or who they're looking for?"

"Milo, you've seen the terrain, right? They might call it the Diamond Coast, but it's essentially desert—no towns, no people, no lights. You'd be driving a dirt road to the border about two miles east of the main crossing point. Your headlights would be visible for miles. You don't have night vision, so you'd have no choice but to use headlights. You'd be a sitting duck if anyone decides to investigate."

He was right. Damn it!

"Could we go further east, maybe? Or cross at dawn?" I asked, hesitant to alter the plan but equally reluctant to stay in South Africa longer than necessary.

"We could, but it would be more difficult and would leave you even more exposed. Only two dirt roads branch off the R382 heading north from your current location to the border. Both are visible at night from either the manned crossing at the Ernest Oppenheimer Bridge or the small airstrip east of there. I'm not sure if the airstrip is staffed at night, probably not, but do you really want to take that chance? You'd be the only vehicle out there after dark."

"I see your point," I admitted.

"And going even farther east," Stitch continued, "you'd have to head east out of Port Nolloth instead of north. Several dirt roads lead up to the border, but you'd be traveling fifty to a hundred miles on some of the roughest terrain imaginable. You'd be just as exposed, only for even longer."

"Agreed," I replied. "Our original plan is now too high-risk. Do you have an alternative in mind?"

Like any former Delta Force senior NCO, I knew Stitch wouldn't bring me problems without also offering a solution.

"I do," Stitch confirmed. "And you didn't even let me get to the risks north of the border. There's only one real highway to Windhoek without traversing Moon Valley, which would take at least a full day." He paused briefly before continuing. "As much as I'm tempted to quote lyrics about a desert highway, cool wind in our hair, traveling by road across southern Namibia would create too much of a funnel we couldn't escape if spotted. Here's my solution: I'm just east of Aus on the B4 highway. I was about to turn south on the C13 toward the border, but if I stay on the B4, I can be in Luderitz in an hour."

"What's in Luderitz?" I asked. "Isn't that a fishing port?"

"Exactly," Stitch replied. "I'll charter a fishing boat. If I push the captain a bit, we can be off Port Nolloth by late morning tomorrow."

"Okay," I said, considering this new development on the three-dimensional chessboard. "Are you worried we'll get stuck on a boat? What if the authorities catch us?"

"That's the point, Milo. If they catch you in your vehicle, it'll be the South Africans, and the Chinese have us by the balls there. But once you and Caitlin are on a boat, we'll be out of South African territorial waters within an hour. Milo, Port Nolloth doesn't even have a coast guard. There are dozens of fishing boats that run up and down the coast every day. We'll blend right in."

I was beginning to see the merits of Stitch's plan.

"Okay," I said. "And you and Stacy agree this is our best option?"

"We do," said Stitch. "I even talked to Nate in the last hour, as he's done a few operations in Namibia. Some of this was his idea, and he's fully supportive that this is the way to go."

"Then let's do it. What do you need from Caitlin and me?"

"Stay in the house, and be ready to roll between ten and noon tomorrow. I'll call when I'm offshore and heading in on their smaller boat. I have your location, so the fallback contingency is I'll just knock on your door."

"Sounds good," I said. "Keep it simple, stupid. I like it."

"If anything goes wrong," Stitch added, "just hang tight in the house getting fat, and we'll figure out another way to get you out."

35

6 MARCH 2005 HRS

PORT NOLLOTH, **Northern Cape, South Africa**

The calls with her father always began the same way—gentle voices that soon frayed into tension—and always ended with Caitlin fighting back tears. Tonight was no different.

He sounded distracted, detached, like his mind was elsewhere. She tried to imagine the weight he carried as Secretary Bishop—every briefing, every decision—yet still it hurt to feel like one more variable in some larger equation.

"Are you safe?" he asked before she could even say hello.

"Yes, Dad," she said. "I think so."

"You *think* so?" His voice rose, sharp and incredulous. "What do you mean? Where are you?"

"Milo thinks it's better if I don't say."

"What?" The word cracked through the sat-phone. "He thinks I can't be trusted? I hired him, for God's sake."

"And you fired him, remember?" she replied, calm but firm. "Let's not forget what happened." She paused, steadying her breath. "You said yourself he's the best person to keep me safe. So let's trust his judgment."

Silence hung for a heartbeat before he exhaled, the sound weary. "You're right. I understand, sweetie. It's just...there's so much you don't know."

"Then tell me," Caitlin said. "It might help us figure out who's after me."

A pause. Then only the faint hiss of the line.

"Dad?"

"It'll all be over in less than a week," he said at last. "I can explain everything then. You won't be in danger anymore."

"You're scaring me," she whispered. "What's happening in a week?"

More silence. Caitlin pressed her lips together and waited him out.

"Listen, honey," he said. "You have to trust me. There's a lot going on, but I have it under control. Now that you're safe, everything will work out."

"But I'm *not* safe!" she blurted. "Scarface may not have me locked up anymore, but people are still out there. Don't you get that?"

"I told you I'd send a plane anywhere in the world," Bishop shot back. "You said you'd be safer with Milo, and I agreed. There's a leak somewhere, but I'm handling it. Just stay put, do as Milo says, and in a week this will all be behind us."

"What happens in a week?"

He hesitated, then forced a brittle chuckle. "You focus on staying safe. Let me worry about the big picture. I'm the Dad, remember?"

The laugh didn't land. Caitlin's throat tightened; she blinked hard to stop the tears.

"Call me or Jessica if you need anything," he said. "Anything, Caitlin. I mean that. I love you."

"I love you too, Dad. I'll call in the morning."

The call ended. The room went very still.

Milo sat beside her on the sofa, close enough that she could feel his presence even before she looked up. He'd listened quietly to every word, his face unreadable.

Without thinking, she leaned into him, pressing her face to his chest. His muscles tensed beneath her cheek; she felt him wince when her arm brushed the bandaged shoulder, yet he didn't pull away. His arms came around her, steady and protective.

She began to sob—deep, uncontrolled, a release she hadn't known she needed.

"Shhh," Milo murmured, his voice low and even. "It's all right. We'll be out of this tomorrow."

For half a minute, she cried against him, feeling the day's strain drain out of her. The solidity of his chest beneath her palm calmed her. She noticed the rhythm of his breathing, the warmth of him. When she looked up, she saw those eyes—green, but never the same green twice. Sea-glass one moment, mossy forest the next. They seemed alive, shifting with mood and light.

She wondered what it would be like to kiss him. To surrender, just for a second, to the pull that had been building between them since Sudan. His gaze lingered, and she could see the same thought flicker in him. She leaned forward slightly, so did he, until, at the last moment, he drew back.

"Are you okay?" he asked, his tone neutral, professional again.

"Yeah," she said, forcing a smile. "I just wish we knew what this was all about."

"You and me both," he said, standing.

He crossed to the fridge, opened a bottle of water, and drank half of it in one pull. His movements were brisk, controlled, the discipline of a man who didn't allow himself to linger on temptation.

Caitlin watched him. The late-afternoon light slanted through the blinds, painting stripes across the room and across his face. He looked exhausted. He *was* exhausted. The gash on his shoulder, the sleepless night, the constant vigilance—it all showed in the set of his jaw.

She, on the other hand, felt strangely alive. The four-hour nap earlier had cleared her fog. She remembered waking to the scent of simmering tomatoes and garlic, wandering into the kitchen to find

Milo at the stove, stirring a pot of bolognese. Pappardelle bubbled beside it, and she'd joined him, buttering bread and laughing at his terrible Italian accent.

They'd eaten together, talking sports to avoid talking danger. Milo had surprised her with how much he knew about Boston teams; they'd traded stories about Fenway and the Garden until the dishes were washed and the illusion of normal life dissolved.

Then his tone changed. "Let's talk about tomorrow," he said.

"Okay," she replied, instantly alert. "I thought we were driving tonight. You said we might have to cross the border on foot."

"That was before the update. The plan's changed. We're leaving by boat."

"By boat?" she repeated. "Where are we supposed to get a boat?"

"We're not," he said. "It's coming for us. Stitch left Namibia on a fishing vessel, a big one, the kind that stays out for weeks. He'll run down the coast and pick us up. Should be here by mid-morning."

"*Should be?*" she asked.

"Depends on how fast the captain's willing to push her. They're about a hundred-sixty nautical miles north—call it sixteen hours."

"And that's safer than driving to the border?"

"Much," Milo said. "The South Africans have tightened every checkpoint. They're looking for me and for a female American, no name given. Your description's close enough."

Her stomach tightened. "Jesus. That's not good."

"No. And the terrain's no help. You haven't seen much of it, but it's flat desert out there. Our headlights would be visible for miles. There are only two dirt tracks leading north, both easy to monitor."

"Seriously?" she said. "Only one real highway between here and Namibia?"

He nodded. "That stretch is called Moon Valley. Nothing but sand and rock. To the west you've got a park the size of Massachusetts—pure dunes, no roads, no people. Totally restricted."

"Okay," she sighed. "I get it. Desert equals death trap. Boat equals maybe not."

He smiled. "Exactly. Stitch will text at midnight with an ETA. We'll pack light—sweatshirt, water, whatever you need for the tender run."

"Got it."

She studied him. The weariness around his eyes told its own story. After the long drive and the firefight that had nearly killed them, he looked ready to collapse.

He grabbed a paperback from the shelf and disappeared into the master bedroom. She lingered on the couch with an old magazine about Cape Town, flipping through glossy photos of the V&A Waterfront. The images, harbor lights and laughing tourists, felt like postcards from another life.

She imagined walking those docks with Milo. No chase, no threat, just sunlight, wine, and the easy rhythm of conversation. The memory of his hand in her hair returned, and with it a pulse of heat that surprised her.

It had been a long time since she'd been close to anyone. Her last boyfriend belonged to another lifetime, a college romance that had faded before she left for South Sudan. Milo was different—older, grounded, capable of command. She admired that control, but part of her wanted to see it crack.

Before she could talk herself out of it, she set the magazine down and padded to the bedroom doorway.

The bedside lamp cast a soft amber glow. Milo lay on his back atop the coverlet, the paperback splayed across his chest, his hands folded loosely over it. He looked asleep, but she could feel him watching her even before one eyelid lifted.

She smiled, caught. "Sorry," she whispered. "Mind if I join you? I don't want to be alone."

He said nothing, just lifted his right arm in quiet invitation.

Caitlin crossed the room and slid onto the bed, fitting herself against his side. His arm wrapped around her shoulders; her head found its place on his chest. She heard his heartbeat, steady as surf. Her hand rested on his stomach, feeling the slow rise and fall.

For a moment, everything else—fear, pursuit, questions—fell away.

She closed her eyes, letting herself drift in that impossible calm. Then curiosity tugged at her. She opened her eyes and glanced down the length of him.

He wasn't asleep. And the unmistakable tension in his body told her why.

Her pulse quickened. Before reason could intervene, she slid her hand lower and cupped him through the fabric of his pants.

Milo reacted instantly, sitting up, disentangling her arms from him. "Whoa." His voice was firm but gentle. "Caitlin...stop."

She froze, stunned. "What? I just thought—"

"I know what you thought," he said, catching her shoulders. "Believe me, I was thinking the same thing. But we can't."

Her cheeks burned. "Oh my God. You have a girlfriend."

He actually laughed, the sound breaking the tension for a heartbeat. "No. Nothing like that."

"Then what? Because you're older? I don't care."

He smiled sadly. "It's not that either."

"Then what?" she demanded, voice cracking. "Did I do something wrong? Do you not—"

"Caitlin." His tone softened but carried authority. "You didn't do anything wrong. And yes, I find you incredibly attractive." He squeezed her arms lightly. "But we're still in hostile territory. I need both of us focused. If we lose that now, we could lose everything."

She tried to grin, to deflect the sting. "I think I can keep you focused."

He laughed again, shaking his head. "Rain check. Dinner, when this is over. We'll see where it leads. I promise."

She searched his face, saw the sincerity there, and knew she couldn't push him further. "Fine," she said softly.

He exhaled, relieved. "Good. Now let's try for a few hours' sleep. Stitch's update should come through around midnight."

Caitlin nodded. She lay back beside him, eyes open to the shadows rippling on the ceiling, listening to the slow rhythm of his breathing until, at last, exhaustion carried her away.

36

PORT NOLLOTH, Northern Cape, South Africa

A faint clatter from the other room nudged me awake—Caitlin, most likely, moving around the kitchen, the smell of instant coffee cutting through the salt-heavy air. I'd slept in short bursts through the night, dozing between updates from Stitch. His last message, not long before dawn, said he was making better time than expected. If the weather held, he'd be just off the coast after nine. Two more hours, and we'd be gone from this place for good.

I stretched on the bed, trying to enjoy a final moment of stillness before the day's chaos resumed. That's when the satphone buzzed on the nightstand. Stacy.

"What's up?" I answered, voice still thick from sleep.

"You need to get out of the house, Milo. Now."

Her tone cut through the last remnants of fatigue.

"What happened?" I swung my legs off the bed and was already moving.

"A plane owned by one of Jinhai's shell companies landed at Kleinsee forty minutes ago. Thirty-five kilometers south of you. Normally an hour's drive, but if they push it..."

"I understand," I said, grabbing the Z88 from the bed and

jamming it into my waistband. My heart rate quickened, but my voice stayed level. "I'll tell Caitlin. We'll move out. I'll call once we're clear."

I ended the call and strode toward the door.

"Caitlin," I called as I stepped into the main room.

I didn't get another word out.

The hit came from nowhere, a streak of metal and motion. I turned my head instinctively, and the steel bar meant for my temple slammed into my cheekbone and ear instead. The world exploded white with pain. I dropped to my knees, dazed but conscious. If that blow had landed square on, I'd have been out cold, maybe worse.

From the kitchen, Caitlin screamed—high, sharp, terrified. I caught a glimpse of her, an arm in black fabric across her throat, a gloved hand muffling her mouth. My attacker loomed above me, bringing the weapon up again for the killing strike.

Every muscle screamed to protect my head. But instinct—hard-earned, drilled deep—told me otherwise. Raising an arm would only give him the chance to shatter bone and end it on the next swing. Instead, I rolled sideways and forward, just as the second strike came down. The rod crashed into my shoulder, pain flaring like lightning through my back as my bullet wound tore open again. I knew I had seconds, maybe less, before he corrected his stance and swung again.

But by then, my right hand was already on the pistol.

I didn't think, didn't plan—I simply acted. I brought the weapon around from my side and drove the muzzle up between his legs, firing twice.

Men can fight through almost anything—pain, shock, fear. But not that. Not two rounds through the family jewels. The man folded instantly, a strangled grunt escaping his throat as blood spread dark and fast across his pants.

I slid backward into the doorway for cover, raising the pistol again. One more shot, clean to the bridge of his nose. The round cracked through the room and ended him where he lay.

One down.

I rose, keeping the gun up as I pressed my back to the wall. The pounding in my head faded behind the rhythm of breathing, the focused calm that follows the first shots. I eased around the doorway, "slicing the pie," revealing the room degree by degree.

The threat came into view almost immediately.

Caitlin stood in the kitchen, rigid, Liu's arm locked across her neck. His face half-hidden behind her shoulder, a sliver of that same smirk I'd seen in Juba curling his lip. I could still hear his voice in memory, smooth and smug. Now it was replaced by the faint, wheezing drag of his breath.

Caitlin stopped struggling the moment she saw me. The instant she understood I was there, gun in hand, her body went still—calm, deliberate.

Liu shifted just enough to show part of his face. "Put your gun down or I'll—"

The rest of his sentence never came.

The crack of the Z88 split the air, louder in the confined space. The hollow-point hit him square in the forehead. The back of his skull vanished against the tile. His body dropped like a string cut loose.

Caitlin gasped but didn't scream.

I advanced fast, gun still up, ready to fire again if he so much as twitched. He didn't. Liu's body sprawled across the tile, his eyes open and glassy. One of them, what remained of it, was nothing but a ruined jelly. Blood and brain matter pooled around the base of the counter, a grotesque halo spreading wider with each heartbeat.

Caitlin stumbled forward, throwing her arms around me. She wasn't sobbing, just trembling—shock distilled into motion.

I held her close, the gun still in my right hand, finger off the trigger but ready.

You'd think my first thought would have been about the noise—the gunfire echoing through thin walls, the neighbors who might already be reaching for their phones. Or maybe relief that Caitlin was alive. Maybe even guilt over the two bodies cooling on the floor.

But no. My first thought was how every movie, every book I'd ever read about a moment like this had some kind of exchange—the villain and the hero trading last words. Threats, philosophy, humor. I had none of that. No questions answered, no explanations.

It would have been nice to ask Liu how he'd found us, who had sent him, why he'd taken Caitlin in the first place. Maybe I should've shot him in the leg, kept him breathing long enough to talk. But I'd been trained otherwise: hesitation gets people killed.

He showed his head. I took the shot.

That's the difference between fiction and survival.

Now Liu was dead, and so was our cover. The safe house was burned.

I glanced at my watch. 0700 exactly. Stitch wouldn't reach the coastline for at least two more hours.

Caitlin stared down at Liu's body, her face pale but composed. I guided her a few steps into the dining room to keep her out of the spreading blood.

"Look at me," I said, gripping her shoulders firmly. Her eyes snapped up to mine. "We're leaving in sixty seconds. Shoes, sweat-shirt, hat, sunglasses. Go."

She nodded, all business now. Whatever fear she'd felt, she'd buried it deep. "Where are we going?" she asked, voice steady.

"To find ourselves a boat," I said.

PORT NOLLOTH, **Nothern Cape, South Africa**

I put sunglasses on and stepped out of the front door, locking it behind me. Caitlin was by my side, wearing a broad-brimmed straw sunhat and large sunglasses, a shopping bag with several water bottles in her hand.

I'd pulled the one Asian man's body into the master bedroom as I'd put on my shoes, retrieved the satphone, and threw my always-ready backpack over my shoulder. The bedroom's blinds were already drawn, so I wasn't concerned about anyone looking through the window and seeing the body.

Jimmy Liu was a different story, and I had neither the time nor the inclination to move his dead body. I pushed him up against the kitchen cabinets, threw a throw rug from the living room over the pool of blood, and strategically closed several window shades.

Anyone looking into the home would find it unoccupied with nothing amiss.

I had little doubt that someone had heard the gunfire and called it in. This early in the morning, unless someone happened to be outside and hear the gunfire come from our house, I hoped the police would not have a specific address to check. They might knock on doors as part of their investigation, but I hoped we'd have at least a thirty-minute head start before someone got bold enough to break into our Airbnb.

I'd been forced to make a quick decision on whether to flee by foot or by car. Having no idea whether Jimmy Liu had reinforcements waiting somewhere up the block, I opted for walking. There was only one road into and out of town, and if the Chinese or South African authorities had information about our vehicle, they'd be able to find us immediately.

Port Nolloth was a tourist town, so I thought: let's become tourists. The Port Nolloth Harbor was just over one kilometer to our south, so I grabbed Caitlin's hand, and we walked along the sandy road to a point where we could pass through the dunes and descend to the beach. Once on the beach, we'd be below the sightline of anyone traveling in a car on the road. In ten minutes, we'd be at the harbor.

At least, that was my plan.

It was shaping up to be a lovely day, but it was only about sixty degrees Fahrenheit at the moment. A crisp onshore breeze brought the clean salt smell of the Atlantic, and the sea looked relatively calm. It was much more tranquil than yesterday when a strong southerly wind pushed wave after wave of white-capped rollers into the beach.

I'd purposely not donned a baseball hat, as I wanted anyone watching from a distance to see a very blond man walking on the beach. This wouldn't match my description, and hopefully, any interested party would look elsewhere. Caitlin held my hand tightly, and as we hit the hard-packed sand just above the waterline, we picked up our pace to walk as fast as we could.

I pulled out the satphone and dialed Stacy.

"Where are you?" She asked without greeting.

"Walking south along the beach from the safe house. Jimmy Liu and one of his associates are dead. They broke in while we slept. I have no other information. We're operating blind here, Stacy. I've never even seen a detailed map of this town."

That was true. I'd scoured the Airbnb for any brochures on the town, hoping to find a map that might point out restaurants or shops. I concluded that since this was a one-road town, there was no need for a map. I wasn't sure if that was good or bad.

"Okay," said Stacy. "I'm looking at recent satellite imagery of the town. If you're heading south along the beach, in about three hundred yards, you're going to hit some rocks. It won't be passable along the beach, but if you go up to the road, there is a paved walking path that parallels it. Get on that, and it will take you directly to the harbor."

"Got it," I said. "What about Stitch? Is he still expected here at oh-nine-hundred?"

"Yes," she answered. "I just spoke with Stitch. He's going to try to see if the captain will goose the engines a bit, but he doesn't think it will make much of a difference. Plan on nine o'clock. He said for you to either flee north in the car and find a spot on the beach to hide or do what you're doing now: find a boat and meet him offshore."

"The vehicle option is a no-go," I said. "It's too wide open, and there'd be no place to hide. We wouldn't have the ability to get away from wherever we abandoned the vehicle, and from your description, there's no place to hide one. Anyone looking for us would find us instantly."

"Agreed. You made the right call, Milo. What can I do?"

"Nothing I can think of. I just wanted you to know. Stitch gave me the info on his vessel so we can find him if we get offshore. Tell Stitch that if we lose our comms, I'll try to find a meetup point one mile offshore from the harbor."

"Okay," Stacy said. "Good luck. I'll be standing by the phone."

"Thanks," I said. "We're going to need it."

Caitlin pointed out the rocks in our path, and we angled ourselves to head up to the paved walkway. So far, we hadn't seen another person, but I saw several small fishing boats on the water, which was a good sign.

We were no longer alone as soon as we stepped on the path. Three women walked toward us on the walkway. They were dressed informally and seemed in no hurry, so my assumption was they were out for a morning walk, or maybe they'd just walked their children to the nearby school. They were heading right for us, and we'd pass in less than a minute.

As we approached the three women, I glanced to my left to see a SAPS police car heading down a side street toward the water, pointing directly at us. The white sedan with the blue and yellow markings and lights on top was unmistakable. Caitlin noticed it at the same time and squeezed my hand.

"Talk to me and laugh," I said to her.

Caitlin didn't need any more coaching and grabbed my arm gaily.

"Oh, Milo, such a lovely day for a stroll," she said. She twirled around me as if she hadn't a care in the world. I laughed along with her.

Our mood must have been infectious. We were now only twenty meters from three women, and they smiled as they saw us laughing.

"Guten Morgen, schöne Damen," I said in my poor attempt at sounding German. I bowed my head slightly in greeting as Caitlin nodded hello. To cap off my acting job, I waved and smiled at the police car as it turned north back toward our Airbnb. The SAPS officer in the car barely glanced at us.

Caitlin squeezed my arm as we continued walking south, neither of us daring to speak.

Sixty seconds later, we were off the promenade and now on a proper sidewalk a few blocks north of the harbor. We could see it clearly and walked directly onto the concrete pier that formed the principal protection for the harbor.

"I didn't know you spoke German," Caitlin said, smiling despite the stress of the moment.

"I don't," I said, smiling back. "But I can say 'good morning, lovely ladies' in about twenty languages."

She relaxed her grip on my arm, her stride a bit less tense, hopefully thinking we were on our way out of this mess. At least that's what I hoped she was thinking—myself, I wasn't so sure.

There didn't appear to be much action: maybe a dozen small, weathered fishing boats moored in the narrow harbor and a single large fishing boat, perhaps seventy feet long, tied up at the end of the pier. None of the boats, including the large one, appeared exceptionally seaworthy. Of more significant concern was a gate across the entrance to the dock, barring admissions to those unauthorized, and there didn't appear to be anyone walking around that we could speak with.

"Shit," I said as we walked up to the gate. "I'm not sure if nothing's open or that there just isn't any type of customer service here."

"What should we do?"

"Well, I don't see us swimming out to one of those boats and hot-wiring it. The water's too cold, and I don't know how to hot-wire a boat."

"They don't teach you that in super-secret Army snake eater school?"

"Not when I went through," I said, smiling and looking around. There had to be an option.

Behind us, there were several commercial buildings opposite the harbor. There were no signs, but they looked like they had something to do with the harbor. We walked over to the one-story building, and it was clear that people were working inside.

"What do you think?" I asked Caitlin.

"Maybe you should wait here, and I'll go inside?" She offered. "No one is officially looking for me, and a white woman might be more disarming than a German porn star."

"Okay," I smiled. "You win. I'll sit on this bench and keep a lookout. See if you can get us a morning tour of Port Nolloth by boat. Leaving ASAP."

"Roger," she said, giving a half-assed military salute.

Caitlin opened the door and went inside. The door closed behind her, and I couldn't hear anything. I waited patiently, confident in Caitlin's people skills.

One minute turned into five. My patience was beginning to whither.

I looked to my right and saw another SAPS patrol car turn onto Beach Street, a few blocks to my north. Not wanting to chance another contact, I turned and walked through the door Caitlin had entered.

She was standing in front of me, speaking into a cell phone. Two black men and a woman stood behind a counter, looking at us. They smiled at me as I entered. Maybe they recognized me from a German porn video.

"Ah, yes, that would be great," Caitlin said, nodding as the person on the other end of the line replied.

"Okay. Your price is acceptable. We will wait for you. Yes, we'd like to get going as soon as possible," She said, pausing. "Yes. See you soon."

Caitlin clicked the button to terminate the call and then handed it back to the man closest to her. "Thank you so much," Caitlin said. "He's going to be on his way here in a few minutes."

"You're welcome," said the man. "We are happy to help you."

"This is my partner, Hans. Is it okay if we wait here for Ezra?"

All three locals nodded and turned to go back to what they were doing. I looked around, and the place seemed to be some type of fish supply company.

"What's up?" I said to Caitlin when the others were out of earshot.

"That was Ezra of Ezra's Boat Rides and Fishing. Apparently, Ezra is the only game in town when it comes to renting a boat."

"And Ezra has agreed to take us out?"

"Yes," Caitlin replied. "He said he'd be here in fifteen minutes."

"Okay," I said. Every minute we stayed here was a minute closer to the police finding the bodies. Once they did, they'd lock down the town.

Twenty minutes later, Ezra arrived. It was a very long twenty minutes. There were no windows in the office, and our only portal to the outside world was through the glass of the front door, which looked directly out onto the harbor. We had no visibility over anything happening behind the building, which was the center of Port Nolloth.

We knew it was Ezra pulling up as his battered truck had hand-painted lettering proclaiming "Ezra's Boat Rides," and below that, painted in a different color in different handwriting, the word "Fishing." The lettering made me smile as I was pretty sure Ezra would be a true businessman open to negotiation.

Caitlin and I walked out to greet him. I turned as we walked, glancing back toward town and half-expecting a dozen police cruisers with lights flashing to be lined up along Beach Road. Luckily, there wasn't a police car in sight.

"Hello, I'm Hans," I greeted Ezra, shaking his hand and introducing Caitlin as Gwen, the name she'd used when calling Ezra.

"Good morning to you both," Ezra said. He was a carefree fellow in his fifties, skin as black as night, with a balding head and tufts of curly black hair sprouting over his ears. He wore an old collared shirt with a ratty wool sweater. I thought he might be dressed a bit too warm, especially as his forehead already had a sheen of perspiration, but then I remembered it was going to be much colder out on the water.

"We're ready when you are?"

"Where would you like to go? Anyplace specific?" Ezra asked.

"To be honest, Ezra. We're from Cape Town and spent all day yesterday in the car. We're looking for a few hours of fresh air out on the ocean. No place specific...just show us the sights."

"Sharp, sharp," said Ezra. "Follow me."

We walked south of the pier, not going anywhere near the gated entrance. In front of us was a rocky beach strewn with a couple of dozen rowboats and skiffs. Ezra walked directly to an ancient wooden rowboat. It was painted red—my guess the last time in the 1970s—and to me, it didn't appear seaworthy. However, Ezra didn't hesitate to pull it to the waters edge. He wore black gumboots that came up to just below his knee, and he maneuvered the boat so just the front half was on the beach.

"Hop in," he said.

I helped Caitlin step over the gunwale and then pushed the boat back toward the water to help our new friend Ezra. Surprisingly, it floated. At the last second, I jumped into the boat, managing to only got one foot soaking wet. The water was frigid. Ezra took his time climbing aboard, and in less than a minute, he was rowing us out toward where a cluster of boats were moored in the harbor.

We transferred to Ezra's fishing boat without incident. The boat reminded me very much of the small lobster boats ubiquitous to the New England coastline. It had a covered bridge open to the stern and a small shrouded compartment at the bow that contained supplies and equipment necessary to run the boat. The interior would provide shelter in a pinch, but it wasn't set up for luxury. The bridge had a steering wheel, basic instruments, a captain's chair, and a wider padded chair next to it that would seat two people scrunched together. I was glad to see a GPS. The gunwales on the stern had a built-in bench seat, and Ezra also had four collapsible lawn chairs for those trips with more than a few people on board.

Ezra's boat started immediately, and the engine sounded smooth. I was hopeful we'd at least be able to get out of the harbor. Telling us to hold on, Ezra put the boat in gear and motored away from the other ships, pointing the bow due west and heading out to sea.

As we cleared the mouth of the harbor, I asked Ezra to keep heading away from town but to turn to a more northerly heading. A half-mile offshore and a half-mile north of Port Nolloth Harbor, Caitlin and I sat silently at the stern, watching the shoreline. The sea was calmer than I expected, and the boat handled the rolling swells admirably.

Caitlin pointed.

It was difficult to make out from this distance, but four SAPS patrol cars appeared parked around one house north of town. It looked very similar to our Airbnb.

"How fast does this thing go, Ezra?" I asked.

ROME, **Italy**

The best French croissant I've ever had was in Rome. Go figure. The pain au chocolat didn't so much flake as dissolve—thin lacquered layers giving way to warm, buttery air—and the double cappuccino hit like a small, merciful sunrise. For a minute, the entire last week receded to the edge of the table with the sugar grains.

"I could be talked into moving to Rome," I told Caitlin, balancing on an undersized and unstable wire-framed chair designed by someone who hated knees. The café's tiny table looked like a stage prop. It felt like one, too.

"Don't try the gelato," she said. "You'll never leave."

We sat on the sidewalk along Via Vittorio Veneto, trees trading shadows with the late-morning sun, the Palazzo Margherita peeking between branches. The clink of cups, the steady hiss of milk on steam, a fluency of languages riding the air—Rome in full ease. The last forty-eight hours had been anything but. We had climbed slowly, quietly, more than seven thousand miles north from Port Nolloth, and the trip had stitched itself into my spine.

Ezra had been better than good, he'd been professional. After I'd told him our "tour" of the coast needed to be one-way, he didn't blink.

A man who paints "Boat Rides" on his truck and adds "Fishing" later in a different hand knows how to adjust. We negotiated; we all smiled. Seventy minutes after leaving the harbor, we'd put alongside the MFV *Bogenfels Arch*, a twenty-meter fishing boat out of Lüderitz, Namibia. Stitch hauled me aboard like a lost brother and turned instantly protective around Caitlin. We paid Ezra, hugged him like family, and watched his little boat shrink to a red fleck on the sea.

The next sixteen hours were a lesson in humility. Caitlin, veteran of Vineyard breezes and Cape Cod currents, took the Atlantic's roll like she'd been born to it. I had joined the Army for a reason. The *Bogenfels Arch* smelled like old fish and cold metal and rocked with a cadence that had me rotating through sleep and vomiting with military efficiency. Privacy was non-existent; our words had to wait until land.

We nosed into Lüderitz at three in the morning. Deserted dock. No questions. Perfect.

Stitch drove the three of us to the airport, where Stacy's plan had already found traction and wheels: a long-range jet was fueled and waiting for our arrival. We lifted at first light.

Nine hours to Naples gave us the one thing you can't schedule into a crisis: space. Stacy rode shotgun via satphone. We walked Caitlin through everything—South Sudan to Juba to Yambio to Port Nolloth—and she filled in what our angles hadn't captured. There were tears, more of them than laughter, and I watched her take in the names we hadn't yet laid on her: the deaths of Crispus and Melissa. I'd held those back, not to shield her from truth, but to get her to the next thing alive.

Now the truth was the next thing.

Stacy asked a hundred questions, anchoring on Caitlin's days before Gangura—details that sounded tangential until you remembered Stacy doesn't ask for color; she paints the whole picture. I fed the answers into the chessboard in my head and moved pieces I couldn't yet see.

The question whose answer proved most elusive was *why*.

Why would Lin Jinhai order a kidnapping of the Secretary of State's daughter and then keep coming when it all went to shit? Understanding the LRA's animus in South Sudan mattered too, but until we answered the first question, the second was a footnote.

Without this answer, Caitlin and I weren't safe; we were simply not yet dead.

We weren't alone on the Via Veneto. Stitch and Nate sat at a twin table a few feet away, sentries disguised as tourists, sipping their coffee and watching the street the way wolves watch a treeline. While they were spinning the Lüderitz logistics, Stacy had been working a second thread—talking to Nate and Jessica in Maputo. She'd directed them to Rome; Jessica checked in at the embassy and pulled whatever levers needed pulling to make sure my passport would be clean at Italian immigration. Nate broke off and met us in Naples when the jet's wheels kissed tarmac.

Caitlin waved our waiter back and ordered rapid-fire in Italian. The only words I caught were "pain au jambon," which, as far as I knew, weren't Italian at all. A minute later, a plate arrived—croissant warm enough to fog the air, ham and Comté melting into one another.

"This is amazing," I said around a mouthful. I nearly added "delightful," then decided to keep my vocabulary from going soft. Some words get your Man Card revoked on sight.

"I know, right?" Caitlin said, smiling over her cup.

"Who knew you had to come to Italy for French pastries?"

"My father used to say that about England...that Oxford had the best Chinese and Indian food in the world," she said, sipping her cappuccino.

I looked up, things starting to click. "I didn't know your father went to Oxford."

"He did. A semester abroad in the mid-seventies while he was at Harvard."

"Interesting," I said. Oxford had been a crucible for me—a PhD, a handful of friendships that had outlived bad years and better ones.

The puzzle pieces always look obvious once they're snapped into place; before that, they just lie on the table, hiding in plain view. "Are you ready to see him? He doesn't know you're coming, right?"

"I haven't told him," she said. "But that doesn't mean he doesn't know." She set her cup down. "I'm ready to hear the why, Milo. I want last week to be a story we tell, not a thing we're still in."

"I hear you," I said. "Any questions about the next forty-eight hours? Once we hand you over, we won't have direct contact. Ask now."

We'd spent last night in a rented estate outside Cassino, in the foothills east of Rome—stone walls, quiet fields, a place designed for solitude. Stacy had put a framework together; we'd filled it with contingencies until it held. Step one was obvious and non-negotiable: deliver Caitlin into the protection of the U.S. Embassy in Rome.

"I'm good," she said. Then she leaned back and added, "And I can't wait to see you tomorrow. You promised we'd talk when this was over, and I'm going to hold you to it." The wink was small and reckless, and it pulled me back to a bed in Port Nolloth and the bright line I'd drawn there.

"Excellent," I said, ignoring the hook and paying the bill with more euros than the pastries demanded. Better to be generous and gone.

A familiar figure was coming up the sidewalk. I glanced at Stitch; he gave a single, economical nod. We rose as one and shifted left, the three of us moving so our bodies naturally bracketed Caitlin. To anyone watching, it would look like friends gathering their things. To anyone trained, it would read like a protective detail.

I stepped out ahead to meet him. "Tex," I said, hand out. "Thanks for meeting us. Everything good?"

"Yeah, Milo," he said, gripping my hand with that old Infantry mix of warmth and assessment. "Good to see you. You ready?"

"She's ready," I said.

He spoke into a cuff mic so discreet it might as well have been magic. An earpiece tucked into his right ear caught the reply. "Fancy," I said.

"Only the best for you," Tex deadpanned. "You said to be prepared."

"I did," I said, meaning it. "I'm glad you are."

Two Marines rounded the corner to our east, uniforms immaculate, expressions professionally blank. We were half a block from the embassy on Via Vittorio Veneto. Tex was DSS now, Regional Security Officer in this patch of Rome, but I still saw the 502nd Infantry lieutenant in the way he read the street. We'd served together once, a lifetime ago, when problems could be solved with a platoon and a map.

A van drifted into view behind us, slow, unhurried.

"The van's with me," Tex said. "More Marines. Just in case."

We moved east. The Marines ahead adjusted their pace to keep thirty meters in front, an elastic band pulling us forward. The embassy's side gate came into sight—stone and steel and American order set into Roman history. At the gate, Caitlin turned to us, handed out quick hugs, then followed Tex through the secure door and into the embassy's interior.

She was safe. I'd done the job I was hired to do.

Except I hadn't.

BUDVA, Montenegro

Yesterday, I reconvened the Council of Trent.

That's what I called the informal advisory board I'd created to keep me honest when it came to Relief Solutions' most sensitive missions—the kind that didn't appear in annual reports, and never would. As a company, I was the sole shareholder and ultimate decision-maker. But decisions made in a vacuum invite disaster, and my late wife had made me promise to never let that happen again.

Stacy, Stitch, and Nate were the visible face of Relief Solutions— my core staff—supported by a small, rotating team of specialists. On paper, we provided discreet crisis management, kidnap-and-ransom support, investigations, and what we euphemistically described as *strategic problem resolution*. In reality, we also handled a very different category of request, one whispered between former officials, ambassadors, and directors, the kind that required the utmost secrecy, discretion, and deniability. Those were the "quiet calls," the ones that came when an intelligence agency couldn't act but still needed something done.

Before my wife died, she'd extracted two promises from me about those kinds of missions.

First: *Never do it for the money*. Only if I believed, absolutely, that it was the right thing to do.

Second: *Never do it alone*. I was to assemble an advisory board—seasoned, moral, unflinching—and make sure any such mission required unanimous approval. A safeguard against hubris and the blindness of conviction.

After her death, and the inheritance that followed, I had more money than I'd ever need. That first rule was easy. The second one became the Council of Trent.

I'll admit, I didn't really know what the original Council of Trent had been. Something about Church reform, I thought—priests, indulgences, maybe the Reformation. I later learned it had taken place in Italy, not England, which tells you everything about my sense of naming. But the moniker stuck.

The council consisted of three men, each one a legend in his own field and a mentor in mine.

General Jack Donovan, former commander of the 5th Special Forces Group and later SOCOM itself. A man who'd carried both the torch and the scars of decades of covert conflict.

Major General Jon Leer, my old battalion commander from 3rd Ranger Battalion, who'd gone on to command the 75th Ranger Regiment. Tough, deliberate, brilliant under fire. A West Pointer whose integrity was beyond question.

And Raymond Conrad, former Deputy Director of Operations for the CIA, a man whose calm could still a war room and whose silence often meant more than his words.

All three had guided me at different turns of my career, and when I'd pitched them the idea of Relief Solutions, they'd said yes without hesitation.

Yesterday, Stacy convened the Council at my request. She flew to Raleigh to meet Donovan in person; Conrad drove down from Charlottesville, Leer up from Savannah. I joined by secure video link from Montenegro, my face half-lit by the laptop glow in a villa we were using as our current safe house.

I briefed them from the beginning: my first call from Secretary of State Bishop on March 2nd; Caitlin's abduction in South Sudan; the firefight at Gangura; the Chinese footprints that trailed us from Juba to Port Nolloth; and the threads now tying Jinhai's syndicate to something far larger. My conclusion was simple: our mission wasn't over. Not until we knew *why* Jinhai had targeted Caitlin and how deep his influence ran into the U.S. government.

Relief Solutions couldn't walk away while those questions were still unanswered.

I outlined the 3D chessboard as I saw it—each move, each counter—and proposed a final play designed to secure Caitlin's safety and expose whatever was festering inside the upper tiers of government. We debated for nearly three hours. The Council asked hard questions, not out of doubt, but precision. Donovan wanted to know the end state. Leer wanted to know the risk thresholds. Conrad, ever the strategist, helped refine the operation's framework, paring it down until only the essential remained.

By the end, I had what I needed: unanimous approval.

Operation *Checkmate* was greenlit.

Our opportunity centered on the upcoming Bilderberg Meeting —the modern world's most famous secret. An annual gathering of a hundred global power brokers: politicians, CEOs, defense contractors, and financiers. No press. No recordings. Just quiet rooms and consequential whispers. Conspiracy theorists called it a shadow government. Realists called it what it was: an exclusive, off-the-record conference where the elite could speak candidly about shaping the future.

This year's meeting was set for two days from now, at Sveti Stefan, the Adriatic jewel of Montenegro. An island resort so private it made Camp David look like a bus terminal.

Last night, Stitch, Nate, and I had left Cassino in a rented SUV, driving across the rugged spine of Italy to the coastal town of Bari. We boarded the overnight car ferry to Bar, Montenegro—a slower, but stealthier route. Stacy had been adamant: *No airports.* She didn't want our passports showing up in a single Schengen-linked database. The ferry, she reasoned, was invisible to anyone scanning for international arrivals. Montenegro wasn't part of the EU system, and its port records barely qualified as digital.

By the time we rolled off the ferry ramp, the sun was climbing above the Dinaric Alps. We drove straight to the safe house, a sprawling villa tucked into the hills above the city of Bar, and dispersed to our assignments.

Nate took logistics: vehicles, communications, and site reconnaissance.

Stitch took procurement, code for "everything you can't buy in a store." Having spent years in the Balkans during his time in the Unit, he had the contacts. He crossed into Albania before noon, destination: Shkodër, capital of organized crime and marketplace for anything that shouldn't legally exist.

My task was more personal.

I was to meet with Dragan "Vuc" Vucović and call in a favor.

Vuc was a mountain of a man, and not just in size. At six-six and somewhere north of three hundred pounds, he looked like a Slavic bear stuffed into a polo shirt. His hair was an unruly tangle of brown, his goatee trimmed just enough to suggest civility. A former police officer turned security magnate, Vuc now ran the largest private protection firm in Montenegro.

We met at a tiny restaurant tucked along a sidestreet in Budva, a seaside town of thirty thousand, and the gateway to Sveti Stefan. The place was the kind that didn't bother with English menus. Two o'clock in the afternoon, locals only, and quiet enough for a conversation that needed to stay that way.

Vuc stood the moment I entered, his grin as wide as his shoulders. He engulfed me in a hug that smelled faintly of espresso and tobacco.

"Milo! My friend!" he boomed. His English was fluent but flavored by the hard consonants of the Balkans, a language built for argument and affection alike. "You look... different. I like the blond hair. Very *cinema adult*," he said, chuckling.

I couldn't help laughing. "Seems like that's the global consensus."

We sat, ordered coffee, and began the dance of Balkan hospitality, fifteen minutes of ritual before business could be named. Family, football, weather. He talked about his teenage son's obsession with *The Wire* and *Breaking Bad*, shows from which he'd apparently learned his English vocabulary. I let the conversation meander; Vuc, as host, would decide when to turn the key.

After our second round of macchiatos, he leaned back and studied me. "So, tell me, Milo," he said, that sly grin returning. "What brings you to Budva? I know it must be important to interrupt me in the middle of the biggest security contract of my career."

He wasn't wrong. His company had landed the contract to provide perimeter security for the Bilderberg Meeting. Which was exactly why I was here.

"Vuc," I began carefully, "you know I'd never ask a favor unless I had no other option. The short version is this: I'm in something delicate. My safety, and the safety of an innocent young woman, depends on it. I need a favor. I can't tell you the details, and you can't ask. But I swear on my word, nothing bad will ever come back on you. You have my guarantee."

He didn't answer immediately. He lifted his cup, took a slow sip, and stared at me over the rim. As he set the cup down, he said, deadpan: "Whose car we gonna take?"

For half a heartbeat, I didn't move.

Then it hit me, the line from the movie: *The Town.*

Jeremy Renner to Ben Affleck after Affleck's character asks him for help with something he can never ask questions about. That rare kind of loyalty that doesn't ask for context. I laughed, genuinely, the sound catching even me by surprise.

"You'll do it? Without knowing what it is?"

"Of course," he said, smiling like a bear that had just claimed a honey pot. "You saved my daughter from a life in chains. I owe you everything. You say it, I do it."

He thumped his chest once, hard enough to rattle the cups. "Now tell me, my friend—what trouble are we making?"

40

10 MARCH 1400 HRS

SVETI STEFAN, **Montenegro**

I sat in the car park above the crescent of beach and the islet of Sveti Stefan, headlights off, engine ticking as it cooled. The gibbous moon laid a sheet of pewter over the Adriatic, and the island's fifteenth-century stone houses, terraced up the rock and roofed in red, glowed like a postcard someone had pinned to the night. In the quiet, with the wind moving through cypress and pine, I believed I finally understood most of the multi-dimensional chess game we'd all been playing. The next few hours would tell me if I'd moved my pieces well, or into a trap of my own making.

Sveti Stefan is unlike anywhere else: barely three acres of pale rock rising steeply from the sea a hundred meters offshore, connected to two pink-sand beaches by a narrow isthmus—a tombolo is the proper word, though that makes the concrete path riding its spine sound grander than it is. The path is just wide enough for one vehicle; anything larger would scrape the stone. From sea level, the island is a small citadel; from the landward side, the beaches flare north and south from the causeway like an admiralty anchor cast on the shore.

To the north, the sand gives way to ten acres of manicured grounds and a stone mansion set back from the water, a 1930s relic called Villa Miločer, the summer home of Queen Marija Karađorđe-vić. Its lawns and the causeway are now part of the resort's domain. To the south lies the town of Sveti Stefan proper—low hotels, cafés, bars, and souvenir shops all facing the water, their lights blinking in slow conversation with the tide.

It was time.

This was the hard part: the piece of the plan where control thinned to a wire and the outcome hinged on human nature—mine and someone else's. Stitch didn't think it would be difficult and had complete faith that I was the right man to do it, which said something about his compass. His compass was a little more Machiavellian than mine.

I stepped out, locked the car, and started across the causeway. March air off the Adriatic was clear and cool, upper fifties and falling. I wore dress slacks and a tweed sport coat over a dark polo, the uniform of a man who wanted to look like he belonged without looking like he was trying. Around my neck hung a key card with my picture that Vuc had issued; on my wrist, a magnetic band that would open most doors; and in my pocket, the brass master key for those doors the band wouldn't. The weight of the Z88 was gone. I'd thrown it into the harbor back in Lüderitz. I had argued with myself about that decision more than once today. Tonight, with what I intended to do, I felt naked without it.

Vuc's map—marked with buildings, alleys, staff passages, and the small, hidden routes that make islands like this function—was committed to memory. Every stairwell, every turn. As the path met stone and the island rose under my feet, I let that picture overlay the reality. Trust the map, trust the lights, trust that security would read my credentials more than my face.

I took the narrow branch road left and walked toward the main reception. The building was well lit, windows throwing warm pools into the night. Inside, a short corridor opened into a high room with a dining area to the rear and a long bar spanning the front windows, the glass filled with the town's lights skittering over black water. The bar was crowded, a few men with ties loosened, voices lowered. I watched without staring, careful and quick. The face I wanted wasn't there.

I figured as much. I moved on.

Just past the lounge, a spiral stair folded into the stone, scarcely more than a helix carved by time. A small sign, BAR, in letters that might have been older than I was, pointed down. The air cooled with each turn. At the bottom, the stairs opened onto a low room with no windows and a square mahogany bar sitting in the center like a table altar. No tables. A ring of leather-topped stools, three or four to a side, each with a view of the door and everyone else.

Two men sat opposite, one of America's richest, jaw like a bulldozer, and a politician I was fairly sure chaired one of the EU's alphabet committees. They spoke in the confidential way powerful men do when they're pretending not to be seen. On the near side, back to me, a woman with a rocks glass and her attention half on her phone: Jessica Reid.

"Can I buy the lady a drink?" I said, sliding onto the adjacent stool.

Her head snapped toward me. Surprise flashed, cooled, then warmed into something I wanted to call affection but didn't dare.

"Drinks are free," she said with a smirk, raising the half-full glass. "How'd you—"

She didn't finish the sentence. She stood, and before I could make a joke or a plan, her arms were around me. She hugged with both arms and all of herself, and my left shoulder lit up where her forearm pressed into recent damage. I hugged back anyway. Then she pulled away, held my face in both hands, and kissed me. It wasn't quick, and it wasn't chaste. Her hand slid to the back of my head and pulled; her tongue was insistent. My body reacted before my brain could catch up. Five seconds of heat, and I let myself have them.

"Jesus," I said, easing her back. "If I'd known I'd get that sort of welcome, I'd have disappeared to South Africa years ago."

She laughed and slid back onto her stool. I sat and ordered whatever she was having. For a second, I wondered if I had lipstick on my mouth and decided this was the sort of bar where it would be considered a credential.

"You like the kiss?" she asked, teasing in the way that dares you to say no.

"Has anyone ever said no to that question?" I asked.

"Not yet," she said, letting the mischief shade toward something hungrier.

"Then I won't be the first," I said lightly.

Her eyes flicked to the side, toward the reflection in the bottle glass, then back to me. The switch to business was instant. "Why are you here, Milo?"

"I'm here to see you," I said, because in one sense, that was true.

"You completed your contract," she said, voice even. "You delivered Caitlin safely. You could have met me in D.C. if you just wanted to see me. So I'll ask again—why are you here? And how did you even get in?"

This was the fulcrum. The mission lived or died here.

"I told you. I'm here to see you," I said, holding her gaze and letting my voice lower a shade. "I need your help."

A beat. The mischief softened.

"What kind of help?" she asked. "It must be important if you hunted me down to a five-hundred-year-old basement bar."

"I need an audience with Secretary Bishop," I said, "and, ideally, with Lin Jinhai present. There's something I learned in Juba and Goma they both need to hear. It's critical."

"What is it?" Hook set.

"It's delicate," I said. "I need to say it to both of them, together, before things get out of control."

"And you can't tell me?" She pouted, but only a little. "You want me to call in a favor with my boss without telling me why."

"I told you why. I can't tell you what," I said. "Jessica, I've been chased through three countries for what people think I know. If I tell you, I put you in the same crosshairs. I won't do that."

Her face changed—some mix of calculation, trust, and the memory of a younger version of herself who liked risk. "I can get Secretary Bishop to meet," she said. "I have no line to Lin. I know he's here on the island, but that's all."

Before I could answer, she leaned in and kissed me again, quick and electric. Her fingers swept down, bold, pressing against me through the fabric, and then her mouth was at my ear. "I have a room," she whispered.

"I know," I said, because of course she did and of course I did.

"Let's go," she said, standing. "We'll talk details. I've got the Secretary's schedule on my laptop."

She kissed me once more, and I saw the tech billionaire across the bar watching us over his glass, a man cataloguing leverage even when he doesn't need it. I slid off my stool and took Jessica's hand.

"After you," I said.

You don't get to accuse me of not taking one for the team.

41

11 MARCH 1248 HRS

SVETI STEFAN, Montenegro

The sea outside Villa Miločer shimmered like liquid glass, each small wave edged in silver light. From where I stood at the tall windows on the second floor, I could see Sveti Stefan island just two hundred meters offshore—a private fortress of wealth and secrecy perched above the Adriatic. The water between us was a deep, impossible green, the sand nearly pink where it curved around the tiny peninsula. The afternoon air had that rare clarity of the Montenegrin coast in early spring—salt, pine, and the faint, earthy scent of the red soil that clung to everything.

I tapped a knuckle against the windowpane. The sound was thin, hollow. Modern glass, replacements, not originals. These windows might look old, but they lacked the imperfections, the tiny ripples of true antique glass. Someone had gone to great lengths to restore the villa to its former glory, but like so much in Eastern Europe, authenticity had been replaced with a convincing imitation. Craftsmanship, real craftsmanship, was hard to come by these days.

Villa Miločer had once been a royal summer retreat—eight guest suites, each lavishly furnished, with frescoed ceilings, Persian rugs, and fireplaces trimmed in marble. The grand ballroom below was roughly the size of a basketball court and smelled faintly of lemon oil and age. For the current Bilderberg Conference, the mansion had been transformed from luxury lodging into a fortress of influence, each suite converted into a private conference chamber for the powerful men and women who quietly shaped the world.

Our meeting today would take place in the library, a stately room in the front right corner of the second floor overlooking the Adriatic. It was roughly thirty feet long by fifteen across, its walls paneled in dark oak and lined with shelves stacked to the ceiling with leather-bound tomes. The air carried a faint mustiness of paper and polish. Two separate sitting areas filled the space, arranged around a central coffee table carved from walnut and scarred from age. I'd arrived early to adjust the chairs. The placement mattered. In my line of work, everything did.

When the first knock came, I felt a prickle of anticipation but no surprise. The door opened, and Secretary George Bishop stepped in, flanked by Caitlin and Jessica. The contrast between the three of them struck me instantly—Bishop with his careful statesman's composure, Caitlin with her wary empathy barely masked by poise, and Jessica Reid, quiet, deliberate, her expression unreadable.

Caitlin crossed the room and hugged me. She smelled faintly of citrus shampoo and travel. Bishop and Jessica followed with polite handshakes, all formality restored. We still had ten minutes before our next guest's arrival. I used them wisely.

"Please, sir," I said, motioning to the sofa positioned with its back to the window. "Sit. I think this arrangement will give us the best view."

Bishop complied, lowering himself with a statesman's stiffness. Caitlin sat beside him, her eyes darting between us, uncertain of what this meeting would bring. I took the chair to Bishop's left, forcing Jessica to occupy the single seat at his right. That left the opposite sofa—empty, waiting—for who was to come.

"Thank you again for all you've done for Caitlin," Bishop said.

His tone was measured but genuine. He'd said the same words over the phone the day before, but here in person they carried more weight.

"You're welcome, Mr. Secretary," I said. "I'm still trying to find answers to certain questions. I appreciate you agreeing to meet with me."

Bishop's mouth tightened. His earlier warmth drained away, replaced by the frosted professionalism of a man used to control.

"What business is this of yours, deCogan?" he said evenly. "Your contract is complete. I'll pay your invoice as soon as you submit it."

"I appreciate that, sir," I said. "But when two of my close friends are killed, I consider the matter unfinished."

"And what's an acceptable outcome to you?" His tone was sharp now. "Because from where I sit, this looks like one big mistake...and a tragedy for the families involved."

He didn't respond immediately. His expression stayed neutral, but the slight twitch of his jaw told me he didn't like being cornered.

I let the silence stretch before speaking again. "You're probably wondering why I asked for this meeting," I said. "The truth is, I needed you here...and I needed Jinhai here. Together."

Bishop's brow furrowed. "Why would you need that?"

"Because that's the only way this ends cleanly," I said. "You two share more history than either of you would admit publicly, or separately. Whatever this started as—a business arrangement, an understanding—it's gone off the rails. And it's left a lot of bodies behind."

Bishop's eyes narrowed. "You seem remarkably informed for a security consultant."

"I make it my business to be," I said. "And I made it clear to Jessica that I believed this meeting could help bring both sides to the table. She seemed to agree. In fact, she was the one who reached out to Lin Jinhai's office on your behalf."

His gaze flicked briefly toward Jessica, who kept her eyes fixed on some invisible point across the room.

"Yes," I continued. "I told her this meeting might be the only way to prevent things from escalating further—to 'resolve' certain misunderstandings before they reached Washington or Beijing." I allowed the faintest trace of irony to edge my voice. "Apparently that was persuasive enough."

Bishop's tone cooled another degree. "You went through Jessica?"

I nodded. "I knew she could make it happen. And she did."

He studied me carefully. "You make it sound as though you knew she had... connections."

"I'd prefer to say that I understand people and their motivations," I said. "Everyone wants to believe they're serving a greater purpose. Jessica's no different."

For the first time, Caitlin shifted uncomfortably beside her father, sensing the undercurrent neither of them could fully name.

"So this meeting," Bishop said, voice low. "You orchestrated it?"

"I facilitated it," I corrected. "The purpose was to get everyone in the same room. To let the truth sort itself out." I leaned back slightly, giving him just enough of a pause to misinterpret the gesture as relaxation. "What happens next depends on how honest everyone decides to be."

Before I could explain further, the door opened again. The air in the room seemed to change.

A small woman entered first—Chinese, early thirties, dressed in a charcoal skirt and fitted jacket. Her black hair was drawn back tight, her movements precise, her expression blank. She carried a slim leather valise, which she set neatly on a nearby table before pushing the door wide.

Behind her came Lin Jinhai.

Lin's presence filled the room before his voice ever did. He was shorter than I expected, no more than five foot six, but carried himself with the coiled energy of a man accustomed to power. His frame was lean, his skin tanned and taut, his movements athletic and fluid despite his seventy years. The muscles in his neck flexed as he turned his head. His forearms, visible beneath a fitted navy polo, looked like those of a younger man. While Bishop wore a gray suit and silk tie, Lin had chosen pale golf slacks and soft leather loafers. The choice wasn't casual, it was calculated. A man at ease in a room of enemies.

He crossed to Bishop with quick, unhurried steps. "Good afternoon, George," Lin said, his accent faint, his voice smooth as silk drawn across stone.

"Lin." Bishop's reply was flat. The chill between them was immediate, almost visible. Whatever history they shared, it wasn't one built on trust.

"Please," I said, motioning toward the open sofa. "Have a seat, Mr. Lin."

He didn't look at me but obeyed. His assistant—Wu Meilin, though he hadn't introduced her—sat beside him, folding her hands primly in her lap.

The six of us settled. Bishop and Caitlin sat with their backs to the window; Lin and Wu faced them. Jessica remained motionless at Bishop's right hand, eyes on no one. The coffee table between us was polished to a dull sheen, reflecting the afternoon light like still water.

"Thank you for joining us, Mr. Lin," I began.

His gaze snapped to me, sharp and appraising. "Who are you," he said, "and why are you speaking?"

"You know who I am," I said. "We've both read the same files."

We stared at each other. His eyes were black glass, empty of reflection. I didn't blink. Eventually, Lin looked away, pretending to study the sea beyond the window.

"I know you and Secretary Bishop go way back," I continued, "but I'd like to introduce his daughter Caitlin and his assistant Jessica."

Lin's smile was thin. "I've never met anyone in this room," he said. "I came here out of courtesy. I received a formal invitation from the Secretary of State this morning. Nothing more."

I tilted my head. "That's how you want to play it? Seems a little late in the game to feign ignorance."

"I have no idea what you're talking about." Lin rose, his irritation barely contained. "If you'd like to continue this privately, Secretary Bishop—"

"I suggest you sit down, Mr. Lin," I said. "You'll want to hear this."

Bishop turned toward me. "What's going on, deCogan?"

I didn't answer immediately. The silence stretched.

"On the morning of March first," I began, "the World Refugee Camp at Gangura was attacked by rebel forces of the Lord's Resistance Army. During the attack—"

"We know this," Bishop interrupted, his voice curt. "You're wasting our time."

"You know the facts," I said. "But you've said you don't know the reason." I turned slightly, fixing him with a look. "I know why the rebels attacked Gangura, Mr. Secretary. And I know that you know too...at least now you do."

Caitlin's brow furrowed. "Dad, what's Milo talking about?"

"I have no idea, sweetheart," Bishop said.

"Yes, you do," I said. "On February 28th, Melissa was working intake with Sebastian Forrester and Festus, the Sudanese camp manager. That afternoon, a new group of refugees arrived from northeastern DRC. Nothing unusual about that. But their story was. They came from a village near one of the major mining operations— your operation, Mr. Lin. The villagers had protested over pay. A truckload of Chinese soldiers arrived the next morning, lined up half the men in the village, and executed them. One hundred and fifty men dead."

"That's absurd," Bishop said, his face tightening.

"It's true, Dad," Caitlin said. "Melissa and Sebastian were shaken. They were somewhat skeptical at first, but multiple people corroborated the same story. They were planning to file a formal complaint, to ask the UN mission in Juba to investigate. I heard about it just before I went to bed, and with the attack the next morning, I'd forgotten all about it."

I took a slow breath, letting the weight of her words settle before I spoke. "And that's where everything shifted," I said. "What happened in that village wasn't just another tragic incident in a forgotten warzone; it was a massacre. And it was egregious enough, documented enough, that if it had reached the international press, the backlash would have been immediate and catastrophic. The world's patience for corporate mercenaries masquerading as humanitarian partners was already thin. Once the evidence connected Green River Mining and its security subcontractors to the killings—companies in which you, Mr. Secretary, held a vested interest—it would have detonated across every headline on the planet."

I leaned forward, my voice steady but edged with precision. "You wouldn't just have lost your post at State. The political fallout would have burned through the administration and scorched Beijing in the process. Lin Jinhai wouldn't be sitting in this villa—he'd be on a flight to The Hague, waiting for an ICC tribunal. And China, already treading thin diplomatic ice in Africa, would be facing an expulsion from South Sudan and probably the DRC as well. The loss of access, the humiliation—it would have been fatal to Lin's career, maybe his life. There was no coming back from that kind of disgrace. The attack on the WRC compound was to silence the witnesses. Caitlin's abduction was just an insurance policy to keep Secretary Bishop in line."

Bishop's jaw flexed. "And what reason would I have for covering that up?"

"I never said you covered it up," I said. "But since you've brought it up, maybe you should tell your daughter why you did."

His eyes turned cold. He hadn't looked at Lin once.

"Well?" I said. "Because you're a part owner in the mining concession that controls that site."

He stiffened. "What the hell are you—"

"Enough, Mr. Secretary." I raised a hand. "You've been in business with Lin Jinhai since the late seventies. There's no need to pretend otherwise."

Bishop glared at me, silent. Caitlin turned to him. "Is that true, Dad?"

"It is," I said, answering for him. "You mentioned something in Rome about French pastries in Italy—that reminded me of Oxford. Your father and Mr. Lin met there. Friends first, then partners. I don't know whether Lin was acting independently or as an agent of Beijing, but together they control a sizable share of sub-Saharan Africa's mineral wealth."

"I don't know what he's talking about," Bishop said finally.

"There's no need to keep secrets from your daughter," Lin interjected, his tone suddenly genial. "We have nothing to hide, George."

Bishop looked from Lin to Caitlin, then back to me. His expression wasn't guilt; it was fatigue, the look of a man too tired to keep lying.

"Dad?" Caitlin whispered.

"It's true I have business interests in Africa," Bishop admitted. "And it's true some of those companies overlap with Jinhai's. And yes, we met at Oxford. But I've done nothing illegal."

"Covering up a massacre," Caitlin said, trembling. "You don't think that's illegal? Danny would be ashamed of you."

Bishop flinched at the name. For a heartbeat, the mask cracked.

"That's where deCogan's wrong," Bishop said. "I wasn't covering it up. I was working to expose it. That's why you were kidnapped, Caitlin. I couldn't make it public, not while they had you."

Caitlin turned to me, eyes wide. "Is that true, Milo?"

"I think it is," I said. "He was trying to do the right thing. Torn between his duty and his daughter."

"I'm sorry, Caitlin," Bishop said, his voice breaking. "I couldn't lose another child. I thought I could control Lin, that I could use his greed against him."

Lin slammed a palm on the table. "Enough!" His voice snapped through the room like a whip. "I'm disappointed, George. You've lost your nerve. Jimmy Liu wasn't going to harm your daughter. We only needed time to handle matters in the DRC. By now, it's already over. No one will find evidence of an atrocity. And if they do, they'll find it points to the Lord's Resistance Army. My people protect those villages. Always have."

There it was. The confession I'd waited for.

Lin turned to me, his anger cooling into condescension. "Mr. deCogan here has proven to be quite the nuisance. May I call you Milo?"

"Of course," I said. "We're all friends here. Right?"

He studied me for a long moment, his expression unreadable. "Tell me something, Milo," he said finally, his tone almost conversational. "How did you figure it out? Jimmy Liu was thorough. He covered every track. Every file, every message, every witness. You shouldn't have been able to piece together anything."

I met his gaze, unblinking. "That was the problem," I said. "There were no tracks."

His brow furrowed slightly.

"The erasing itself was the clue," I continued. "When I was informed Melissa had died, I was told it was sepsis. But Melissa was beaten badly, and her injuries weren't life-threatening. I'd met with her doctor. I knew her prognosis—her body would heal relatively quickly; it was her mind that would take the longest to recover. It didn't add up. And I knew Liu—his methods, his arrogance. If she'd been killed, it wasn't random. It was because she'd seen something she shouldn't have."

Lin tilted his head, intrigued despite himself.

"So I reached out to a few contacts I trust...people in Goma, and in Juba," I went on. "Asked them to dig quietly into reports coming out of the northeast. What they found painted a picture you couldn't scrub clean: villagers gone missing, satellite images showing burn patterns, and rumors of Chinese security personnel seen near a mining concession north of Gangura. Then came the witness accounts, the survivors who'd fled across the border. They all told the same story."

I paused for effect. "Melissa didn't die of sepsis. She was silenced. And the moment I learned that, everything else fell into place."

Caitlin held back a sob, tears beginning to stream down her face, Melissa's death still hitting her hard. Bishop attempted to comfort her by putting his arm around her, but she shrugged him off.

Lin's faint smile returned, thin and joyless. "You're an observant man, Mr. deCogan," he said. "Maybe too observant for your own good."

"I've been told that before," I replied.

He smirked. "Then you must also know that Bilderberg security forbids private protection inside the perimeter. All guards, all weapons, left outside. That's why you feel safe holding this little meeting. You assumed I came alone."

I smiled. "Assumptions are dangerous things."

"Jimmy Liu was right," Lin said. "You're smug and reckless."

"I prefer the term self-assured," I said. "But do go on."

"My point," he said, leaning forward, "is that when you leave this villa, you'll be taken. Or shot. Either way, your body will be found at the bottom of Lake Shkodra tomorrow morning."

Caitlin gasped. Bishop's face twisted with helpless fury. Jessica didn't flinch. She hadn't spoken once, and that silence told me everything.

I brushed an invisible thread from my lapel, adjusting the fold of my Infantry-blue pocket square, and met Lin's eyes.

"I hope your men are better than Jimmy," I said. "He didn't make it past breakfast."

Lin's face hardened. For the first time, I saw something behind his eyes—not fear, but calculation. He was weighing outcomes. The meeting was nearing its end, and every one of us knew it, but how the ending played out was still unknown to everyone in the room. Everyone but me.

In my mind, the chessboard was already complete—every piece where it belonged.

I tugged the pocket square from my breast pocket.

I'd never be certain later whether it was the crack of the shot, the explosion of glass, or the faint hiss of feathers that I noticed first—but in that instant, the air itself seemed to tear open, dividing what came before from everything after.

Lin's head snapped back, then forward, as the .300 Winchester Magnum round tore through his chest. His body slumped sideways, his mouth open, his eyes staring at something no one else could see. Blood spread across his polo in a dark bloom.

Caitlin screamed. Bishop lunged, pulling her down.

A second shot.

Jessica's head jerked violently as the bullet punched through her temple. She was dead before she hit the floor.

For a heartbeat, only the whisper of the sea outside filled the silence. The smell of cordite drifted faintly through the shattered window.

"It's over," I said, lowering my voice. "You can get up. No more shots."

Bishop stared at me, horror mixing with rage. "What the hell have you done?"

I crossed the room, crouched beside Jessica, and checked her pulse. Nothing. Her eyes were open, glassy. I reached up and closed them gently. "What had to be done," I said.

Back in my chair, I faced the three who remained—Bishop, Caitlin, and Wu Meilin.

"I'm sorry it happened this way," I said. "But you both understand why. Secretary Bishop, I know you tried to do the right thing. You got trapped in something too big to control. You were protecting your daughter. That's a motive I'll never condemn."

He nodded once, hollowly.

I turned to Wu. "You'll return to your team. Tell them this ends here. There will be no retaliation. Your operations in Africa remain untouched—but you will provide restitution to the villagers in northeastern DRC. Secretary Bishop will transfer his holdings into a charitable trust. That trust will become your new partner. Do you agree, Mr. Secretary?"

"Yes," Bishop said. "I don't need the goddamn money. I just want this over."

"Do you understand, Ms. Wu? Some very powerful people sanctioned this outcome. Make sure your superiors understand that."

"I understand," she said softly, the first words she'd spoken all afternoon.

"You may go."

She rose, walked to the door, then hesitated. "If I may ask... what happens to Mr. Lin?"

"You tell me," I said. "Would you prefer he died of a heart attack, or that he disappears completely?"

Her eyes flicked to the body. "He should go home. His family will want him."

"Agreed," I said. "Please have your security detail retrieve him after we leave. Coordinate with Dragan Vuković, the head of security."

"Thank you, Mr. deCogan," she said, bowing slightly before slipping out.

The door clicked shut behind her. The air seemed heavier now, filled with the scent of gunpowder and something else—finality.

"Jesus Christ, deCogan," Bishop said, his composure unraveling into fury. "Why did you kill Jessica?"

Technically, I hadn't.

Stitch had fired both rounds from an untraceable rifle using a long-range hide site we'd set up in an empty apartment on the island's third floor. By now, he'd packed the weapon and was slipping down a back stairwell toward a waiting speedboat where Nate would be idling, ready to exfiltrate him out to sea before anyone knew what had happened. No one would ever look inside the Sveti Stefan castle, as its security during the Bilderberg conference was so tight that even contemplating such a breach was unthinkable.

Not to mention that this assassination never happened—at least to anyone not in the room at the time.

"She was a traitor, wasn't she?" Caitlin asked, tears in her eyes.

"Yes," I said. "She betrayed your father. She betrayed you. She was responsible for Dominic's death, and she gave us up to Jimmy Liu."

"How do you know?" Caitlin asked.

"Stacy put the pieces together," I said. "Did you know, Mr. Secretary, that Jessica studied abroad while an undergrad at Georgetown? I remembered this tidbit of information about her only after Caitlin mentioned Oxford."

Bishop shook his head. "No. I didn't know. She was already at the State Department when I hired her."

"She interned at a think tank in Beijing," I said. "Guess who sits on its board."

"Lin Jinhai," Caitlin whispered.

"Exactly. Stacy found photos of them together at events. And when we were compromised in Port Nolloth, only one person outside our team knew our location—Jessica. Jessica endlessly pestered Nate about where I was and Caitlin's status, and when she didn't get any answers from Nate, she called Stacy. Stacy, trying to reassure her and thinking Jessica's help might be crucial to getting us out through Namibia's immigration control, told her that Caitlin and I would be crossing into Namibia shortly. She passed that information on to Liu during one of the numerous calls she told Nate was having with Secretary Bishop, and that was enough for Liu's hackers to find our Airbnb reservation. And the rest, you know."

Caitlin's voice was small. "So for that she had to die? Like this?"

"I'm sorry," I said. "But there was no evidence that would hold up in court. What she did cost lives—Dominic's, and nearly yours. I confirmed it with her last night. Justice comes in different forms. This was the only one available. This evening, Montenegrin authorities will notify the U.S. Embassy that one of their employees, a Ms. Jessica Reid, died tragically in a fiery single-car accident on the Kotor Serpentine—a treacherous stretch of the P1 highway that's unfortunately been the location of too many fatal car crashes. Her body will be repatriated back to the United States in the next several days."

The silence that followed was heavy, but not hopeless.

"What now?" Caitlin asked finally.

"That's up to your father," I said. "My advice? Go home. Take time. Maybe somewhere quiet. You've both been through hell. You survived it. That's more than most can say."

Bishop looked out toward the broken window, at the island shimmering in the distance.

"Was it worth it?" he asked, already knowing the answer.

EPILOGUE
ONE MONTH LATER

BUDAPEST, Hungary

I leaned back into the warmth of the midday sun, its gentle rays draping across my face like a comforting blanket. From my seat outside the bustling café on Andrássy Avenue, I took in the vibrant panorama of one of Europe's most enchanting cities. Ornate baroque facades lined the boulevard, their pastel colors glowing in the golden light that reflected off tall, stately windows. Cobblestone streets wound between them, radiating that old-world charm I'd always appreciated from a distance but rarely had the luxury to enjoy. Linden trees offered dappled shade to the passing crowd—a steady stream of tourists, locals, and lovers who looked like they'd never known the word danger.

The air carried the easy hum of conversation, the clinking of cutlery, and the faint, haunting sound of a street violinist playing something that could only be Liszt. The music fit the city perfectly— refined, a little melancholic, but full of quiet passion. The scent of espresso and warm pastries drifted from the café behind me, mingling with the cool breeze coming off the Danube. For a moment, it was hard to imagine there was any other world beyond this one.

Across from me sat an empty chair, waiting for my companion's return. I smiled at the sight of it. A month ago, my life had been defined by chaos. Now, I was surrounded by sunlight, elegance, and peace. The contrast felt almost obscene, as if I'd stumbled into someone else's life by mistake.

I lifted my espresso, savoring a slow sip. The bitterness grounded me. I'd never pictured myself here, of all places—Budapest, on a spontaneous getaway. It was the kind of thing other people did, not me. But lately, the old rules didn't apply. After everything that had happened, giving in to a little spontaneity felt less like indulgence and more like survival.

I glanced at my watch, a habit that had survived every firefight and mission, and checked the time out of reflex. She'd been gone just under ten minutes. I'd told her I'd wait while she explored the boutique next door, but she'd turned to me with that sparkle in her eyes and said she'd "only be a few minutes." I'd believed her, even though I knew better.

That sparkle, it had caught me off guard more than once. It was the kind of light I'd trained myself not to notice, the kind that could slip past all the armor you build up over a lifetime. I still couldn't quite believe any of this was happening—that I was here, in this city, at this table, waiting for her. The disciplined world I'd lived in for years had no place for this kind of calm. But she did. Somehow, she'd made it fit.

I spotted movement across the boulevard and instinctively straightened. Old habits die hard. Then I saw her.

Rosalie stepped out of the boutique and into the sunlight. Even in a city filled with elegance, she commanded the street. The violet dress she'd chosen fluttered lightly around her knees with each step, and the sunlight seemed to follow her, catching the smooth lines of her shoulders and the graceful curve of her neck. Heads turned as she passed—men, women, everyone. Her beauty was palpable, and she carried herself like a woman who knew exactly who she was and what power that gave her.

A young waiter walking past froze mid-stride to stare. Rosalie met his gaze and offered him a gentle, forgiving smile. He flushed crimson and hurried away, muttering apologies. I chuckled under my breath. I knew exactly how he felt.

As she crossed the avenue toward me, I stood, setting my cup down and pulling out her chair.

"Thank you, Milo," she said, her voice smooth as ever.

"My pleasure," I replied.

She sat gracefully, crossing one leg over the other with the kind of elegance that drew the eye without demanding it. When she looked at me, her eyes—emerald green and full of mischief—caught the light.

"Budapest suits you," I said. "You look... happy."

Her lips curved into a smile. "It's beautiful here. It's been a long time since I've let myself simply enjoy a day."

"You deserve it," I said.

She nodded. "We both do."

I nodded. There was more truth in those three words than either of us wanted to unpack right now. I never would've guessed, months ago, that I'd be sitting at an outdoor café in Budapest with Rosalie Muhire—the Umwamikazi herself. But life had its own sense of irony. Sometimes cruel, sometimes merciful, always unpredictable.

"I got you something," she said suddenly, breaking the silence and reaching into her shopping bag.

"Oh no," I said, half-laughing. "You didn't have to—"

"I know," she interrupted. "But I wanted to. It's time you let people do nice things for you."

She placed a small black box tied with a silver ribbon in front of me. I hesitated for a beat before untying it, careful not to tear the ribbon. Inside was a wristwatch—beautifully crafted, understated, timeless.

"It reminded me of you," she said. "Steady, precise, maybe a little old-fashioned." Then, with a grin: "And surprisingly stylish."

I laughed, reaching across the table to take her hand. "Thank you, Rosalie. Truly."

She squeezed my hand. "My pleasure."

We sat for a while in comfortable silence, listening to the low rhythm of the city—the violinist, the chatter, the distant tram bells echoing down the avenue. For once, I wasn't thinking about what came next. Neither of us was. The past was too heavy to carry, and the future was too uncertain to plan. Right now was enough.

It was Rosalie who finally spoke. "So, Milo," she said with that half-smile, "what do we do now?"

I looked at her across the table, the sun reflected in her eyes, and for the first time in a long time, I felt something close to peace.

"We let ourselves enjoy this," I said. "We've earned it."

She lifted her glass, a spark of playfulness in her gaze. "To life," she said. "And unexpected journeys."

I raised my espresso cup and clinked it lightly against hers.

"To unexpected journeys," I echoed.

Author's Note

My years working in and around African conflict zones have left an indelible mark on me. The landscapes, the people, and the unthinkable tragedies I've witnessed have shaped not only my view of the world but the way I write about it. Many of the places and experiences woven through *Diamond Coast* are drawn from that reality. The stories of those who live and die in the margins of conflict deserve to be remembered, and I will continue to bring them forward in future Milo deCogan thrillers.

Of all the places I have known, Rwanda holds a singular place in my heart. It was there that I first began to comprehend the depths of human savagery and the uncomfortable truth that such brutality lies only a thin distance beneath the surface of even the most "civilized" societies.

Ntarama Church is a real place. I encourage anyone who has the opportunity to visit it. It will change your life. So too will a visit to the Murambi Technical School, where an estimated 50,000 Tutsis were systematically murdered over the course of several days. At Ntarama, the bones of the dead remain as silent witnesses. At Murambi, the victims were bulldozed almost immediately into mass graves—graves that French troops later paved over to create a volleyball court, an act meant to conceal the enormity of what had occurred there. Those same French forces, who had been "protecting" the Tutsis, conveniently withdrew on the day the massacre began, April 21, 1994, only to return in June as part of Operation Turquoise to apparently play volleyball.

The character Father Wenceslas Muyemana in this novel is based on a real man: Father Wenceslas Munyeshyaka. Like his fictional counterpart, Munyeshyaka initially provided refuge to Tutsis seeking sanctuary, only to betray them to the Hutu militias. A Rwandan military tribunal later found him guilty of rape and of aiding in the slaughter of hundreds of Tutsi refugees at the Holy Family Cathedral in Kigali, where he had served as head priest. Yet he remained free in France, shielded by the Roman Catholic Church, which rewarded him with his own parish in Gisors. His eventual excommunication, some twenty-seven years after his crimes, came not for his role in genocide, but for breaking his vow of celibacy and fathering a child.

If there is a corollary to man's inhumanity to man, it is the righteousness with which people, and institutions, so often protect the corrupt, the cruel, and the morally bankrupt. That truth, more than any other, is what drives me to write stories like *Diamond Coast*.

— Robert Cole

Thank You

Since you've made it this far, I want to pause and sincerely thank you for reading *Diamond Coast*. This novel was deeply personal to write—both challenging and rewarding—and I'm grateful you chose to spend your time with Milo deCogan and the dangerous world he inhabits. My hope is that the story entertained you, but also pulled back the curtain on a part of the world most people never see, where humanitarian work, power politics, and moral choice collide far from public view.

If you enjoyed *Diamond Coast*, or if you've read and liked my work in the *Matt Sheridan* or *Fractured Union* series, I would truly appreciate it if you took a moment to leave a review on Amazon. Reviews—especially 5-star reviews—play an outsized role in helping new readers discover books like this, and they make an enormous difference for independent authors. Even a sentence or two helps more than you might realize.

And if something didn't work for you, or you feel compelled to leave a lower rating, I'd ask that you consider reaching out to me directly instead at Robert@OfficialRobertCole.com. I read every message personally and genuinely value thoughtful feedback, whether positive or critical. Your input helps shape future books in this series.

Thank you again for reading, and for being part of this journey.

Best regards,

Robert

Acknowledgment

I ultimately wrote *Diamond Coast* because it was the kind of thriller I love to read—fast-moving, character-driven, and immersive, with just enough real-world texture to make the danger feel authentic. Above all, my goal was to tell a gripping story that pulled you forward, kept the pages turning, and made you want to see what happened next.

To readers who have followed my work from the *Matt Sheridan* series or the *Fractured Union* novels into this new world, thank you. Your trust means more than I can adequately express. I am especially grateful to those who approach these books as stories first—fiction that explores difficult terrain without demanding easy conclusions.

Any factual errors in these pages are mine alone. Some liberties were taken deliberately in service of the narrative; others may reflect oversight or ignorance. In all cases, responsibility rests entirely with me.

I owe sincere thanks to those who read early drafts and offered candid, thoughtful feedback. Your insights, encouragement, and critiques strengthened this book in ways that may not be immediately visible on the page, but are deeply felt by the author. I am also grateful to friends, colleagues, and extended family whose conversations, experiences, and perspectives quietly informed the characters and situations in this story. I hope you recognize echoes of yourselves and smile at them.

To my parents, thank you for instilling in me a love of reading, curiosity about the world, and the confidence to pursue work that demands both discipline and imagination.

Most of all, I owe my deepest gratitude to my wife and children. Your patience, love, and understanding make this work possible. Thank you for the sacrifices you make—often unseen—so I can spend long hours writing, revising, and chasing stories that matter to me. This book, like all the others, is better because of you.

AUTHOR'S NOTE

My years working in and around African conflict zones have left an indelible mark on me. The landscapes, the people, and the unthinkable tragedies I've witnessed have shaped not only my view of the world but the way I write about it. Many of the places and experiences woven through *Diamond Coast* are drawn from that reality. The stories of those who live and die in the margins of conflict deserve to be remembered, and I will continue to bring them forward in future Milo deCogan thrillers.

Of all the places I have known, Rwanda holds a singular place in my heart. It was there that I first began to comprehend the depths of human savagery and the uncomfortable truth that such brutality lies only a thin distance beneath the surface of even the most "civilized" societies.

Ntarama Church is a real place. I encourage anyone who has the opportunity to visit it. It will change your life. So too will a visit to the Murambi Technical School, where an estimated 50,000 Tutsis were systematically murdered over the course of several days. At Ntarama, the bones of the dead remain as silent witnesses. At Murambi, the victims were bulldozed almost immediately into mass graves—graves that French troops later paved over to create a volleyball court, an act meant to conceal the enormity of what had occurred there. Those same French forces, who had been "protecting" the Tutsis, conveniently withdrew on the day the massacre began, April 21, 1994, only to return in June as part of Operation Turquoise to apparently play volleyball.

The character Father Wenceslas Muyemana in this novel is based on a real man: Father Wenceslas Munyeshyaka. Like his fictional counterpart, Munyeshyaka initially provided refuge to Tutsis seeking sanctuary, only to betray them to the Hutu militias. A Rwandan military tribunal later found him guilty of rape and of aiding in the slaughter of hundreds of Tutsi refugees at the Holy Family Cathedral in Kigali, where he had served as head priest. Yet he remained free in France, shielded by the Roman Catholic Church, which rewarded him with his own parish in Gisors. His eventual excommunication, some twenty-seven years after his crimes, came not for his role in genocide, but for breaking his vow of celibacy and fathering a child.

If there is a corollary to man's inhumanity to man, it is the righteousness with which people, and institutions, so often protect the corrupt, the cruel, and the morally bankrupt. That truth, more than any other, is what drives me to write stories like *Diamond Coast*.

— Robert Cole

THANK YOU

Since you've made it this far, I want to pause and sincerely thank you for reading *Diamond Coast*. This novel was deeply personal to write —both challenging and rewarding—and I'm grateful you chose to spend your time with Milo deCogan and the dangerous world he inhabits. My hope is that the story entertained you, but also pulled back the curtain on a part of the world most people never see, where humanitarian work, power politics, and moral choice collide far from public view.

If you enjoyed *Diamond Coast*, or if you've read and liked my work in the *Matt Sheridan* or *Fractured Union* series, I would truly appreciate it if you took a moment to leave a review on Amazon. Reviews—especially 5-star reviews—play an outsized role in helping new readers discover books like this, and they make an enormous difference for independent authors. Even a sentence or two helps more than you might realize.

And if something didn't work for you, or you feel compelled to leave a lower rating, I'd ask that you consider reaching out to me directly instead at Robert@OfficialRobertCole.com. I read every message personally and genuinely value thoughtful feedback, whether positive or critical. Your input helps shape future books in this series.

Thank you again for reading, and for being part of this journey.

Best regards,

Robert

ACKNOWLEDGMENTS

I ultimately wrote *Diamond Coast* because it was the kind of thriller I love to read—fast-moving, character-driven, and immersive, with just enough real-world texture to make the danger feel authentic. Above all, my goal was to tell a gripping story that pulled you forward, kept the pages turning, and made you want to see what happened next.

To readers who have followed my work from the *Matt Sheridan* series or the *Fractured Union* novels into this new world, thank you. Your trust means more than I can adequately express. I am especially grateful to those who approach these books as stories first—fiction that explores difficult terrain without demanding easy conclusions.

Any factual errors in these pages are mine alone. Some liberties were taken deliberately in service of the narrative; others may reflect oversight or ignorance. In all cases, responsibility rests entirely with me.

I owe sincere thanks to those who read early drafts and offered candid, thoughtful feedback. Your insights, encouragement, and critiques strengthened this book in ways that may not be immediately visible on the page, but are deeply felt by the author. I am also grateful to friends, colleagues, and extended family whose conversations, experiences, and perspectives quietly informed the characters and situations in this story. I hope you recognize echoes of yourselves and smile at them.

To my parents, thank you for instilling in me a love of reading, curiosity about the world, and the confidence to pursue work that demands both discipline and imagination.

Most of all, I owe my deepest gratitude to my wife and children. Your patience, love, and understanding make this work possible. Thank you for the sacrifices you make—often unseen—so I can spend long hours writing, revising, and chasing stories that matter to me. This book, like all the others, is better because of you.

ABOUT THE AUTHOR

Robert Cole is a former U.S. Army infantry officer having served with some of the Army's most elite units. His fiction draws heavily on his real-world military, political, and geopolitical experience. He is the author of the acclaimed post-apocalyptic Matt Sheridan series and the Fractured Union political thriller series. Known for blending authentic operational detail with complex global stakes, Cole's novels explore power, conflict, and the human cost of decisions made in the shadows. *Diamond Coast* launches a new thriller series centered on modern humanitarian crises and the dangerous forces that exploit them.

To learn more, visit www.officialrobertcole.com. Subscribe to his newsletter for occasional updates on future novels—no spam, just stories worth waiting for.

ALSO BY ROBERT COLE: